PRAISE FOR *DRUNK ON LOVE*

"The queen of contemporary romance is back with a new tale and group of characters, this time set against the gorgeous backdrop of Napa, California."
—Shondaland

"As if we didn't already wish we can live in a Jasmine Guillory novel, the iconic author is back with another romance that will absolutely sweep you off your feet."
—*Cosmopolitan*

"[Guillory] demonstrates why she's a bestselling author as she weaves in more serious threads about race and identity, about what it means to be recognized and what it means to be successful. You'll be cheering for Margot and Luke until you turn the last page."
—*USA Today*

"Suffused with tenderness and delight, this is Guillory's best book yet."
—*Booklist* (starred review)

"The lush background and Guillory's signature blend of sexy, sweet, and funny keeps the pages flying. This is a gem."
—*Publishers Weekly* (starred review)

"Guillory's latest, imbued with her signature heat, wit, and scene-stealing secondary characters, is sure to be popular."
—*Library Journal* (starred review)

TITLES BY JASMINE GUILLORY

....

FLIRTING LESSONS

JASMINE GUILLORY

BERKLEY • NEW YORK

BERKLEY
An imprint of Penguin Random House LLC
1745 Broadway, New York, NY 10019
penguinrandomhouse.com

Book design by Daniel Brount

The Library of Congress has cataloged the Berkley Romance
trade paperback edition of this book as follows:

Names: Guillory, Jasmine, author.
Title: Flirting lessons / Jasmine Guillory.
Description: First edition. | New York: Berkley Romance, 2025.
Identifiers: LCCN 2024031762 (print) | LCCN 2024031763 (ebook) |
ISBN 9780593100912 (trade paperback) | ISBN 9780593100905 (hardcover) |
ISBN 9780593100929 (epub)
Subjects: LCGFT: Romance fiction. | Novels.
Classification: LCC PS3607.U48553 F55 2025 (print) |
LCC PS3607.U48553 (ebook) | DDC 813/.6—dc23/eng/20240715
LC record available at https://lccn.loc.gov/2024031762
LC ebook record available at https://lccn.loc.gov/2024031763

Printed in the United States of America
1st Printing

The authorized representative in the EU for product safety and compliance is
Penguin Random House Ireland, Morrison Chambers, 32 Nassau Street,
Dublin D02 YH68, Ireland, https://eu-contact.penguin.ie.

For Amy Spalding and Kayla Cagan.
I hope we have many more years of sitting
in the hot tub together under the full moon.

FLIRTING
LESSONS

ONE

TAYLOR CAMERON WAS HOT. SHE PICKED UP AN ICE CUBE, slipped it down the back of her tank top, and sighed with relief as it slid down her back. Why had she worn jeans today when she knew she had to be outside all day in the middle of the summer, serving hundreds of glasses of wine to guests at the Noble Family Vineyards anniversary party? Sure, this pair of jeans was comfortable, and one of her favorites, but still.

She laughed at herself as she greeted the next person in line. She knew why she'd worn these jeans. They made her ass look fantastic, and she knew she'd see a whole lot of people today, that's why. She was single again, after all.

"Welcome to Noble Family Vineyards," she said, picking up the bottle in front of her. "Would you like some rosé?"

As she poured wine, smiled, chatted with guests, and checked them off the list, she looked around the party to see how it was going. A lot of people were already there, though none of her friends had arrived yet. That didn't surprise her; her friends weren't the arriving-early type. But despite her boss Margot's anxiety about the party, Taylor wasn't worried. Noble had recently been on a bunch of lists of up-and-coming wineries in Napa Valley, and she was pretty sure there would be a fun crowd.

Luke walked by and waved at her. She grinned and waved back. Up until about a month ago, Luke worked here at the winery with her; Taylor assumed he was at the party today because he still had an enormous crush on Margot. She wondered if anything would ever happen with that. He was here with Avery Jensen, one of his best friends and a local event planner whom Taylor had met a few times at other jobs. Taylor gave herself a moment to—respectfully!—ogle Avery. She was always so immaculate, so perfectly dressed from head to toe; the kind of woman who could wear a white dress at a garden winery party and go home spotless. And that dress looked great on her; her golden brown skin stood out against the stark whiteness of the dress that clung to her long legs as she walked, and her hair was caught up in a knot at the nape of her neck that Taylor ached to unravel. Granted, if Taylor had her way, that dress wouldn't be buttoned up quite so high, but hey, you couldn't win them all.

Luke always talked about Avery, but he never mentioned how gorgeous she was. Taylor shook her head. Men. No matter how great they were, if they weren't interested in sleeping with a woman, they didn't even register how attractive she was. Taylor was . . . not like that.

"There you are!" a very familiar voice said. Taylor looked away from Avery and threw her arms around her best friend Erica.

"What are you guys doing here so early?" she said to Erica and her wife, Sam. "I didn't expect you until at least an hour from now."

Erica glared at her, but her eyes betrayed her amusement.

"Are you trying to say that I'm always late to things? Because if so, I resent that!"

Taylor laughed as she poured glasses of wine for each of them.

"Erica. Please. We would have been late to your own wedding if your mom hadn't forcibly removed us from the kitchen that morning. And yes, I know what you're going to say, I am the exact same way. The difference is I don't deny it."

Erica's attempt to keep a straight face failed.

"Okay, you have a good point. And it was Sam who got us here early, of course. She's got work to do this afternoon, so we can't stay long."

Sam was a partner at a law firm in San Francisco and worked constantly. Despite that, Taylor liked her a lot and was glad Erica had found someone who cared about her so much. It still felt weird to her, though, that Erica was so . . . settled now. They'd met and become friends in their early twenties, when they were both pretty wild and carefree. Now Erica was married, to a corporate lawyer, of all things. And a few months ago, Erica and Sam had moved out of the apartment complex that the three of them had all lived in and bought a house a few miles away. A whole house! Taylor didn't think she'd ever own a house, especially not in Napa Valley.

"Sucks that you have to leave early, but don't worry, I'll take good care of you before you go," she said, and handed full wineglasses to Erica and Sam. Erica, though, immediately handed her glass to Sam, with a significant look.

"No wine for me today," Erica said to Taylor. And then a wide grin spread across her face. "Because I'm pregnant!"

Taylor yelled, immediately attracting the attention of every-one in line, and threw her arms around Erica again. She turned to her boss, whose concerned expression softened into a smile.

"Margot, can I have a second? You've met my friend Erica; I've got to go freak out with her and her wife about their news."

Margot waved her away, and Taylor pulled Erica and Sam over into the corner and then into a three-person hug.

"Ahhh, I'm so happy for you both! How are you feeling? When are you due? And all those other questions that people who know stuff about babies would ask!"

Taylor was very much not a baby person, but she knew Erica was, and she also knew how much Erica had wanted this.

"I'm due in November, I'm twenty-one weeks along now and feeling good!" She took a step back and put her hand on her stomach, which Taylor could now tell was more rounded than usual. "I've done a pretty good job of hiding it, since it's not like my belly is small at normal times, and I've been wearing lots of oversized stuff, but I'm relieved I can stop that now that it's so hot out. I was sure you already knew, though, after I canceled with you a few times when I was pretty sick in the early stages."

Taylor shook her head.

"I had no idea. Wait, you've been pregnant for twenty-one weeks and you didn't tell me?"

Erica's smile faded.

"I know, I'm sorry. But after the last time, we thought . . . we didn't . . ."

Taylor nodded and pulled Erica back into a hug.

"Right, it's okay, I get it." Erica had gotten pregnant last fall and lost the baby. That time, they'd told everyone about it in the very early stages. Taylor had assumed she would still be in the inner circle of those who found out about something like this early, but now wasn't the time to bring that up.

"We wanted to wait until we got the all clear from the doctor," Sam said.

Erica squeezed Taylor hard before she stepped back.

"Which, full disclosure, we got last week, but I wanted to tell you in person, and you've been so busy lately that this was the first opportunity, so we had to take it." Erica waggled her eyebrows at Taylor. "I assume you've been making the most of your newly single state?"

Taylor shrugged.

"I guess so." Taylor had broken up with her most recent ex-girlfriend just a few weeks ago. "I mean, sort of. Not that I regret the breakup," she said quickly, after seeing the hopeful look on Erica's face. Erica had always liked Gemma. Taylor had, too, just . . . not enough. "But I don't know, I'm just tired of the drama. While I like the *idea* of dating someone new, actually dating doesn't sound fun anymore. Maybe I just need a break."

Erica shook her head.

"I can't believe Taylor Cameron, the hottest catch in Northern California, is already bored of being single. Here's something to make it fun: Pick a hot girl at this party. Any one of them. I bet you that you can get her into bed."

Taylor thought about Avery, just for a second, but shook her head.

"Okay, I *could* do that, but I'm not going to bet against myself like that. Plus, I said I wanted less drama, not more. But also, that's kind of mean to do to someone—I don't want her to find out that I slept with her because of a bet!"

"She has a point there, you know," Sam said.

Erica sighed. She and Taylor constantly bet each other about random stuff, mostly ridiculous things like this.

"Good point. Okay, then, here's a bet that's mean only to you. If you're bored with being single already, let's make it a little more challenging: I bet you that you can't make it through the summer without sleeping with someone."

Taylor's eyes widened involuntarily.

"The whole summer?"

Erica nodded with a very smug look on her face.

"Until Labor Day. You said you wanted less drama; that's a good way to accomplish it."

Taylor had never turned down a bet from Erica and vice versa (which had caused the two of them to spend one very memorable overnight in an IKEA after they'd bet each other to do it), and unfortunately her pride wouldn't let her turn down this bet. She held out a hand to Erica.

"Done," she said as she and Erica shook hands. "Margot is swamped, so I need to run back to the bar, but you'd better come up with a good prize for me for when I win this bet."

She heard Erica's laughter behind her as she raced back to the bar.

AVERY TOOK A SIP OF WINE AS SHE LOOKED AROUND THE WINery from her slightly out-of-the-way corner. It was nice to not have to work this party like she usually did—when you were an event planner, most parties that you went to were work. Instead, she could just relax and observe. People watching at parties was so much fun: she got to see who was checking each other out, who was flirting with whom, the couples who had clearly had a fight right before they'd gotten out of the car but were pretending they were so happy together, the person everyone was trying to go home with, that person who just really needed to break up with her boyfriend.

She let out a long, relieved sigh. She had been that last person, just a few months ago. Thank God, she'd finally done it. Everything would be different today if they were still together, if he were here with her. It had always been so stressful to be at parties with him. If it was a party with her friends, he always wanted to leave early; if it was a party with his friends, he never introduced her to anyone, and she was bored the whole time. But most of all, he never seemed particularly happy to be with her, no matter what she did. Until she'd broken up with him, she hadn't realized how much happier she'd be without him.

Even though it seemed like everyone else in her life had.

She shook those thoughts off. Today, she was going to just enjoy this party. Free wine, good snacks, beautiful weather, and a day off. And not only free wine, free *good* wine; free wine was easy to come by when you lived and worked in Napa Valley, but free good wine was a different story.

She glanced over at the makeshift bar, where the Noble staff was pouring wine for the growing crowd. Speaking of the person everyone at the party wanted to go home with, there she was: Taylor Cameron, pouring wine, laughing, gently flirting with the guest in front of her. Everyone walked away from her with a smile on their face, and most of them looked back at her to see if she was still looking at them. Avery had met Taylor a few times but mostly knew her by reputation. Her best friend Luke had talked about her, of course, when he'd worked with her here at the winery, but that wasn't just it. Taylor had dated at least half of the eligible women in Napa Valley—okay, that was a bit of an exaggeration, but only a bit of one. People were always falling for Taylor, and most of them got their hearts broken—that, she did know.

Avery watched her, trying not to be obvious about it. She was short, in a black tank top that showed off the tattoos on her upper arm as well as her significant curves, and jeans that clung to her wide hips and round butt. She had short curly hair and light brown skin. Avery hoped she was wearing sunscreen; too many people thought just because you were Black you didn't have to. That was a good reminder; she should reapply some soon.

Taylor grinned at the person she was talking to, and Avery smiled at her. Oh my God, what was she doing, Taylor wasn't even looking at her! Was Taylor just so magnetic that Avery was smiling at her from across the party? Apparently, yes! No wonder she had that reputation, goodness. Avery turned away.

"Avery! It's so lovely to see you!"

Avery hoped her face didn't show her surprise at being accosted by her old English teacher.

"Hi, Ms. Cunningham, it's so nice to see you," she said.

Her teacher laughed.

"You can call me Liza now, you're an adult, you know!"

Why did old teachers always say this? She would never be grown-up enough to call Ms. Cunningham by her first name.

"How are you?" her teacher asked. And then she laughed again. "Though I don't even have to ask, your mom tells me all about how you're doing." Her mom was a teacher at her former high school. "She always talks about you; you're the same as you've been since you were a teenager. You were always so well-behaved and reliable, and now you're such an upstanding member of our community. We're so proud of you, Avery."

Avery smiled automatically.

"Thank you so much, Ms. Cunningham. I try."

"Liza! And how's that boyfriend of yours? Things going well there?"

Yes, right, her mom still didn't know about her breakup, because she'd been too stressed out at the time to have that conversation, and just . . . kept procrastinating it.

"Um, oh, he's—"

"Oh, there's my husband waving at me. We have to head to a wedding, but we wanted to stop in to Noble before we left, and I keep running into people I know, he's going to kill me if I delay us any more. Great to see you, Avery!"

"Great to see you, too," Avery said.

As soon as Ms. Cunningham walked away, Avery fled to the taco stand. It wasn't that she didn't like Ms. Cunningham, she did, she always had. But "well behaved"? "Reliable"? Yes, fine, it was true, it was all true, but Ms. Cunningham may as well have said, *Avery, you were always such a boring teenager, and now you're a boring adult! Congratulations!*

And that was true, too. She was steady, focused, dependable, and boring as hell. What a fucking legacy. She'd stayed in a bad relationship for far too long because she was so reliable that she'd assumed that by sheer force of will, she could make it become a good one. That, or because she was so boring that she'd assumed no one else would ever want to date her—one or the other.

Wasn't she too young to be this boring? No, probably not, boring had no age level, and that made it even worse. It wasn't that she wanted her life to just be organizing her new apartment and working and very little in between, but everything else that she could do— everything else that she wanted to do—felt uncertain, risky, scary.

She grabbed a plate of tacos and wandered over to the wine table. Her glass had been empty from the moment Ms. Cunningham had called her an upstanding member of the community.

Taylor was still there, still pouring wine. And, right at that second, she was opening another bottle. She bit her bottom lip as she concentrated on it, and Avery couldn't stop herself from staring at that lip. Good Lord, why was she so focused on Taylor today?

"It's Avery, right?"

Avery looked up to find Taylor looking straight at her. Great, on top of everything else, Taylor would think she was a creep. Oh wait, thank goodness, she had sunglasses on; maybe Taylor hadn't realized she'd been staring at her.

"Yeah, I'm Avery. Hi." She was glad her voice seemed normal. "And you're Taylor? Luke forgot to introduce us earlier. I think we've met at other events, but he's also told me a lot about you."

Taylor grinned, and her eyes lingered on Avery.

That was why people fell for her. It was the way she looked at you, like the two of you had a little secret from everyone else.

"He's told me a lot about you, too." Taylor held up a bottle of rosé. "Need more of this?"

Avery held out her glass.

"I thought you'd never ask."

"How are the tacos?" she asked, with a glance at Avery's plate. "I haven't gotten a chance to try them yet. I've been glued to this table since they started serving."

"And no one has brought you one?" Avery asked. "That seems cruel. They're great."

Taylor grinned at her again.

"I agree, that is cruel."

The crowd around the wine table had thinned, so Avery didn't feel bad monopolizing Taylor's time.

"Well, we can't have that." Avery held out her plate. "Here, have this one."

What in the world was she doing? Why was she giving this woman—whom she barely knew—her last taco?

Whatever, it was fine, Taylor would know she was just being polite and wouldn't take it.

"Thanks, you're a treasure." Taylor picked up the taco with her fingers.

Oh. Okay. But, well, if Taylor was going to call her a treasure like that, it was worth her last taco.

She downed it in two bites, and then let out a deep sigh.

"Wow," she said. "That was really good." She licked her fingers slowly, and Avery couldn't stop staring. Until Taylor looked up at her and slowly licked her lips.

At least, that's what she did in Avery's imagination.

Did she have heatstroke? She needed to get hold of herself. She took a gulp of her wine.

"I, um . . . Do you need some help?"

Taylor raised an eyebrow at her abrupt question. Oh, she could do that eyebrow move, too. Of course.

"Help pouring wine? I know you're an event planner, but today you're the guest! This party is for you to have fun and drink wine and relax."

"Yeah, I know." Avery sighed. "The thing is . . . I'm not great at relaxing. I was trying, just now, and instead I counted the number of people here and looked at the food lines to see if there was something I could do to make them more efficient, and if that sounds insulting, I'm sorry. I thought I could turn off the event planner in me, but apparently, I can't. So, if I can pour wine or unpack wineglasses or direct people to the bathrooms or something, it might make me feel better." Oh God, why was she still talking? The wine had obviously already gone to her head.

Taylor laughed at her.

"Not great at relaxing? I wish I had that problem. You should work on that, you know."

Avery took another sip of wine.

"Yes, so I've been told. Repeatedly. Especially by my mother."

Taylor flinched dramatically.

"I am so sorry to echo a criticism of your mother's," Taylor said.

"But yeah, sure, come over here. But you have to promise that if my boss gets mad at me for this, you'll tell her that you begged to help me and gave me no choice."

Avery stepped around to the other side of the table to stand next to Taylor.

"Will do."

"Here, let me at least fill up that glass of yours again."

While Taylor greeted the next group of guests, Avery straightened the glasses on the table into neat rows and turned them all so that the Noble Family Vineyards logo was facing out.

"Wow." Taylor looked down at the glasses after the guests had all walked into the party. "I don't understand at all why your mom said you needed to work on relaxing."

Avery looked into Taylor's amused eyes and couldn't help but laugh.

"Okay fine, my mom may have had a *tiny* point." She looked back down at the wineglasses. "But doesn't that look nice?"

Taylor poured more rosé into Avery's glass.

"It looks very nice," she said, in the same tone of voice you'd use to compliment a toddler on their Lego creation. From most people, Avery would have bristled at that tone, but when Taylor grinned at her, Avery had to laugh.

"If it helps, I hate that I'm like this, too," Avery said.

Taylor tapped her gently on the hand.

"Hey, no negative self-talk. I don't hate that you're like this, and you shouldn't, either. It's always good to have orderly people in a world full of chaotic people like me. Plus, I've worked events that you've planned. They go off without a hitch, every time."

Avery smiled back at her. It was kind of amazing that Taylor had noticed that.

"Thanks, I appreciate that." She sighed. "No, you're right, I don't hate that I'm like this, it's just . . . I wish this wasn't all that I was."

Taylor raised an eyebrow again.

"What do you mean?"

Avery opened her mouth to answer her but took another sip of wine instead.

"Forget I said anything, you're busy, you're working, it's nothing."

Taylor gestured to the empty space in front of them.

"We're in a lull, we might as well make use of it. There's going to be another rush soon; this is the universe giving you an opportunity to tell me what you mean." When Avery hesitated, Taylor smiled at her. "Also, you don't have to tell me anything. Just call me a nosy bitch who you barely even know, and you can take your wine and leave. Or you can stay here, and you can tell me all about being an event planner. I bet you have the best stories."

Avery smiled at her. Something in Taylor's eyes made the tension drain from her body.

"I do have some good stories, yeah," she said. She took another sip of wine. Oh, the hell with it. "It's just that I ran into one of my old high school teachers—that's the problem with living in the town where you grew up. And she's great, I like her a lot, but she kept talking about how reliable I am, how I was such a well-behaved teenager, and grew up into such a dependable and upstanding adult, and I'm so sick of being well behaved and dependable and *boring*."

The passion in her own voice surprised her, and she almost stopped. But then she saw Taylor's eyes light up with interest. She went on.

"I broke up with my terrible boyfriend a few months ago, which was the best thing I've done for myself in years, and also the most out-of-character thing, and I've been so happy about it, really, I have been. I have so much space in my life now to have fun, be wild, get some hobbies, make new friends, flirt with, like, dozens of people at parties like this, all those things that people are supposed to do in their twenties, but I never did. I'm going to turn thirty at the end of the year. Does that mean that I'm stuck being the same boring person I've been forever?"

Avery took another sip of wine, or at least tried to, but somehow her glass was already empty. Oh no. It had taken only three glasses of wine before she'd shouted a diatribe about her life to Taylor Cameron. Now Taylor would do one of two things: call Luke over so he could take his drunk and uncharacteristically chatty friend home, or call over some of her coworkers to gently escort Avery to get some more food to help sober her up.

"Of course you're not stuck being the same person you've been forever, and you're not boring." Taylor paused. "What's stopping you from doing all those things? The hobbies, the friends, the flirting, all of that?"

Avery looked up, surprised again.

"Oh, I thought you would . . . I'm sorry for saying all of that, you don't have to—"

Taylor waved that away.

"Answer the question: What's stopping you?"

Avery sighed.

"I don't know how to do any of that, that's what's stopping me! As you've seen, I'm not good at relaxing! I'm also not good at hobbies! I had hobbies in high school, but they were all things to put on my college applications and then I stopped when I got to college. And I don't know how to flirt with people, I've never known how to do that! Plus, I don't know how a person who works for herself and isn't in school goes about doing things like making new friends. All the friends I've ever made I either worked with or went to school with. I don't have time to go around doing needlepoint or making pottery or whatever, I'm trying to run a business, the one thing I seem to sort of know how to do!"

Taylor reached over and took the wineglass out of her hand. Avery felt outraged for a moment, and then she realized she'd been gesturing wildly while holding the glass. Good thing it was empty.

"You don't know how to flirt?" Taylor asked. "We can work on that. Some of those other things, too, actually—I'm an expert at relaxation, I'm sure I can teach you a few things there as well. Relationships, now, if what you wanted to learn was how to be good at relationships, that I couldn't help you with, but flirting? That I can do. Do you want to be able to flirt with men or women?"

Oh. Avery should have expected that question.

"Um. Either? Both?" she answered. "But, I guess, especially the latter?"

"Have you dated women before?" Taylor asked casually.

Avery shook her head without exactly meeting Taylor's eyes.

"If I knew how to flirt with women, I might have dated one by now, but I don't, so . . ."

Taylor tossed an arm around her shoulders.

"Avery, my friend, you came to the right place. I'm going to teach you how to flirt."

TWO

AVERY PACED AROUND HER APARTMENT. WHAT THE HELL should she wear for her first flirting class with Taylor? How the hell had she gotten herself into this?

She'd spent the rest of the party attempting to convince Taylor that no, she didn't need flirting lessons, she'd be just fine without them, she would manage to figure out some sort of hobby, wasn't that good enough? Taylor had just laughed at her arguments and demanded her phone number.

She'd texted the very next day.

TAYLOR

> tuesday. 6:30 pm. be ready. what's
> your address? i'll pick you up

Avery texted back.

AVERY

> You really don't have to do this!

Taylor had just sent a laugh reaction.

TAYLOR

address please

Avery gave in and sent her address. Oh God, Taylor was really going to make her do this, wasn't she?

AVERY

Where are we going? What should I wear?

Those were both, she thought, perfectly reasonable questions. Had Taylor answered either of them? Obviously not.

TAYLOR

hmmm, i think where we're going should remain a surprise, don't you?

AVERY

No. I don't think so.

TAYLOR

lol

And then she hadn't said anything else! Finally, Avery had texted her earlier that day and asked, again, what she should wear. Taylor had responded immediately.

TAYLOR

oh you were serious about that question
ok. ummmm wear something kind of
nerdy but also approachable. does
that help?

AVERY

Taylor had just sent the laugh reaction again. And that was the last Avery had heard from her.

It had felt good to tell Taylor that she wanted to date women. That wasn't something she talked about with most people; it wasn't a secret, just that she was usually private about her love life. Luke knew, of course, as did some of her old friends back in L.A. But since she'd moved home to Napa, it hadn't really come up, especially since she'd been dating Derek for a lot of that time.

But she was still *very* nervous about how the night would go.

"Where are we going?" Avery asked as soon as she got in Taylor's car.

"You'll see," Taylor said. Of course she did.

"Is it time for the makeover montage?" Avery asked as she settled herself into the car. "New clothes and hair and makeup so I can attract women to my side like bees to honey?"

Taylor looked her slowly up and down before she finally met her eyes. Avery blushed at the look on Taylor's face.

"Avery. My smoking hot friend over here. You don't need a makeover. You look fantastic. You might need a confidence implant, but your clothes and hair and makeup are all just fine. More importantly, *you* are fine as hell."

Avery blushed again and looked out the window.

"Um. That's very nice of you to say."

Taylor laughed as she started the car.

"I can see this is going to be a process. I really need to teach you how to take a compliment. But first, and this is important." She waited until Avery turned to face her. "That was a genuine compliment. I'm not bullshitting you. And that leads to the bigger thing: I'm in this to win it. I want you to turn into a fantastic flirt, I know you've got it in you. But this isn't going to work if you don't trust me. I wouldn't tell you I thought you were hot if I didn't think so, and I'm not going to tell you that you did a great job flirting with someone if I don't think that. I'm going to be honest with you, okay? And I want you to be able to be honest with me about how you're feeling, or what you don't want to do, or anything else. Okay?"

Avery dropped her eyes.

"Um, okay."

Taylor nodded and pulled out into the street.

"In the interest of honesty," Avery said, "I want you to know it's killing me that I don't know where we're going and what we're doing tonight."

Taylor laughed. It was more of an evil cackle, actually.

"Oh, I know," she said.

That didn't help.

"Okay, but, I don't even know what the structure of this is going to be."

That made Taylor actually giggle.

"The structure of this? Oh, Avery, you're a delight. What kind of structure do you mean?"

What Avery really wanted was a syllabus, lesson plans, readings, but she supposed Taylor wasn't going to give her any of that.

"I mean, are you going to give me an assignment for tonight or something? Or are you just going to throw me into a scary situation, like speed dating or ax throwing or a candy-making party, and I'll have to go through it by myself while you watch me?"

Taylor turned to her again.

"First of all, I would never. And you know that. You wouldn't have gotten into a car with me if you thought I'd do that."

Well. That was true.

"Second, you don't have to do this, you know. When you were trying to talk me out of this on Sunday, I got the impression you actually wanted to do it, so I wasn't going to let you off the hook. But if you really don't want to, just say the word, and I'll take you home."

Avery sighed. She was anxious about this. The whole prospect was scary. The thought of attempting to flirt with people freaked her out. She already knew she was bad at it, she was sure she'd do something stupid and humiliating in front of Taylor, who made flirting with people look so effortless. Avery had seen her do it over and over again throughout the party. And she had no idea what Taylor was going to make her do.

But . . . she was also kind of excited. To do something different, to change things up about her life, and to hang out with Taylor, who was fun and hot and relaxed and confident, a whole bunch of things that Avery was not. Taylor was probably never uncertain about anything and probably never worried about what other people thought.

She gestured at the road in front of them.

"Fine. I'm in. Take me wherever you want to go."

Taylor smiled that slightly smug smile of hers and drove on.

"And third of all," she continued, "'a candy-making party'? What the hell is a candy-making party? 'Ax throwing'? Like, actually throwing axes around? Who do you think I am?'"

"Look, I was brainstorming, okay?" Avery said. "I obviously don't know what I'm doing here!"

Taylor smirked.

"Mm-hmm. I can tell."

Avery narrowed her eyes.

"Has anyone ever told you that you're annoying?"

Taylor nodded, a grin on her face.

"All the time, as a matter of fact. I never pay attention."

"That's clear," Avery said under her breath.

"What was that?" Taylor asked.

"Nothing," Avery said. Taylor just laughed.

"Okay, so here are a few flirting tips to keep in mind," Taylor said as she got on the freeway. "First of all, and I know it sounds basic, but bear with me: Make eye contact, at least briefly. Don't stare—at least not until you get a little more advanced at this—but you want people to know that you're looking at them. Second: Smile. You don't have to give everyone the exact same smile, it doesn't have to show all of your teeth or whatever, but people like to spend time talking to someone who seems friendly. And third: Ask people their name and try to remember it. Say it back to them right away, say it a few times in the conversation to keep it in your head. Remembering names makes a difference; people are really flattered by it."

Avery wanted to pull out her phone and write all of this down, but she thought Taylor might make fun of her if she did. Then she thought about what Taylor had said about being honest. Taylor was right; she didn't want to do this if she was going to worry at every moment that Taylor was going to make fun of her. And if

Taylor did make fun of her, fine, she'd just go home. She pulled out her phone and started a new note.

"Okay: eye contact, smile, remember names, anything else?"

Taylor glanced down at Avery's phone and smiled.

"I also don't remember anything unless I write it down. Hmm, okay: Ask people questions about themselves, and really listen to the answers. If they say something interesting, keep asking more questions. I know, I know, this is Conversation 101, but sometimes people think of flirting as something different and freeze up, when it's just a category of conversation. You seem like you have the potential to freeze up."

Avery let out a breath.

"You are correct about that." She added *ask questions, then more questions* to her list.

"But also," Taylor continued, "flirting isn't one size fits all. Pay attention to who you're talking to and how they interact with you. People like to be flirted with the same way they flirt." She laughed. "That goes for other things, too, but I digress. Some of what I said won't work for everyone. Some people don't like eye contact but will hang around and keep talking to you, some people hate being casually touched while others are super into it. What matters is what you like—if you're not vibing with someone, don't force it."

- *Not one size fits all*
- *Pay attention*
- *Like to be flirted with the same way they flirt*

Oh God, this was already so many things. How was she going to remember all of it?

"And I can already feel your shoulders getting tense over there, so please don't try to memorize this all now and think there's going to be a pop quiz or something, little miss A-plus student."

Avery tried to relax her shoulders.

"A quiz would be easier than having to do this in real life," she said.

Taylor ignored that.

"Oh, and this is the most important thing: Only flirt with people that you actually want to flirt with. Where there's some attraction, or they seem friendly, or they say something funny, or they're just very hot, whatever. This is supposed to be fun, and attempting to flirt with people you don't want to flirt with is no fun."

Avery stared at her.

"I'm supposed to do all of this and also have fun?"

Taylor laughed.

"You don't have to do all of it at once! Try to do one or two things, and let the rest come. I'll remember not to give you too much information in the future; I should have known that you would want to ace it all."

There was no chance of her being able to do that.

"Okay, we're here," Taylor said a few minutes later.

"Where are we? What are we doing here?" Avery asked as Taylor pulled into a parking space.

"So suspicious," Taylor said with laughter in her voice. "If you get out of the car, maybe we can go see what we're doing here."

Avery grumbled a little as she unbuckled her seat belt.

"This isn't some escape room or magic show or anything, is it? Because if so, I'm—"

"Avery. I know we don't know each other very well, but do you really think I would take you to a *magic show*? Especially with no warning? Come on. And no, just the thought of escape rooms makes me claustrophobic. But keep throwing out these nightmare scenarios, please. I'll start taking notes for the future." She held a finger up. "Now that I think about it, speed dating would be a good idea." Avery blanched, and Taylor grinned. "Come on. Let's go."

They got out of the car and followed a stream of other women heading in the same direction. Even though Avery had been—slightly—playing up her desire to know what they were doing tonight, she was now deeply curious. Where could these women be going? Was it, like, a jewelry trunk show? No, Taylor wouldn't bring her to that. A major designer sale? No, again, this was Taylor. And plus, that wasn't the vibe of the women around here. They had more of a friendly, young librarian kind of energy. Some sort of a . . . cult meeting? Now she was just grasping at straws.

They turned a corner, and she saw where all of the women were heading.

"We're going to a bookstore?"

Taylor nodded.

"There's this writer I like, Holly Brock. She writes queer romances, she has a new book out, and—"

Avery's mouth dropped open.

"I love her books! Wait, is she here tonight?"

Taylor looked smug again, but Avery didn't even care.

"She is. I thought it would be a good opportunity for you to do some socializing and light flirting with some like-minded strangers. Ease into all of this. Everyone else here will be excited, and you'll have a built-in topic for conversation."

This was much less scary than she'd anticipated.

"A book event," Avery said. "I think I can do that."

"You're welcome," Taylor said.

Avery looked at the women around them again and laughed.

"Oh, nerdy but approachable, I get it." She looked down at her sleeveless blue-and-white-pinstripe shirtdress. "I think I fit the brief?"

Taylor patted her on the arm.

"You do. But remember, you have to talk to people, too. You can't be all wallflower in the corner like I know you want to be."

How did Taylor know that's exactly what she wanted to do? Ah, because that's how she'd gotten into this thing in the first place. She stopped a few feet from the bookstore.

"Do I really have to?" she whispered to Taylor.

Taylor shrugged.

"Like I said, you don't have to do anything you don't want to."

Now Avery felt like an asshole for all the whining she'd been doing since she got in Taylor's car. Taylor was doing this for her to be nice, and she'd just complained the whole way.

"I know, I know. Okay. Let's go." She took a step and then stopped again. "I do better with specific measurables. How many people do I have to talk to?"

"'Specific measurables.'" Taylor shook her head slowly. "Good Lord, you need my help. Okay, fine—five people."

"Five!" Avery tried not to shriek. "I thought you were going to say, like, two! Maybe three!"

"Five," Taylor said firmly. "And you get extra credit for any more than five."

Extra credit? Avery liked the sound of that. She was the queen of extra credit.

Avery took a deep breath.

"Okay. Okay."

"But saying 'hi' or 'excuse me' or whatever doesn't count," Taylor said. "Five actual conversations. And here's one more tip: a compliment is a great conversation starter."

Avery took her phone back out and added *compliments* to the list.

Then she took a breath and walked into the bookstore. There was already a good-size crowd there with some women sitting down, some milling around the store, and others gathered by a table along the side wall. That must be the snack table. If she knew one thing about parties, it was that people often gathered around the food.

Granted, this was a bookstore event, not a party, but she was pretty sure the same principle applied. She walked over to the snack table and turned to ask Taylor if she wanted anything, but Taylor was no longer next to her. Avery glanced around the bookstore, until she finally saw Taylor by the new-fiction shelf. She gave Avery a thumbs-up and an encouraging grin. Oh, so Taylor was going to make her do this all by herself? Great.

Avery took a glass of prosecco, and then put some cheese and crackers on her plate. The other women by the snack table were all in cute colorful dresses and cardigans. Did they all know one another and decide to dress alike? Or was that the unwritten uniform for book events? Or maybe there was a dress code, and Taylor hadn't told her? Taylor didn't seem like the type of person who would care about a dress code.

Okay, now she was just spiraling. She was supposed to be talking to people, remember?

"I love your dress," she blurted out to the woman standing next to her. Oh God, that was awkward. The poor woman looked startled, probably because Avery had almost shouted at her. But Avery hadn't lied, she *did* love her orange and pink maxi dress.

"Oh, thank you," she said. "I just got it. I feel a little overdressed, but I love Holly Brock's books, so I thought it was a great first occasion for it."

Taylor was right, people did love compliments.

"I love her books, too. I'm really excited for this one," Avery said. "Um, also, hi, I'm Avery."

Yep, introducing herself to a stranger who probably wasn't at all interested in talking to her felt just as weird and awkward as she'd anticipated.

"Hi, Avery," the woman said. "I'm Pam. Nice to meet you." And she smiled at Avery—in a stiff way, yes, but it was still a smile.

"Nice to meet you, too, Pam."

Pam walked off with her drink, and Avery took a deep breath. She'd done it. One down.

She glanced in Taylor's direction, and Taylor winked at her. Avery felt a little tingly inside. She threw caution to the wind.

"Those cookies are so cute," she said to the woman across the table. Two in a row!

"Oh my God, they're so good," the woman said. "I've already had one, and I'm hoping they're going to bring out more so that I don't feel guilty for taking two."

Avery laughed as she looked down at the book-shaped cookies.

"Okay, thank you, because sometimes the cutest baked goods taste like nothing, and it's so disappointing."

The woman nodded.

"I know, I hate that. These are great, I promise."

Avery picked one up.

"I'll have to grab one now before they're all gone." She grinned. "Or two. One for my friend over there."

"Good thinking," the cookie enthusiast said. "Thank me later."

Avery put the cookies on her plate and walked back toward the seats. She found two next to a woman wearing a blue dress with an ice-cream cone pattern on it—anyone who wore a dress with ice-cream cones on it must be friendly, right? Avery put the plate of food on the seat next to hers to save it for Taylor.

Then she looked around the room again. A bunch of people already had the book in their laps. Were they supposed to buy the books before the event started, or afterward? She had no idea. See, this was why she didn't like going to events when she hadn't prepared in advance.

Even though she very much did not like confessing her ignorance about anything to anyone, this question might be a good opening. Time for number three. She turned to the woman in the ice-cream cone dress.

"Do you know if we're supposed to buy the book before the event starts? I've never been here before."

Ice-Cream Cone Dress turned to her with an eager expression on her face.

"Oh, either before or after works. But there will be a signing line afterward, and it's usually faster to get in the line if you buy the book first."

Avery was sure Taylor would make her get in the signing line.

"Oh, thanks, I'd better do it now." She started to stand up, and then turned to Ice-Cream Cone Dress again. "Will you save my seats? For me and my friend. Is that weird? I'm Avery."

Oh God, she was so awkward. Was she in kindergarten with this seat-saving thing? This was why she shouldn't be allowed to do things like this.

But Ice-Cream Cone Dress immediately put her bag on Avery's seat.

"Of course. Not weird at all. Nice to meet you, Avery. I'm Mallory."

Avery smiled at Mallory and then turned to find the register. Right, of course, she should have noticed the line of people near the register, all clutching books to their chests. Avery grabbed two copies of the book and joined the line.

Speaking of Taylor . . . aah, there she was, flipping through books in the personal growth section. She glanced up and waved at Avery. Avery smiled at her and waved back.

Fine, this may not have been a terrible plan. She absolutely wouldn't tell Taylor that, though. Especially after how pouty she'd been in the car on the way here; please, how embarrassing would it be to tell Taylor that she'd been right?

Should she try to do one more? It would feel great to get four conversations over with before the book event even started. Granted, nothing she'd done with any of the first three women could in any way be described as flirting, but still, you had to walk before you could run.

She was grateful that Taylor's mission for her tonight had been to just talk to people; thank goodness she would get to ease into flirting.

Oh, look! She had a conversation starter for the woman in front of her. She took a deep breath. Time for number four.

"I've been thinking about getting those sneakers," she said. "They're so cute, are they comfortable?"

The woman turned around, an animated look on her face. She had warm brown skin, and long braids piled up in a big topknot.

"Yes! I'm evangelical about them, honestly. I just moved here, and I wore them all day when we moved in, and my feet weren't sore at all. That's the biggest testament to them, don't you think?"

Avery nodded.

"Absolutely." She remembered what Taylor had said. Follow-up questions. "You just moved here? From where? I'm Avery, by the way."

The woman held out her hand.

"Hi, Avery, I'm Beth. I moved from L.A. My girlfriend . . . well, fiancée and I moved up here for her job; she works for one of the big hotels. She's over there saving our seats. We figured that instead of staying in and trying to organize things, which I absolutely didn't want to do, we'd try to get out and do something fun, see the lay of the land in our new home. So far, it seems good. Do you also live around here?"

Beth seemed better at this conversation thing than Avery was. Thank goodness; someone had to be good at it.

"Yeah, in Napa. Born and raised, though I did leave for a while before coming back."

Beth smiled at her.

"We're neighbors. Well, maybe not neighbors, Napa isn't that small of a town, but you know what I mean. I'm deep into researching things to do in Napa, which has been harder than I thought it would be, because all of the lists are for tourists. There's only so much wine I can drink on a day-to-day basis, you know?"

"Have you discovered anything that sounds good?" Avery asked. She wasn't just asking to keep the conversation going; she really wanted to know. "The problem with growing up in a place is that you get very stuck in your ways and don't experience a lot of new things. At least, that's how it is for me."

"Yeah, I get that," Beth said. "Lots of knitting groups, but I've been working on the same scarf for years, so I'm not sure if I'm the right person for that. A few book clubs, but I like to know at least one person in a book club before I commit—I need to make sure that it's not one of those book clubs where they take it all super seriously, you know? I like to chat about the book, sure, but I don't want it to feel like homework. And there's a gardening club at a local community garden that sounds fun—it meets every Sunday, and I guess the experienced people help the newbies, which I would need. It's already July, so I have no idea if people can still show up for it, but I want to."

"I don't even think I knew we had a local community garden," Avery said. "That sounds like fun. I have a bunch of indoor plants, and I've gotten kind of obsessed with them, but I don't have any outdoor space."

"Oh, you should come to the garden club!" Beth said. "Maybe then I wouldn't be the only new person. I also want to look into some volunteer work, and—"

"Excuse me?" the person at the cash register said. Beth and Avery both looked around and then realized it was Beth's turn to pay.

"Oh! Sorry about that!" Beth said, stepping up to the counter. "Nice to meet you, Avery! I hope I see you at the garden club!" she said after she paid for her books.

"Nice to meet you, too," Avery said. It was only after Beth walked away that Avery realized she should have asked her where the community garden was. Oh well. At least she'd finally had a good conversation with someone.

When Avery got back to their seats, she looked around for Taylor and saw her deep in conversation with someone in the cookbook section. She probably hadn't seen Avery sit down or witnessed her long talk with Beth. But a few minutes later, Taylor slid into the seat next to her.

"Four people, good job," Taylor said in a low voice.

So she had been paying attention. Avery glanced her way.

"You mean five."

That little grin appeared on Taylor's lips again.

"The cashier doesn't count."

Damn it. Avery had hoped she could get away with that.

"Fair," she said.

A woman at the front of the store cleared her throat for attention, and everyone settled into their seats before she introduced both writers. Avery didn't know what she had expected from a book event like this—something like an English class in high school, maybe? But with more pretentious, snotty adults in the audience who could tell this was her first book event and looked down on her? She didn't know why she'd thought that. Especially since she'd always liked English class in high school! But the conversation between the writers wasn't like that at all—relaxed, interesting, and actually kind of funny. And no one in the audience was snotty or pretentious; they were all just nice and friendly and kind of awkward.

Well, not everyone. A few people seemed shy, and a few were hot and aloof. Then there was the very hot and not at all aloof person sitting next to her. She hadn't failed to notice just how many people checked Taylor out and then checked *her* out when they saw that Taylor was with her.

Not *with her* with her, which was probably easy for people to figure out as soon as they watched her and Taylor together. Partly it was because they clearly interacted as just friends (and they were barely friends at that). But mostly it was because someone as magnetic and attractive and fun obviously wouldn't be *with* someone like her, Avery Jensen. She knew she was relatively good-looking, but in a boring, uptight sort of way, and boring and uptight were polar opposites of Taylor.

She wasn't even sure if Taylor noticed all the people looking at her. Was she so used to people checking her out that it didn't even faze her, or was she just oblivious? Avery had no idea, but she was enjoying being in Taylor's reflected glory.

She also was enjoying being with Taylor, and not just because of that. Yes, she oozed sex appeal, but she was also very funny and managed to put Avery at ease in a way few people did.

It had still been humiliating to open herself up so much to a virtual stranger, and embarrassing to smile and make stupid small talk here with people she didn't know, though she had felt kind of triumphant when she'd done it. Even from across the room, it felt like she'd been able to sense Taylor's approval. Maybe she was making that up, though. She probably was. But . . . Taylor *had* paid attention to how many people she'd talked to.

The whole crowd—including Taylor—laughed at something, and Avery mentally shook herself. She'd been sitting here thinking about Taylor instead of listening; that wasn't like her. She had to focus. What if Taylor wanted to talk on the way home about whatever had made everyone laugh? She turned her attention back to the front of the room.

TAYLOR WATCHED AVERY WATCHING THE CROWD. SHE'D PRO-posed these flirting lessons for Avery on a whim, and then she'd half encouraged, half forced her into them mostly because the whole idea of them tickled her. Besides, Avery seemed like she desperately needed her help. Taylor also needed something to keep herself busy for the rest of the summer after her bet with Erica. And okay, maybe it was also a *tiny* bit because she found Avery wildly attractive, in her uptight, buttoned-up kind of way, but it wasn't like she could act on it, because of that damn bet again.

She was a little irritated at Erica about that bet. Mostly because of how smug she'd been in the days since the party, with her little comments about how she was sure she'd win, since Taylor would *never* be able to make it that long. Yes, it would be a challenge, but was that how Erica really thought of her?

Avery laughed at one of the audience questions, and Taylor smiled as she glanced over at her. She'd managed to eavesdrop on Avery during some of her chats with people around the snack table, and the way she'd stuck to the tips that Taylor had given her had been very awkward but also deeply endearing.

The question-and-answer portion of the book talk ended, and Taylor leaned over to Avery.

"Ready to do some flirting in the signing line?"

Avery sighed dramatically.

"That's a yes, I assume?" Taylor asked. She didn't even bother to hold back her grin.

Avery stood up.

"That was a 'ready as I'll ever be.'" She handed a book to Taylor. "Here's your book, by the way."

Taylor looked down at the book Avery had given her.

"Oh, thank you. You didn't have to do that, I could have—"

Avery shrugged.

"I know, but you didn't have to do any of this."

She turned to get in the signing line. Well, that was very sweet.

Avery talked to four more people as they waited in line, and even offered to take pictures of the woman in front of them as she met the author. She was a little stilted and self-conscious at first, but she relaxed some by the end. When Avery got her book signed, she blushed and stammered a bit as she talked to Holly while Taylor snapped a few pictures of them together. It warmed her heart to see the shy smile on Avery's face in the photos.

When they got back into Taylor's car, she turned to Avery.

"You hungry? We could grab something to eat before I drop you off unless your social battery is depleted."

Avery shook her head.

"My social battery is low but not quite in the red yet. And, more importantly, I'm starving. That cookie was delicious, but it wasn't dinner."

Taylor started the car.

"Just tell me where you want to go—dinner is my treat because of all that extra credit you got."

Avery looked over at her.

"You don't have to . . ." She stopped and shook her head. "You know what? No, I'm not going to look this gift horse in the mouth."

Taylor laughed.

"Excellent. It would be no good, anyway."

Avery was mostly quiet on the road, but when they sat down at a corner booth at Taylor's favorite taqueria, she grinned at their tray full of tacos.

"I *did* get a lot of extra credit, didn't I?"

Taylor couldn't help but smile at the proud look on her face.

"So much extra credit," she said. "Eight people, plus both authors. Great job."

She meant that, too. She could tell that it had been hard for Avery to strike up conversations with people, especially at the beginning, but she'd done it, and she'd kept doing it.

"Thanks," Avery said. That was all she said, but Taylor could tell she'd meant it. She'd expected Avery to act like it wasn't a big deal, or that this hadn't been a challenge for her, or even just change the subject. Or that she'd be grumpy in the way that she had been in the car on the way to the bookstore. So, when she just gave Taylor that little smile, and then looked away, it was pretty adorable.

"Did you have any fun?" Taylor asked. "In addition to getting that extra credit, I mean."

Avery let out one of those deep sighs again.

"'Fun' would be overstating it. But, yes, it was enjoyable, I guess." Then she shook her head. "No, sorry, that was ungracious of me. I apologize. I did have a good time. Thanks for thinking of this. And for doing this with me."

Taylor hadn't expected that. She'd assumed Avery would be grumpy and irritable all night, just to hide her vulnerability. Clearly, it had been hard for Avery to say that—she hadn't quite made eye contact with Taylor during that speech—which made it feel all the more genuine.

"You're welcome. But I'm not completely selfless here—I love both of those authors, and I'd been wanting to go to that event. So thanks for coming along with me, and for being a good sport about me making you do this."

Now Avery did look at her.

"But was I a good sport? *Really?*"

They both laughed.

"Okay, well, not at first," Taylor said. "Maybe not even at *second*. But you got there. And it wasn't that bad, was it? This is going to be a breeze for you. You'll be hitting on people and asking them out in no time."

Avery burst out laughing. "I absolutely won't be hitting on people in no time. As for asking people out? Oh God no. Because, wow, that was most definitely not a breeze for me."

At first Taylor laughed at the expression on Avery's face, but then it worried her.

"Was the bookstore really that hard for you?" Was she putting Avery through hell? "It seemed like you were having fun while we were there."

Avery looked up quickly with remorse on her face.

"No, no, I really did. I'm sorry for being such a buzzkill about all of this. I really did have a good time at the bookstore, and I'm so grateful that you thought of this and brought me there, truly. I mean it."

She sounded like she meant it, but Taylor still didn't know her that well. Avery was hard to read.

"You don't have to apologize, but I guess I just want to understand more. You seemed good at chatting with people tonight, and you obviously do it a lot for work, and I'm sure you're great at that. What's so hard about this for you?" Taylor shook her head. "Forget I said it that way, I sounded like an asshole. I just mean—"

"No, you don't sound like an asshole, I get what you mean." Avery's expression had relaxed from the rigid look she'd gotten while Taylor had been talking.

"I guess it's a few things," she said. "This isn't the biggest one, but ugh, the small talk! It's so stupid, I don't know how you do it all day. I mean, I guess I do know—you must have a system like I do when I'm doing it for work. And yeah, I do it for work, but I hate it so much. I do it the same every damn time: blah blah talk about the weather, the traffic, 'ooh, I love your shoes.' But it's so inefficient! I would rather just cut to the chase and get business done, you know?"

Oh God, Avery was one of *those* people.

"No, I don't know," Taylor said. She set down her horchata. "And also no, I don't think small talk is stupid, either. That's the way people get to know one another, trust one another, find common ground in things. What's so great about efficiency anyway? No one is going to trust you to do business with them if they don't think you're someone who will respect them, listen to them and their needs and concerns, take them seriously. Small talk is the way people learn about one another in social contexts. No one is going to want to be friends with you—or go home with you that night—if they can't have a fun little conversation with you about cookies or books or music or whatever. Well, some people would want to go home with you without doing that, but no one you'd be interested in taking home, I bet. How do you think people learn to trust other people with the big talk if they don't start with small talk to warm things up?"

Avery stared wide-eyed at her, and Taylor realized she'd been getting progressively more and more passionate as she talked.

"Sorry, I didn't mean to get so worked up," she said, "but I guess this is something I care a lot about. People are always so dismissive of small talk and the getting-to-know-you type of conversation, and it irritates the hell out of me. Especially since I work in hospitality, and it's one of the things that I do all day, as you noted. And I *like* that about my job. I get to know so many new and different people. Sure, sometimes it's boring, or the people are annoying, but other times those same questions and conversation starters can lead to such interesting stories."

Avery didn't say anything for a moment.

"Don't apologize," she said stiffly. But then Avery always seemed stiff; maybe it was that perfect posture of hers. "I insulted what you do without even thinking about it. I'm sorry. And you've given me something to think about."

Avery looked uncomfortable, and for a moment, Taylor regretted her monologue. Then she pushed that regret away—she and Avery had to be honest with each other, like she'd said, right?

"Good, I'm glad," Taylor said. "Don't worry about insulting me—I mean, don't do it again, for sure—but lots of people feel this way. I think most of the time, it's because they're just nervous in social situations with people they don't know, and maybe a little awkward and self-conscious, so they resent having to do any of that because they hate feeling uncomfortable and bad about themselves. And they blame it on 'small talk' in general, instead of any of the reasons that they feel like that."

Great, right after she'd gone on a rant about what Avery had said, she then turned it back around and made it about Avery being self-conscious and awkward, the very things she was trying to make Avery not feel like.

"I didn't mean that you—"

Avery cut her off.

"You did, and you were right. I *am* awkward and self-conscious in situations like tonight. That's one of the reasons I wanted—sort of—to do these . . . flirting classes or whatever with you."

"Okay, you're definitely not as awkward as you think you are, though you may be very self-conscious. Also, you're not always self-conscious, right? I mean, I've seen you work events, you're great at those. And I saw you talking to other people at the winery party, you seemed to do well there."

"Oh, but see, I know how to do those things," Avery said. "I'm used to events, I'm prepared, I know what to wear"—Taylor grinned at her, and she smiled back—"and who is going to be there and what they're going to be like. Plus, I know what my role is for all of those things. But . . ." She stopped and shook her head. "Never mind, it's nothing."

Taylor gave her a long look.

"Don't do that. It's not nothing. If you don't want to talk about this, just tell me that, but don't say it's nothing."

Avery stared down at the table, her lips in a tight line. Well, this might be it for their flirting lessons.

"I don't really want to talk about this, but fine," she said eventually. "I don't know what I'm supposed to do when it comes to flirting. And I guess I'm worried that people will say—in so many words—'why the hell are *you* talking to *me*,' and then just turn around and walk away."

Taylor laughed softly.

"Ah, so just a perfectly normal fear of rejection, got it. And I totally understand. But the thing about flirting with people—and about making friends, for that matter, since I know that's something else you want to do—is that you have to put yourself out there. Which is hard. But also worth it, because you don't get anything if you don't try. Remember that you're in the driver's seat in this, too. It's not all about you putting yourself out there and waiting for people to reject you—part of this is for you to get more comfortable talking to people, so you can decide if they're even worth your time. Like, do you want to keep talking to *them*? Trust your instincts with people."

Avery shook her head.

"No. My instincts are off. I have a terrible ex-boyfriend, remember?"

Now Taylor was even more determined to help Avery find the great new girlfriend she deserved.

"Yeah, but didn't you know in your heart that he was terrible? And you ignored your instincts? This is what I mean: listen to yourself next time. Like, think about the people you talked to tonight. There were conversations that went better than others, weren't there?"

Avery thought for a moment, then nodded.

"I guess so. Especially one woman I talked to in line to get the books. She's new to Napa, she moved here with her fiancée and doesn't know anyone, and she talked about maybe doing a class at the local community garden, which I didn't even know existed.

And she sort of invited me to go along with her, but then it was her turn to pay, so I'm not sure if she was serious, or . . ."

"Go!" Taylor said. "Yeah, you don't know if she was serious, but isn't it better to go and maybe do something fun, rather than stay home out of fear? This is low stakes, it's a gardening class. If it's weird or whatever, you just leave! And I get it, rejection sucks and is scary. But the only thing to make it less scary is to face it, over and over."

Avery put her head in her hands.

"That sounds terrible."

"I know. But really, that's how you learn that it's not all that bad, that life will go on afterward. So, okay, some of our lessons have to work on that fear of rejection. I have some ideas about how we'll do that."

Avery raised her head. She looked alarmed, as Taylor had known she would.

"And might I ask what those ideas are?"

Taylor grinned.

"You can certainly *ask*."

Avery groaned.

THREE

TAYLOR'S PHONE BUZZED IN HER POCKET AS SHE LEFT THE winery on Thursday evening. She glanced at it to see texts from Erica.

ERICA

You free for dinner? If so, come over!

Or wait, are you busy? Have I already won the bet?

Taylor rolled her eyes.

TAYLOR

i am free for dinner, but if i wasn't that wouldn't mean you won. having dinner with someone does not equal sleeping with them

Erica responded to that before Taylor had even gotten to her car.

ERICA

When it's you it does.

Anyway, come over. Sam is away for work and I just ordered an enormous amount of pizza because I'm hungry for everything right now. Plus, you haven't seen our new deck and backyard yet!

TAYLOR

hmm. what kind of pizza?

Taylor got into her car and laughed at the outrage that she knew would be on Erica's face when she saw that text. Sure enough, she responded with a middle finger emoji.

Her relaxed, easy text conversation with Erica made her think about the much less easy conversation she'd had with Avery at dinner. Had she pushed Avery too far to talk about why flirting was hard for her? She'd seemed reluctant, and maybe embarrassed, to talk about that. Taylor wondered if this was all too much for her, if Avery would call all of this off. She really hoped not.

She stopped at a bakery on the way to Erica's house and picked up a half dozen brownies at end-of-the-day prices. She wasn't sure what Erica's pregnancy cravings were, since she'd just found out that Erica was pregnant, but brownies never hurt.

It was weird enough that Erica and Sam had bought an actual house, but their home was on a perfectly manicured street, where all the houses had rose gardens or succulent gardens or flowering jasmine or all three, and some had actual white picket fences. If you'd driven her and Erica down this street five years ago and said that Erica would live there in a matter of years, they'd both be hysterical with laughter. And yet.

She and Erica had known each other for over ten years; they'd been friends since Erica's first day on the job at the restaurant in Berkeley where Taylor worked. Up until then, Taylor had been the only Black server; they'd gone out for drinks after that first shift and had been friends ever since. That had been the only time they'd worked together, but their friendship had stayed solid. Taylor bounced around, working at a bunch of different cafés and restaurants as a barista, server, and bartender, while Erica had gotten her aesthetician's license and worked in a spa during the day and at restaurants at night. About five years ago, they'd both moved up to Napa Valley—Erica because she'd gotten a job at a hotel spa, and Taylor because Erica had floated the idea that she come along since rent was so much cheaper and they were both sick of their roommates. Taylor had shrugged and said, "Why not?"

She'd had no trouble getting jobs up in Napa; there were tons of restaurants and bars, she worked hard and was good at her job, and customers always loved her. She'd gotten her first job at a winery when one of her favorite customers had an opening and asked her if she'd be interested. The job at the winery started as just a lark, one that she did on the side, but slowly—and especially after she moved to Noble, which paid well to start off, and then promoted her—she started cutting back on her hours at her restaurant jobs. Now, she worked at restaurants only occasionally, usually when she got a panicked phone call from one of her old bosses that they were shorthanded and please, please, could she work tonight?

Taylor hadn't expected to be in Napa for long, but she was happier than she ever thought she'd be, so she'd stayed. Even after she and Erica stopped being roommates, they'd still lived in the same apartment building. And after Erica met Sam, nothing major had changed; Erica and Sam had just moved into a larger apartment in the building.

Then they'd gotten married, and then Erica and Sam had bought this house, and it felt like everything changed. She couldn't help but feel sometimes like they were the grown-ups and she was the kid, still dating around, with no interest in getting married or even a serious relationship, still in an apartment, still in a service job. She loved her job, that wasn't it, but was everyone else miles ahead of her as she just trailed behind?

She shook that off and got out of the car. Erica met her at the front door and immediately looked down at the pink bakery box in her hands.

"Is that for me? See, I was going to be all mad at you for not even telling me for sure that you were coming, and then you show up with . . ." Taylor flipped the box open. "*Brownies?* Ugh, you're the worst. Thank God for you, come in."

She led Taylor straight into the kitchen, where both pizzas were on the counter.

"In answer to your question, one Hawaiian; one pepperoni, mushroom, and hot honey. I was craving that salty-sweet thing, you know, and I couldn't decide between the two, so I ordered both. I also ordered a salad, since I'm supposed to be eating vegetables for the baby, I guess, but all I'm craving is baked goods and salty things. Though"—she grinned—"I guess that's what the baby wants, and who am I to disobey a baby's commands?"

Taylor grabbed flatware out of a drawer.

"How's our little one doing in there?"

Wow, that was awkward. *Our little one?* What did that even

mean? Well, they hadn't found out whether it was a boy or a girl yet, so she couldn't call it him or her. Not that Taylor believed in enforced gender roles. And she couldn't call the baby "it"—she'd made that mistake once, and people seemed to get *really* upset when you used *it* for a baby.

"Good, at least that's what the doctor said last week. I can't believe I'm only halfway through this." Erica put pizza on her plate, and they walked into the living room.

"They say the baby is the size of a mango now," Erica said. Taylor almost choked on her slice of pizza.

"A mango? Why are you supposed to imagine your unborn baby as a mango?"

Erica laughed.

"Oh, it's a whole thing! I guess because people can imagine that size? Every week it's a different fruit or vegetable. Sort of helpful, very weird."

Very weird seemed like a good description of most things having to do with pregnancy and babies, Taylor was discovering. Speaking of. She went to the kitchen, and when she came back, she presented Erica with a plate heaped full of greens.

"Salad time, my friend," she said. "Sam will kill me if she comes home and all you've eaten are pizza and brownies."

Erica rolled her eyes but obediently took a bite of salad.

"I even got a salad with broccoli in it, see how committed I am to this vegetable thing?" She brandished a piece of broccoli at Taylor, who laughed and started eating her own salad.

"I'm very impressed. And just for that, you can have a brownie for dessert."

Erica giggled.

"I'm not going to stop at one. But also! That's not how you're supposed to do it anymore with kids. The experts say not to force them to eat things they don't like or make food they do like a reward for eating something they don't. It turns food into a power struggle and can lead to body image issues and other problems with food. I learned about this from a parenting book my friend Sloane gave me."

"Sloane? You have a friend named Sloane?" Taylor asked.

"Yes, you remember her! You met her at my housewarming party," Erica said. "We've had this conversation before."

Well, Sloane clearly hadn't made any impression on Taylor.

"I'm glad she gave you that book, and I will definitely never turn food into a power struggle with our forthcoming little mango, and I certainly won't allow anyone else to do it, either," Taylor said. "You're going to have to coach me; you know I don't know much about babies. Can I say, 'You are such a good little mango, eating all of your broccoli like that'? Wait!" Her eyes widened. "What if you think of your kid as a mango and then you serve them mangoes? What if you think of your kid as a broccoli and then you serve them broccoli? OH GOD, what if you think of your kid as a potato? That will ruin potatoes forever!"

Erica was laughing so hard she almost choked on her broccoli.

"Oh no, I've created a monster," she said. "You're going to call this baby 'mango' for the rest of their life, aren't you?"

Taylor considered that.

"Well, at least until our little mango in there has a real name . . . and okay, yes, maybe for a while after that."

Erica shook her head.

"Thank goodness we didn't have this conversation a few weeks from now," she said. "Soon the baby will be the size of a rutabaga."

They both let out peals of laughter.

"Rutabaga!" Taylor said as soon as she could speak. She put her hand on Erica's belly. "How's my little rutabaga in there?" Erica bent double with laughter. Seeing her laugh so hard set Taylor off again, and soon she was wiping tears from her eyes.

Taylor looked sternly at Erica when she was mostly recovered.

"Are you trying to distract me? I notice you aren't eating your broccoli."

Erica pouted and picked up her fork.

"That's better," Taylor said. She looked at the stack of parenting books sitting on the coffee table and grinned. Erica grinned back at her as she stabbed broccoli with her fork.

"I know, I know, it's really early to think about this now, but you know me—I've been reading every parenting book I can. I like to be prepared."

Taylor had assumed this. She *did* know Erica.

"Oh, speaking of, I ran into what's-her-name at the bookstore the other day."

"Camille? She always had such a thing for you. Did she ask you out when you saw her at the bookstore?'"

"Well, as a matter of fact . . ."

Erica laughed.

"Was 'the other day' before or after our bet? Have I already won?"

Did Erica think she couldn't look at a woman without sleeping with her? She wasn't that bad.

At least, not all the time.

"It was after our bet, and no, you haven't won. I told her that it wasn't the right time—which was true—but that I'd be happy to grab a drink or coffee with her anytime."

It had been weird, to have that conversation while she was out with Avery. Not that she was on a date with Avery, but still.

"See, this bet is good for you," Erica said. "It's making you stop and think about dating people. Not to be an old married lady, but—"

That never prefaced anything good.

"I feel like you just have to give a real relationship a chance," Erica continued.

Taylor picked up another piece of pizza so she wouldn't actively roll her eyes. This pregnancy had made Erica want the whole world to settle down.

"That's exactly what Gemma said when I broke up with her. I 'didn't give our relationship a chance.' Maybe I'm just not a relationship person. Not everyone has to be one, you know."

Erica sighed.

"I know, of course I know that. I just—"

Taylor didn't want to hear this. It was going to be something like *I just want you to grow up and get married in a big fancy wedding and buy a house and have a baby like me*, when Taylor knew that's not what she wanted.

"*I* think you should eat more of that salad, so Little Rutabaga in there doesn't get scurvy."

Erica burst out laughing.

"I don't think you can get scurvy before you're even born, but point taken." She stabbed the salad with her fork and shoved it in her mouth. "See?"

Taylor nodded.

"Finish that, and then we can talk. Speaking of this bet, I've been thinking about what I'll win. This is a big one, so I think I get a big prize."

Erica laughed.

"I had a brilliant idea about what my prize will be when *I* win. You'll have to throw my baby shower!"

Taylor recoiled.

"Throw your what? Didn't we go through this when you got married?" Taylor had been happy to be Erica's maid of honor but had drawn a firm line when it came to throwing a shower.

"Yeah, but you threw us a really great party, even though you refused to call it a shower." A sort of firm line. "I bet you'd throw as great a baby shower as you did the wedding shower."

Taylor shook her head.

"I would not! You need to know things about babies to throw baby showers! Like . . . onesies and diapers and things. I've never been to a baby shower in my life, I can't start out by throwing one! And your mom will insist on being there, and she terrifies me."

Erica shivered.

"She terrifies all of us, and yes, you're right, she'll insist on being there. But that's it, that's what you'll have to do if—when—I win."

Taylor reached for another piece of pizza.

"Okay, fine, then. When *I* win, you have to get me a spa day. A whole day, mind you, and not just a facial or massage, but the whole 'mud bath, steam room, scrub-down' kind of thing."

Erica reached out a hand.

"Deal."

They shook on it with identical smug grins on their faces.

"Anyway," Taylor said. "Now that my evenings are empty, because of you, I'm occupying my time by giving flirting classes." That was, if Avery didn't change her mind.

Erica dropped her fork.

"You're doing what? Where? Also, why didn't you ever give *me* these classes, I could have used them!"

"Finish your salad," Taylor said. "They aren't formal classes—or that formal, anyway. Do you know Avery Jensen? She's a friend of Luke's, they went to high school together, she's an event planner . . . anyway. She had a bad breakup recently, and she's never really dated women, and she wants to but doesn't know how or where to start. She was telling me about all of this at the winery party, and long story short, we had our first lesson on Tuesday night."

Erica narrowed her eyes.

"Wait, was she that woman with the long hair and the immaculate white dress who was helping you over at the bar?"

Taylor nodded. She still didn't understand how Avery had managed to drink wine and eat tacos outside and keep that dress perfect.

Erica's eyebrows raised in amusement.

"Taylor Cameron. You come up with a different way of seducing people every single time. This is some sort of long con to get her into bed, isn't it? This poor woman, she doesn't even know what hit her."

Taylor glared at her.

"'Seducing people'? Who do you think I am, some old-school movie villain? I'm not trying to seduce her! I'm just helping to bring her out of her shell a bit." Yes, fine, she was *attracted* to Avery, but she wasn't trying to get her into bed or anything. Even aside from the bet, Avery didn't seem like she was ready for that. "I'm just trying to help someone learn how to date women. It's my gift to the queer community, which has given so much to me."

That sent them both into another fit of laughter.

"Okay, how are you doing this?" Erica asked. "Tell me everything."

"That's why I was at the bookstore, actually. I brought her there for a book event for a queer author and made her talk to people there. Not quite flirting yet, but baby steps."

Erica put another piece of broccoli into her mouth.

"I can't *wait* to see how this goes," Erica said. "And I especially can't wait to see what happens when our friends—and some of your exes . . . two groups that overlap quite a bit—see you going on these flirting dates. Please, keep me posted."

Taylor grinned.

"Oh, I will."

AFTER AVERY GOT HOME ON TUESDAY NIGHT, SHE'D PICKED UP her phone at least three or four times to text Taylor. She was going to say thank you for everything, but she didn't want to keep learning how to flirt. This was going to be too hard, too stressful. She could tell Taylor had gone easy on her this time, and yet she'd had to talk about her fear of people making fun of her and her fear of rejection? How humiliating.

But then she'd thought about what Taylor would say—and what Taylor would *think* but not say—if she got that text from Avery. She wouldn't say anything bad; she'd let Avery off the hook easy and would probably text back something like *ok, no problem, good luck*, and that would make Avery feel even more terrible. Ugh.

The fourth time she picked up her phone, she made herself look up community gardens in Napa, just to see what Beth had been talking about. The garden was only a few blocks away from her building, and the class Beth had mentioned was at two on Sunday afternoon. Should she go? Gardening was a hobby, wasn't it? And she'd liked Beth, who was also trying to do new things and meet new people around here.

For days, she'd gone back and forth about whether to go to the garden, even on Sunday, while she was getting dressed in her oldest jeans and a plain gray T-shirt. (That's what people wore to garden, right?) She hesitated again right before leaving her apartment. Why was she doing this, anyway? The whole prospect of it seemed overwhelming, chaotic, dirty. Shouldn't she just stay home and rearrange her bookshelves again?

She thought of what Taylor would say if she knew that Avery had chickened out about something so simple as walking into a community garden. She wouldn't say anything mean, or judgmental— Avery barely knew Taylor, but she knew that much by now. No, she would just ask Avery, in that friendly, open way of hers, why she hadn't gone, and Avery would have to tell her that the prospect of going to a garden seemed too much for her. Avery let out a frustrated sigh. *Fine, Taylor. You win this one.* She pulled open her front door and walked outside.

She followed the directions on her phone to the garden, just to make sure she went the right way, even though she'd driven down that street a million times. She'd never noticed the garden there, after all; maybe there was some secret to finding it.

As it turned out, it had been hiding in plain sight all along. There was an unobtrusive wooden gate, with a sign that read COMMUNITY GARDEN on top. Avery could hear what sounded like friendly chatter behind the gate. She paused before opening it. Like Taylor said, she could always just leave if she hated it or if people were unfriendly. That's why cell phones had been invented, so you could pretend you got an emergency call and escape. She made herself push the gate open and walk inside.

She stopped just by the garden, her eyes wide. How had she never known this place was here? It was wild and overgrown, neat and orderly, busy and calm, all at once. There were rows and rows of raised garden beds, most of which had many varieties of plants growing in them, of different shapes and sizes. Some were drooping over the edges of the beds, spilling their leaves and fruit almost to the ground; others were standing up high, full of bright red and yellow and orange and white flowers. The dirt paths were neatly raked, but growing along the sides were tiny plants. (Or weeds? She had no idea.) Trees lined the perimeter of the garden, a few of which were clearly fruit trees. Maybe they all were. In the middle of the golden-brown, sun-bleached Northern California summer, where they hadn't seen rain in months, this place was lush and green and vibrant. She'd lived around here for so long, had driven by countless times, and this garden was just here all along?

There was a buzz of activity, with people industriously hoeing or weeding or whatever you did to plants, at many of the beds and more people milling around the exterior of the garden. Some gardeners were chatting and smiling and showing one another plants with more excitement in their faces than Avery thought possible. Only a few were just silently working in their beds. It was very cool to see this level of activity at a place in her neighborhood that she hadn't even known existed. Almost everyone looked friendly and like they were having fun, and like they might be welcoming to a new person.

But . . . where was she supposed to go for the garden club? Honestly, she hated being in situations where she didn't know what she was doing, so this situation was like one of her anxiety dreams. Should she turn around and leave right now?

"You seem confused. Are you here for the garden club?" Avery looked down, and a petite woman with short gray hair and more muscles in one arm than Avery had ever had in her whole body was standing in front of her.

"Um, yes?" Avery said.

"This way." The woman set off down one of the long dirt paths at a fast clip. She was wearing oversize khaki cargo pants and a slim-fitting green T-shirt, and she carried a large canvas tote bag over her arm, with all sorts of gloves and tools sticking out of it. She walked so fast that Avery scurried to catch up with her, but she didn't look back to see if Avery was following her. She stopped abruptly near the center of the garden, where a small group was gathered under a tree. One of the women in the group turned around when they approached, and Avery was both thrilled and relieved to see that it was Beth. She'd liked her as soon as she'd met her; she was so glad she was here. But wait, oh no, would Beth think she was stalking her or hitting on her or something?

But a wide smile spread across Beth's face as soon as she saw Avery.

"Hi! Oh my goodness, I'm so glad you came. Now I know at least one person. You're Avery, right?"

Avery smiled back at her. Taylor had said to trust her instincts about people; maybe Taylor was right.

"Yeah. You're Beth, aren't you? I never even knew this place existed; thanks for mentioning it. It always takes new people to show you stuff about the place you live." She lowered her voice and leaned closer to Beth. "But I have to confess: I don't know anything about gardening."

Beth grinned at her.

"That's okay, we can learn together."

"Garden club!" Everyone immediately quieted down and turned to the woman who had led Avery over there. She had that kind of voice. "I see that we have some new members today, welcome." She nodded in the direction of Avery and Beth, and everyone in the group turned to look at them. Avery tried to smile, to look friendly, but she probably just looked terrified. "For those of you who don't know me, I'm James Kincaid, I'm a Napa County Master Gardener, and I'm the president of the garden club here. It sounds like a very big title, but simply means I'm here all the time, and I'm always available for your garden questions. We meet here on Sundays because many of us have beds here, and sometimes at members' homes and gardens throughout the area for lectures and discussions. For the new people"—she turned to stare straight at Avery and Beth—"as you can see, we're deep into summer growing, and the vast majority of the garden is all planted up. But if you two are willing to share, we just had one garden bed open up for the rest of the year. Do you want it?"

Way to put us on the spot, James. Avery had a lot of questions: What did taking over one garden bed entail? Did they have to pay for it? What were they supposed to plant? Did they get graded on their plants? Could they fail out of the garden if their plants died? Was it a cursed garden plot since it opened up in the middle of the summer?

As she tried to decide which question to start with, she saw Beth looking at her with raised eyebrows. Right, okay, this was a yes-or-no question. She nodded at Beth, and Beth turned to James.

"We'd love to share, thank you! And we'll take advice and guidance from anyone who is willing; we're both very inexperienced at this."

James nodded to them.

"Good." She handed them each a form. "Fill that out and pay the city online. I'll take you to your bed shortly. Now, who wants to go first?"

Avery had no idea what that was in reference to, but apparently everyone else in the garden club did, because one person toward the front of the group raised their hand.

"Lillian, thank you," James said. "Lead us to your bed."

Beth turned to Avery, her eyes full of mirth. She pulled Avery down so she could whisper in her ear.

"If she doesn't stop saying 'your bed' like that, I am one hundred percent going to lose it. So far, it's been that we have to share a bed, she's going to show us our bed, and now 'lead us to your bed'? This is too much for me."

Avery held back a giggle as they followed the group to Lillian's bed. Lillian pointed out her vegetables and flowers and told the group about the problems she was having with them, and then the group gave her advice. And then James asked for the next person to go, and a man named Damien raised his hand, and they went through the same routine with his . . . bed. This was apparently the way the Sunday meetings worked, at least this time of year. They walked around and talked about people's gardens, which, honestly, was very soothing. Everyone used words that Avery didn't know, like *black spot* and *germination* and *leaf curl*, and there was a lot of headshaking or excitement about things she'd never heard of. A few people standing around her and Beth must have seen the confusion on their faces, because they explained things to them in low voices, which was very sweet. Avery understood only about a quarter of their explanations, but she thanked them and filed away her questions for later.

Once they were done walking around to the different beds, James pointed at her and Beth.

"You two. Come with me. I'll take you to your bed."

Avery did not make eye contact with Beth, knowing that if she did, they'd both start giggling. James led them to a plot in the far corner of the garden. It already had a bunch of plants in it, most of which Avery couldn't identify, but a few were definitely tomato plants. She could tell by the tiny green tomatoes hanging on them.

"We usually have a long waiting list for plots here, but this is a special case. Henrietta had to move away for the rest of the year, but she's hoping to be back next year, so she didn't want to give her plot up. She already planted some tomatoes and peppers before she moved; I've been tending to them, but I'll pass this bed over to you two for the rest of the year. You can add—or take away—anything you want, and you can ask me or anyone else at the garden for assistance if you have any questions. Here." She pulled two cards out of one of her voluminous pockets and handed one to both Avery and Beth. "We get discounts at the local garden center, show them that for anything you want to buy."

"Oh, thank you," Avery said. She slipped the card into her pocket but wasn't sure how much she'd use it. Would she really end up buying that many plants? She glanced over at Beth, but Beth wasn't looking at her. She was staring down at her phone with a weird look on her face.

"If you want to remove anything from the bed, don't throw it away," James said so forcefully that Avery immediately felt guilty, like she'd already been planning to dig up and throw out the entire bed to start from scratch.

"Oh, no, of course not," Beth said. Okay, good, it made Beth feel guilty, too. "What, um, should we do with it instead?"

"There's a plant exchange here, just pot it up and put it on the shelf by the entrance, someone will take it. You should look over there before you go to the garden center, someone might have what you want."

A plant exchange. Adorable.

"I'll leave you two now to take stock of your bed."

And with that, James stalked away, and left Avery and Beth standing next to their bed.

"She kind of scares me, you?" Avery asked Beth in a low voice.

Beth nodded but didn't look at Avery. She stared down into their garden bed, with a distant look on her face.

"Um, yeah, me, too," she said.

Oof, okay. Avery had meant that as a joke, a we're-in-this-together kind of thing, but apparently it hadn't landed. Maybe she'd read this all wrong. She'd thought she and Beth were bonding, that maybe she'd found someone who could be a new friend. Did Beth not want that? Was she being too friendly too early? Did Beth not want her to get the idea that just because they were sharing a garden bed—*garden plot* was maybe a better way to say that—that they could be friends? Yeah, that was probably it.

"I think I'll head home now," she said. "I'll, um, go to the garden store or whatever sometime this week."

Beth sat down at the edge of their plot.

"Yeah, okay," she said.

Avery turned to walk away. And then she remembered something Taylor had said the other night. *The thing about flirting with people—and about making friends, for that matter—is that you have to put yourself out there. Which is hard! But also worth it, because you don't get anything if you don't try.* Ugh, fine. If this crashes and burns, it will be all Taylor's fault.

She turned back to Beth.

"Um, is everything okay?"

Beth had been staring at the ground. She looked up at her with tears in her eyes.

"I'm sorry, I don't mean to be such a buzzkill. I'll be fine, it's just that . . ." She shook her head. "Sorry, you don't want to hear all of this."

Avery sat down next to her.

"I wouldn't have asked if I didn't want to hear it. You don't have to tell me if you don't want to, though."

Beth turned to face her.

"No, that's not it. It's so stupid, I mean, I feel stupid about it, it's no big deal, even though it feels like one. It's just that Greta and I keep fighting about what we want our wedding to be. And it's not even like the normal fights that people have, because I know what she would want and she knows what I would want. I keep insisting that it's fine for us to just elope at the courthouse because I know she doesn't want a big wedding or to deal with her family because her mom will want to take over, and she keeps insisting that it's fine for us to have an actual wedding because she knows I really want my family there because I'm so close to them. I feel like no matter what we do, one of us is going to be miserable, and that's not what I want for our wedding, you know? And she just texted me to tell me about the discount she gets to have for big events at her hotel, and it made me sad all over again." Beth wiped her eyes. "See? So stupid."

Avery patted her on the back. Awkwardly, yes, but at least it made Beth smile.

"It's not stupid. Of course it's a big deal; weddings matter to people. It doesn't make you stupid to care about it."

"I wish she would just let us elope! I know that's what she wants to do! She mentioned a long time ago, before we even started dating, that the only way she'd want to get married is for only her and her partner to know about it ahead of time, so she wouldn't have to deal with all of the stress of her family and other people and everything. And I know she still feels that way. She's being so stubborn!"

Avery pressed her hands together. The event planner in her turned on. There must be a solution to this.

"So, it's just that she doesn't want people to know in advance?"

"Yeah. I thought maybe a compromise could be we could elope, then have a party later, but I know she'd say that I'd be sad that my family wasn't there for the actual marriage, which is true, but I could get over it! But I bet her mom would try to take over planning the party—especially once she knew we'd eloped—so I didn't even bring that up."

"I have a better idea," Avery said. "What about a surprise wedding? Sort of an elopement, sort of a wedding—you tell everyone that it's an engagement party, or birthday party, or something, to get them there. No one knows in advance, your families are all there, you have snacks and champagne, you both go up to the front of the venue with whoever is officiating, and boom, the party turns into a wedding!"

Avery bit her lip after she finished talking. She'd forgotten for a second that she wasn't talking to a client who had asked for her opinion, but to Beth, someone who she barely knew. Would it upset Beth that she was butting in, giving advice?

"Um, I *love* this idea," Beth said. "Oh my God, especially since Greta's birthday is on Christmas Day; we could make it a New Year's Eve wedding, and I'd tell everyone she's finally having a big birthday party so they have to come." She stood up. "I have to go home right now and see how she feels about this before I get too excited. And even if she doesn't love it, thank you for this, you've given me hope that we can figure this out." She threw her arms around Avery and gave her a hard hug, and then took off for the exit.

"Thanks again!" she shouted when she was halfway there. "Meet you here on Wednesday?"

"Okay, see you then!" Avery shouted back.

Later that same night, Avery got a text from an unknown number.

BETH

> Hi! This is Beth, from the garden—I got your number from James, I hope that's ok? I just wanted to text because Greta LOVES the surprise idea, and we can't thank you enough! Want to meet at the plant store tomorrow to buy some plants for our bed???

Avery smiled down at her phone. She wasn't sure about this hobby thing, but maybe, just maybe, she'd found a new friend.

FOUR

"GUESS WHAT?" AVERY SAID WHEN SHE GOT INTO TAYLOR'S car on Tuesday night.

"What?!" Taylor opened her eyes dramatically. Avery knew Taylor was gently making fun of her, but the smile in her eyes took the sting away.

"I, um, went to the garden on Sunday," she said.

Taylor's fake excitement left her face, replaced by a big, and real, smile.

"You did it! That's awesome. How did it go?"

Taylor smiled at her like she was proud of her. That felt good, especially since Avery was proud of herself. She'd almost texted Taylor about this on Sunday night, but she wasn't sure if she and Taylor were texting friends. All they'd ever texted about so far was Taylor telling her what time she was going to pick her up and what to wear. Plus, it felt good to tell her about this in person.

"It was sort of fun? Beth, from the bookstore, was there, and the very bossy head gardener assigned us a garden bed together."

"A garden *bed*?" Taylor said. "Avery, you minx."

Avery laughed.

"That's exactly how Beth and I both reacted. My God, Taylor, she kept saying things like 'I'll take you to your bed' and 'are you two willing to share a bed,' and we almost died."

"Hmmm, there's hope for you," Taylor said.

"What was that?" Avery asked.

Taylor shook her head with a grin.

"Nothing, continue."

God, that grin of Taylor's was deadly. No wonder Avery had overheard her friend call her the hottest catch in Napa Valley.

Wait, they were talking about the garden, remember?

"Anyway, the garden stuff was actually fun. I'm not sure how I feel about gardening, it seems both more work and also more confusing than I thought it would be, but like you said, this is low stakes, right? And Beth and I planned what we're going to plant—we met up at the garden store yesterday. It's no big deal, we're just planting some seeds and little baby plants and stuff, but—"

"It feels like it's a big deal," Taylor said. "Especially since—I mean, I don't know you very well, so correct me if I'm wrong—but I get the impression that you don't like doing things you're not already good at."

"Of course I don't," Avery said. "Does anyone?"

Taylor laughed. Definitely at her, this time.

"Most people don't mind it as much as you do. You have to be bad at things while you learn how to do them. At least, most people do."

"Hmmm." Avery thought about that for a moment. "Yeah, nope, still sounds terrible."

Taylor chuckled as she started the car.

"And, on that note, time to head out to tonight's big event. I hope we aren't late."

Avery looked sideways at her.

"Late to where?"

Taylor just grinned at her.

A little while later, they pulled into the parking lot of a community center in Napa. The lot was almost full, and people were still streaming in. Avery looked at their outfits, and then looked down at herself with a frown.

"You told me to wear something I could move in, so I wore leggings and a tank top. Look at all these people wearing flowy dresses! Where are we?"

Taylor gave her a teasing little smile.

"This is a community center! I didn't realize it was here, either, all tucked away in this backstreet, but—"

"That's not what I meant, and you know it!"

Taylor smirked at her.

"Yep. Come on."

Avery got out of the car, her mind turning over possibilities of what could be inside that community center.

"Maybe the people in dresses are going somewhere different than we are, and they're just a misdirection to trip me up. Is this an aerobics class or something? Are you going to make me flirt with people while I do aerobics?"

"An *aerobics* class?" Taylor asked with an indignant tone. "Do I look like a person who would make you go to an aerobics class?" She stopped and turned to Avery. "I need to know the answer to that right now before I go any farther."

Avery looked Taylor up and down. She was in a snug black tank top, cutoff denim shorts, and stylish black sneakers. Infuriating, sexy, and impossibly cool—that was Taylor. Aerobics class, she was not. She let out an aggravated sigh.

"Fine, no, you don't look like a person who would make me go to an aerobics class. If not aerobics, then yoga? Is it yoga? You seem like a yoga kind of person, all relaxed and chill about everything. Only you would wear jean shorts to yoga, but I can see it."

"No one else in the world would describe me as relaxed and chill, but I guess compared to you, I am," Taylor said. "But I feel like *you* seem like a yoga kind of person, all tense and anxious. People like you flock to yoga and wear perfectly put-together outfits like the one you're wearing right now." Taylor gestured to Avery's black leggings, pink tank top, and white ballet-style sweater. "'Something you can easily move in' doesn't need to be full-on designer athleisure, you know."

Avery laughed at her.

"This is all from Target, thank you very much, but I appreciate the backhanded compliment."

Taylor rolled her eyes. "You know what I mean."

Yeah, she knew what Taylor meant.

"You're one of those yoga people, aren't you?" Taylor asked. "I can tell. I only know what the outfits look like because I see all of the women flocking to the yoga studio on my block, racing to be first in line for class. It's like they're in a competition to see who can be the most flexible, or the most meditative, or who can win the prize of best friends with Adriene."

Avery pointed at her and cackled.

"Aha! I was right! You gave yourself away with the Adriene reference. You *do* do yoga! You want to be best friends with Adriene and everything! Is that what we're doing tonight? Is it a yoga class?"

Taylor sighed, but with a grudging smile on her face.

"As soon as that came out of my mouth, I knew I'd given myself away. Fine, I have been known to do yoga with Adriene *occasionally*. But no, it's not yoga."

Taylor looked around as they kept walking toward the community center, and then she turned to Avery and lowered her voice.

"Okay, I can tell why you thought it was going to be a yoga class, because like half of the people here are in either outfits like yours or what I call *sexy* athleisure—the kind where you can tell that outfit has never actually been worn for exercise, it's just to make the wearer look as hot as possible. All bare midriffs and slightly too-small sports bras and pristine sheer leggings."

Avery knew what Taylor meant and held back a giggle.

"Give them the benefit of the doubt! Maybe they are exercising in those outfits, and they just take care of them very well."

Taylor waggled her eyebrows.

"Oh, I'm not complaining. Didn't I say they're wearing them just to make themselves look as hot as possible? It's working. I'm glad I'm here for the show."

Avery elbowed Taylor and kept walking.

"You should be ashamed of yourself."

Taylor walked along with her, a big smile on her face.

"Oh, I am, I absolutely am."

Did Taylor think *her* outfit made her look as hot as possible? No, probably not—she'd clearly differentiated Avery's outfit from the sexy athleisure that other people were wearing.

Whatever. It didn't matter.

A carful of people pulled into a spot right in front of the community center, and everyone who got out of it was wearing brightly colored dresses with full skirts. Avery turned to Taylor in a panic.

"Okay, now I feel very underdressed, and if there's one thing I hate, it's being underdressed. You've got to tell me why some people look like they're going to the most fun wedding in the world, and some people—people like me—look like we're going to yoga class."

Taylor patted her on the shoulder.

"Thank you for telling me you hate being underdressed. I should have figured that out, but I'll remember it for the future. But you're dressed just fine, and you'll find out the answer to your question in literally just a few seconds, so come on."

Avery groaned but kept walking, and once they got close enough, she read the sign on the door.

"'Queer Salsa Dancing,'" she read out loud. Oh no.

"Isn't it a fun idea?" Taylor said. "I heard about it a while ago, but I've never been. There's a class once a month."

Avery opened the door for her.

"A really fun idea," she said, because it was, in theory. Would it be fun for her? Absolutely not. She bit her lip and looked at Taylor. "The thing is . . . I don't know how to salsa dance. Like, at all."

Taylor grinned back at her.

"Neither do I. We're both learning something new tonight." She paused. "Well, you're learning more than one thing tonight, but who's counting?"

"You definitely seem to be," Avery muttered.

"Some ground rules first," Taylor said. Rules, okay, good. She liked rules. "You have to dance with strangers, so if there's anyone here you know, you can't dance with them, including me." She grinned again, that slightly evil grin that Avery was starting to both anticipate and dread. "You also have to be the one to approach people to dance with, *and* it has to be someone you find attractive."

Of course Taylor would raise the difficulty of their second lesson exponentially.

"How did you manage to make this sound even scarier than it already was?"

Taylor threw an arm around her.

"You're going to be great at this. I have faith in you!"

"Has anyone ever told you that you should have been a cheer-leader?"

Taylor let out a bark of laughter.

"Not even once. Come on."

As they walked toward the registration table, Avery kept look-ing around. She nudged Taylor and inclined her head toward the center of the room, where two older women were practicing moves.

"Look at those two. They really know what they're doing."

Taylor stopped, and they watched them together for a while. Their brightly colored dresses flowed back and forth with them as they moved. Everyone had backed away to give them space.

"Fantastic," Taylor said. "This is going to be fun."

They walked up to the registration table, and Taylor gave the woman their names.

"You both are beginners, yes?"

"Yes, and some of us"—Taylor inclined her head toward Avery—"are a little nervous." Of course Taylor would embarrass her like this. The woman at the desk gave them a warm smile and grabbed both of their hands. She looked straight into Taylor's eyes, then Avery's.

"Beauties like the two of you? Nervous? Impossible. I can al-ready tell you'll be the stars of the class today." She probably said that to everyone, but in that moment, Avery believed her.

They both smiled back at her.

"Thank you," Avery said. "We'll do our best."

The woman released their hands and beamed at them. "I know

you will," she said. "Class will begin in about fifteen minutes. We're thrilled to have you."

Taylor thanked her and put her arm through Avery's.

"Let's go over here. I have some friends here that I want to introduce you to." She turned to Avery and anticipated the question Avery was about to ask. "And no, I didn't know they were going to be here."

They walked over to a cluster of people. When they spotted Taylor, they all hooted like she was a celebrity.

"Why didn't you tell us you'd be here?" one of them asked as she pulled Taylor into a hug. Taylor kissed her on the cheek and laughed.

"Because I didn't know you guys were coming." She took a step back and gestured to Avery. "Callie, Liz, Rex, this is my friend Avery. Avery, Callie, Liz, Rex." Taylor pointed to each person as she said their names.

"Nice to meet all of you," Avery said.

"Likewise," one of them said, and the other two smiled at her. Shit, she'd already forgotten who was who. That was one of the first things Taylor had told her—to remember names, that people were always flattered by that. She was a flirting school failure already.

"I'm the one who told you about this class, you should have known I was coming," the person who had hugged Taylor said.

"With everything you know about me, Liz, did you really expect me to remember who told me about these classes?" Taylor asked her. "But I've been wanting to come to one of these for a while; I'm glad I finally made it."

Oh good, so Liz was the white woman with the long dark brown hair and very short bangs. She had on a blue and white sleeveless floral dress with a full skirt. Not Avery's style, but she still liked it. And it made her wish more that she wasn't in her boring athleisure.

Though, did she have anything in her closet that she would have worn if she'd known this was a salsa dancing class? No, and she would have torn her closet apart and been stressed as hell about what to wear if she had known. Okay, this might be *one* situation where ignorance was probably better.

"Hey, there's wine over there," Taylor said. "I didn't even see it; I must have been distracted by that queen at the registration table. I'll go get some. Avery, do you want some?"

"Um, okay," she said. Wait, did that mean that Taylor was going to walk over to get wine and just . . . leave her here? With three strangers? Oh God, this was what she'd signed up for when she'd agreed to this, wasn't it?

"I'll go with you," Liz said. Now it was two strangers, but Avery wasn't sure if that made it better or worse. "Callie, Rex, you want some?"

Both Callie and Rex shook their heads, which was incredibly frustrating. If one of them had wanted wine, and one hadn't, that would have made her life much easier. Taylor touched her on the arm before she and Liz walked off. That touch felt like Taylor knew what she was thinking, that she was giving Avery a small *you've got this*. It made her breathe a little easier.

As soon as Taylor and Liz walked away, Callie and Rex both turned to her. One of them looked Latina, with long, bright pink hair and lipstick to match, and had on a black jumpsuit; the other was of Asian descent, with short dark hair, glasses, and wore a pink floral button-down shirt with long shorts. Black Jumpsuit had a big smile on her face, while Floral Button-Down looked a little more standoffish, but not unfriendly.

Black Jumpsuit leaned closer to her.

"I'm sorry, but I'll explode if I don't ask this. Are you and Taylor together, or . . . ?"

"Oh. No." Avery shook her head. "Just friends." This question embarrassed her, only because Taylor had never given her the slightest signal that she wanted to be anything more than just friends. Taylor flirted with her, sure, but Taylor flirted with literally everyone; that didn't mean anything. And yes, she'd told Avery that she was hot, but she hadn't said it like she was attracted to her or anything, more like she wanted to give Avery a confidence boost. Which she had.

Obviously, *she* was attracted to Taylor, how could she not be? How could anyone not be? But that was the whole thing—Taylor could date anyone she wanted to, why would she date someone like Avery, who didn't even know how to flirt with her, much less do anything else?

Oh God, either Callie or Rex was talking to her, and she wasn't listening, because she'd been too busy thinking about Taylor. She was here to try to flirt with people, people who weren't Taylor Cameron. *Focus, Avery.*

"Makes sense. I probably would have heard the weeping of every lesbian north of San Francisco if Taylor was off the market again that quickly. Though I'm surprised I haven't heard about her with anyone. I bet people are waiting in line for her. She doesn't stay with people long, but while she does . . ."

Avery had no idea how to respond to this, so she went to the Taylor playbook. A question.

"What about you?" Avery asked. "Are either of you with anyone?"

Was that too bold a question, right off the bat?

"Not right now," Black Jumpsuit said.

"Me neither," Floral Button-Down said.

Black Jumpsuit threw an arm around Floral Button-Down.

"Proud of you for getting out of that," Black Jumpsuit said, and then turned to Avery. "They just had a hard breakup, but it was really for the best."

"Me, too," Avery said.

Floral Button-Down gave her a warm smile.

"You get it, then," they said. "That's why we're here—to have a little fun, post-breakup."

Avery smiled at both of them.

"Well, I hope this night is fun for all of us." Okay, she just couldn't take it anymore. "Okay, now *I'm* going to explode if I don't ask this. Which one of you is Callie, and which one of you is Rex?"

They both burst out laughing.

"She's Callie," Floral Button-Down said, pointing at Black Jumpsuit.

"And they are Rex," Black Jumpsuit said.

"Nice to meet you again, Callie and Rex," Avery said.

———

"THAT WAS FAST, EVEN FOR YOU," LIZ SAID TO TAYLOR AS THEY walked over to get the wine.

"What?" Taylor asked. She wasn't paying her that much attention. Had she been wrong to leave Avery alone with Callie and Rex? Not that she thought Avery shouldn't be able to handle talking to two strangers without her around, and that's what they were here for, after all. Still, throwing someone into a situation where everyone but you knew one another was never a fun time. Callie and Rex were great, though; they'd be nice to her. Maybe this would be a way to ease Avery into meeting new people tonight, even though she hadn't planned it this way.

"You and Avery," Liz said. "I didn't know you were dating someone new."

Taylor laughed.

"Oh—no, it's not like that. We're just friends."

"Oh," Liz said. "I just thought . . . bringing someone to queer salsa lessons definitely seems like a date kind of thing."

Taylor shook her head again.

"Nah, I just remembered about these classes, and when I mentioned it to Avery, she decided to come along." That was a lie, but it wasn't like Taylor was going to tell the world she was teaching Avery to flirt. That was Avery's story to tell. And if she told most of her friends about this, they would think that she was only doing it to get into Avery's pants.

Yes, she *did* want to get into Avery's pants, but she couldn't get into anyone's pants for a while, so she might as well try to have other—lesser—kinds of fun.

"Oh. Well. I hope tonight is fun," Liz said. "Have you seen Gemma around lately?"

They got up to the front of the line just then, so Taylor didn't have to get into a conversation with one of her exes about another of her exes. She thought she and Gemma would be able to be friends, eventually, in the same way she and Liz were friends. But Gemma had made it clear that she didn't want to see or hear from Taylor for a while, and Taylor would respect that.

Avery, Callie, and Rex were all laughing when Taylor and Liz got back to them. Good, that had gone well.

"Here you go," she said, handing off the wine to Avery. "I think we have about five more minutes before they start, from what I heard them saying over there."

Avery took a gulp of her wine, and Taylor held back a grin. It's not that she thought it was funny that Avery was nervous about this; it just seemed so contrary to how confident and self-assured Avery was in other contexts. She put her hand on Avery's back for just a second, and she could feel Avery take a deep breath.

"You're going to be great," she said under her breath. "A beauty like you?"

Avery's stoic face relaxed into a smile at the reminder of the woman at the check-in.

"I want to grow up and be just like that woman," she said. "I'm half in love with her already."

Taylor nodded.

"Oh absolutely."

"Attention!" They all turned to the commanding voice at the front of the room, and there she was, a microphone in her hand and a huge smile on her face. "Welcome to our queer salsa class! I am Elena, and this is my partner, Alisha. We are delighted to see so many of you here today, especially all of you here for the first time! Now, let's begin: at first, we will have the beginners dance with the experts and intermediates, and then we will swap it around. So, beginners, to the green corner! Intermediates, to the pink corner! And, experts, to the red corner!" There was some looking around to see where the green, pink, and red corners were, and some shuffling, but it was apparently too slow for her. "NOW!"

Everyone moved quickly to their correct corner of the room. Taylor grabbed Avery so they wouldn't get separated as everyone moved around, though they lost Liz, Callie, and Rex. Honestly, Taylor was grateful for that since this wasn't meant to be a group excursion; tonight was for her and Avery.

"Excellent job, everyone!" Elena said. "Now, Alisha and I will demonstrate the first dance for today, and then you'll all pair up. We will go slowly at first so you can see the steps, and then we'll show you how the dance is supposed to look." She beamed at them all for a second. Then she called out, "MUSIC!"

The music started immediately after her command.

"I wish I could yell like that and have things happen immediately," Avery said in Taylor's ear. "Imagine how great that would be."

"What an absolutely you thing to say." Taylor turned to her with a grin.

Avery's eyes laughed into hers.

"You already know me so well," she said. They smiled at each other for a few seconds longer. She really liked that challenging, confident look on Avery's face. She needed to do more to boost Avery's confidence in the flirting and dating arena.

Elena started talking again, and they both snapped their attention to the front of the room.

"Now, we will show you the salsa." Elena moved her body to the beat in a way Taylor both envied and lusted after. "The salsa can be many things, but it's nothing without this basic step. It's the building block of everything, you hear me?" Everyone nodded in unison.

"Now. Watch our feet." She and Alisha faced the audience. They swayed from side to side for a few beats, and at some unseen cue, started dancing at the same time. "One two THREE four, five six SEVEN eight! You got that? No, of course, many of you didn't get that, but that's okay, we'll keep going! One two THREE four, five six SEVEN eight!"

"I would like that woman to do very dirty things to me," Taylor said in Avery's ear.

"Taylor!" Avery whispered in a scandalized voice. Taylor just giggled.

"Now, it's time for you to do it!" Elena said. "I'm going to do another count of eight, and Alisha and I will dance it again, and then at the second count of eight, you all join in, okay? Some of you will have never done this before; for others, it may have been a while, especially if it's been since our last class here. If you know it, you can help me demonstrate. Okay! One two three four five six seven eight. One two three four five six seven eight!"

The whole room moved along with her on the second count of eight, some people more successfully than others. Avery was definitely one of the more successful ones.

"And again! One two three four five six seven eight, one two three four five six seven eight. Wonderful job! I can already tell this is going to be an excellent class!"

Taylor nudged Avery when they had all gotten back (sort of) into place.

"What were you talking about, you don't know how to salsa? You seem like you knew what you were doing there."

Avery shrugged, a shy smile on her face.

"I just take direction well, that's all."

"Oh, do you?" Taylor said. And then she stopped herself. No, she couldn't go there. Even if she really wanted to.

"Next," Elena said, rescuing her from Avery's raised eyebrows. "You'll all split up into pairs. Once you find your partner, we will demonstrate how to do this together, okay? Beginners! Go find a partner. Don't be shy, you can do it!"

Who knew that instead of making rules for Avery, all she'd needed to do was rely on Elena.

"Go get 'em," she said to Avery. At first, Avery didn't move. But then she took a deep breath and walked across the room, stopping next to a woman with dark brown skin and bright red lipstick. Taylor was too far away to know what Avery said to her, but the woman smiled back at her and nodded, and then took her arm. Okay, one mission accomplished, at least.

Taylor scanned the room, then walked over to an older woman in a very ruffly floral dress and asked her to dance.

"Of course, my dear!" she said. "I'd be delighted. Won't this be fun? I love these classes. I'm Val."

Taylor smiled at her.

"Hi, Val. I'm Taylor. Nice to meet you."

They faced the front of the room. Taylor positioned them close enough to Avery so that she could see how it was going for her, but not so close that Avery would see her watching. Avery would be at least a little self-conscious no matter what; Taylor didn't want to make it worse.

She looked at the woman Avery had selected. Was that Avery's type? It must be. Taylor had told her she had to ask someone to dance that she was attracted to, and as Avery had said, she was definitely a rule follower.

She seemed a little more . . . femme than she thought Avery would be into. Well, she didn't actually have any real idea *what* kind of woman Avery would be into. The bookstore event hadn't helped with that because it was full of bookish femme types—not that there was anything wrong with that; Taylor was a big fan of bookish femme types. But it had meant that Taylor hadn't been able to figure out what Avery was looking for.

"Attention!" Elena said from the front of the room. "Now we will show you how to dance the salsa with a partner. Intermediates and experts, remember, you will lead! Beginners, that means you will dance backward! I promise, you can do it; watch me and do the steps like this. MUSIC." Surely, at some point, Taylor would get used to Elena's voice becoming a megaphone without any warning. "We'll start by going backward. Again, Alisha and I will show you, and you'll join us on the second count of eight. One two three four five six seven eight. ONE two three four five six seven eight." She stopped and nodded at them. "Excellent job. Now that you have the building blocks, Alisha and I will show you how to dance together."

She took Alisha's hand, and they stared into each other's eyes for a full count, and then, again without any clear signal, they began to dance together, first in place, and then around the stage. When they finished, they both curtsied to the class, who cheered wildly, with plenty of hooting and hollering. Taylor did her share of both; she saw Avery turn and look back at her, a slightly indulgent smile on her face. Taylor winked at her, and she laughed, and then she turned and said something to her dance partner. Was it *That's my friend, isn't she great, she's a delight to be with, and super hot, too?* Or was it *No, I don't know that person, I don't know what you're talking about?* Probably something in between.

"Thank you, thank you, you're very kind, though yes, we deserve all of that," Elena said to much laughter in the room, and even more cheering. "Now it's time for what you've all been waiting for: time for you to dance! Turn to face your partner!"

Taylor grinned at Val as she turned to face her. Val smiled back at her.

"Take your partner's hand," Elena said. Taylor put her hand in Val's.

Val was just a little bit shorter than her, even with her high heels on, which was kind of adorable. She squeezed Taylor's hand gently.

"Don't be nervous, you'll be great," Val said. Hmm, maybe Avery should be with Val. She was so encouraging.

No, Taylor—the point of tonight was for Avery to flirt, not just to learn how to salsa dance, remember?

Taylor glanced over at Avery and her partner. Avery's hand was on her partner's shoulder, and her partner's hand was on Avery's waist, and they were hand in hand, just like they were supposed to be. But Avery was very stiff, and at least from behind, she still looked nervous. Though Avery had incredible posture, she always looked stiff.

"Wonderful, you all look beautiful," Elena said. "MUSIC! I'm going to count again, and you'll start on my second count of eight. If you mess up, which many of you will, that's okay, just stop until you get to the one again, and start again. Alisha and I will walk around and help you. Now . . . one two three four five six seven eight, ONE two three four five six seven eight."

Step, step, step, pause; step, step, step, pause. At first, Taylor was too busy dancing herself and trying to follow Val to even look at Avery. Elena and Alisha had made this look so much easier.

After a few rounds, though, Taylor managed to look up and over at Avery and her partner. Avery still had ramrod straight posture, but she no longer looked as anxious. She was dancing away with her partner, like she'd been doing this for years. Her partner's hand was now more toward the middle of Avery's back, and . . . were they closer together?

Taylor stepped forward when she should have stepped backward and landed on Val's toe.

"Sorry, sorry," Taylor said.

"That's okay, sweetie, don't worry about it!" Val said. "Remember what Elena said, we'll just stop and start back up again. And . . . one two three four five six seven eight."

Avery laughed at something her partner said, and her partner smiled at her. Huh, that was going much better than she thought it would, at least this early on.

Taylor almost stumbled again, but Val held on to her so securely that she found her footing. Thank goodness Val knew what she was doing; Taylor was weirdly distracted by watching Avery and her partner. Why did that distract her so much? She had to focus.

Avery's partner leaned closer to her, and Taylor stumbled again. And then it all became clear.

She was jealous! That was all. She wasn't the jealous type, but she was so sexually frustrated because of this stupid bet; *she* wanted to be the one with her hands on Avery, watching her body move, smiling at her and making her laugh. It all made sense now. Well, she'd deal with that problem with her favorite vibrator later tonight. That would calm her down.

Once she diagnosed the problem, Taylor did a much better job dancing with Val and her other partners. After an hour and a half of dancing with only quick breaks to change partners and learn a few more moves from Elena and Alisha, the music stopped.

"My friends, my darlings, my wonderful dancers!" Elena said. "It breaks my heart to say this, but our class is over for this evening. You all were a joy, especially you beginners, who exceeded my already high expectations for you. Thank you, thank you for everything for this evening, and please come back to our class next month!"

The class broke out into applause, and there was even more cheering than the first time. After one particularly loud "woooooo" on her part, Taylor felt a tap at her shoulder.

"Remind me to have you in the audience if I'm ever performing at anything," Avery said.

"I wouldn't miss it for the world," Taylor said.

The crowd was loud and friendly and euphoric on the way out of the community center. Taylor and Avery both stopped to thank their partners on the way out of class, and Avery had a big smile on her face as they exited the community center. Taylor turned to Avery.

"Did you—"

"Taylor!" They both turned to find Liz, Callie, and Rex behind them. "Hey!" Liz said. "Did you guys have fun? We're heading out to get a drink and something to eat now. I'm starving after that—do you want to join us?"

Taylor was also starving, and she would usually say yes to that, but she wanted to do the class debrief alone with Avery.

"I wish," Taylor said. "I have to get up early tomorrow morning, so I think I'm going to go home and crash. Next time, though."

The three of them looked disappointed, but they all exchanged hugs and goodbyes and *nice to meet you*s with Avery before Taylor and Avery walked off toward Taylor's car.

"I don't actually have to get up early tomorrow morning," Taylor said as soon as they got in the car, "but I figured you might need a break, and I didn't want you to think you were still on the flirting clock if we went out with them."

Avery laughed as she clicked in her seat belt.

"Thank you. Tonight was fun, but going home to eat something and crash sounds great to me. But your friends all seemed nice; I'd love to hang out with them again another time."

This was maybe the most enthusiastic Taylor had seen Avery so far. Even more so than when they'd been at the winery party and Avery had been about five glasses of wine in.

"We'll do that sometime," Taylor said. "Did you have fun tonight? I can't believe you were even slightly nervous about this; you looked great while you were dancing."

Avery laughed again, an adorable bubbly laugh that Taylor had heard from her only once or twice before.

"Like I said, I take direction well, and luckily, I had good partners. But yeah, once I got the hang of it, I wasn't nervous anymore. And I think it helped to be in that space—everyone was so warm and welcoming, so I wasn't stressed about messing up in front of them. And . . ."

Her voice trailed off, but Taylor waited instead of prompting her. After a few beats, she started talking again.

"And I guess because it was in a queer space, I just felt so much more comfortable. Like, I wasn't worried about people judging me, or hitting on me in a way that would feel creepy, or making me feel bad about myself. It was just . . . it was really nice, that's all. Thank you for bringing me."

"I'm so glad," Taylor said. Was there a way that she could express how touched she felt by what Avery had just said? She had no idea, and she didn't want to make Avery feel weird, so she didn't even try.

"There's, um, there's one other thing, though," Avery said after another pause. Was she going to say she didn't want to do this anymore? That Taylor had given her enough flirting lessons and she could now carry on with this all by herself?

"What is it?" Taylor asked.

"I had a great time tonight, and I talked to my partners, and we danced and stuff, but . . . I don't know if I quite 'flirted' with them? I still don't feel like I'm any good at the flirting part of this. I don't think I'm doing any of it right. Am I failing flirting lessons? I'm failing at flirting lessons, aren't I?"

Taylor couldn't help but laugh.

"You are such an overachiever. Of course you would think you were failing at flirting after only two lessons. You're not getting graded on this, you know!"

Avery scoffed.

"Obviously I'm not getting graded on this; why would you think I would think that?"

She looked at Taylor, and now they both erupted into laughter.

"Okay, I understand why you'd think I would think that," Avery said. "But . . . do you have any feedback for me, or things I could do better, or . . . I don't know."

Taylor patted her hand.

"I've been trying to ease you into this, but okay, I can give you some feedback. But first I have a few questions: How did you feel about the people you danced with? Did you have fun dancing with them? Did you have fun talking to them? Did anyone in particular stand out?"

Avery thought for a second, and then nodded.

"Yeah, I mean, I had fun with all of them, though I had more fun as the night went on, mostly because I relaxed about everything. But as for anyone who stood out, that woman with the short overalls on, the one who hugged me on the way out . . . she was great."

Taylor nodded. She'd sort of suspected that.

"Okay, so, you do this thing when you're nervous, or someone gives you a compliment, and you don't know what to do about it or whatever. You kind of withdraw from them. You look away, don't really respond, sometimes you change the subject. And that makes most people think that you aren't interested, that you don't like them. I saw you doing it with that woman, both while you were dancing and when she hugged you when we left. She said how much fun she had dancing with you, and you looked away and mumbled that you had fun, too, and then walked away from her. That was an opportunity to keep flirting, that's what she wanted, and from what you say, that's what you wanted, too, but you didn't do that."

Avery was silent for a moment. Had Taylor said too much? Had she made Avery feel bad about all of this? Would Avery not want to do this anymore?

But then Avery nodded.

"You're right. It feels so . . . bold to keep looking at someone when they give me a compliment. Like I think I deserve it."

"You *do* deserve it!" Taylor said. It blew her mind that someone like Avery felt that way.

Avery didn't respond to that, and just went on.

"And I guess I worry that if I hold eye contact with them, or try to flirt with them, or show them that I'm interested, they'll laugh at me or something, so I freeze up." When Taylor tried to interrupt her, she said quickly, "Even though I know that probably won't happen. That's in the back of my mind."

Taylor didn't say anything for a minute. She could tell it had been hard for Avery to tell her that. It felt good that Avery could be honest with her.

"I get it," she said. "We can work on that. We've got time."

Avery groaned.

"Oh no, how much time is it going to take to make me even slightly passable?"

Taylor laughed.

"First of all, you're already more than passable. I'm going to make you great. Also, we aren't on any timeline here." She thought for a moment and then smiled. This was going to be fun. "Okay, I have an idea for next week that I think will help."

"Oh no, that sounds scary," Avery said. "What is wrong with me? I shouldn't have said anything."

Taylor shook her head.

"After the past two weeks, when you came in all suspicious and you ended up having a great time, can't you give me the benefit of the doubt that you'll have fun? Trust me."

Avery let out a deep sigh.

"I do trust you, but I never know what to expect with you!" she said.

Taylor grinned at her.

"That's what they all say."

FIVE

AVERY LOOKED AT HERSELF IN THE MIRROR AFTER SHE GOT dressed for her now regular Tuesday night with Taylor and bit her lip. She had no idea what they were doing tonight. All Taylor had said about what to wear this time was to "lean risqué." What did that even mean? Not helpful, Taylor! After she'd mentally surveyed her entire wardrobe (twice), she'd decided on a button-down sundress; she'd undone one button at the top, and enough from the bottom to have a slit up to her thigh. She looked at herself in the mirror, and her face got hot. Wasn't this too much?

No. She was going to do it. She was pretty sure this was a challenge from Taylor, and she wanted to win it. Yeah, she wasn't getting graded on this, but she did want to surprise Taylor, show that she had more gumption than Taylor might give her credit for.

And she wanted Taylor to know that she was taking this seriously. After the past two weeks, when she'd whined and complained as soon as Taylor had picked her up—and ended up having a good time—she wanted to start tonight with a better attitude.

So far, Taylor hadn't made her do any of the scary stuff she'd worried about, like go to bars and makc her go talk to women, or buy them drinks, or get their phone numbers. But even scarier had been the idea that Taylor would judge her on what she did, and she hadn't done that, either.

Granted, Taylor had given her feedback last week, but it wasn't mean, just friendly. Kind. A little funny, slightly mocking, sure, but in a way that hadn't made her feel bad. Just like Taylor always was.

"Okay, what is it today?" she asked as she got into Taylor's car. "Also, I can drive sometimes, you know. I feel bad that you drive every time."

Taylor shook her head.

"That's okay, I like driving. Plus, if you drove, I'd have to tell you in advance where we were going."

Avery grinned at her.

"I know."

Taylor grinned back.

"Nice try, though." Her smile got bigger as she glanced over at Avery's outfit, her eyes lingering, just for a second, at the slit in her dress. How could she make Avery's whole body tingle just from a look? "I will say this, good work with tonight's dress code."

Avery smiled shyly and looked away. And then she remembered what Taylor had said last week and made herself turn to face her.

"Thank you," she said, looking straight at Taylor.

Taylor looked into her eyes as she nodded slowly.

"You're welcome," she said. "You were right, you are a quick study."

It never felt weird or uncomfortable when Taylor looked at her like that, it just made her feel good. Maybe because her look was appreciative, not leering.

"Here's another tip," Taylor said as she started the car. "If someone gives you a compliment, and you want to flirt with them, you give them a compliment in return."

"Oh." Avery looked closer at Taylor's outfit. Oh no. Taylor was so sexy on a normal day, without even really trying, that it was honestly hard to look at her dressed like this. She had on a short-sleeved black jumpsuit that zipped up the front; if Avery had thought she was being adventurous by unbuttoning one button of her dress, that was nothing compared to how far down Taylor's jumpsuit was unzipped. There was a little bit of her bra peeking out, and a faint glistening of sweat from the heat of the day in the hollow of her breasts. Avery had to look away.

"Um, I like your outfit, too."

Taylor burst out laughing.

"Oh, sweetheart, your compliments have to sound like you mean them."

"I did mean it! I just didn't mean to say it like that." Avery had known, even as she heard herself say it, that it was the wrong thing, but what was she supposed to say? *You're the sexiest person I've ever met, and that is very evident tonight?* She couldn't say that. She wasn't supposed to be flirting with Taylor, first of all. And secondly, while she knew Taylor wouldn't laugh at her, she would probably just pat her on her hand and tell her that was very sweet but Avery wasn't her type, which would be humiliating.

It wasn't like Avery wanted to date Taylor, anyway! Taylor was for the 400-level class; Avery was very firmly still in Flirting 101.

Taylor turned to her with a smile. Good, Taylor hadn't taken offense at her unconvincing compliment.

"Well, thank you," Taylor said, laughter in her voice. "We'll work on that delivery. On a different topic: Margot and Luke are together, huh? I always knew he had a thing for her."

"Oh, she told you?" Avery grinned. "I'm happy for them."

"She didn't exactly tell me, but he picked her up from the winery the other day and it was very clear," Taylor said. "It explains why Margot has been smiling so much lately—it freaked me out."

They drove over to Sonoma and parked on a side street, a few blocks off the main square. Avery followed Taylor out of the car and toward a divey-looking bar not too far away. She noticed other women were walking in the same direction. Were they going to a lesbian bar? Was she dressed correctly for a lesbian bar? Was a sundress with a high slit and flat sandals the right outfit?

It must be; Taylor had complimented her on the outfit.

Oh God. Maybe Taylor *was* going to make her hit on women tonight. Should she put more lipstick on? Or take what she had on off? Taylor would tell her if she should, right?

She saw the big chalkboard sign outside the bar and stopped. Then she laughed out loud and turned to Taylor, who had a big grin on her face.

"Burlesque?" she said, still laughing. "We're going to a burlesque show? Oh my God."

Taylor patted her on the shoulder.

"I thought it would be a little outside your comfort zone," she said. "But I wasn't sure if it would be so far out of your comfort zone that you'd run away screaming; I'm glad that you haven't done that . . . yet."

Avery put an injured expression on her face, even though it was pretty far outside her comfort zone. She'd never been to a burlesque show before—obviously—but what if it was the kind of thing where they did lap dances or things like that? She would die. Or what if it was, like, stand-up comedy where they tried to get audience participation? She would die all over again.

She couldn't let Taylor know that these scenarios were running through her head, though.

"You think that little of me?" she asked Taylor.

Taylor slid an arm through hers.

"Mmm—I notice we're still standing outside."

Avery tossed her head with a bravado that she didn't feel.

"I was waiting for you. Let's go inside; we want to get a good seat for the show."

Taylor laughed again as they walked inside.

It definitely was a lesbian bar; that was clear from the clientele. But it was a very diverse one—women and nonbinary people of many races, ethnicities, and styles of dress. And thank goodness, her outfit wouldn't be totally out of place here; she saw at least a few other femmes in cute sundresses and lipstick, though most of them also wore Birkenstocks instead of strappy flat sandals like hers. She had Birkenstocks! Next time, she'd wear them. She was probably the only person in the room without a tattoo, but hell, as far as any of them knew, she had a tattoo in a place none of them could see!

Taylor seemed to know quite a few people here, too, from the number of them waving at her from across the room. Taylor knew people everywhere. She nodded back at a few, and then turned to Avery, a sly little smile on her face.

"You said you wanted a good seat—there are still plenty up front?"

Avery blanched, but after what she'd said outside, she felt like she had to do it.

"Sure, okay, yeah, yes, of course. We should definitely grab one of the seats up front. I've never been to one of these before; I've got to get a good view, after all."

Taylor looked amused, which irritated Avery a little. Did she think Avery was scared to sit up front? Before she could make fun of her more, Avery charged ahead and settled into one of the little tables near the stage. Taylor followed her a few seconds later.

"Do you want a drink?" Taylor asked. "I'll head over to the bar to get them—I know the bartender working tonight."

Of course she did.

"Yeah, sure," Avery said. "Gin and tonic, please."

Taylor strolled over to the bar, and Avery bit her lip. Should she have ordered something else? Was a gin and tonic too much of a straight-girl drink? Should she have gotten something with bourbon or a beer or even a cider instead? Was the bartender, the one with the ripped T-shirt and tons of tattoos, whom Taylor was talking to right now, going to roll her eyes when Taylor ordered it and say, *Why are you here with someone who would order a gin and tonic?*

Well. Then Taylor would just say, *I'm not* here *with her. We're just friends.* And the bartender would laugh and say, *Obviously, I should have known.*

Avery looked away from the bar and tried to shake her insecurities off. She was here because she wanted new experiences, remember? She was at a burlesque show at a lesbian bar! Those were both brand-new experiences!

She looked around at the crowd. She felt kind of nervous, sitting up here at a table in front all alone, but it was excellent for people watching. Some people here were casually dressed, but she could tell that quite a few had dressed specifically for this event, in outfits they wanted the world to see. They'd put care into what they were wearing, matched their pink lipstick with their pink highlights just so, put on that cute pair of shoes they'd been waiting for a chance to wear. The women in these outfits had clearly chosen them to give themselves a boost, to make themselves happy, to feel good in that dress that showed all that cleavage, in that peacock eye makeup that they'd watched dozens of tutorials to figure out how to do, in those studded combat boots they'd saved up for and finally splurged on.

Did she ever dress like that? Just to please herself, to show off a part of herself that she liked, to make herself feel attractive, to pump herself up? She had her various self-imposed uniforms that she wore for work, but that didn't count; that was all to make herself feel professional and competent, or make her clients trust her, which usually worked. But outside of work, her clothes were mostly boring, conservative, to make herself blend in with the world. This sundress was as adventurous as she usually got, and this was the first time she'd unbuttoned it at all. She should really buy some more fun clothes.

"One gin and tonic, with a lime," Taylor said as she set Avery's drink in front of her.

"Thanks," Avery said. She took a gulp of the drink, partly because it was hot in here and the drink looked refreshing with that ice, and partly because she was still nervous. "Um, when does the show start, do you know?"

Taylor sat down with her own drink, which was also some sort of tall, iced thing, with lemon instead of lime. Avery didn't know if Taylor had ordered her own straight-girl drink just to make her feel better, or if that's the kind of drink she always ordered, but either way, it made her feel better.

"Technically in about five minutes, probably more like thirty minutes or so. We made surprisingly good time; I thought we'd get here just as the show started, but now we have time to relax." She grinned at Avery again. "And we had time to get good seats."

Avery narrowed her eyes at Taylor.

"I'm not sure if I like that look on your face. What is it about these seats? Is something bad going to happen to me?"

Taylor laughed.

"I love how suspicious you are. Can we please let the record show that you're the one who wanted this table, not me? Anything that happens as a result of this is NOT my fault."

Avery just put her head in her hands, and Taylor laughed harder.

"Okay, but no, really," Taylor said, the laughter gone from her voice. "There can sometimes be an . . . audience participation element when you're up front. If you don't want to deal with that, which I imagine you don't, we can move. It's no big deal." She patted Avery on the shoulder. "I promise."

Avery was touched by the serious expression on Taylor's face. She knew that Taylor meant it, that they could move to a table in the back, that Taylor wouldn't make fun of her, would never bring it up again. She sat up straight.

"That's okay," she said. "Let's stay here. If I'm going to do this, I'm going to do it all the way."

Taylor's hand slid down her shoulder and gripped her upper arm. She looked at Avery and smiled slowly.

"That's my girl." She dropped her hand, but the imprint of it was still on Avery's skin. Avery smiled back at Taylor and felt a little burble of pride in herself.

"Also," Taylor said. "This table is a great people-watching vantage point, and we need to take advantage of it. Let's decide on who we think the hottest people in this room are—other than the two of us, obviously. Oh, and what our favorite outfits are tonight, because there are a lot of great ones."

"Before I answer that first question, I need to know: Are you going to make me flirt with whoever I say the hottest people in the room are?" Avery asked.

Taylor shook her head slowly.

"Avery. When are you going to realize that I'm not going to make you do anything that you don't want to do?"

Avery let out a sigh.

"No, I know. I do realize that. I'm just . . . paranoid, that's all." She tried to make herself relax and answered Taylor's question. "Okay, your bartender friend is definitely one of the hottest people in this room."

Taylor grinned knowingly.

"Roxy? You're correct about that one. Okay, yes, she goes on the list. What do you think about Polka-Dotted Crop Top over there?"

Avery turned to her left and saw a woman with long, multicolored hair, wide-leg jeans, and the aforementioned polka-dotted crop top lean over and kiss another woman on the cheek. She tossed her hair back and laughed, and her friends laughed with her. She had a round little belly that poked out between her crop top and her jeans; Avery envied her whole attitude.

"Hot, yes," Avery said, "though not my type. I mostly just want to be friends with her."

"Hmm, that raises a question that I've been meaning to ask you," Taylor said. "What *is* your type?"

Avery bit her lip.

"Great question." She was stalling. But she didn't know how to answer. Partly because the only thing she was absolutely sure about was that her "type" included Taylor.

"If you don't really know, that's all right," Taylor said. "But, okay, do you like women more femme, like you, or toward the butch end of the spectrum, or—"

"Not like me," Avery said. "But also, um . . ."

Taylor lifted a hand to stop her.

"Actually, wait, here's a better way to do this. Okay, we agree that Roxy is hot; I think you'll agree with me that Leather Skirt to your left is hot as hell?"

Avery glanced in that direction and her eyes widened.

"Wow, yes, I do agree with you."

Taylor smirked and nodded.

"Excellent. Okay, what about Pink Mesh Dress over by the bar?"

Avery looked at the tall, thin, brown-skinned woman with short blond hair and shook her head.

"Very attractive, obviously, but not my type."

Taylor nodded again.

"These are good data points. How do you feel about Ripped Jeans and Black Muscle Tee by the door?"

Avery turned again, and a slow smile spread over her face. Taylor laughed.

"Well, there's my answer."

Oh God, was she that obvious? Avery looked down at her drink. But then she made herself look up at Taylor, whose eyes were fixed on her. She grinned, and Taylor grinned back.

"She's so hot I can barely look at her," Avery said, which made Taylor giggle.

"I think I may already know the answer to this question," she said, "but how about Rainbow Petticoats over there?"

Avery swung her head in that direction.

"Beautiful, but not for me. But wait, why am I the only one answering these questions? What about you? What's your type?"

Taylor laughed.

"Oh, I have too many types. I think all of these people are hot, that's the problem."

Avery opened her mouth to ask another question, when a rumble went through the crowd.

Taylor glanced up at the stage and took another sip of her drink.

"Show's about to start." Apprehension must have shown on Avery's face, because Taylor then gestured to Avery's drink. "You ready for this? Should I have made that a double?"

Avery laughed and shook her head.

"Absolutely not, to both questions."

WHY HAD TAYLOR BROUGHT AVERY TO THIS SHOW TONIGHT? She was already intensely sexually frustrated from this fucking bet with Erica, so why did she come up with the brilliant idea to (a) tell Avery to wear something risqué, (b) come to a place where she knew many hot women would be hanging out, and (c) also where a number of said hot women would be some of her exes with whom she'd had very excellent sex in the past? Any one of those things could have easily set her off; all that combined made her want to explode.

She couldn't exactly regret this, though. Because hanging out here with Avery was just . . . fun. The car ride, the people watching, the conversation. To be true to their mission, Taylor probably should have encouraged Avery to go up to the bar to order a drink from Roxy, or beckoned her ex Gillian and her crowd over so Avery could try to flirt with them. But even though that was what she'd planned to do tonight, she didn't want to push Avery. She wanted this to be fun for Avery, too, after all.

The lights went down, and a big cheer went up throughout the bar. Taylor let out a huge "Wooooooooooo," and Avery giggled. Taylor pursed her lips at her.

"I'm a very enthusiastic audience member, okay? No performer is ever going to say they had a bad audience on a night I was there."

Avery nodded, a smile on her face.

"I can see that," she said.

A dancer ran out onto the makeshift stage, and the cheers got louder. She was in a skintight sparkly red catsuit, with matching sparkly red lipstick, and a very large hot pink wig. The audience laughed and cheered through her opening number, and then three more dancers ran onstage to join her. Taylor paid enough attention to know when to cheer, but she mostly watched Avery's reactions. At first, her smile looked tentative, obligatory, one that would fool most people that it was real, but not Taylor, at least not anymore. She could tell Avery was still nervous about whether her front-row seat would force her to be a part of the show. But when one of the performers made an extremely off-color joke, a half-horrified and half-delighted laugh burbled out of Avery, and Taylor laughed along with her.

It wasn't until the fourth number that it happened. One of the performers, known only as the Goddess, who had on a bunch of expertly draped feather boas, stepped off the "stage" and greeted the four people sitting at the closest table.

"Hellooo, don't you look sexy tonight!" She took a step back and looked each of them up and down. "Oh yeah, at least two of you are dressed to hook up later. The other two . . . hey, maybe you'll get lucky." The crowd laughed, and the people at the table joined in—though Taylor noticed that they all looked around at one another, clearly wondering which of them she'd been talking about. The performer patted one woman on the shoulder. "Don't worry, baby, you know you've got this in the bag." She moved on, while the woman at the table blushed but also preened a little.

"Now, who is going home with who tonight?" the Goddess asked a table of three. "Or, maybe all three of you are going home together, and if so, more power to you!"

She wandered around the audience doing her patter with the crowd, and Taylor felt Avery tense up next to her. She felt guilty for a moment that she hadn't moved them to another table under the guise of introducing her to some of her friends so Avery wouldn't have to do this, but she reminded herself that this had been Avery's choice.

"Oohhhhhh," the Goddess said, an arch tone in her voice. Taylor looked up, but she had her eyes on Avery. "I think I've found the person I've been looking for all night."

Avery cleared her throat.

"Me?" she asked. Taylor felt unreasonably proud of her. There was no nervousness in her voice, her posture was as upright and ramrod straight as usual, and she'd even managed to have some of that same archness in her voice that the Goddess had in hers.

"Yes, you, oh yes indeed," the Goddess said. She looked Avery up and down in the same way she'd done to the other table, except the look on her face was even more lascivious, if that were possible. "I think you're just who I need to help me. You see, you look very competent, like you always know what you're doing, like you'll be honest with me, no matter what, and that's just the kind of person I need right now. Can you help me?"

Taylor touched Avery's elbow, trying to communicate to her that Avery could always say no and that she didn't have to do this if she didn't want to. Avery patted her hand without looking at her, and then smiled up at the Goddess.

"I'd love to," she said.

Taylor tried to hide her smile. This was going to be entertaining.

"It's my costume," the Goddess said. "It's a new one, and I'm not quite sure about it."

Avery looked her up and down, almost as boldly as the Goddess had done. This time Taylor couldn't keep the grin off her face.

"What aren't you sure about?" Avery asked. "I love a boa." She turned to the crowd. "Don't you all love a boa?" The crowd cheered, and Avery grinned. She was getting the crowd on her side, amazing. Taylor knew she was beaming at Avery like she was a proud dance mom whose kid had won a pageant, but she didn't even care.

The Goddess grinned back at Avery.

"I also love a boa; as a matter of fact, as you can see, I love boas, plural. But are you sure this isn't . . . too many boas?"

Avery shook her head.

"Impossible. You can never have too many boas."

Taylor laughed out loud. Avery met her eyes for just a second and gave her a tiny smirk before she looked back at the Goddess. Incredible. Avery was actually enjoying this, despite her anxiety earlier.

People in the crowd shouted, "Yes, girl," "She's right," and "Love the boas." But then someone in the back yelled, "Take it off!" which turned into a full-blown chant.

"Take it off, take it off, take it off!"

The Goddess looked at the crowd, then back at Avery.

"You hear what the people say. I think I need to take at least one off, or they'll be so disappointed. So I need your help to decide which color to take off."

Oh no. Taylor could see where this was going. At this point all she could do was sit back and hope Avery wouldn't be so mortified that she would literally sink into the floor. So far, however, she was doing great.

Avery sat back and surveyed the Goddess again, so Taylor looked her over, too. The boas were in every color of the rainbow, along with a gold one and a silver one. She had no idea which one Avery would pick, or why.

"I think the silver one," Avery said. "Gold is really more your color than silver."

The Goddess gasped dramatically, and Taylor could tell Avery was trying hard not to grin. She, of course, succeeded; Avery was excellent at keeping a straight face.

"You know, I could choose to be insulted by that," the Goddess said. "But you're right—see, I knew I picked the correct person to help me. I really am more of a warm-toned person." She reached for the silver boa, which was draped around her neck. "Now I need to take it off right now." The Goddess paused and held out a hand to Avery. "Actually, this is very embarrassing, but I need your help to get it off. It's attached back here, can you do it for me?"

"Of course." Avery stood up, without a glance at Taylor. Taylor didn't know if that was because she had no idea what was about to happen, or if she was already mortified and couldn't look at Taylor for fear she'd burst into either laughter or tears.

No, not tears, Taylor couldn't imagine Avery doing something so revealing as crying in public.

"It's right . . . there," the Goddess said as Avery disconnected the silver boa from the rest of them. "Perfect, you've got it. Here, let me make this easier on you." And then the Goddess spun in a circle and the silver boa unraveled from around her neck. She plucked it up off the floor and draped it tenderly around Avery's neck.

"Oh, that looks great on you," the Goddess said. "Silver is definitely your color, even if it isn't mine." She looked down at herself and then frowned. "Hmm, but there's still a problem. Hold on to this, will you?" She handed Avery the end of the gold boa, and then twirled faster and faster, as first the gold boa, then the red, then the pink, then the rest of them unraveled from her body. The crowd started clapping as the gold boa fell away, and got louder as the rest fell to the floor. When she was finally devoid of boas, the cheer was deafening. She faced Avery and shimmied back and forth, wearing just sparkly hot pants and bright blue tasseled pasties. The tassels at the ends of her substantial breasts swung back and forth and then around in a circle as she moved, and Taylor couldn't help the giggle that came out of her mouth.

"There, now, isn't this better?" she asked the crowd. The crowd cheered and hooted and called out "Swing those titties," "Yesss, girl, yesss," and "Tig ol' bitties!" Taylor couldn't help herself from yelling out, "Yeahhh, baby." She saw the corners of Avery's mouth twitch.

"What do you think, Ms. Thing?" the Goddess asked Avery. "Isn't this better?"

Taylor had no idea how Avery would respond.

"Well, you know how much I love a boa, so I didn't think it was possible to get better than what you had before, but . . ." Avery paused and looked from one tassel to the other. "That little loop de loop blew my mind."

The Goddess shouted with laughter, kissed Avery on the forehead, pushed her back down into her seat, and shook her boobs in her face one last time for good measure. Avery's cheeks were bright red, but she laughed and clapped for the Goddess along with the rest of the crowd as she gathered her boas—except for the silver one—back up and gave one more twirl with them before she disappeared.

Once another set of dancers had taken the stage and the attention of the crowd was off their table, Taylor looked over at Avery, who was staring at the stage with that silver boa still around her shoulders. Taylor touched Avery on the knee.

"Do you hate me for not making us change tables?" she asked under her breath.

Avery met her eyes and paused for a long few seconds, before she laughed out loud and shook her head.

"I could never hate you. I mean, yes, of course, I was completely mortified, but it was sort of fun?"

Taylor grinned at her.

"If it helps, I don't think anyone else in this place had any idea that you were mortified. Other than me, I mean. You did a great job."

Avery shook her head again.

"'Great' might be overstating it, but as long as I didn't embarrass myself, I'll call it a win."

Taylor threw an arm around her.

"Not only did you not embarrass yourself, but you surprised even me. I did *not* think you were going to go there with the tassel thing, and you did."

Avery pulled the boa tighter around her neck with a wide smile.

"Okay, but, Taylor, I couldn't help myself! Did you SEE the tassels swing in the little circle like that? How did she make them do that? That was total wizardry there!"

"That kind of thing is either years and years of training, or just sheer talent," Taylor said.

They both laughed again, and then Avery picked up what was left of her drink.

"Um, I have one more question, and it's a serious one," she said.

Taylor sat back.

"Go for it," Taylor said.

What was she going to ask? Something about why Taylor had brought her here tonight and was just hanging out with her instead of giving her flirting lessons, like they'd agreed on? Or if she was Taylor's type? Or if they could leave right now and go back to Taylor's place? Or . . .

Avery looked from side to side and lowered her voice.

"Do I get to keep this boa?"

Taylor dissolved into giggles.

SIX

THE NEXT AFTERNOON, AS AVERY WALKED OVER TO THE COM-munity garden after work, she still felt a glow from last night. She'd been stupidly nervous before the burlesque show—*No, Avery, no bad self-talk, remember?* Okay, she'd been *very* nervous before the burlesque show. She'd never gone to anything like that, and it had stressed her out to be there with Taylor, who was so cool that she'd probably been to zillions of these things, and who probably knew the performers and knew what she was supposed to act like and how and why. And then she'd had the ridiculous idea to sit up front?

But she realized during the show that she hadn't given Taylor nearly enough credit. Taylor had been so supportive—smiling at her, cheering for her, moving a little closer to her when she could tell that Avery was anxious. It had made her want to bring Taylor along to all stressful events, to everything that she thought she couldn't really do, just to have Taylor there to be her cheerleader. She felt like she could accomplish anything with Taylor by her side.

Even though Taylor wasn't actually cheering for her—she was

only doing this because . . . Wait, why was she doing this, anyway? Because she was having fun doing it? It must be that, right? Taylor didn't do things she didn't want to; she'd made that very clear. And Avery had gotten to know Taylor pretty well in the past month; she wasn't the type of person to blow smoke up someone's ass. Taylor was only giving her flirting lessons because she wanted to. She must be cheering her on because she actually believed in her. All of those compliments Taylor had given her on the ride home from the burlesque show about how funny she'd been and how well she'd done must be because she'd meant it, right?

Though, wow, Avery got embarrassed all over again just thinking about the moment when the Goddess had shaken her blue-tasseled boobs in her face. She'd had the urge to reach out and ring the tassels like they were bells. That had made her blush even harder than she had before, and made her scared to make eye contact with either the Goddess or Taylor, out of fear that they'd know what she'd been thinking. And then *that* had made her wonder what Taylor's boobs looked like, and what they would look like swinging back and forth, and what it would feel like if the hand Taylor had put on her knee moved up just a little bit higher, and, well, she'd had trouble making eye contact with Taylor for a *while* after that.

Fine, she'd admit to herself that she had a tiny crush on Taylor. That was normal, wasn't it? Especially since they were spending so much time together, getting to know each other, and Taylor was teaching her how to flirt. Plus, Taylor was the kind of person that *everyone* had a crush on. She was hot; she was confident in her own skin; she knew how to talk to everyone; she sometimes looked at people with those warm eyes and slow smile like she really, really liked what she saw; she walked and danced in that unselfconscious, open way that meant she was probably *very* good in bed . . .

In a word, Taylor was fucking sexy. Fine, that was two words, but it was true. Obviously, she would have a crush on her, especially since she was just starting this whole dating-women era of her life.

But that didn't mean anything. It was no big deal. She'd let this crush go on and keep that energy to continue learning how to flirt with other people, and maybe she'd eventually go on an actual date with an actual woman and put those skills to use.

She pushed open the gates to the community garden. Maybe gardening would take her mind off Taylor.

"Hey, Avery!" Beth waved at her from their shared garden plot, and Avery waved back. She was weirdly excited to see the garden today. She hadn't been there since the weekend, and even then there had been so many changes; she wondered what would be there today.

"Oh my God, look at the zucchini!" she said to Beth when she got to their plot. "I feel like it's grown a foot in the last few days!"

Then she laughed at herself.

"Sorry, I feel ridiculous getting so excited about zucchini, I don't know what's gotten into me," she said to Beth.

Beth shook her head.

"Please do not apologize, you're making me feel better for scaring the birds away with my shout of glee when I saw the radish seeds we planted."

Avery walked down to the other end of the garden plot. She got to the corner where they'd planted the radishes, and looked up at Beth, her eyes wide.

"Wait. Are these huge sprouts our radish seeds?"

Beth grinned at her and nodded.

"Isn't it amazing?"

Avery pulled her phone out of her pocket.

"I don't care how dorky it is, I need to document this."

"Oh, good idea," Beth said, and reached for her phone, too.

They spent the next hour working in the garden together, weeding and watering and planting and asking James and some of their fellow gardeners questions, but most of all, laughing and chatting. They didn't talk about anything important, only what they'd done the week before and what vegetables and flowers they wanted to learn more about next and what they both thought of the book from that bookstore event, but Avery enjoyed every moment of being in the sunshine and working in the dirt and talking.

After they were done with their plot, they walked together around the garden to check out what everyone else was growing.

"Wow, they harvested onions over there," Beth said. "I wonder how long those took to grow."

Avery nudged her.

"Those sunflowers are enormous. And look at those straw-berries."

Beth bent over the strawberries and then took a step away.

"I can't get too close, otherwise I'll just start picking them and eating them, they look so good. We should definitely grow those next year."

It felt nice, for Beth to say "we" like that, for her to assume that of course they would share a garden plot next year, too, that they were in this together. That's how Avery felt. She was glad Beth felt the same way. She had a sudden impulse to acknowledge this somehow. Taylor *had* told her to put herself out there.

"Speaking of wanting to pick and eat those strawberries, I'm hungry," Avery said. "What are you doing after this? Want to grab something to eat?" As soon as she said it, she questioned herself. Had she sounded as nervous as she felt? Maybe Beth just thought of Avery as a gardening buddy, but not an actual (or even potential) friend; a person she only ever wanted to see inside the walls of the community garden. Avery had had work friends like that, people whom she got along great with at work but where she was perfectly happy to leave that friendship at the office. She and those friends now wished one another happy birthday every year on Facebook but otherwise never interacted.

Maybe Beth would say no and roll her eyes and think it was weird for Avery to ask her to get food, and then things would be awkward between them at the garden from then on. Oh God, she never should have said anything.

"God yes, definitely," Beth said. "I'm starving, and Greta is working late tonight, so I'm on my own for dinner. What do you want to eat?"

Avery held back her sigh of relief.

"I'll eat anything—all I had today was the random snacks I had in my office. So long as it's not a mini granola bar from an airplane, or a handful of candy from last Halloween, I'll be happy."

Beth laughed.

"How about pizza? Are there any places that you like around here that won't care if we show up with dirt under our fingernails?" She looked at Avery's gardening gloves and grinned. "Metaphorically speaking, I mean."

Avery pulled off her gloves with a smile.

"Our main product here in Napa Valley is agriculture, after all."

Fifteen minutes later, they were ensconced at a corner table in the back garden of one of Avery's favorite places.

"I've been coming here since I was in high school," Avery said. She looked around and then laughed. "And, unlike almost everywhere else I went in high school, this place is both still standing and also still good."

Beth looked around, then gestured to the restaurant or the sky, Avery couldn't tell which.

"If I grew up in a place like this, I'd never want to leave," she said. "I couldn't wait to get out of my hometown and never go back."

Avery laughed.

"You'd be surprised at how many people feel like that about growing up here. Most people either never want to leave, or they leave and never come back." She shrugged. "And then there are those of us who thought we'd be the latter and came back anyway."

Beth picked up a piece of pizza and paused with it halfway to her mouth.

"Okay, look, I know there's probably a better way to do this, but I'm just going to ask so I stop wondering: You *are* queer, aren't you? Because I thought so, but Greta said no, that you were obviously straight, and I need to know which one of us is right, and we may have even bet about it . . . and I'm making a mess of this, aren't I? Let me know if I need to get up and leave because I will, even without taking a bite of this pizza that looks and smells very delicious."

Avery burst out laughing.

"This is definitely the first time that anyone has ever had a bet about my sexual orientation."

Beth held up a finger.

"That you know of."

Avery stopped to consider that.

"That I know of, yeah, I guess you're right. And, um, you win the bet."

It felt both weird and good to say that. Despite going out with Taylor once a week for the past month or so, she hadn't really talked to many people about this, outside of the people she'd met around Taylor.

It also felt both weird and good that Beth had thought she was queer and cared enough to have a discussion and a bet with her fiancée about it.

A huge grin broke out across Beth's face.

"I knew it," she said. "I can't wait to tell Greta." She made a face. "Oh no, I'm making it weird again, aren't I?"

Avery nodded.

"Yeah, but I don't really care." She took a careful bite of her own slice of pizza. "Can I tell you something?"

Oh no. Why had she said that? She hadn't meant to say that. Why did she keep doing this?

"Most definitely." Beth looked very interested. Of course she did. And of course that would be her answer. No one would say no when someone said, *Can I tell you something?* unless they were a sociopath or a complete misanthrope, and Beth was neither. By now she knew Beth well enough to know that she would absolutely be interested in what someone would tell her when they asked her *Can I tell you something?* in that tone of voice. So now she had no choice but to tell her.

"I, um, have never really dated women, even though I've wanted to," she said, watching Beth's face for scorn or pity. She saw neither there, just friendly interest, so she went on. "And earlier this summer I told that to my friend Taylor—well, she wasn't really my friend then, but I guess she is now—also that I didn't really know how to flirt with women. I mean, I don't really know how to flirt with anyone, but especially women. So, Taylor has been teaching me how to flirt this summer."

Beth's eyes were wide as saucers.

"Wait, I love this. What is she teaching you? How's it going?"

Avery felt a very strange combination of abject embarrassment and glee.

"It's going well, I think? I'm not totally sure. But it's been fun so far, at least? We've only had a few classes or whatever so far; that bookstore event was actually the first one, then we went to queer salsa dancing, and last night was a burlesque show. She gives me tips on what to do, and I talk to people and get embarrassed about it, rinse and repeat. I don't think I'm particularly good at flirting yet—or even okay at it—but at least I'm less terrified about it, which is progress."

Beth nodded.

"Definite progress. But, okay, I need to know more about your friend Taylor! Why is she qualified to teach flirting classes?"

Avery laughed.

"Oh, you wouldn't ask this question if you'd met Taylor at the bookstore. She was hiding away in the corner most of the night, I think so I wouldn't feel overshadowed, which was very nice of her, but she's basically a magnet for women. She's really good at flirting, but not in a superficial way—she's just good at talking to people, you know? Which I guess I am in a work context, but not when it comes to personal stuff. And she also seems to know every queer woman in the area, so she knows good places to take me and, like, people to introduce me to. And also she's . . . I don't know, really kind about it all. Which is good because I still can't believe I'm doing this."

She also couldn't believe she was telling Beth about it. Maybe it was heatstroke after spending two hours gardening in the sun.

"Well, I'm glad you're doing it, and I can't wait to hear more about this," Beth said. "And I also desperately want to meet this clearly very hot friend of yours. Obviously, I'm taken, but I can still look, can't I?"

Avery laughed. As they ate their pizza, they talked in more detail about the flirting lessons (Beth laughed until she cried when Avery told her about the boa incident), about plans for Beth and Greta's surprise wedding, and how Greta was liking her new job. Avery walked back home later that night proud of herself for inviting Beth to dinner, for maybe even making a new friend. Taylor was right; putting yourself out there was worth it.

TAYLOR TEXTED AVERY ON SATURDAY MORNING.

TAYLOR

> want to go to a birthday party tonight? it's for callie, from the salsa class, she said to bring you along if you want to come. there will be great snacks and many people to practice flirting with . . .

There would also likely be many people who would ask Avery a million questions about what was going on between her and Taylor, which was why she'd hesitated to invite her. But Callie had specifically told her to invite Avery, and Taylor knew that would be a nice little confidence boost that Avery needed.

AVERY

> Ugh I totally would have but I can't, I'm working an event tonight and by the time I get done it'll probably be too late. Tell Callie I said happy birthday!

Taylor felt a flash of disappointment, which was ridiculous. Her fixation on Avery was obviously just because of this stupid celibacy bet. She'd been spending more time with Avery than almost anyone else lately, so of course she couldn't stop thinking about how much she wanted to sleep with her. It wasn't anything about Avery, exactly, just her own hormones. If things had been normal, she would sleep with someone else and not give Avery another thought.

Well, if things had been normal, Erica wouldn't have bet her to do something ridiculous like stay celibate for months. This was all Erica's fault.

Was Erica even coming to the party tonight? Taylor hated that she didn't know the answer to that. In the old days—a year ago—she would have known this. She and Erica used to see each other all the time, talk almost every day; there's no way she wouldn't have known. But now she had no idea. She and Sam were probably hanging out with Sloane and their other grown-up friends, talking about, like, mortgages and the stock market and property taxes, things that Taylor was too immature to know anything about.

But to her surprise, Erica and Sam were at the party when Taylor walked in.

"Hey, stranger," Taylor said, and immediately regretted it. She didn't want to be all passive-aggressive about this; she wasn't that kind of person. So when Erica pulled her into a hug, she gave her a fierce embrace. Then she stepped back and laughed.

"Oh wow, the little rutabaga is really starting to make herself known, huh?"

Erica patted her belly.

"I'm really showing now, aren't I? It's great—I'm not sick anymore, I'm not exhausted all the time like I was for the first few months, I have a ton of energy. This part is fun."

Sam sighed.

"A little too much energy, if you ask me." She gave Taylor a quick hug. "She's spending all of her time organizing things with Sloane. I swear, if one more thing in our house gets a cute little label on it, I'm going to be afraid that I'll wake up one day and look in the mirror and right there on my forehead there'll be a little handwritten label in perfect script with 'Sam' on it."

Ugh, of course Sloane had perfect script and would put handwritten labels on everything. She probably put them all on cute little baskets all over her house.

Erica just swatted her wife on the shoulder and laughed.

"I'm not *that* bad. We might as well get our house all in order before crunch time. We hadn't really gotten ourselves organized since the move, and we needed to! And it's so nice to be able to find everything." She turned to Taylor, her face all animated. "Did I text you pictures of our linen closet? It's so great now; we have designated labeled shelves for everything, and little baskets for washcloths and toilet paper and extra beauty supplies." Baskets. Yep. "And what used to be our junk closet now has baskets for the random cords we have and lightbulbs and batteries and instruction books and all of that stuff. Someday, I'm going to bring Sloane over to your apartment and we can do this for you."

Taylor burst out laughing. Erica just shook her head.

"You laugh now, but just you wait. Next time you come over, you'll see how convenient it all is. It maximizes so much space. Plus, I can write so much of this off on our taxes because it's for the home office."

You know who would probably be fascinated by this organization talk? Avery. She was far more of an adult than Taylor was. She probably had baskets and labels and stuff, too.

"I need to get to the food before it's all gone," Taylor said. "Come tell me more about these organized cords or maybe even, for the love of God, something more interesting while I get some food and say hi to Callie."

Callie's parties always had great food. That's why Taylor had to get some right now before whatever the best thing was disappeared into the stomachs of the people who had gotten there before her.

Sam pulled out her phone and made the *I have to take a call* gesture, while Erica followed Taylor outside.

"It's the little phyllo dough turnovers," Erica said under her breath. "They're the best thing this year. Everything is great, obviously, but those are incredible. She has them with a spinach and feta filling, and a sausage filling; get both. I've already had probably ten of each."

Taylor widened her eyes.

"There's always someone who eats all of the best snacks at Callie's party in the first hour. Has it always been you?"

Erica shook her head and laughed.

"No, no, it's not usually me, I swear. But I'm pregnant! I'm always starving! And I can't eat any of the charcuterie and most of the cheese, and you know how tempting her cheese and charcuterie platters always are, so I had to just . . ."

"Go to town on the turnovers?"

Erica grinned.

"Exactly." Then a mischievous look came over her face. "You should get the recipe from Callie so you can make them for my baby shower. You know, when you have to throw it for me. Have I won that bet yet, by the way?"

"Nope, and you're not going to. I can't wait to hear all about that baby shower as I lounge at my spa day."

Erica looked smug.

"Feeling very confident, aren't you? And yet, I've already seen you exchanging looks with at least two people at this party. You'll cave soon, I know it."

Taylor slid three of each kind of turnover onto her plate.

"First of all, I was not 'exchanging looks' with anyone, I was simply smiling a hello to people who smiled hellos to me. Do you want me to be rude? And secondly, wow, you have so little faith in me."

She tried to make that sound like a joke, but it wasn't really. It *did* kind of hurt her feelings that Erica thought like this about her. It stung that she thought Taylor was so childish or so ruled by her hormones that she had to be celibate for months to, what, learn how to be a grown-up like Erica?

Erica just laughed.

"You know that's not true; I have all the faith in the world in you. I know that you can get literally any woman that you want if you set your mind to it. Your power is too strong; the queer women of Northern California need a break, that's all!"

Taylor ignored that as they walked over to Callie.

"Happy birthday!" She gave Callie a hug. "Avery couldn't come, but she wanted me to say happy birthday, too. She has a work event tonight, but she told me to tell you she wished she could be here, and she hopes you have a great birthday."

Erica gasped. "You met Avery?" she asked Callie. "What's she like?"

Callie grinned at Taylor.

"So there *is* something going on between the two of you! We all thought so!"

Erica turned to stare at Taylor, and Taylor shook her head at both of them.

"There is nothing going on between the two of us, and you know that," she said, with a pointed glance at Erica. She hoped that glance said, *You're the only one who knows about the flirting lessons, keep your mouth shut.* But now Callie was looking at her, wanting to know what Erica had meant. Fuck. She had to explain that, but how? Then she had a brain wave. "I am simply helping introduce her to queer society, that's all. She had a dunce of a boyfriend for years, and now she's gotten rid of him and is ready to date women. It's like she's a debutante, and I'm her chaperone."

Callie, who has a weakness for historical romance novels, grinned. Taylor had to look away from Erica; her trying-not-to-laugh face was going to make Taylor crack up.

"That makes sense," Callie said. "There's no one better than you to launch someone into queer society. But how'd Avery manage to get *you* for that job?"

"Oh, I felt bad for her, that's all. Plus, she's great. I hope she finds some people to date who are good enough for her, they'll be lucky."

Someone else came up to hug Callie, and Erica dragged Taylor back to the food.

"Oh no, the turnovers are gone." Erica shrugged. "I guess I'll just have to get some of these adorable little sliders, then." She loaded three onto her plate. "But also, I need to hear more about 'introducing Avery to queer society.'"

Taylor grinned.

"Sorry, I just feel like Avery probably wouldn't want me to tell the world that I'm teaching her how to flirt with women, so please, don't tell everyone that. Callie and Liz and Rex met her because we ran into them when we did queer salsa lessons, and we also went to a bookstore event and a burlesque show. And I think next week—"

"You went to a burlesque show with her! Oh my God, Taylor, you didn't tell me you did that!"

You didn't ask. Maybe if you weren't so absorbed by your new bestie Sloane and her little baskets and her perfect handwriting, I would have told you.

"Oh, it's a better story for in person," Taylor said instead.

"Taylor!" She heard Liz's voice, and then felt Liz grab and hug her from behind. "I was wondering when you were going to show up!"

Taylor turned to her and returned the hug.

"I'd never get to one of Callie's parties late; you miss all of the good snacks that way."

Erica drifted off to the other side of the backyard; she and Liz had never been huge fans of each other. Taylor chatted with Liz, with Dani and Charlie, with Anya (one of the people Erica had accused her of "exchanging looks with") and Zoe (the other person). Which, okay, fine, Taylor *had* sort of given them each a look that *possibly* said that she'd like to see them naked. And yes, fine, Zoe had whispered a little something in her ear that indicated that Taylor could do that—and many other things to her—as early as tonight. But she wasn't planning on doing any of those things until after Labor Day. She did not want to lose this bet with Erica.

Speaking of Erica . . . Taylor looked around the party for her and didn't see either her or Sam. Maybe they were hanging out inside? She poked her head in, but she still didn't see them. They must have left. And even before Callie cut her cake, which was a travesty. Callie's cakes were always fantastic.

Erica hadn't even said goodbye to her. So much for her wanting so badly to know about how stuff with Avery was going.

Taylor looked across the party and saw Kelsey checking her out. She grinned at her as she tried to brush off the hurt she felt. It wasn't like Erica owed her anything. It was fine for her to not say goodbye when she left a party, she was an adult, she had a wife now, she didn't need to check in with Taylor when she left somewhere and when she got home like they used to do.

But still, it stung. She pulled out her phone to see if maybe Erica had texted. She hadn't. But Avery had.

AVERY

How's the party? What are the good snacks? Who is flirting with who and is there anything I could be learning from this? There are at least two more hours in this event before I can go home, and I need all the hot gossip.

Taylor laughed out loud and immediately texted Avery back.

TAYLOR

oh my friend, everyone is flirting with everyone, i'm sad you aren't here, it would be so educational

but don't worry, i have a plan

Taylor knew what Avery's response would be. Sure enough.

AVERY

Oh no.

Taylor laughed at her phone. This week with Avery would be fun.

SEVEN

AVERY SHOOK HER HEAD AT TAYLOR'S "CASUAL BUT SEXY" IN-structions in response to her "what should I wear???" text. Last time, it was risqué; now sexy? Not for the first time, she wondered what she'd gotten herself into.

The good thing was she'd bought a bunch of new clothes recently, some for her Taylor adventures, which was how she'd come to think of them, and some for the garden club. She now had more casual sundresses, tops that showed a lot more cleavage than her other clothes did, and, in general, more clothes that she could wear out of the house for occasions other than work. She thought for a moment and pulled on her new pair of denim shorts that somehow managed to both be comfortable and make her butt look great, and a white button-down from the work wardrobe side of her closet. She buttoned one fewer than she normally would, rolled up the sleeves to her elbows, *and* tied the bottom to show a little midriff. There. With some flat brown sandals, that should be good no matter where they were going. At least, she hoped so.

She worried that she didn't look queer enough, but maybe being with Taylor gave her some sort of cred? She still had no real idea what she was doing, but after her first few weeks of total anxiety, the burlesque show had cracked through that wall. Taylor had said the goal was to have fun, and she *was* having fun. And as a bonus, she got to hang out with Taylor at least once a week.

Sure, she had a crush on Taylor, but she also knew how Taylor operated. Everyone did because, from what she had observed, *everyone* had a crush on Taylor. She knew it, Taylor knew it, the rest of them knew it, so they just lived with their crushes and perked up every time Taylor smiled at them or flirted with them. And Taylor flirted with her, of course, both because she was literally teaching her how to flirt, and because she was Taylor and she couldn't help it. Avery simply wouldn't take it seriously, that's all.

Anyway, it was fun to have a crush, for the first time in a long time. After she'd been so beaten down by her relationship with Derek, she'd wondered if she'd ever find anything fun about all of this again, if dating and relationships and love and sex were only about stress and pain and stifling yourself. Or if the good parts about it were reserved for other people, not her. But she felt butterflies again every time Taylor texted her, or when she got in Taylor's car on their Tuesday nights, or when Taylor laughed at one of her jokes. She hadn't had that feeling in a very long time. She was going to try to enjoy it.

She looked at herself in the mirror again right before Taylor got there. Oh, to hell with it. She unfastened one more button and walked out of her apartment before she could change her mind.

"How do I look?" she asked Taylor when she got into the car.

Taylor looked her up and down. Avery felt a little tingle go through her body the way it always did when Taylor did that.

"You're going for prep school hottie tonight, I see," Taylor said.

Admittedly, she had been fishing for a compliment, but she hadn't expected that.

"Um, that wasn't my aim, no. I think of prep school hottie as, like, short little plaid skirt. You know, like Britney in that video."

Taylor laughed.

"I do know, and while I agree that you'd look great in that outfit, too, that's the young version of the prep school hottie. Yours is the all-grown-up, polished, even hotter version."

Avery smiled over at Taylor.

"You do amazing things to my confidence. Thank you. And you look pretty hot yourself tonight."

That "tonight" was superfluous. Taylor always looked hot, but she was currently wearing the ur-Taylor hot outfit: jeans, a black belt, and a snug black tank top, with many earrings jangling in her ears. She'd gotten browner in the summer sun—it was almost impossible not to here in Napa—and her skin looked so smooth and supple. Avery wanted to stroke her arm. She made herself look up at Taylor's face and smile.

"You're getting good at this," Taylor said. "Nice job there, returning the compliment."

Avery tossed her hair.

"Remember? I'm a quick study." She leaned back in her seat. "Plus, it has the advantage of being true."

What had gotten into her tonight? Just because she'd made peace with her crush on Taylor didn't mean that she had to overdo it!

But Taylor laughed and blew a kiss in her direction.

"Oh, how was Callie's party?" Avery asked.

Taylor sighed, her smile dropping slightly.

"Oh, it was fun. Lots of people came, and I got there in time to have her phyllo dough turnovers, which were wildly delicious. Definitely the star of the party this year."

That sigh didn't seem like Taylor. Avery started to ask about that, but Taylor kept talking.

"Oh! And just so you know—I told Callie that I was introducing you to queer society, you know, like an old-timey chaperone but, like, modern and queer. Just FYI."

Avery turned to stare at Taylor.

"You told Callie *what?*"

Taylor made a face.

"You're right, without any context that sounds unhinged, let me explain. She was asking questions about you and why we were suddenly hanging out a lot and if we were dating, blah blah. I had to tell her something, but I didn't want to tell her about the flirting lessons, since that seemed personal and I didn't want to tell the world about that without talking to you first, so I kind of riffed on it? And telling Callie would be telling the world, trust me. Wait, are you mad? I probably shouldn't have said that, either. I'm sorry."

Mad? Avery was flattered that Taylor's friends had asked Taylor if they were dating, especially since they'd already asked her that. It felt good that they thought she'd be good enough for Taylor.

"No, of course I'm not mad. Thanks for not telling everyone about the flirting lessons; I appreciate it. I'm impressed you came up with 'queer chaperone' on the spur of the moment." Avery giggled. "Wait. Does that make me a queer debutante? Do I get a coming-out ball?"

Taylor grinned at her.

"Say the word, and I'll throw you one."

A few minutes later, Taylor pulled into a parking spot in downtown Napa. Avery followed Taylor down the street to a bar and read the sign on the door.

"'Trivia night,'" Avery read. And then smiled.

Taylor smiled back at her.

"I had a feeling you'd be good at trivia. You seem like that kind of person."

Avery glared at her.

"That sounds like you're trying to insult me, but I'm going to take it as a compliment."

Taylor laced her arm through Avery's.

"You *should* take it as a compliment. Come on, this way."

Avery looked over to where Taylor was leading her. Aah, this made more sense now. Taylor's friends were over there. That must be why Taylor had told her about the queer debutante thing on the way here.

"Avery, you've met Callie and Rex. This is Dani and Nadia," Taylor said, gesturing at first Dani, then Nadia, thank goodness.

"Hi, all. Good to see you again," Avery said as she nodded toward Rex and Callie. "Nice to meet you Dani, Nadia." Dani was gorgeous; she was tall, with light brown skin, and looked like a retired professional soccer player or something. Nadia had dark skin that looked amazing with her bright yellow dress, and was very curvy. Avery tried to smile at them naturally, like she wasn't nervous walking into a group of people who knew one another and were friends and probably saw her as an interloper. Was it weird how she'd tried to say hi to all of them and "good to see you again" to just some of them?

Why was it easier to unbutton her shirt one extra button than it was to not feel anxious in a social situation?

Everyone smiled at her, though, and Callie pulled her into a hug.

"Good to see you too, Avery!"

"Over here!" a woman shouted in their direction.

"Excellent, Liz got us a table," Taylor said.

They all sat down, and Avery ended up between Liz and Callie. She wished she were next to Taylor, but the whole point of doing this was to flirt, learn to talk to strangers, maybe go on an actual date with a woman, and not be so fucking anxious in social situations that were new to her. It might be counterproductive to sit next to Taylor, whom she already knew, and whom she obviously would not be going out on a date with. If Taylor wanted that, it could have happened at any time in the past month.

"We missed you at the party this weekend, Avery." Callie turned to her and put her hand on Avery's arm.

It was likely for the best that she hadn't been there, because otherwise Avery probably would have blurted out the truth about why she and Taylor were spending time together. And she didn't really want all of Taylor's friends to know that Taylor was teaching her how to flirt. That made her sound pathetic.

"I was sorry to have missed it," Avery said. "Happy belated birthday, and thanks for inviting me. Taylor said it was great, and that the food was amazing."

Callie preened from the compliment.

"I go all out on the food at my parties. I used to cook in restaurants, but that got exhausting, so I haven't cooked professionally in years. Whenever I have people over, I get to go a little wild."

Callie's hand was still on her arm. Avery froze. Was Callie flirting with her? Shit. What was she supposed to do now? She couldn't remember anything.

From the corner of her eye, she saw Taylor at the other end of the table. Knowing she was there made Avery relax a little. Now she remembered. Smile. Don't freeze up. Make eye contact. Ask questions. Okay, she could do this.

"So, Callie, what do you do?" Yes, *What do you do?* was a boring question, but she had to start somewhere. Small talk, remember?

"I own a plant store in St. Helena."

Huh, that wasn't what Avery expected her to say. But then, she supposed, she didn't know what she'd expected.

"Oh wow, how did you get into that? Plants, I mean." *Plants, I mean.* Why was she so incredibly awkward? "Sorry, that sounded weird, what I meant was that I recently started getting into gardening and I've loved it so far."

"I guess the way most people get into them," Callie said. "I got obsessed with having plants in my too-small apartment, and then in our too-small house, and I was constantly moving them around to figure out which ones need full sun and which need filtered sun, how much water they all need and how to repot them and why and everything else. At first, it was just fun, and then I got super into it, and I was at some of my local plant stores so often that all of the staff knew me. So when there was a part-time job available at one, I took it, mostly just to make extra money that I could spend on plants." She laughed, a little self-consciously. "And then, a few years later, right when I'd decided that I was done working in restaurants and catering companies and needed to figure out something else to do with my life, the owner of the store was retiring and selling the business, and I made the very risky decision to buy it from her."

"That's amazing," Avery said. "It sounds a lot like my business origin story, except not with a plant store."

Callie raised her eyebrows at Avery.

"What's your story? What do you do?"

"I'm an event planner. I used to work at hotels, doing their event planning stuff, and I got laid off during the pandemic." Callie made sympathetic noises. "A few months later, a local event planner who I'd worked with reached out to see if I could work for her part-time, helping with virtual events since she didn't know how to deal with them. And then when she retired, I made the very risky decision to buy her business."

"That is similar," Callie said. "How's it going?"

"Really well, actually," Avery said. "I'm working a lot, though. I've been thinking about hiring an assistant, but I'm a little worried that I'd make a terrible boss."

Avery saw Taylor grin when she said that.

"Oh, I thought I would be, too," Callie said. "Luckily, it's turned out great—which I'm only sure of because I have some employees who have been around since I bought the place, and absolutely would tell me if I was a nightmare. There were definitely some bumps in the road initially, but we figured it out. If you end up hiring that assistant, let me know if you have any questions about being a boss, happy to help."

"That's so nice of you," Avery said. "I might take you up on that." She knew a lot of other small-business owners in Napa Valley, but many she'd met at events, or given her business card to when she'd dropped by their store; they all sent business one another's way, but she often had to fake it till she made it with them and be the smart, successful, hardworking, intrepid entrepreneur. She couldn't ask them questions like how it felt to be a boss, and how to make sure she was demanding excellence from an employee without micromanaging them. That fear had kept her from hiring someone, but it meant that she was constantly overworked. But wouldn't she be overworked when she had to train someone new and also do all the stuff she was already doing? See, this was the kind of thing she needed to ask someone else.

"So, tell us, how did you meet Taylor?" Liz broke in. "She was pretty vague about that."

Avery laughed. She hoped it was a casual laugh, and not one that said, *Why are you asking me this, do you think there's something weird about Taylor bringing me here?*

"That's no mystery: my best friend Luke used to work with Taylor. I think he was intimidated by her, which is excellent. More women need to intimidate straight men, it's good for them." Even the best of straight men, which Luke is, need that sometimes.

"Taylor can do that," Callie said, laughing.

Liz nodded.

"It's true, she can." She grinned at Avery. "She breaks a lot of hearts, you know." There was a smile on her face, but not in her voice. What was this about?

Callie nodded.

"She does. We once got her to sing 'Heartbreaker' during karaoke, everyone died laughing."

Avery tried to picture Taylor doing karaoke and smiled.

"Yeah, so she's told me," she said. "I can certainly see why, she's a lot of fun."

Liz turned to look at Taylor, who was in the middle of a conversation with Dani.

"Yeah," Liz said. "She is, isn't she?"

Had she just tried to warn Avery off Taylor? Avery couldn't decide whether to be amused or flattered. She guessed it would be a combination of both, since it was both very funny to her and an enormous compliment that anyone could think Taylor would be interested in her.

Okay, now it was her time to change the subject. She couldn't just ask the *What do you do?* question again, could she? Well, why not?

"So, Liz—" she started, when Liz interrupted her.

"What are your big three, Avery?" Oh no. Not astrology. "Wait, let me guess . . . Libra sun, right?"

Avery took a sip of the margarita she'd ordered and shook her head.

"Hmmm, I could have sworn . . . Well, you must have Libra as a rising sign. Leo?"

Avery shook her head again. She had the sudden evil impulse to see how long this would go on if she just kept shaking her head and giving Liz nothing. Was it because Liz had irritated her a bit with that implied warning about Taylor? Maybe. She also hated when people tried to distill her personality traits—or what they knew of them—down to when she was born.

"Okay, well—hmmm." Avery glanced over to the other end of the table and saw the smirk on Taylor's face. Their eyes met, and Taylor winked at her. Avery couldn't help but grin. "Aha! Scorpio!" Liz said. "You must have that somewhere in your birth chart."

"Do we want to order some nachos?" Taylor asked their end of the table. "One vegetarian and one with meat?"

There were universal nods, so Taylor got up. She came around to their side of the table.

"Liz, did you open a tab?" Taylor asked. She rested a hand on Avery's shoulder as she talked to Liz. "If so, you should come to the bar with me and get your card back, I'll get this round." Avery took the last sip of her margarita and started to lean back against Taylor before she caught herself. She tried to pretend that Taylor's touch was no big deal, didn't make her feel anything at all, totally normal.

Liz jumped out of her chair.

"Oh yeah, thanks, Taylor."

When Taylor came back, she slid into the seat next to Avery.

"I had to save you from that astrology conversation," she said in Avery's ear. "I knew that it would go on forever if I didn't do something. I've got to say, usually you're great at a poker face, but that time . . ."

"Wait, what was wrong with the look on my face?" Avery asked.

"Nothing was *wrong* with it, exactly, it was just clear that she was getting on your nerves."

Avery had to laugh.

"She wasn't getting on my nerves! She's nice! Though I was kind of enjoying fucking with her." Oops, she had *not* meant for that to come out of her mouth. She looked around to see if anyone had overheard her, but thankfully it didn't seem like it.

Taylor grinned sideways at her.

"I could tell."

"My mom is super into astrology, and I guess one of my small bits of rebellion is to resist everything about it."

Taylor leaned closer to her.

"Wait, if your mom is super into astrology, that means you know your big three. Come on, you can tell me."

Avery sighed, but she couldn't help the smile on her face.

"Capricorn sun, Virgo moon, Taurus rising."

"Oh, Liz was very wrong." Taylor laughed. "Incredible."

"Now you have to tell me yours," Avery said.

"How do you even know I know them?" Taylor asked.

"Because I do," Avery said.

Taylor fluttered her eyelashes.

"Leo sun, Sagittarius moon, Libra rising."

They smiled at each other, both with eyes full of laughter, and Avery suddenly realized how close they were sitting. So close, their hips were touching. So close that if she moved just a little, their arms would be touching, too.

She stayed right where she was. But that tiny space between their arms felt like it was almost pulsing. She could feel the warmth coming from Taylor's skin.

What was she doing, fantasizing about Taylor like this? Taylor wasn't interested in her! Taylor had women throwing themselves at her all the time—as was clear from what Liz and Callie had said. Taylor didn't want someone as inexperienced and awkward as Avery. Taylor was only out with her because she was teaching her how to be not quite so awkward.

Wait, hadn't she decided it was fine to have a crush on Taylor? That it was a nice way to warm herself up, to get some practice in, to make herself feel a bit less awkward around women? That it was an Exciting New Experience and that she was not going to fight it but instead let herself enjoy it?

That was before she was one strong margarita in and sitting this close to her.

"Okay," Taylor said in her ear. An actual tingle went down her spine. How could Avery *not* have a crush on her? "I bet you're very good at trivia," Taylor continued.

Avery turned to look at Taylor. She had a sly little smile on her face.

"Kind of, but I'm making no promises," Avery said. "Are you good at trivia?"

Taylor shook her head.

"No, but I'm good at being able to figure out who knows what they're talking about versus who is bullshitting. Let's see how this goes."

TAYLOR PROBABLY SHOULDN'T HAVE GONE OVER TO AVERY'S side of the table, not with her friends around, watching for any sign that something was going on between the two of them. And she definitely shouldn't have sat down so close to her. But she had to save Avery from Liz, who was clearly annoying Avery and absolutely dying to cross-examine her. The only problem was that Liz was now back and sitting in Taylor's old seat and kept looking at the two of them. Whatever, if Liz stared at them, she stared at them. The important thing was that Avery enjoy herself.

"You having fun?" she asked Avery in a low voice.

Avery nodded quickly, a smile on her face.

"Definitely. Your friends are all fun, and the margaritas are great." Avery took another sip and laughed. "And also very strong—I can't have more than two of these, I have to be up early tomorrow for a breakfast meeting."

Taylor opened her eyes wide.

"A breakfast meeting? Those are two words that should never be paired together."

Taylor saw Dani and Liz exchanging glances at the other end of the table. She sighed internally but shook it off. Whatever, this whole group would gossip about her later, not like that was anything new. She sort of asked for it by bringing Avery around them—though she probably wouldn't have done that if she and Avery hadn't already run into them at the dance class. But the queer community in Napa wasn't all that big; she and Avery definitely would have run into her friends at some point. And once it happened, it made sense to just bring Avery to a group event so the rumor mill wouldn't go quite as wild about what was going on between the two of them.

Still, the knowing looks and raised eyebrows in her direction were getting on her nerves. She didn't love the way they gossiped about her, though she knew none of it was malicious. It had been different when Erica was around the group all the time—then, it had been easier to not be bothered, to laugh it off. Then, it had been fun to be the one there were always stories about, the one who everyone gossiped about, who everyone wanted to know what she was doing . . . or who she was doing, more specifically.

But now Erica was married and pregnant and hanging out

with her friends who had elaborate dinner parties and organized their home offices. If she complained to Erica about the way they were acting about her and Avery, would Erica say something like *Well, you know how you are with women* or even *Come on, tell me, have you slept with her yet?*

At least Erica wouldn't size up Avery like she was fresh meat, like everyone else here was doing. Well, not everyone, Rex wasn't. But Dani and Nadia were staring at her cleavage, Callie was staring at her whole body, and Liz was just staring at her. Granted, Avery's cleavage was on display tonight, which both surprised and impressed Taylor. That wasn't something the Avery of a month ago would have done.

She was glad that she'd waited until this part in their flirting curriculum to bring Avery to hang out with her friends. She was way more relaxed and comfortable with them now than she would have been at first. She hoped Avery would come away from this night buoyed by all the people flirting with her.

As a matter of fact, she should probably move away from Avery so the rest of the group could continue to flirt with her. Slightly reluctant, she stood up.

"I'll get us another pitcher before things get too busy at the bar," she announced to the table at large. She walked over to the bar and nodded at Sofie, who was behind the bar that night.

"Another pitcher of margaritas?" Sofie asked her.

"You know it. See, this is why you're the best bartender in Northern California."

"Only Northern?" Sofie shook her head. "I've obviously got some work to do."

Taylor laughed and handed over her credit card. As she waited for the margaritas, she wondered who would take advantage of her departure to get up to "go to the bathroom" and then quickly come back to sit down next to Avery. She refused to turn around—someone at that table was definitely watching her—so she pulled out her phone to text Erica.

TAYLOR

> i brought avery to trivia night tonight and the whole crowd is flocking to her. i just got up to get drinks, want to bet on who grabs the seat next to her?

Would Erica be too busy with work or her house or Sloane to see and respond to her text?

ERICA

> Ooh yes. Who all is there?

Guess she wasn't too busy tonight.

TAYLOR

> liz, callie, nadia, dani, rex. but callie is already on avery's other side and isn't budging

Who would she bet on? Taylor ran through the group in her mind.

There was definitely a strong probability Liz would try to grab her seat back. However, Dani had already very casually asked Taylor if Avery was single. She was warm and bubbly, so that would be good for Avery; it was really easy to talk to her. Rex, no—they were never interested in people as femme as Avery, so they definitely wouldn't jump up to go sit next to her. Though Taylor kind of wished they would; Rex was calm and low-key—they'd probably be a soothing presence for Avery. Nadia was a wild card—she also wasn't into femmes, but she *loved* gossip, so she might try to get some info out of Avery just for fun.

She smiled to herself as she thought of that quick mental rundown of her friends. It had reminded her of all their good qualities and the reasons why she was friends with this whole crew in the first place. Sure, they gossiped about her; she also gossiped about other people all the damn time. And to be fair to them, she'd probably gossip about herself, too.

She mentally apologized to them; they probably had no idea she'd been a petty bitch about them tonight. Still, she'd put her money on either Liz or Dani to be the one who had leapt from her own seat to sit next to Avery. And since Liz had started the night sitting next to Avery, Taylor was pretty sure that when she turned around in about thirty seconds with the pitcher of margaritas in her hand, Dani would be sitting next to Avery.

TAYLOR

i'll go first: i'm betting on dani

ERICA

Ooh, interesting, I'm betting on Liz

Sofie handed her the pitcher, and Taylor tipped her well. Then she turned around to go back to the table and almost laughed out loud. Yep, there was Dani, sitting next to Avery, chatting animatedly with her. And look at that. Avery was chatting animatedly right back.

TAYLOR

i was right. dani

ERICA

Damn it. That was going to be
my other choice.

By the time Taylor got back to the table, the trivia was in full swing.

"Interstate highways in America that go west to east always end with what number?" the announcer asked over the mic.

"Zero!" Avery said, as did Dani. The two of them grinned at each other.

Taylor didn't contribute much to trivia; she'd never particularly been good at it. Also, she didn't understand why people would want to ruin a nice relaxing night out at a bar with a series of tests. But she'd had a feeling that this would be a good venue for Avery. She'd been right.

"This famous English breeder of roses developed over three hundred rose varieties during his lifetime," the announcer read.

"I know this one," Avery said. "David Austin. People *always* want his roses for weddings."

"Avery, you're so good at this," Dani said, practically trying to sit in her lap. "You should come join our trivia team every week."

Taylor barely stopped herself from rolling her eyes. Yes, Avery was good at this, and it was good to see her blooming under the flattery of Dani and Liz and Callie and everyone else, but could they be any more obvious about this?

Avery looked away for a moment, and Taylor could see her start to withdraw a little. Oh no, was this too much for her? But then Avery turned back to Dani, looked her in the eyes, lowered her lashes, and then looked back up at her.

"Thank you," she said. "It's good to be able to put the random information I've learned throughout my life to good use. I'm glad you appreciate it." She grinned at her slowly. "Do you want to know what the eleven most common allergens are? I know that, too."

Dani burst out laughing, and Taylor let herself grin. Avery was having fun with this. And *Taylor* needed to stop being such a bitch, once again.

Their team came in second, which made everyone at their table cheer loudly—apparently it was the first time they'd come in the top three in months.

"You're our lucky charm, Avery," Callie said. "That just means you've got to come back next week."

Avery looked at Taylor for a second. Was she checking in with her to see if Taylor wanted to come back, or was she trying to get Taylor to give her an excuse not to? Taylor wasn't sure. Avery turned back to Callie.

"I'll see what I can do," she said. "You know how it is to own a small business; work often gets in the way of fun things. And a lot of my stuff is at night, unfortunately. But this was really fun, I'd love to do this again."

After another round of hugs and goodbyes and whispers in Taylor's ears ("Leave it to you to bring around a hottie no one knew" from Dani; "Okay, but seriously, is something going on between you two?" from Nadia; "Bring her back!" from Callie; "I have so many questions" from Liz), all of which she just laughed at. Taylor and Avery walked back to Taylor's car.

"So," Taylor said as soon as they drove away. "*Did* you have fun, and *would* you love to come back, or were you just saying that to Callie?"

Avery had a smile on her face, but then, she'd had a smile on her face most of the night, which was why Taylor already knew the answer to that question.

"Yeah, I had a great time," she said. "You were right, I am good at trivia, I liked it a lot more than I thought I would. And your friends were all super nice to me."

Taylor raised an eyebrow.

"You mean my friends all thought you were hot as hell."

Avery's smile turned just a tiny bit smug.

"Well. I wouldn't have put it that way, but I *did* get some good flirting practice in."

"Oh, I saw," Taylor said. "But what was that look you gave me when Callie said she wanted you to come back?"

"That was just . . ." Avery said. "I wasn't sure how to answer."

"Why not?" Taylor asked. "Didn't you have fun?"

"I did," Avery said. "It's just . . . these are your friends. I didn't know if you would want me to come back and hang out with them. I also didn't know if Callie's invitation was real or just something she says to everyone, and I shouldn't take it seriously. But mostly the first thing."

Taylor was glad they were stopped at a light so she could look at Avery.

"Callie's invitation was definitely real, but why wouldn't I want you to hang out with my friends?"

Avery didn't look at her.

"Sometimes people . . . like to keep circles separate. Plus, we're not . . . I mean, you're doing these flirting lessons for me but that was you taking pity on me, we didn't really know each other before, so I don't want to . . ."

Taylor shook her head.

"Avery. I like you. I'm not doing these flirting lessons for you because I'm 'taking pity' on you—I'm not that kind of person. I'm not that nice! I wouldn't hang out with someone on a weekly basis if I didn't like them. We are friends, and friends help each other out." Taylor paused. "I mean, that's if you want to be. I don't know, maybe you don't like me, in which case I just made a fool of myself, but then I do that often, so—"

By this point, Avery was laughing.

"No, no, I like you, too. I thought we were friends, too. Or hoped. I mostly thought we were; I guess I was just having a moment of insecurity, or, I don't know, mean girls from the past getting into my head about friendship and everything. I'm sorry for being weird."

"No apologies necessary," Taylor said. "Any other questions about tonight?"

"Now that you ask," Avery said. "Is there a story with you and that bartender?"

Taylor let out a loud laugh.

"Why does everyone ask me about Sofie? Yes, we may have hooked up before, but she's taken now."

Taylor could feel Avery's smirk without even looking at her.

"I knew it," she said.

Taylor rolled her eyes.

"Don't you start," she said. "Now you're acting like my friends. Wait, what did they tell you about me?"

"Oh," Avery said. "Just stuff I already knew. Heartbreaker, champion flirt, allergic to long-term relationships, that kind of thing."

Basically, exactly what Taylor had thought they'd say. Taylor, always jumping in and out of relationships. She'd heard it all before.

"Okay, that last thing is true, and fine, maybe the second thing, but I still resist the heartbreaker label, despite what I'm sure they told you about karaoke."

Avery's laugh confirmed that yes, they had told her about karaoke.

Their next flirting lesson was *not* going to include her friends.

EIGHT

ON HER WAY TO AN EVENT ON WEDNESDAY LATE AFTERNOON, Avery got a text from Luke.

LUKE

> You around tonight? I feel like I haven't seen you forever–dinner?

Avery couldn't help but grin. They hadn't seen each other for weeks, but they both knew why. He and Margot were so happy, they were both walking on big fluffy clouds and had eyes for nothing and no one but each other.

Margot must be busy tonight, she typed and then deleted. Margot probably *was* busy that night, but Avery didn't want Luke to think she thought he was abandoning her or whatever to be with Margot. She really was happy for him.

It would be more fun to gently mock him about Margot in person, anyway.

AVERY

As long as you can wait until 8 or so when I'm done with work. Conference cocktail event tonight

LUKE

Sure, 8 works. Sushi?

AVERY

Great, I'll text when I'm leaving the event

Luke caught up to her outside the restaurant right after she parked.

"Hey," he said as he pulled her into a hug. "It's so good to see you."

She returned his hug and kissed him on the cheek.

"It's great to see you, too," she said. "Margot busy tonight?"

He looked embarrassed, but he still couldn't wipe the happy smile off his face.

"How'd you guess?" he said, and she laughed at him as they walked into the restaurant.

"I'm sorry if I've been blowing you off," he said as soon as they sat down. "It's just that I—"

She held up a hand to stop him.

"You have nothing to apologize for."

He didn't look convinced.

"You've had a hard time lately. I don't want you to think that I'm not—"

"Luke. My friend. I know you'd be there for me if I needed you. You know I know that. You and Margot are deep in love, you want to be with her all the time, I get it. I love this for you. Really."

His face relaxed back into his dreamy smile. It would be annoying if she didn't adore Luke with her whole heart. And she hadn't seen him this happy in a very long time.

"Okay. Thanks. And . . . yeah, we are. I mean, I am, and I think she is, too."

Avery laughed.

"You '*think* she is, too'? Taylor told me that Margot got distracted halfway through a winery tour the other day and brought them back to the tasting room like thirty minutes early. It wasn't until Taylor asked her why it went so fast that she realized and brought them back outside; they had to pretend it was a planned thing and give the guests a mid-tour glass of wine so they wouldn't realize what happened. Does that sound like the normal Margot Noble?"

Luke's surprised smile at that was frankly adorable.

"What? Okay, no, that is . . . not like Margot." He suddenly looked up at her. "Wait. *Taylor* told you that? I didn't realize you guys really knew each other."

That was an opening if she'd ever heard one.

"We didn't. But we talked for a while at the anniversary party, and we've been hanging out a lot more since then."

"Oh, that's good," Luke said. "Taylor's great." Then he paused and narrowed his eyes at her. "What's that look on your face? Is something going on with you two? Don't get me wrong, I really like Taylor," Luke continued. "But from what she's said, she seems to, um, date around a lot, and I don't—"

Avery patted him on the shoulder.

"Don't want me to get hurt? That's very sweet, but unnecessary. Don't worry, nothing's going on between the two of us, and I am very aware that she breaks a lot of hearts. No, it's that—" Luke was the one person who would really understand why she was doing this. She could tell him everything. "Okay, let me back up."

Luke's eyebrows were sky-high now.

"I'm listening."

"Are you ready to order?" the server asked. They both jumped; clearly neither of them had heard her approach.

"Let's order now," Avery said. "I'm starving, and this story might take a while." They both glanced at the menu and ordered far too much food. When the server walked away, Avery started again.

"It began when I ran into Ms. Cunningham at the winery party. She said something about how she hears from my mom about how I'm doing and she's so proud of what an upstanding citizen I am and how I was always such a well-behaved teenager blah blah, and all I could hear when she said that is that I've been boring my entire life." She held up a hand when Luke tried to interrupt. "I know what you're going to say; let me finish. I had a little too much wine after that and told Taylor that I was tired of being boring, and I wanted to flirt with people and get hobbies and make more friends and do things that weren't related to work, but then I said I had no idea how to flirt. Then she asked if I wanted to know how to flirt with men or women, and I said both, but especially women, since—"

"Since you've had enough of men for a while, I get it," Luke said.

"I was going to say since I haven't had a lot of experience with women, but your version works, too. So, long story short, Taylor is teaching me how to flirt."

"Are you kidding?" Luke looked at her. "You're not kidding, oh wow. This is very unlike you, I'm impressed. How's it going?"

"It's going well?" She stopped to think about that. "At least, I'm having fun with it. Well, I am now. It won't surprise you that I tried to talk Taylor out of this for a while at first, but she wasn't having it."

Luke grinned at her.

"No, as a matter of fact, that doesn't surprise me at all. About either of you. Tell me more. How has she been teaching you how to flirt?"

Avery had been a little worried that Luke would be weirded out by all of this, but she should have known that all Luke cared about was that she was happy.

"First we went to a bookstore event with an author I like, where she made me talk to other people there, and then we did queer salsa dance lessons, where I had to ask people to dance." Luke was very clearly fighting back a smile, so Avery threw him a glare. "Stop laughing at me."

"I'm not laughing at you," Luke said, with almost a straight face. "It's just that the tone of your voice when you said that you had to ask people to dance . . . I mean, you have to admit that was a little funny."

Avery tried not to smile and completely failed.

"I will admit it was a *little* funny," she said. "Anyway, we've done four total, and they've gotten less terrifying each time, which is nice. Oh! And did you know there's a community garden right by my apartment? I found out about it from a woman I met at the bookstore, and now I'm sharing a garden plot with her there, and we've planted a bunch of vegetables and stuff. Some flowers, too."

Luke smiled at her, with no laughter in his eyes this time. She knew how worried Luke had been about her since her breakup; she could tell how glad he was that she was doing something so out of character for herself, something just for fun.

"That's awesome, A," he said after the waiter dropped the food off at their table. "I can't believe this all happened in the last month. You're learning how to flirt *and* how to garden? So, what else has Taylor taught you? I feel like you've gotten a flirting expert to give you the secrets here; I want to know them, too."

Avery waved a chopstick at him before grabbing a piece of a spicy tuna roll.

"You don't need to know any of them, you have no need for flirting. You've got Margot."

Luke grinned at her.

"Yeah, but I need to *keep* Margot."

Avery smirked at him.

"Didn't we just talk about how you're not in any danger of losing her?" She shrugged. "I don't really know what I'm doing, though I'm getting more comfortable. Every time I try to talk to someone, or someone starts to talk to me, I still feel like a deer in the headlights. I don't freeze up quite as much anymore, but it's kind of embarrassing."

She was pretty sure Taylor would have had a lot more fun at trivia night without having to babysit her. She was grateful to Taylor for bringing her, and yes, some of Taylor's friends had definitely been checking her out, which was gratifying, but still.

"I'm sure you don't have anything to be embarrassed about. Do you want me to ask Taylor? She'll tell me."

"Luke." Avery glared at him.

Luke laughed at the look on her face.

"Don't worry, I was kidding. But seriously, remember, you're not being graded on this, there's no test or anything, this is just for fun, okay? I know how you get sometimes."

This was the problem with Luke. He knew her too well.

"I promise, I'm trying to remember that. I'm trying to have fun, something that is very un-me. Let's hope I can stick to that."

THURSDAY AFTERNOON, TAYLOR GOT A TEXT FROM HER OLD boss, from the restaurant where she'd worked before moving to Noble.

JENNY

Any way you can work a shift tonight? three people called out sick and we're fully booked. I promise I'll give you the easy tables

Taylor laughed. Jenny always said that; sometimes she actually meant it.

TAYLOR

sure but i can't get there until just before 6 probably

JENNY

I'LL TAKE IT

By 5:55 p.m., she had an apron on, and Jenny was frantically running down the specials.

"I think that's it," she said after a few minutes. "Anything else?"

"I've got it, don't worry," Taylor said. "If I have questions, I'll find you."

"I owe you one for this," Jenny said.

"Oh, don't worry, I know." Taylor grinned and tucked a notebook and pen into her pocket. "And I'll hold you to that."

The restaurant was packed, but Taylor quickly fell back into the rhythm of it all. She'd waited tables for years, and while she much preferred her predictable schedule at Noble and her consistent paycheck, she had kind of missed the chaos of a packed restaurant, the frantic rush of the servers and hosts and cooks, the ballet of the way they all moved around one another, the guests' obliviousness to all of it. She quickly memorized the specials, and managed to rave about them even though she hadn't tasted them. To be fair, she'd eaten a lot of this restaurant's food, so it was easy to speak with authority.

She delivered a round of drinks to one table that was clearly a first date, and a struggling one, at that. She wished she knew the backstory on this couple, because they both seemed so shy that she had no idea how they'd ever managed to make it on a date with each other. She had to do what she could to make the date a good one, for both of them.

"Have you decided what you'd like to order?" she asked them. "Does either of you need a recommendation? Though you picked two of my favorite wines on the menu, so you probably don't need me."

The woman smiled at her, and the man sat up straighter. A compliment always helped.

"Oh, thank you," the woman said. "Actually, I was deciding between the kale and lemon pasta, or the Early Girl tomato and burrata pasta. Do you, um, have a recommendation?"

"I was deciding between both of those, too," the man said.

Taylor beamed at them.

"Those are two of our best pastas, but the tomato one is really special; the tomatoes are so good this year. But if you're interested in sharing, I'd say get both."

They both hesitated.

"Um, I'd be happy to share?" the man said. "But if you don't, we can just—"

"Oh no, that's a great idea," the woman said. "Thank you."

"Is there an appetizer that you recommend as well?" the man asked her. "We're both vegetarians, so nothing with meat."

"I eat everything, but some of my favorite items on the menu here are vegetarian. Are you in more of a salad mood or a cheesy mood? No judgment either way."

They both laughed a little, like she'd meant for them to do. She lingered at the table for a while, chatting with them about the menu and asking them a few questions about themselves. By the time she walked away, they were talking to each other, both wearing tentative smiles. There. That was her good deed for the night.

About an hour later, she stepped up to a table of two women who'd sat down a few moments before.

"Hi, I'm Taylor, I'll be your server tonight, and— Hey!" Erica grinned up at her. She was with a blond woman with soft, beachy waves in her hair and a pale pink cardigan over her shoulders.

"Hi, Tay, I was wondering when you'd notice us. What are you doing here? You remember my friend Sloane, right?"

So, this was the Sloane that Erica kept talking about. Taylor did vaguely remember her from Erica's housewarming party. Vaguely.

"Hi, Taylor, good to see you," Sloane said. "I didn't realize you worked here."

Was that judgment there from Sloane? Like wow, she didn't realize that Taylor worked at a *restaurant*, she thought they were on the same social level.

Okay, she didn't have to be so defensive, Sloane was probably a perfectly nice rich lady.

"Hi, Sloane, nice to meet you again," she said. "I'm just filling in. I used to work here, and occasionally I'll get an SOS from my old boss when she's in a crisis. Do you two want drinks to start? Any questions?"

"Just sparkling water for me," Erica said. "But we definitely want to start with the tomato and cucumber salad, can you put that in for us? I'm famished."

Taylor raised her eyebrows.

"You? Famished? No, really?" She grinned at the look on Erica's face. "Yeah, don't worry, coming right up. Sloane, anything to drink for you?"

Sloane smiled a bland smile at her. No wonder she hadn't remembered meeting Sloane, she was so . . . colorless.

Was she being unfair?

"Just sparkling water for me, too, thanks," Sloane said.

"Great, I'll bring the big bottle."

Taylor flashed a smile at both of them and went back to the bar to put in their drink order, and then to the kitchen to put in the salad, and an extra order of bread for Erica. She flew around the restaurant delivering drinks and salads and charcuterie platters and pasta, all the while trying to shake off the weird, uncomfortable feeling it had given her to see Erica and Sloane together.

Why did this bother her? It wasn't like Erica didn't have other friends, they both did, lots of them. Erica had even gotten *married* the year before, and Taylor had never had an issue about that. She liked Sam, she was happy for Erica, she was happy for both of them. Was it just that she found Sloane boring, someone not worthy of being friends with Erica? Was she worried that Erica would turn into someone like Sloane? No, that was impossible. It was a little weird to her that Erica was suddenly so buddy-buddy with someone Taylor thought she barely knew, but Sloane was probably giving her advice about babies or childbirth or how to get your toddler into the top preschool. It was fine. And when Erica and Sloane left, she gave them both hugs goodbye. See? Fine.

Later that night, she dropped the check off at the table with the shy couple, and they both thanked her for her help and told her they loved their meals. And when they walked out the door together, she saw their hands brush against each other's in a way that she was certain was not accidental. That was a job well done. She couldn't wait to tell Avery about this.

It was wild to think about how much Avery's flirting had improved over the past month, and just how much she'd relaxed during that time. After seeing how tense and nervous she'd seemed walking into the book event, Taylor had worried about the success of this little how-to-flirt project. But Avery had grown by leaps and bounds in the past few weeks. Taylor hadn't needed to tell her to flirt with everyone at trivia this week, she'd done it without being ordered to. Avery had even flirted with her a little, although that may have been accidental.

Oh, this gave her an excellent idea for what their next flirting date should be. Taylor laughed to herself. This should be fun.

NINE

you free tonight? i have an idea

Avery shook her head. Leave it to Taylor to send a text like this on a Friday morning. Slightly stressful, but also kind of exciting, yep, that was Taylor.

Avery glanced at her calendar. She was busy for most of the weekend, but not tonight.

AVERY

I'm free after 7. Should I be scared? I'm scared.

TAYLOR

only a little. pick you up at 8

Avery shook her head. Taylor's taciturn texting style would be the death of her, and they weren't even dating! There must be hundreds of group texts out there trying to decipher what her uncapitalized sentence fragment texts *really* meant.

An hour later, Taylor sent a follow-up:

TAYLOR

> oh right—wear something casual but a little slutty

AVERY

> I don't OWN anything a little slutty!

TAYLOR

> i figured you'd say that. do it anyway

Avery stared at her closet. She'd clearly underestimated Taylor when she shopped for new clothes. And it was too late to buy anything else. Wait, she had an idea. An outfit started from the inside out, didn't it? She put on a lacy red bra that pushed her boobs skyhigh, and matching underwear. She'd bought them toward the end of her relationship with Derek, but she'd broken up with him before even wearing them. Might as well use that energy for something fun.

Over that she pulled on a snug black sundress. She loved this dress, but because her bra straps always showed in it, she always wore it either with a black bra underneath or with something over it, usually both. But Taylor had called for a little slutty, so tonight, she was going to let her red bra straps show.

She put on bright red lipstick, then pulled the pins out of the low bun that her hair had been in all day and tossed her head back and forth. She looked at herself in the mirror and shrugged. Hopefully this was messy in a sexy way.

TAYLOR

here

There was Taylor, exactly on time. Well, five minutes late, but that was exactly on time for Taylor, Avery knew that now.

AVERY

Coming!

As she walked out to Taylor's car, she regretted, once again, what she'd said to Taylor after trivia. She should have just brushed off Taylor's question about why she'd given her that look when Callie had asked her to come back. But she'd been so used to being honest with Taylor about dating and flirting and everything else that it hadn't even occurred to her to hedge. Granted, everything that Taylor had said had reassured her, but she still felt silly for being quite so . . . naked in her insecurity. She didn't usually do things like that.

Just try to act normal, she said to herself as she got into Taylor's car.

"Hey," Taylor said. Her grin widened as she glanced at Avery's outfit. "Red bra, wow."

Avery grinned back at her.

"This was a big step for me, I hope you realize. I'm not really a visible-bra-strap kind of girl."

Taylor patted her on the shoulder.

"Oh, I do realize. I'm very proud."

Avery knew that Taylor was mostly joking about being proud of her, but she still felt a swell of happiness when she said it, as well as at the lingering feeling of Taylor's hand on her bare shoulder.

"Good," Avery said. "Tonight had better be worth this leap of faith."

"It will be," Taylor said. "Don't you worry your pretty little head about that."

Avery giggled at that, as did Taylor.

"My pretty little head? Seriously?"

Taylor drove off as she shook her head at herself.

"Well, you *are* very pretty, but yes, I probably could have worded that a little better. I'm not trying to emulate the Wicked Witch of the West. Whatever, you got what I meant."

Avery felt herself flush at the compliment. Taylor said things like this all the time, in such a casual, direct way. She knew Taylor didn't *mean* anything by it—if she hadn't already known that, Liz and Dani and Callie had made that very clear—but she also knew Taylor wasn't bullshitting her. Avery looked out the side window and tried not to show how pleased she was.

Wait, why was she doing that? She did that all the time—she hid her emotions from people. Not just the bad emotions, the good ones, too. Why?

Because showing her emotions made her vulnerable. Because then people knew how to hurt you. Ouch.

But it's not like that had prevented her from getting hurt in the past.

She'd think about that more later. For now, she tried to let herself bask in Taylor's compliment.

She didn't even bother to ask Taylor where they were going, but she definitely wondered. Where would Taylor take her that prompted her to tell her to dress "a little slutty"? And why had she wanted to go out tonight, instead of waiting until their regular Tuesday?

"You're dying to know where we're going, aren't you?" Taylor asked, looking at her sideways as she drove.

"Me?" Avery said in an outraged tone. "Nope, not at all, not even thinking about it. I'd honestly forgotten that I was in the car with you, as a matter of fact. Just thinking about a fascinating thing that happened at work today."

"Mm-hmm," Taylor said. "And what would that fascinating thing be?"

Avery racked her brain for something slightly believable.

"Uh, tonight's event was for an ophthalmologist conference, you see, and did you know that when they operate on people's eyes, they have to stay awake? Because of—"

"I'm going to stop you right there," Taylor said, and they both burst out laughing.

A few minutes later, Taylor pulled into a parking spot, despite the many tourists out that night in Downtown Napa.

"How do you always manage to do that?" Avery asked as they got out of the car.

"Do what?" Taylor was in her typical uniform of jeans and a tank top, but tonight's jeans were ones that hugged her waist and butt very well, and her black tank top was snug in a way that Avery hadn't quite noticed in the car. Now that she did, though, she knew it was going to distract her all night. Well, depending on what tonight ended up being.

"Find a parking place wherever we go. You barely even have to circle."

Taylor put her hand on Avery's back and turned her in the opposite direction.

"What can I say, we all have gifts, that's mine." Avery looked at her, and Taylor grinned. "Fine, that's *one* of mine."

Avery shook her head.

"You have an unfair number of gifts, you know."

Before too long, Taylor guided her into a packed restaurant, and over to the bar. Miraculously, there were two seats together, right at the back. As they slid into them, Taylor leaned close to her.

"Before you say anything," Taylor said in Avery's ear, "*this* was not one of my gifts—I had Lucy save me two seats at the bar tonight. She owes me a favor."

Avery laughed and tried not to let Taylor's proximity give her butterflies. She had a job to do tonight, remember? Even though she didn't quite know what it was yet.

"Of course she does," Avery said. "I feel like every bartender in both Napa and Sonoma Counties owes you a favor."

Taylor winked at her.

"Not just the bartenders." She turned to Lucy and caught her eyes immediately. "Two gin and tonics please."

Lucy nodded at her and grabbed a bottle of gin—very good gin, Avery noticed—down from the bar. Avery started to watch Lucy make their drinks, but suddenly, she couldn't take it anymore.

"Taylor. Why are we here?" she asked.

Taylor turned to her, a grin on her face.

"I thought you'd never ask." She cleared her throat and folded her hands together. "I realized something the other day: We're about midway through our flirting lesson curriculum, so to speak, which means it's just about time for a flirting midterm. You've been so desperate to be graded this whole time, here's your chance."

Avery just stared at her. Was Taylor serious?

"So, I have to wander around this bar and find random people to flirt with, while knowing the whole time that you're watching me and judging me?" She'd worn her special red bra—and exposed it to the world—for this?

Taylor's face fell as Avery talked, and she put her hand on Avery's upper arm.

"Oh my God, of course not, I would never!"

Avery let out a deep sigh of relief.

"I'm sorry. I just . . . got stressed for a second. I should have known you wouldn't do that to me."

Taylor's hand was still on her arm.

"No, that was my fault. I was trying to be too dramatic and failed. But I promise, this is much better than having to find random people to flirt with at a bar. Instead, you have to flirt with me."

Avery sat up straighter, unsure whether she'd heard Taylor correctly over the din of the bar.

"I have to flirt with . . . you?"

Taylor nodded.

"Yes." When Avery didn't say anything, she dropped her hand and pulled back. "Well, not *have* to. If you don't think this will be fun, we don't have to do any of this. You know that, right? Like any of our other lessons, you can abort at any time, including right now, before we've even started. Just say the word."

Obviously, Avery wanted to flirt with Taylor. But she was intimidated by the idea, too. This was sexy-as-hell Taylor Cameron! The idea of flirting with her on purpose, like, committing to it in a way that Taylor *knew* she was doing it, and then having to figure out how to respond when Taylor flirted with *her* . . . And what if the way she responded made Taylor realize Avery had a crush on her? How humiliating!

But this also seemed like an opportunity she couldn't refuse. And didn't really want to.

She turned to face Taylor, made eye contact with her, and smiled.

"Oh, I absolutely think this will be fun. I'm glad you do, too."

Taylor smirked, just for a second, and then picked up her drink.

"I'm happy you agree with me," she said. "So, what was your work event tonight?" she asked, her eyes locked on Avery's. "Something about ophthalmologists, you said?"

Avery nodded. She tried to make herself relax into this, but she still felt wound up by what Taylor had said, by her proximity, by the way Taylor was looking at her.

"Yeah," she said. "It was, um—they're having a conference in St. Helena, and I guess between talking about eye surgeries or whatever they do, they also like to drink a lot of wine." She shifted in her seat so that her knee was just barely touching Taylor's. "So, I organized three wineries to come so they could do wine tastings from a range of Napa Valley wines. Noble was one of them, actually."

Was she doing this right? Just talking about normal stuff, but making her voice and eyes and body do the flirting work for her? Or, at least, *attempting* to do that? She thought so, but now she was questioning everything.

As soon as Avery heard Taylor laugh, she relaxed. This was just Taylor. Taylor wasn't going to care what she did or how she looked at her or how much she touched her. Despite all of her talk about grading her, they both knew that was just a joke; Taylor wouldn't judge her on how she did—or didn't—do anything tonight. Taylor probably already knew Avery had a crush on her and didn't care. This was just for fun.

"Oh, right," Taylor said. "I helped Margot pack up the wines to

go to that event. She didn't tell me that you'd organized it, though."
Avery couldn't tell if she'd shifted in her seat or if Taylor had, but
now her knee was a lot more than just barely touching Taylor's; it
had moved to the inside of Taylor's knee. Even in her long dress,
and with Taylor in jeans, she could feel the warmth of Taylor's
body through the fabric. Why hadn't she worn a knee-length
dress? If she had, it would have slid up just enough so her bare
knee would be touching Taylor's.

Avery had to laugh at herself. Why was she eroticizing knees,
for God's sake?

"Yeah, Margot was the first person I called when they agreed
to my plan to have wineries come to their event," Avery said. She
pushed her hair back behind her right shoulder. She saw Taylor's
eyes linger on her bare shoulder and let herself smile. What had
Taylor told her a long time ago? Pay attention to the person
you're flirting with. Avery pushed her hair back behind her left
shoulder this time, and she could almost feel Taylor's attention
lock onto her. "The event went really well—I got tons of compliments from the people I worked with, and everyone seemed to
enjoy the wine. And the wineries got a bunch of orders, so it was
win-win for all of us."

Taylor picked up her drink and ran her finger along the condensation on the glass. Avery got goose bumps watching the slow,
gentle movement of her finger.

"That's fantastic," Taylor said. What was fantastic? Avery had
forgotten what they were talking about. "I'm sure I'll hear the details from Margot tomorrow." Right, the event.

"Yeah, I'm glad I got to organize it," Avery said. "I got to do one
of my favorite things, which is to work together with places I love
here in the valley and get business for everyone in the process."
Taylor took a sip of her drink as Avery talked, and one tiny droplet

of condensation fell right onto the center of her cleavage. Oh God, Avery couldn't watch it, she had to look away. As much as she wanted to, she couldn't watch that little drop slide down . . . and down . . . and down. That wouldn't be flirting, it would just be ogling at that point. Avery picked up her own drink, partly to give herself something else to do, and partly to cool herself down a little. She could feel her cheeks getting hot.

She had to get Taylor talking again. That was the only way not to stare at her cleavage. She looked back up at Taylor, who had a knowing smile. She couldn't have made that little drop of liquid slide into her cleavage . . . could she? No, impossible.

"Um, how's your friend Erica doing?" Avery asked.

Taylor sighed and her smile fell.

"She's fine, I guess. I don't know, really. We've been friends for so long, but it suddenly feels like . . ." Taylor looked away. "I don't know, like there's a gulf growing between us, you know? I sort of feel like whenever I text her, I'm bothering her or something. To be honest, I'm worried she's firmly in the married-women-with-babies demographic now and not into the whole single-queer-women scene anymore, and I'm a casualty of that."

Avery wanted to take Taylor's hand, put her arm around her, do something to comfort her and drive away that sad look in her eyes. She was just about to, when Taylor suddenly laughed and put her hand on Avery's. "Oh, but she and I did text when we were at trivia—we bet on who was going to win the race to sit next to you after I got up to go to the bar."

The pressure of Taylor's warm hand on hers almost made her not pay attention to what Taylor was saying. Almost, but not quite.

"Wait, really?" Avery sat up straight, moving slightly away from Taylor in the process. She didn't move her hand from underneath Taylor's, though. "You bet on who was going to try to sit next to me? Erica doesn't even know me."

Taylor patted her hand.

"I know, but she knows the rest of that whole crowd. Plus, that's kind of our thing—Erica and I bet on random stuff all the time."

"Who won the bet on Tuesday?" Avery asked. "Since it was about me, don't I get to know?" She turned her hand over halfway, so they were sort of, but not quite, holding hands. She hadn't even meant to do it, but it just felt natural at this point. When Taylor had first suggested actual flirting tonight, Avery had thought it would feel weird or hard or scary to flirt with her, but that couldn't be further from the truth. It just felt easy, exciting, even comfortable. She couldn't believe she'd existed for this long and had spent so much time with Taylor without touching her like this, looking at her like this.

Did Taylor feel the same way?

No, of course not. But that didn't matter right now. Right now, Avery would pretend that she did.

"I won," Taylor said with a laugh in her voice. Her thumb caressed the center of Avery's palm. "Erica said it would be Liz, but I bet on Dani, and I was right. Granted, I'd seen the way Dani had been looking at you earlier, and Erica hadn't, but she knows both Liz and Dani pretty well, so it seemed like a fair contest."

Avery desperately wanted to know what the history was between Taylor and Liz . . . and Taylor and Dani . . . and Taylor and the rest of that group, for that matter. She swallowed the question, but Taylor gave her that knowing look again.

"Go on," she said. "Ask me what you were about to ask me."

Avery tilted her head.

"Are you and Liz . . . I mean, have you ever . . . ?"

Taylor laughed and picked up her drink with her free hand.

"We're not now, obviously, but yes, we have. It was a long time ago, and we've been friends ever since. And to answer your next question, the same answer goes for Dani, but that was just last year. It was just a quick thing, though; we are clearly not for each other, but I like Dani a lot." Taylor raised an eyebrow. "Why, are you interested in either of them? Or any of the rest of that crowd?"

TAYLOR WISHED SHE HADN'T ASKED THAT. SHE'D DONE IT BE-cause it was the kind of half-teasing, half-serious question that she would naturally ask Avery, so it just came out. The problem was right now—with Avery sitting here with her knee in between Taylor's, and her hand in Taylor's, and with Taylor's eyes constantly going in between that flash of a red bra strap, Avery's big soft lips, and her just-out-of-bed curls—she didn't know what she would do if Avery said yes. All she knew was that she felt a flash of jealousy just thinking about it.

Avery shook her head.

"Not really, though I have to admit, the attention from them on Tuesday night was flattering."

Taylor hated the rush of relief she felt. This was unlike her. She wasn't the jealous type, which was something that had seemed to bother at least a few of her past girlfriends. It was probably this stupid bet with Erica making her act weird. This was like how she'd felt at trivia when she'd wanted to claim Avery as hers, to pull her away from her friends, to sit somewhere with her, just the two of them, and no one else.

And now that's exactly what they were doing.

Shit. She'd thought that a flirting midterm was a brilliant idea; that it would be a fun night, where Avery would try to flirt with her and she'd flirt back and give her critiques and that would be all. But now she was in much deeper than she'd planned to be.

And the worst part was, she wanted to stay right there.

"But I liked them both a lot, and it was a really fun night," Avery continued. "It's been a while . . . a long time, really, since I enjoyed a night out in a big group like that. It felt nice to be in a group where everyone was friends, everyone was relaxed with one another, no one was trying to, like, make an impression or one-up one another or edge someone else out of a circle. Sure, there was some interpersonal conflict and history that I could feel but didn't know the details of, but it wasn't a big deal."

Now Taylor felt even more guilty for mentally being such a bitch about her friends on Tuesday night. Next time they all went out, she'd buy the first round, as an apology that none of them would ever know they were getting.

"Yeah, it's a good group," she said. "We've all been through a lot together, and we know one another really well. So even when people have little spats, it blows over quickly."

Avery picked up her drink and took a sip.

"Yeah, it felt like that. Usually when I've been in a big group, it's either for a work thing, where I'm organizing it or networking the whole time, or it was a party with Derek and his friends, where I never felt like I fit in, and I was always trying to be the perfect girlfriend or whatever." She shook her head. "God, I can't believe I stayed with him for so long."

Taylor patted her knee. She let her hand linger there.

"That's okay," she said. "There's no point in beating yourself up for it now; the important thing is that you figured it out, and you moved on."

Avery smiled at her, long and slow.

"I definitely have moved on," she said. She curled her thumb around Taylor's. "And I'm feeling great about it."

Taylor was feeling pretty great about it right now as well. She realized she'd been holding herself back from flirting with Avery—*really* flirting with Avery—for weeks now. And it felt so good to finally be able to flirt like hell with her. Finally, she got to caress her hand like this, lightly, so lightly, and think about touching her like that all over her body. Finally, she got to see that heavy-lidded look in her eyes that told Taylor that Avery was imagining how she'd touch her like that elsewhere. Finally, she got to let her glance linger on that red bra strap, and at the tiny hint of red lace she could see under Avery's dress when she moved. Finally, she got to let the attraction she felt for Avery run free.

And if she was a good judge of women in general and Avery in particular—and she was—she was almost certain that Avery was just as attracted to her. She knew Avery was attracted to her; obviously she knew that, she'd known it for a long time. But there was a difference between being attracted to someone, in a general sense, and wanting to act on it. Did Avery want to act on this? Right now, in this second, Taylor thought she did.

She probably wouldn't, though. Because Avery was smart, and acting on this attraction between the two of them wasn't the smart thing to do. Plus, Avery's whole thing was that she wanted to flirt in general, yes, but she also wanted to date women, plural, to sow her wild oats or whatever she'd said.

And Taylor couldn't act on this. Even though right now, in this second, she really wanted to. She felt protective of Avery and how new she was to this. Taylor didn't want to take advantage of her.

Also, by this time, she knew Avery well enough to know that if anything happened between the two of them, Avery would want too much, more than Taylor could give her. Taylor didn't want to start something she couldn't finish, at least, not in the way Avery would want. That wouldn't be fair to her.

And the bet! How could she forget, even briefly, about that fucking bet with Erica? Erica would be all smug and say, *I told you so*, about how Taylor couldn't even make it a few months. And she absolutely did not want to organize a baby shower; what a nightmare that would be. She must be really getting carried away to forget about the bet. Absolutely nothing could happen tonight.

She had to change the subject, ask Avery about something different, something boring, so that she could still do this, but not make it quite as dangerous for herself.

"How's the garden stuff going?"

Avery's face lit up. Damn it. She looked too excited for this to tamp down Taylor's roaring libido.

"It's good! Beth and I are both having a lot of fun with it. One of us is at the garden almost every day, and we're usually there at the same time at least twice a week, always on Sundays. This is so dorky, but we're always texting each other pictures of what the garden looks like when one of us is there alone and updating the other one about our plants and stuff. Our first cherry tomatoes ripened this week, and it was so exciting. Even though we didn't plant the tomato plants, we've taken care of them for a month, so they feel like ours. And, I don't know, there's something about being outside, smelling the plants and leaves, getting my hands in the dirt, but I always come home from the garden in such a good mood." She shook her head. "I can't believe that everyone who preaches about how great the outdoors is for your mental health is right. How depressing."

Taylor laughed, and Avery laughed with her. Partly at what Avery said, but also because it felt really good to see Avery looking so happy. Taylor didn't credit herself with this change in Avery; of course it wasn't because of her. In a way it might be because of their flirting lessons, but only because Avery had thrown herself into them and worked hard at opening herself up to people.

"I'm really proud of you," Taylor said. Avery looked at her sideways, and Taylor squeezed her hand. "That seemed like it came out of nowhere, didn't it? It's just . . . you've come a long way. Not only with the flirting, with everything."

Avery looked away for a moment, and Taylor wondered whether that had sounded condescending, if she'd crossed some sort of line. But then Avery looked back at her, and Taylor saw that her eyes were full of tears.

"Thank you," she said. "That means a lot. I . . . I feel like that, too. I've been really trying to push myself out of my comfort zone, and it's been hard, but good. I'm glad you can see it, too."

"I definitely can," Taylor said. "I hope—

"TWO VODKA CRANBERRIES. TWO. VODKA. CRANBER-RIIIIIEEES."

Taylor and Avery both turned and stared up at the man standing far too close to them and shouting far too loudly at the bartender. Taylor looked around to see that the bar was a lot more crowded than it was when they'd arrived. She leaned in closer to Avery.

"You want to get out of here?"

Avery nodded. Taylor pulled cash out of her pocket and tossed it on the bar, and then saw two women standing together behind the loud dude, obviously trying to get the swamped bartender's attention. She caught the eye of one of them, and made the universal *we're leaving, want our seats?* gesture, to which the other woman nodded gratefully. The four of them executed the switch, right under the outraged eyes of the loud man and his buddy, and she and Avery walked to the door. Taylor rested her hand on the small of Avery's back as they moved through the crowd.

"You're so good at that," Avery said.

"So good at what?" Taylor asked as they got to the door of the bar.

Avery smiled.

"You know. Supporting other women."

Taylor felt relieved by that smile. She'd suggested leaving on an impulse, once it got so crowded, and when she'd realized they'd been low-key shouting so they could hear each other for the past fifteen minutes. But once they'd gotten up to leave, she'd wondered if this would be it for tonight, if she and Avery would walk outside and Avery would take a step back from her, give Taylor one of her sweet, infectious laughs, ask for her grade on her flirting midterm, and then Taylor would simply drive her home and wave goodbye.

But Avery was still by her side, still smiling at her, still looking at her like she was a plump, juicy strawberry, just waiting to be gobbled up. Was she looking at Avery like that? Almost certainly yes.

"Where to next?" Avery asked her.

Taylor thought for a second.

"Want to walk down to the Barrel? I don't go there that often, since as much as I adore Margot, she's always there, and I don't need to hang out during my off hours with my boss. But since she and Luke are on their way to San Francisco . . ."

"Perfect. I love that place," Avery said.

Taylor dropped her hand from the small of Avery's back, but they still walked closely together, Avery's skirt brushing against her legs, their hands touching once, twice, three times, until finally their fingers intertwined. Avery's hand was warm and soft, and her grip on Taylor's firm. So different from earlier in the night, when Avery's move to turn her hand over so they were—sort of—holding hands was tentative, something that could be pretended away if Taylor had moved. Now she held on to Taylor's hand with certainty. Taylor liked it. A lot.

They stopped outside the Barrel to let a big group walk by, and Taylor looked up at Avery. She always forgot that Avery was taller than her, since so often they were sitting next to each other, not standing or walking together. Even with Avery in flats, and her in sneakers, Avery was at least four inches taller than her, tall enough that she had to look up at her.

Avery let go of Taylor's hand and lifted hers to Taylor's hair.

"Are you growing this out?" she asked, stroking the shaved area above Taylor's right ear. Taylor's eyes fluttered closed for a second at the gentle tickle as Avery's fingers brushed against the stubble there.

"Not exactly," she said. "I've been lazy about going to get it touched up, and I can't do it myself. I've tried, and it was not a good experiment. I'm not very good at that kind of thing." She raised an eyebrow at Avery, whose fingers were still in her hair. "Should I grow it out? It would definitely make things easier. Less maintenance."

Avery moved her fingers back and forth against Taylor's hair again, in a way that made Taylor's whole body react.

"No," Avery said. "Don't grow it out. I like it."

Avery smiled down at her. Had Avery moved closer to her, or had Taylor moved closer to Avery? Taylor didn't know, but she knew that she wanted them to be even closer.

"Avery."

Avery's eyes were intent on hers.

"Yeah?" she asked, almost in a whisper.

"Now is when you kiss me."

Avery's hand moved from her hair to her cheek, and Avery

bent down to Taylor as Taylor reached up to her. Her lips barely touched Taylor's, a soft brush of them at first, and then gentle pressure that Taylor returned. The kisses got longer, but they were still soft, gentle, light yet tantalizing kisses that reminded Taylor of that way she'd stroked Avery's hand earlier in the night. She wanted to speed it up and pull her close, but she let Avery control this. Every brush of her lips made Taylor's entire body quiver.

She put her hand on Avery's waist, not hard, just so she could touch her more, feel that part of her body, feel the skin underneath her thin dress.

That must have been some sort of signal to Avery that Taylor really wanted this, though she had no idea how Avery could be ignorant of that. Avery's tongue slid into her mouth, and Taylor could have cried out in victory. Instead, she pulled Avery flush against her body, kissed her harder, let her hands grip Avery's waist, then roam upward until her fingers tangled in Avery's hair. Their lips and tongues danced together, soft and hard, gentle and firm, sweet and yearning, all at the same time.

Taylor slid her lips down so she could kiss Avery's throat, her neck, her collarbone. Avery sighed, her hands moving up Taylor's back, gripping tightly and letting go in turn. God, it was going to be fun to learn what she liked.

Then Taylor lifted her head again and went back to Avery's incredible lips. Avery kissed her back, harder than before, more determined, more intent. Taylor liked this side of her a lot.

"Avery?" Taylor said in a low voice.

"Mmm?"

"Do you really want to go inside?"

They laughed softly together.

"I don't think so, no," Avery said. "You?"

Taylor grinned at her.

"For me, it's absolutely not."

Taylor took her hand. As they walked back toward her car, Taylor remembered the whole list of reasons she'd given herself, less than an hour ago, about why absolutely nothing would or could happen between her and Avery tonight. Oh well. She could deal with all of that tomorrow.

WHEN THEY GOT TO TAYLOR'S CAR, AVERY DIDN'T WANT TO LET go of Taylor's hand. Which was silly, she knew it was silly, but she didn't care. She was going to let herself be as silly as she wanted to be tonight, because she was having one of those nights where everything she did was right, and everything she touched turned to gold. She made herself release her probably too-tight grip on Taylor's hand and got in the car. She had no idea what was going to happen after this, but she was going to let the magic continue.

Taylor settled in her seat, and without even thinking about it, Avery leaned over to kiss her. Taylor immediately kissed her back. She was as good a kisser as Avery had expected her to be—probably even better, actually. For half a second, Avery wondered whether she wasn't good enough a kisser for someone like Taylor, but then she lost herself in the kiss. It was impossible to think about anything when Taylor Cameron kissed you other than how good it felt to kiss her, how you wanted to keep kissing her forever.

Too soon, Taylor pulled away and started the car.

"Where to?" she asked.

"Um. My place? It's closest," Avery said. Why was she so uncertain when she said that? Because even though she'd done a lot of things out of her comfort zone lately, this was very far out of it. Even though she wanted this.

Without a word, Taylor pulled out of the parking spot and drove toward Avery's apartment.

Did Taylor want this, want her, just as badly? That felt impossible, until she remembered the way Taylor had looked at her when they were sitting at the bar, that tone in her voice outside of the Barrel when she'd commanded Avery to kiss her, that hunger in her touch.

She hadn't expected this tonight. Not at the beginning of the night, and not even after her flirting midterm had gone so swimmingly. She hadn't expected their chemistry to be so good, especially after weeks of hanging out just as friends, with occasional light flirting, but nothing like this. She'd been attracted to Taylor, and yes, had a crush on Taylor, from the very beginning, but she didn't think that attraction would be returned, not in any real way. Even after they were sitting at the bar hand in hand, with their legs almost intertwined, she didn't really think that Taylor was actually attracted to her. She'd figured that was just Taylor—she had chemistry with everyone, everyone fell for her, that's why she could do things like get phone numbers wherever she went, and have every bartender fall half in love with her, and give flirting lessons, for God's sake. Of course she could turn on flirting like a switch!

So it had been easy to just relax into flirting with Taylor, without wondering what was going to happen next. But then, after they'd left the bar and started walking toward the Barrel, something had changed. Avery had felt it happen, as they'd walked down the street together, when their hands had touched, then clung to each other's like magnets, when they'd moved closer and closer to each other. She could feel that Taylor wanted to be there with her. Not with just someone, but with her, specifically. If she hadn't felt that, she never would have had the courage to touch Taylor's hair in that way, in a way that showed she wanted more.

Despite all those things, she still never would have had the courage to kiss her, not until Taylor told her to do it. She'd wanted to—good Lord, she'd wanted to—but she'd needed something to push her past her fear and uncertainty. Taylor had clearly known that. If Taylor hadn't told her to kiss her, she wouldn't have done it, no matter how Taylor had looked at her, touched her.

She should probably be embarrassed at how little she'd hesitated after Taylor had told her to kiss her, but she wasn't. Not at all. All she had the capacity to feel right now was anticipation about what was going to happen when she and Taylor got back to her apartment.

Well, she was also a *tiny* bit nervous about that. What would they do? What would Taylor expect? What did *she*, Avery, want? She didn't know the answers to any of those questions.

"You're quiet over there," Taylor said as they stopped at a red light.

Avery smiled at her.

"Just wondering when I'll get my grade for my midterm."

Taylor let out her loud, joyful laugh.

"Oh, that was a solid A performance, from beginning to end, but don't even try to pretend you didn't know that."

Avery let her smile become a little smug. Okay, maybe a lot.

"Obviously I knew that, but I wanted to hear you say it."

Taylor's hand squeezed hers.

"Then I'm glad you asked. I'm happy to shout it from the rooftops."

As they walked up the stairs to Avery's apartment, Taylor glanced around the outside of the building.

"It's weird that I've never seen your apartment. I wonder if it's anything like I picture it."

Avery turned to her as she pulled her keys out of her bag.

"How do you picture it? Now I need to know that before you come in."

Taylor sighed, but with a smile on her face.

"See, now I shouldn't have said anything. I'm probably going to get this all wrong and offend you in the process."

Avery waved that away.

"I still want to hear it."

"Fine." Taylor paused for a moment. "This is all just off the top of my head, but: completely immaculate; your closet is organized by color; everything is decorated in, like, warm neutrals but also lots of things that design people refer to as 'pops of color' with those cute and also useful knickknacks that I only see on Instagram; throw pillows everywhere; lots of plants, tons of books." She paused. "Oh, and a perfectly made bed; you strike me as one of those people who makes your bed every morning as soon as you get out of it."

Avery said nothing. She just unlocked her door, pushed it open, and flipped on the lights. She stood there at the door, Taylor by her side, as Taylor looked from her camel-colored couch with four bright throw pillows on it to her brass and pink lamps to her many plants, all in different but coordinating planters. She silently closed the door.

"Well." Avery hung her bag on the carved wooden coatrack on her door. "I guess you've gotten to know me pretty well."

Taylor was silent as she walked around the room. Finally, she stopped next to the basket that Avery kept next to her couch and looked inside it.

"You have a decorative basket . . . filled with blankets." Taylor giggled and dropped down on the couch.

"Why is that so funny?" Avery stood in front of her, her hands on her hips. "It gets so hot here in the summer, but sometimes still chilly at night, and the basket is a great place to put the blankets away but still have them accessible, just in case, and—"

Before she could finish, Taylor grabbed one of her hands and pulled her down onto the couch.

"She's explaining the practicality of the cute but also useful decorative basket," Taylor said to an imaginary audience.

Avery tried not to crack a smile, but it was hard.

"Look, I already told you that you were right about me, you don't need to rub it in."

Taylor grinned at her.

"Your closet?"

Avery nodded.

"In order by color, then subdivided by occasion. So, like, work clothes in one section, weekend clothes in another. I'm never quite sure where pink is supposed to go in the color order, though. I put it in right after red, though some people put it in at the beginning of the purple section; that just feels wrong to me."

Taylor's face was full of mirth.

"Your bed."

Avery cleared her throat.

"I make it every morning," she said. "Though, this morning . . ."

"Wait, don't tell me—you were in a rush, so you didn't plump up the pillows?"

Avery rolled her eyes.

"Of course not, I would never not plump up the pillows. No, I was in a rush, so I didn't refold the decorative blanket that lives at the foot of the bed."

Taylor let out a loud shout, and finally Avery couldn't help but join her. "I'm sorry that I'm so predictable," Avery said.

Taylor shook her head.

"You have nothing to apologize for, you're perfect."

Avery laughed at that.

"I'm perfect? Sure, okay."

Taylor smiled and touched her softly on the cheek. She wasn't laughing anymore.

"Of course you are."

She leaned forward and kissed Avery. When their lips came together, Avery almost sighed in relief. She knew that's what they were coming back to her apartment for, but she'd made the first move at several points that night, including kissing Taylor first. She just couldn't do it one more time. This time she needed Taylor to do it, she was ready for Taylor to take back a little bit of the control, and thank God she did.

Holy shit, could this woman kiss. If Avery had been doubtful in any way of how and why Taylor was such a magnet for women, just one kiss would have cleared it all up. But she quickly discovered that being kissed by Taylor standing up on the street was a very different experience from being kissed by Taylor sitting down on the couch in her apartment. It wasn't just about lips or tongues, rather a full-body experience.

She shifted in Taylor's arms and then pulled her closer, so they were snug there together on her very comfortable new couch. She lifted her fingers to Taylor's hair and caressed that stubble at the side of her head. Taylor smiled against her mouth.

"You could tell I liked that, couldn't you?" Taylor murmured. "You're very perceptive, you know."

Avery kissed her cheek.

"You're going to turn my head with these compliments. 'Perfect,' 'perceptive,' 'gorgeous,' and those are just compliments you've given me tonight. I'm going to get conceited."

Taylor lifted a finger and traced the outline of her lips.

"Your head could use a little turning, as far as I'm concerned," Taylor said. "You deserve to be far more conceited than you are. But you've come to the right place; I can get you there. Because I meant every word. And a lot more that you'll probably hear shortly."

Avery didn't really believe Taylor's compliments, but she believed that Taylor meant them, which was almost as good. Maybe that was one of the secrets to Taylor's magnetism: she gave lavish compliments—and she meant them all. With her, it wasn't bullshit. Avery knew that; Taylor wasn't the type of person who was fake about that kind of thing.

Taylor brushed her hair gently to the side and moved her lips down to Avery's neck. Avery sighed softly and leaned her head back.

"I love the way you do that," she said.

Taylor slid her tongue in circles.

"I can tell."

In all the times that Avery had fantasized about making out with Taylor—and there had been an embarrassing amount of them at this point—she'd always pictured Taylor just like this in her head: sexy, commanding, sure of herself. So none of that was a surprise. What was a surprise to her, though, was her own reaction. She would have assumed she'd be awkward, fumbling, uncertain, but it wasn't like that tonight. *She* wasn't like that tonight. Maybe it was because of the work she and Taylor had been doing with the flirting lessons this summer, or maybe it was about Taylor herself; it was probably some combination of both. Tonight, with Taylor, she felt comfortable, relaxed, and very, very turned on.

She was maybe a little too in her own head, but what else was new?

She should try to do something about that.

She remembered something that Taylor had told her on the way to their first flirting lesson: *people generally like to be flirted with the same way that they flirt*. And then she'd laughed and said that was true for other things, too. As much as she was enjoying the way Taylor touched her, it was time to see if Taylor was right about that as well.

She pulled Taylor back up to her mouth and kissed her again, a little harder than she'd been kissing her before, in the way she'd noticed Taylor doing when she'd kissed her neck. Taylor sighed softly, so Avery increased the pressure, and let her hands roam up and down Taylor's body. Taylor was so warm and soft in her arms, and God, she smelled so good, like some sort of rich brandy, and it made Avery just want to lick her.

So that's exactly what she did. She moved her way down to Taylor's neck, first kissing her on her collarbone, and then tracing a thin line with her tongue back up to Taylor's lips. Then she kissed and sucked her way back down to Taylor's collarbone in the same way Taylor had done to her earlier. Taylor's fluttering lashes and gentle sighs as Avery did this were the same reaction she'd had outside the Barrel, when Avery had stroked her hair. Yes, she definitely liked being kissed the way that she kissed Avery.

God, it felt good to know that Taylor's reactions—including those hard points of her nipples that Avery could see through her thin tank top—were all due to something she was doing. It felt incredible, actually.

Taylor must have seen—or felt—Avery looking at her nipples. Taylor's hands moved up her body, and her thumbs brushed against Avery's hard nipples in a way that felt so good that she jumped, and then giggled. Taylor smirked and did it again.

"It feels so good to finally get to touch these," Taylor said.

"Finally?" Avery asked. She was a little embarrassed at how breathy her voice sounded, but Taylor didn't laugh at her. Then, Taylor never would.

Taylor brushed her lips softly against Avery's.

"Of course finally, you ridiculous, hot, silly woman." She let out her low chuckle. "Come on, I *know* you saw me staring at your boobs tonight, you can't even pretend that you didn't."

Well, yes, Avery had noticed that. She smiled.

"I mean yes, tonight, but . . ."

Taylor rolled her eyes as she flicked her thumb back and forth across Avery's nipple, causing incredible sensations throughout her body, and a delicious jolt between her legs.

"Hmmm, did you notice me looking at your boobs on Tuesday night, when I complimented you on that button you left unbuttoned? Or last week, at the bar, when I told you how good you looked in that dress? Or when we went to the dance class, when I looked you up and down when we got out of the car and said you interpreted my what-to-wear instructions perfectly, or . . ."

Avery leaned forward and kissed her.

"Okay, okay, I noticed those other times, too, but I just thought you were complimenting me on how well I dressed for each occasion. And that you were trying to boost my confidence."

Taylor bent down and kissed Avery right above the V of her neckline.

"Mmm, yes, that was a lovely side effect. But mostly it was because every time I saw you showing off those boobs of yours, I wanted to do this." She hooked her finger around the strap of Avery's dress and tugged it off her shoulder, and then pushed the top of her dress on that side down enough so that Avery's red lace–clad breast was revealed. A hungry smile spread across her face. She reached toward Avery's bra, then stopped.

"This is okay, isn't it?" she asked softly. "You know, don't you, that if anything isn't okay, you just have to say the word?"

Avery nodded.

"Yeah." She nodded again. "I mean, yeah, I know that. And yeah, it's okay. More than okay." She put her hand on Taylor's. "Please."

Taylor grinned at her.

"Well, since you asked so nicely." She traced the edges of Avery's bra with her index finger gently, almost reverently, before sliding her finger underneath the edge of it. She stroked the skin right there at first, and then slowly lowered her lips to be where her finger had been. Avery let out a deep sigh when her lips finally landed there. Then Taylor pushed Avery's bra strap off her shoulder, and tugged the lace of her bra down, down.

"Ah, there we are," Taylor said when she stopped. Her thumb stroked Avery's bare nipple, at last. "So beautiful."

The combination of the way Taylor touched her, of that aroused, intent look on her face, and that deep, almost hoarse tone in her voice, made Avery let out a low moan.

"That just . . . it feels so good," she said to Taylor, a little embarrassed. She never made noises like this, especially not this early. But Taylor smiled at her.

"Good," she said. "I was hoping it did." Then her eyes locked onto Avery's. "I always want you to tell me when something feels good. And I especially want you to tell me if something ever doesn't feel good."

Avery nodded, though she couldn't imagine anything Taylor could do to her that wouldn't feel good.

"You make it easy to tell you," she said.

Taylor touched her cheek, and the expression in her eyes softened.

"Thank you," she said. "That's a really big compliment, especially coming from you."

She moved down Avery's body. They were now half sitting, half lying on the couch, and Taylor swung her legs up onto it, pushing Avery's legs up in the process.

"There," she said. "Now, isn't that more comfortable?" They lay next to each other, Avery's hand resting on Taylor's hip, Taylor's thumb and forefinger gently flicking and squeezing Avery's nipple, their eyes intent on each other's.

"Mm. Yes." Avery arched her back and leaned to the side. "That feels fucking incredible, I hope you know."

Taylor chuckled again.

"I do know. But I really like it when you tell me."

Avery looked at Taylor, really looked at her for a moment, and almost had to pinch herself. She was actually doing this. She was here on her couch, making out with a woman who was attracted to her and whom she was very attracted to. And not just any woman, but Taylor Cameron, who she'd thought was hot from the first moment she'd seen her.

Taylor moved down her body, her eyes on Avery's the whole time. Avery had an idea of what she was about to do, but as soon as Taylor's tongue reached out and touched her nipple, she knew she hadn't been prepared for how good this was going to be. What was it about Taylor's tongue that made her whole body react like this?

"Oh . . . wow," was all she could say. Taylor just chuckled softly, and sucked Avery's nipple completely into her mouth.

When she'd had sex with men in the past, they'd always made a big deal of her boobs, too, but they hadn't made her feel like *this* about them. They'd spent a few minutes clumsily groping them, if that, and then moved on to the main event (taking their pants off and pulling their dicks out). And she'd had to pretend that she enjoyed that.

They hadn't caressed them like this, kissed them like this, sucked them like this, they hadn't made her feel like she was a goddess and her boobs were a part of her body to be worshipped. But that's how Taylor made her feel.

As Taylor kissed and sucked one breast, she squeezed the other nipple between her thumb and forefinger, and Avery didn't have to pretend at all. All she had to do was enjoy the hell out of this.

After a while, Taylor pulled back slightly and reached for the hem of Avery's dress.

"Can this come off?"

Everything in Avery froze up. She stared at Taylor, unable to say anything.

It wasn't like she hadn't realized what might happen when they'd come back to her place. She'd thought she was prepared for it. She was even excited about it! But being prepared for it and excited about it in the abstract was very different from realizing that she was about to have sex with a woman for the first time.

"Avery?" Taylor pulled back and sat up. "Is something wrong?"

Avery reached for her hand before Taylor could pull away completely.

"No," Avery said. "Nothing's wrong. It isn't. It's just that, um . . . I've never done this before."

Taylor nodded.

"I sort of figured that," she said. "If you're not ready—"

Avery shook her head.

"That's not it. I'm ready. I want to. But, um, I don't really know what I'm doing. And you—you do."

Taylor leaned forward and kissed her.

"It's okay," she said. "We'll figure it out together. You tell me what you like, what feels good to you, I'll tell you what I like, what feels good to me, and we'll go from there. We'll just have fun figuring it out. Okay?"

How did Taylor always know the perfect thing to say? That's why Taylor was Taylor, probably.

"Okay," Avery said. The relief at Taylor's words was probably all over her face, but she didn't care. She took a deep breath. Then she stood up, grabbed the hem of her dress, and pulled it over her head. Then she unhooked her bra, and pulled that off for good measure.

Taylor stood up, too, and reached for her, but Avery shook her head. She marshaled her courage again and put a hand on Taylor's belt.

"Um, you, too," she said, looking at Taylor, who still had all of her clothes on.

A smile spread across Taylor's face.

"I thought you'd never ask." She looked down at Avery's hand on her belt. "Will you? Please?"

Avery's fingers fumbled as she unhooked Taylor's belt, but she got it open. And then, because Taylor didn't move to do it herself, she put her hand on the waistband of Taylor's jeans.

"Can I?" she asked.

Taylor's eyes were on Avery's hands.

"Please," she said again.

Avery unbuttoned and unzipped Taylor's jeans, and pushed them down her body. It felt so intimate, undressing her like this. Slowly, carefully, bit by bit, not rushing through it, getting to see every part of Taylor's body revealed to her.

Taylor stepped out of her jeans, then Avery took hold of the hem of her tank top. Taylor kissed her again, before she could pull it off, and raised her arms above her head. Avery took the hint, pulled Taylor's tank top off, and dropped it on the couch. She looked at Taylor, almost in awe. She'd seen other women's bodies, obviously, hundreds of them, in changing rooms and locker rooms and at beaches and pools. But this felt different. Taylor was revealing her body to *her* in a way that was just for her, and it felt wonderful.

Avery stepped closer to Taylor and reached around her body for the clasp of her bra. She worried that she would fumble with that, too, since she'd never done that for another woman, not like this. But luckily, she'd taken her own bra off so many thousands of times in her life that even though this felt so momentous, she had no trouble.

She dropped Taylor's bra to the floor, and there they stood, both naked except for their underwear. Avery looked at Taylor: her heavy breasts; her round, soft belly; her wide hips; her tan lines right down the middle of her shoulder from those ubiquitous sleeveless tops. She couldn't believe this was happening.

"You are so amazing," Avery said. In response, Taylor cupped Avery's face with her hands and kissed her.

That kiss made the tension leave Avery's body. All throughout undressing Taylor, she'd still worried that, despite what Taylor had said, despite how much she herself was enjoying this, that she would do something wrong, something Taylor wouldn't like, something that would make her not enjoy this anymore. But Taylor's kiss was even hotter than before. After a few seconds, her hands moved down Avery's body, to her breasts, her hips, her butt. And that gave Avery permission to do what she'd wanted to do all night—all summer, really. She moved her hands up Taylor's body and cupped Taylor's breasts.

Taylor kissed her harder, so she let her fingers brush over Taylor's nipples. For a while, she just played with them—experimenting with what she liked, figuring out what Taylor liked. She rolled them between her fingers, circled them with one finger, then two, pinched them softly, then harder. When she did that, Taylor backed her up against the couch.

"We're going to have to sit back down if you're going to do that," she said.

Avery laughed and sat down on the couch, pulling Taylor down onto her lap. Taylor repositioned herself so she was straddling Avery.

"Aren't you getting bold," she said. She kissed Avery again. "I like it. A lot."

Maybe it was because Taylor had said to have fun with this, but Avery was having a lot of fun exploring Taylor's breasts, even more than she expected to. They were bigger than hers, and fuller; one nipple pointed up and one pointed down, in a way that Avery found deeply charming. Her areolae and nipples were big, and dark brown against her light brown skin. She clearly enjoyed being touched there, too, which was good, because Avery felt like she could touch them, kiss them, lick them for hours.

Once they were back on the couch, everything moved a lot faster. Their hands were everywhere; their lips and tongues followed suit. Avery forgot to be anxious about whether she was doing the right thing, and let herself relax into this. They stopped talking, and communicated by sighs, moans, pauses, raised eyebrows, more kisses. Taylor pulled Avery's head up to hers so she could kiss her and play with her breasts, then Avery grabbed Taylor's ass and pulled her closer. Taylor chuckled and moved her hips slowly against Avery's, then faster.

"Holy shit, Taylor," Avery either thought or said, she wasn't sure which. In response to either her statement or the look on her face, Taylor moved her hand down in between them, and slid a finger underneath the red lace of Avery's underwear. She paused, but Avery didn't wait for her to ask the question.

"Yes," she said in Taylor's ear. "Please."

Taylor leaned forward, sucked Avery's tongue into her mouth, and at the same time, slid a finger inside of her. Avery opened her legs wider, and moved against Taylor's hand, almost without meaning to.

Taylor moved slowly at first; Avery couldn't tell if she was trying to slow things down, or if she was just exploring Avery and how she felt, what she liked and what she *really* liked, in the same way Avery had done earlier. Either way, this all felt so good she was in a daze. But after a while, Taylor slid off her lap and knelt in front of her on the floor.

"As gorgeous as these are, they need to come off for me to do this properly," she said, her fingers on the thin lace on the sides of Avery's underwear. Avery lifted her hips, and Taylor pulled them off and tossed them on the floor. She pushed Avery's legs open and smiled up at her.

"Now," she said. Avery felt a flash of anxiety. Did she smell okay? Was she too wet? Not wet enough? Did she have too much hair down there? Not enough? But she didn't have a lot of time to worry, because almost immediately, Taylor's mouth was on her, and Taylor's fingers were inside of her. And then all she could do was tangle her fingers in Taylor's hair, open her legs wide, and lean backward against her couch cushions. Holy fuck, that felt good.

After a few moments of pure bliss, Taylor shifted her position, just a little, and her tongue and fingers moved faster, and Avery could feel everything in herself build. She gripped Taylor's hair harder, and Taylor went faster, and then even faster, until Avery's whole body shook, and all she could do was hold on to this feeling, this magic, this peak, for as long as possible. She gasped once, twice, then fell back against the couch, breathing hard.

Taylor sat next to her, and Avery pulled her into her arms.

"Wow, I . . . that was . . . oh God."

Taylor laughed softly and kissed her neck.

"Good."

They lay there together for a few minutes until Avery stood up and pulled Taylor up along with her.

"Come into my bedroom so I can return the favor?" she asked. "You know how I feel about extra credit."

Taylor grinned at her.

"Who am I to deny you your chance for an A-plus?"

TEN

THE NEXT MORNING, TAYLOR WOKE UP IN AVERY'S WARM, SNUG, incredibly comfortable bed. She turned to look at Avery, curled up next to her.

The night before had been great. A huge fucking mistake, but great. She and Avery had chemistry in the bedroom (and living room) as well as at the bar, something you could never be sure of. And it had been delightful to have sex with her. What Avery had lacked in experience, she'd made up for in enthusiasm, so it had been a satisfying evening on all counts.

However. All the reasons that she'd listed for herself last night at the bar—before she'd gotten drunk on Avery's plump lips and red bra and the touch of her fingers—about why she and Avery should not hook up were still true, and now she was going to have to deal with the repercussions.

The worst one—even worse than having to host a fucking baby shower—was that she was going to have to figure out a way to let Avery down gently without crushing her. The night before had been a ton of fun, she wished she could hook up with Avery again, but she did not want to be responsible for breaking Avery's heart.

Ugh, hadn't she told Erica that she wanted a drama-free summer? Wasn't that the whole reason for that stupid bet in the first place? Well, she'd probably just fucked that up for herself.

Also . . . she liked Avery. She enjoyed being around her, she loved teaching her how to flirt. She didn't want all of that to end.

Fuck, fuck, fuck.

Avery must have felt her mental tumult in her sleep, because she stirred, then turned to face Taylor.

"Morning," she said in a scratchy voice, her eyes narrow and squinty, a sleepy smile on her face.

"Morning," Taylor said back. She couldn't help but smile at the sight of Avery's face, creased by her pillow, her bare shoulders, the top part of her breast exposed above these luxurious sheets that felt so good against the skin.

Avery half smiled back at her, before reaching over to her nightstand. She slid a pair of glasses on, then turned back to Taylor and sat up straight.

"Now I can see you."

Taylor sat up.

"I didn't know you wore glasses."

Avery took her hair out of its messy bun, and then twisted it back into a slightly neater bun.

"Oh yeah, I've worn them most of my life. I can barely see without them. I took my contacts out after you fell asleep last night."

She looked so cute with her glasses on and her hair—despite her efforts to tame it—still tousled from sleep, with that pristine white sheet covering her, that Taylor had to lean over and kiss her softly on the lips.

"Those glasses are very sexy."

Avery laughed and kissed her back.

"*You* are very sexy."

At first it was just a quick, soft, easy, no-big-deal good-morning kiss. But, even though this was not at all what Taylor had intended, it turned into a lot more. Taylor pulled Avery back down onto the bed.

"I only wish most people found my glasses to be this much of a turn-on," Avery said, her hand on Taylor's waist. "I wouldn't have needed flirting lessons from you if that was the case."

Taylor was too busy kissing Avery's neck to answer her.

Just as Avery's hand cupped Taylor's breast, a loud buzzing interrupted them.

"What is that terrible noise?" Taylor closed her eyes, like that would make it stop. It didn't.

Avery turned to her nightstand.

"Oh sorry, that's my alarm." She kissed Taylor again, then got out of bed. "Which unfortunately means I have to get in the shower."

Taylor sat up again. She was unreasonably disappointed, despite her plan to let Avery down easy and leave.

"I have no idea what time it is, but it feels very early for an alarm to be going off on a Saturday," she said, in a much grumpier voice than she'd intended.

Avery just laughed and pulled a robe out of her closet. Taylor should have known she was the type to be super chipper in the morning.

"It's seven, which I agree is very early for a Saturday, but unfortunately, life as an event planner means I often have to get up early on Saturdays. I have a fiftieth anniversary brunch this morning, and a corporate dinner tonight, so it's a busy day." She put her robe on and walked to her bedroom door, and then stopped. "Do you need the bathroom before I get in the shower?"

Taylor nodded and stood up.

"I'll be quick," she said.

She couldn't help but squeeze one of Avery's breasts as she walked by. Avery's laughter followed Taylor into the bathroom.

Taylor splashed water on her face and shook her head at herself. She shouldn't have done any of that. The kiss, the far more than a kiss, the boob grabbing, none of it. Ugh, she had to say something to Avery before she left and Avery thought they were together now or something. She was dreading this. She was always so fucking bad at this part.

She came out of the bathroom, ready to start this conversation. All she could do was be kind but honest; that would be the best thing for both of them. But before she could say anything, Avery whisked into the bathroom.

"Don't worry, I'm fast in the shower!" she yelled through the door.

That hadn't been what Taylor had been worried about, but okay.

Taylor shrugged and went into the living room to retrieve her clothes as well as her phone from her jeans pocket. She'd expected to find them thrown on the floor and couch, but they weren't there.

She stood at the bathroom door and shouted over the sound of the shower.

"Do you know what happened to my clothes?"

"Bedroom!" Avery shouted back.

Bedroom? She had definitely taken the majority of her clothes off before they'd made it into the bedroom, she absolutely remembered that. But when she walked back into Avery's bedroom, there were her clothes, folded neatly on the bench at the foot of Avery's bed. Taylor laughed to herself and shook her head. Avery must have done some post-sex tidying after Taylor had fallen asleep.

When Avery got out of the shower and came back to the bedroom, she threw open the doors to her closet.

"No wonder I have to give you guidance on what to wear every week," Taylor said. "You have more clothes than I've ever seen outside of a department store!"

Avery rolled her eyes at her as she pulled on her bra and underwear.

"Just because your wardrobe is wholly made up of fourteen black shirts and twelve pairs of jeans, that does not make my perfectly normal wardrobe extreme."

"Excuse me, but I do also have some gray shirts, and I have hoodies for when it gets cold."

Avery just laughed at her, grabbed a dress out of the closet, and pulled it over her head.

"How did you do that so fast? Doesn't it take you forever to decide what to wear?"

Avery shook her head.

"This is my event clothes section of the closet. I have specific kinds of clothes that I wear when I'm running events, as opposed to meeting with clients or with vendors, and of course, my work clothes are in a totally different part of my closet than my clothes for fun or for relaxing."

"Mmm, of course, totally different sections, yeah, me too," Taylor said with a straight face. Avery threw a pillow at her, and they both started giggling. It was very entertaining to make gentle fun of Avery.

"*Anyway,* that takes a lot of the decision-making out of the process," Avery said, moving to the mirror. She quickly put at least four layers of skin care products on her face, then put her hair up in a very tidy bun. Taylor went to stand behind Avery as she started doing her makeup. She had to get this over with.

"Uh, Avery, I wanted to . . ." She shook her head at herself and started again. "I, um, didn't mean for last night to happen; it's not like I secretly planned that or whatever when I made it your flirting lesson midterm or anything."

Avery patted on a layer of eyeshadow.

"No, I know. I didn't think you did."

Okay, that wasn't Taylor's main worry, but still, she hadn't wanted Avery to think that this whole flirting lesson thing had been about getting in her pants.

"Great, I'm glad. But I . . ." She just had to say it. "Last night was so fun, but you know I'm legendarily hopeless at relationships, and I don't think we should . . . I mean, I don't want you to think that we're—" Oof, that was clumsy. She was about to start again when Avery interrupted her.

"No. No, of course I don't." Avery turned around to face her, eyeshadow brush still in her hand. "Don't worry, I know you too well for that. And I'm definitely not ready to date anyone, you know that."

Taylor sighed with relief.

"I mean yeah, but I didn't want us to have any misunderstandings. I wanted to make sure we were on the same page."

Avery patted her hand.

"We are. Absolutely. Last night was great, I passed my flirting midterm with flying colors, I can't wait to test out the skills I've learned, no misunderstandings here." She turned back to the mirror and picked up an eyeliner. "Now, go home and get some more sleep before you have to go to work. See you Tuesday?"

Taylor blinked. This conversation had gone so differently than she'd expected that she didn't know what Avery was even talking about.

"Tuesday?"

Avery looked at her in the mirror.

"For flirting lessons?" Avery said slowly, like Taylor was confused. Which, she guessed, she was.

"Oh yeah, of course," Taylor said. "I wasn't sure if you still wanted to do the flirting lessons, like, if you thought you still needed them, after passing your midterm with flying colors, like you said." What she really wasn't sure of was if Avery wanted to keep hanging out with her after they'd slept together.

Avery shook her head.

"Oh no, I feel like it would be a big mistake to get cocky and think just because I had one good night that I don't need any more, don't you think? I know I have a ton more to learn."

Huh, okay.

"You had one excellent night, not just a good one," Taylor said. "See you Tuesday night. Don't worry, I won't forget to text you what to wear."

"Perfect," Avery said. She put her mascara down and walked Taylor to the door of her apartment. Taylor wasn't sure whether to give Avery a hug or kiss her on the cheek or what. She wasn't used to feeling so uncertain about this kind of thing, but that conversation with Avery had turned her upside down. Avery gave her a quick hug, and before Taylor could respond, she pulled open the door.

"Sorry I'm in such a rush; I need to be out of the house and on my way in ten minutes."

Taylor stepped out the door and lifted a hand to wave goodbye.

"Yeah, totally. Bye."

Avery's door clicked shut behind her, and Taylor walked down to her car. Why did she feel so . . . perplexed after that conversation? She should be thrilled. She *was* thrilled. That was the easiest "please don't fall in love with me" chat she'd ever had. They were both on the same page, no feelings were hurt, and they'd get to keep doing the flirting lessons. So why did she feel so confused?

Maybe because she'd prepared herself for the worst, and the best had happened instead. Even though it was a good outcome, the oppositeness of it all had her off-kilter.

She glanced at the clock when she got into her car. She might also be feeling this way because it was barely seven on a fucking Saturday morning, way too early to be having difficult conversations. And she hadn't even had coffee yet.

If she was up this early on a Saturday, she might as well take the opportunity to get a great breakfast at one of her favorite spots. It had both excellent food *and* great coffee, which you almost never found in the same place. There was always a nightmare of a line there after nine, but they opened at seven thirty and she'd heard—although never experienced—that it was easy to get a table then.

Yes, that was it. She'd go, sit at the counter, drink three cups of black coffee, eat eggs and fried potatoes, spread her toast very thickly with butter, and then she'd be in the right state of mind to celebrate her triumph of sleeping with Avery while still managing a perfect, no-strings-attached hookup right when she needed one.

Actually. She had to do this part eventually; might as well get it out of the way, and at one of her favorite places. She picked up her phone.

"What's wrong? Is someone sick? Are you at the ER?" Erica asked when she answered the phone.

"No, nothing's wrong, why all the panic?" Taylor asked, as innocently as she could.

"Taylor. How long have we known each other? Ten years? Twelve? Throughout that entire time, you have never called me this early on a Saturday. Not only that, but I've never known you to willingly be awake at this hour when you weren't on your way to work. And I know you're not on your way to work, because (a) you don't get to work this early, and (b) you like silence in the morning. I know this because every time we've ever shared a hotel room and I wake up before you—which I always do—you try to smother me with a pillow if I so much as make a slight creaking noise on my way to the bathroom."

Taylor stifled her giggles.

"I have never tried to smother you with a pillow. I may have put a pillow over your head *one* time, but that was when you started singing 'The Hills Are Alive' in your sleep and wouldn't stop. And I am calling because I happened to wake up super early this morning, and I thought, 'You know who else is almost certainly awake? My friend Erica, who wakes up at six a.m. every single day year-round, except for the days when she wakes up at five. I wonder if she would like to join me at the Homemade Café for a delicious breakfast at a time when we don't have to fight the lines.' So—"

"Give me fifteen minutes."

Erica hung up, and Taylor smiled to herself, satisfied. She hadn't been sure if Erica would join her for breakfast like this at the last minute, since she was all married and pregnant and friends with Sloane and needed to "calendar" hanging out with her best friend. But she was glad she'd called Erica; if Taylor was going to confess that she'd lost the bet, she might as well have fun with it.

Exactly fifteen minutes later, Taylor was seated at a window table at Homemade, when she saw Erica at the door and waved. Erica came over to the table, shaking her head.

"I wondered if I would get here and realize you'd pulled a very mean prank on me, but amazingly, you're here," Erica said as Taylor got up to hug her.

"I would never joke about something that involved fried potatoes," Taylor said. "Or actually, breakfast in general. That would make me undeserving of the best meal of the day."

Erica laughed and put her hand on her belly as she sat down. She picked up the cup of coffee sitting in front of her, looked at it for a second, then put it down.

"It's decaf, don't worry," Taylor said.

"Oh!" Erica picked her cup back up. "I didn't know if you'd remembered, that's all."

"Of course I remembered," Taylor said. "Gotta do everything we can to keep Little Rutabaga safe and healthy."

Erica looked relieved and took a gulp of coffee.

"Thanks, I appreciate that. Technically I can have a cup of caffeinated every day, but it made me anxious, you know? Better safe than sorry."

Taylor nodded understandingly. At least, she hoped her nod looked understanding. Better safe than sorry was rarely a motto she lived by—more often it was the opposite—but hey, life was a rich tapestry, people lived in different ways, and even though Erica never used to live by that motto, it didn't matter. People changed, right?

Taylor laughed at herself. Wow, she was in a *much* better mood than she'd been for weeks. She was never going to take a vow of celibacy again.

"I get it," Taylor said. "You're what, six months now?"

"Almost twenty-five weeks," Erica said.

Why did people measure things in weeks like that? No one ever said, *This kid is one hundred and two weeks old*, so why did they say it about pregnant women and babies? Whatever, it didn't matter; after years of bartending, she was good at doing math in her head.

"Sloane said to enjoy this part, so I'm trying to, and Sam is trying to plan a babymoon for us . . ."

"That sounds fun," Taylor said.

"Yeah . . ." Erica's voice trailed away as the server stopped at their table.

"You two ready to order?"

Taylor nodded.

"Two eggs over easy with chorizo, the potatoes crispy, please, and sourdough toast."

She looked at Erica, who glanced down at the menu, nodded, then closed it.

"A short stack of blueberry pancakes, please. Oh, and more decaf."

Taylor raised an eyebrow after the server walked away.

"Just a short stack of pancakes? Aren't you eating for two?"

Erica laughed.

"Trust me, I wanted a full stack of pancakes, but my gestational diabetes test is in a few weeks, and I'm stressed about it so I've been avoiding sugar as much as possible. That's why I had to dip out of Callie's party early. I knew once that cake came out that I'd want to dive headfirst into it, I didn't trust myself to stay. But since I amazingly get to have an early breakfast with my best friend, I figured I should treat myself a little."

Taylor was kind of touched by that.

"You should definitely treat yourself," Taylor said. "I'm going to make sure you put syrup on those pancakes, too."

Erica cast her eyes upward.

"We'll see about that. Now, care to explain what you are doing up this early? I mean, have you ever even gotten here before me? I need answers."

Taylor from last week would be annoyed that it took this long for Erica to get to this question, but Taylor from this morning was too relaxed and smug to care. It would honestly make the telling of this story even more fun.

"Please don't expect this to happen again. I'm not going to make a habit of this; while it was great to not have to stand in line to get a table here, I'd still rather be in bed right now." She grinned. "But yes, you need answers. Here's your answer: you win."

"I win what?" Erica asked, nodding her thanks to the server who refilled her coffee mug.

Taylor did roll her eyes this time.

"You know what you win."

Erica looked confused for a second, then let out a shout of laughter that made the whole restaurant turn and look at them. She kept laughing for so long she had to stop and take a sip of water in the middle before starting up again. Taylor sat there and waited for her to finish.

"I win!" she said when she finally settled down. "You have to throw me a baby shower!" She bit her lip. "Though, Sloane has already volunteered to throw it, so you two might have to be cohosts, if that's okay?"

Taylor made a face.

"I guess so. But isn't she a little boring for you? She's so, I don't know, rich and bland. Perfect suburban wife and mom."

Erica shook her head.

"No, she's a lot more than that. You've never really gotten to talk to her, you'll like her, I swear. But we'll talk about that later. I won the bet! Tell me everything. But wait, why does that explain why you were up so early? Shouldn't you still be in bed with your new conquest?"

Taylor sighed.

"I wish I was still in bed with my new conquest, but she had to go to work, unfortunately, and so she very nicely kicked me out of her apartment early this morning, and I thought, 'Who better to enjoy a surprise early Saturday morning with than my best friend Erica?'"

"Who is this mystery woman?" Erica asked. "Where did you meet her? How did this happen? Has she professed her love for you yet? Tell me everything."

"I will answer those questions in reverse order. No, she has not, as a matter of fact she said this morning that she knows I'm not ready for a relationship and that she isn't, either. I met her a while ago, but for real earlier this summer. And the mystery woman is . . . Avery."

Erica's reaction could not have been better. Her eyes got huge, her mouth dropped open, and she clapped her hands.

"Don't yell," Taylor said before Erica could say anything.

Erica shut her mouth and nodded repeatedly for a few seconds, her eyes still wide.

"AVERY?!" she finally scream-whispered. "The hot girl you've been teaching how to hit on women all summer?"

Taylor couldn't stop giggling.

"Yes, that Avery," she said. "I only know one."

"You finally gave in and hit on her? Or did you teach her so well that the student became the master?"

"It was a combination of the two, actually," Taylor said, still giggling.

Erica dropped her hands to the table and leaned back in her chair.

"Okay, I'm going to stop asking questions if you're just going to answer them in that cryptic way that makes me have more questions. I need you to start from the beginning and tell me the whole story."

Taylor grinned.

"I made a . . . maybe slight tactical error—or an excellent choice, depending on your perspective—with my selection of a flirting lesson for last night. I told her that it was time for a midterm, and she had to flirt with me."

Erica cackled until the server brought over their food. Taylor thanked him and glared at Erica.

"What is so funny?" she asked once he'd walked away.

Erica picked up her fork and knife.

"You are. Your test for a woman you've wanted to fuck all summer—and don't tell me you haven't—was that she had to flirt with you? They should have named you Taylor 'Playing with Fire' Cameron." She paused, a neat triangle of pancake halfway to her mouth. "Someone who didn't know you as well as I do would think you'd done that on purpose, that you'd set a trap all ready for her to walk right into. But you're neither that crafty nor manipulative; you wouldn't do something like that on purpose."

"Thank you, I think?" Taylor said. She looked down at her breakfast. The potatoes at this place were always the precise amount of crispy she wanted them to be. It made her happy every time.

"You're welcome," Erica said, after she finished chewing her bite of pancake. "The incredible thing about you is that I'm sure you did this genuinely, you thought it would be a good little test for Avery, and you'd tell her at the end that she did a great job and give her a few pointers, and she'd get a great ego boost out of it and that would be that. Right?"

Taylor frowned at her.

"I mean, when you put it like that, it sounds like there was something wrong with it. Obviously there was, but I didn't plan for it to go like that."

Erica patted her on the hand in that slightly condescending way that she did.

"No, no, I know you didn't, that's the whole point. You didn't plan for it to go like that, but literally anyone who has ever met you would know that's exactly how it would go, that is, if this Avery had any game in the slightest, which I guess she did."

Taylor thought back to the night before and grinned.

"She absolutely did, which I didn't expect."

Erica was already halfway through her second pancake.

"She learned from the best, so I'm not surprised. But also—you realize that this means that your goal for a no-drama summer is now lost for good, right? This woman is *definitely* going to fall for you."

Taylor shook her head.

"She won't! We talked about that this morning! I brought it up because I didn't want the prospect of drama hanging over my head, and she laughed at me and said she wasn't ready to date anyone yet and obviously I wasn't, either, so that's not what she wanted or expected. She even said she wanted to continue with the flirting lessons! Everything is fine."

Erica reached across the table for a piece of Taylor's toast, and smeared some strawberry jam on it.

"As you know, what people say and what they mean are often very different."

Did Erica think she'd never interacted with a human being before? Or that she'd never had a difficult conversation with someone she'd just slept with? Of course, sometimes what people said and what they meant were very different, but that wasn't the case here.

"I know that. I also know Avery. Look, I'll check in with her again if it feels necessary, but I can usually tell when there are weird undertones to a conversation, and there weren't to this one. Now, just be excited for me that I finally had sex again. I was getting deeply irritable. I don't ever want that to happen again."

Erica giggled again.

"God, neither do I." Taylor glared at her, which just made her giggle harder. Then she shook herself, set down her coffee, and pulled an exaggerated straight face. "What I meant to say was 'Oh wow, you were irritable? I hadn't noticed.'"

Taylor threw a piece of toast at Erica, who caught it and put more jam on it.

"Do you seriously believe that she's totally fine with this being a one-night stand or whatever, and that she's not all into you now? Because we've both seen it happen many times when a woman falls hard for the first woman she has sex with, and we both have experience with falling hard for our first, I'm just saying."

Taylor found herself getting irritated again. Why did Erica have to ruin this nice, fun, good thing? She'd won the bet, couldn't she just gloat about that and be done with it?

"This is different," she said. "Avery is older than we were when we fell hard for our firsts. And she got out of a bad relationship recently, so I believe her when she said she's not ready for something."

"Oh, I'm sure she's not ready for something, but that doesn't mean that she doesn't *want* something," Erica said. "She couldn't tell you that she has feelings for you, she knows you well enough to know that would be a disaster, but that doesn't mean that she won't want something more from you and make that very clear to you soon. Especially if you keep hanging out with her doing 'flirting lessons' and making her fall for you even more. And then we have to put the Taylor of it all into the picture, which means that I have a feeling that this isn't going to be as easy and drama-free as you want it to be."

Erica slipped into that condescending tone again, first when she'd talked about the flirting lessons, and then when she said "the Taylor of it all," like Taylor had some sort of hypnotic power over women that made them fall for her and cause drama, or worse, like she was the one to cause the drama herself as if it were her goal. Erica should know Taylor too well to think that.

"Relax, it's going to be fine. Avery's not like that. We've spent a lot of time together this summer, we're very honest with each other. I'm not concerned."

"Fine," Erica said, putting her hands up. "I get it, she's perfect, everything's perfect."

Taylor wanted to push back and say that she hadn't been saying that Avery was perfect or that everything was perfect, but couldn't everything be just good? Was it too much to ask for Erica to be happy that things were good for Taylor? You know, her best friend? Did she have to make every small thing into a big one?

She stopped herself, though. She didn't want to get into an argument with Erica today. She just wanted to have a nice, fun breakfast with her best friend and be in a post-sex good mood on a Saturday morning before she had to head to work.

"Thank you," she said. Oh. She knew how to move the conversation back to a more relaxed tone. "Anyway." She let out a big sigh. "When should we set the date for your . . . baby shower?"

Erica's loud cackle made the whole restaurant stare at them again.

AVERY COULD FEEL THE BOUNCE IN HER STEP AS SHE WALKED to the garden on Sunday. She was such a fucking cliché, but she didn't care. The sun was shining, she had the whole afternoon off, her coffee had tasted excellent this morning, and oh right, she'd had fantastic sex with Taylor Cameron two nights ago. The whole world seemed pink and shimmery.

That last thing might be because of her new pink sunglasses, but who cared? She'd worn them today for the first time, and she felt amazing in them. She felt amazing, period.

She wanted to shout to the whole world, *I had sex! With a woman! And it was incredible!* The movie version of her would do that, but the real Avery would never. The real Avery hadn't even told Luke, her best friend of fifteen years.

Though she and Luke never really talked about sex—they had too much of a sibling-like relationship for that. Sure, they told each other when they started dating people, and Luke had told her that he'd had sex with Margot the night before he started work as her employee, but that was so wild that he'd *had* to tell her. But he hadn't told her any of the details, and she was dying to talk to someone about the details of her night with Taylor.

She didn't really have any other friends whom she could tell. She'd lost touch with most of her friends over the past few years, partly because of Derek, partly because of the pandemic, and, if she was being completely honest with herself, partly because of herself. She'd been depressed about the world and her relationship and ashamed to tell any of her friends how she felt, and she let too many texts and voicemails go unanswered, until they stopped coming. She didn't blame her friends for that, and she wanted to see if she could rekindle those friendships, but she didn't exactly think the way to get back in touch was to send a text saying, *Are you around tonight for a phone call so I can tell you about how I had sex with a woman this weekend?* Like, that would for sure get a response, but she was a little too shy to start off that way. Plus, she'd feel like an asshole only texting them to tell them about herself and not actually finding out how they were.

How did a person text a friend they hadn't talked to in over a year? She made a mental note to figure that out after she got home from the garden.

She also wasn't . . . exactly . . . quite so low-key about Taylor's whole brush-off from Saturday morning as she'd pretended to be. She hadn't lied to Taylor, she knew she wasn't ready for a relationship, and she sure as hell knew Taylor didn't want one. She'd given herself a lecture in the shower on Saturday morning about not making a big deal out of this, playing it cool, not getting too attached. But still, it stung a little that Taylor hadn't fallen madly in love with her over the course of a night. Or even fallen madly in lust with her. But she was glad that Taylor had brought it up, and that they'd talked about it. She knew Friday night couldn't happen again, but she wanted to stay friends with Taylor, and keep up the flirting lessons.

And she was really, *really* glad it happened.

When she got to the garden, she raced over to their plot to see what had changed in the past few days.

"Oh my God!" She let out a squeal as she looked at the jalapeño plant at the corner of their plot. They'd planted that pepper seedling together, and had nurtured it for weeks now. On Wednesday there had been a bunch of flowers on it, but suddenly, there were actual, tiny little peppers.

"What are we yelling about?" Beth said as she approached the plot. "Was that a good yell or a bad one, so I can prepare myself?"

"A good one, a good one!" Avery pointed to the pepper plant. "I just got here, but look! Look at all of these baby jalapeños!"

Beth came closer.

"Oh my God!" Beth yelled. Avery grinned at her, and Beth had a huge, equally dorky smile on her face that Avery could feel on her own.

"I know, right?" Avery looked back at the plant. "And there are so many of them!"

The older woman who had a plot a few rows away came over to them, probably confused by the yelling.

"Sorry," Avery said. "We were just excited. By, um, the baby peppers."

She looked at their peppers and smiled.

"Your first year?" she asked, and they both nodded. Her smile got bigger.

"Us old-timers get excited, too, about our first little baby vegetables. It's a pity we started playing it cool at some point and don't yell about it anymore. Keep yelling."

She smiled at them again and walked back over to her plot. Avery and Beth looked at each other.

"Do you also feel like we got visited by the gardening fairy godmother?" Beth whispered to Avery.

Avery nodded.

"One hundred percent. I've always wanted to be visited by a fairy godmother. Who knew I just had to start gardening for it to happen?"

They grinned at each other, and then began their weeding from opposite corners of the plot. It was hard, hot work, and Avery distracted herself by thinking about Friday night and how excellent it had been. Excellent, unexpected, fun, and, surprisingly, very sweet. She'd expected Taylor to be good in bed, but she hadn't anticipated that she would be so kind and thoughtful. When she'd said that thing about how inexperienced she was compared to Taylor, she really liked that Taylor didn't deny it, or brush off her worries, but acknowledged them and made her feel better. After they'd moved to the bedroom, she'd been very nervous, which she was sure Taylor knew, and Taylor had managed to give her direction without making her feel bad or inept. And she'd been very complimentary afterward.

"Okay," Beth said in her ear, making her jump. "That's the third little chuckle you've let out in the last twenty minutes, and I know it wasn't the little jalapeños this time, or the little radishes or the enormous fucking zucchini. What's got you in such a good mood?"

Beth would be the perfect person to talk to about Taylor. She'd already told her about the flirting lessons; she would probably love to hear about what happened at the midterm.

Wait no, she barely knew Beth. She couldn't tell her about this.

"Enormous zucchini?" Avery asked to buy some time. "Where? I haven't gotten there yet."

Beth grabbed her arm and pulled her over to their zucchini plant.

"You can't see it at first, look under the leaves," she said. "I was going to pick it, but I left it for you to see first."

Avery pulled up a few leaves.

"That's . . . the biggest . . . zucchini I've ever seen!" she said between gulps of laughter.

"I could say something very dirty about that vegetable right now, but I'm not going to do it," Beth said. "See how I'm restraining myself from saying that it would be just an incredible dildo? Shit, I said it, didn't I?"

Avery giggled and nodded.

"You sure did."

Beth reached for the zucchini and snapped it off the plant so quickly that Avery gasped, then giggled again.

"Wow, I am really acting like a teenager today, aren't I?" Avery said. "I swear, I'm not usually like this. Um, did you know that zucchini—and all squash, actually—are fruits, not vegetables?"

Beth nodded.

"I did know that, just like I know you haven't answered my question about why you're in such a good mood."

Avery shrugged.

"Oh, it's nothing, I'm just . . ." Her voice trailed off as she looked at Beth's face. Could she tell her?

"What are you doing after this?" she asked.

Beth's eyes got big.

"Having drinks with you?"

"You sure are."

The rest of their time at the garden, as they weeded and dead-headed and plucked hidden zucchini from underneath leaves and chatted with other gardeners, Avery had mingled excitement and anxiety dancing around her stomach. Should she really tell Beth about Friday night with Taylor? At this point, she'd committed, hadn't she?

Well, she didn't *have* to tell her. If she changed her mind, she could tell Beth that she was sorry, she couldn't get drinks after all, and leave quickly, and next week she could make up some story.

But she didn't want to do that. She *wanted* to tell Beth, even though she didn't know her all that well, even though she was nervous about telling her, even though she wasn't in the habit of talking to anyone about stuff like this. She wanted to be different, remember? More open with people?

Beth had been so encouraging when she'd told her about the flirting lessons with Taylor, and she hadn't acted like Avery was weird or her growth as a person was stunted for not knowing everything already. Maybe Beth would be weird about this, though? That was possible. But that's what taking risks was, right? Learning how to deal with it if you weren't completely sure of the outcome? God, that still sounded terrible. But maybe slightly less scary than it had?

After about forty-five minutes, Beth appeared at Avery's shoulder as Avery was frowning over the stunted cilantro plant.

"What's wrong?" she said when she saw Avery's face.

"This cilantro! It doesn't look like it's supposed to. I don't know what we did wrong."

"It's gone to seed," James said as she walked by their plot. "It's the heat. Cilantro is more of a fall plant here; it's too hot and dry in our summers for it. You didn't do anything wrong. Plant more in a month or so."

"Thanks," Avery said. James nodded briskly and kept walking.

"Forget about the cilantro!" Beth said. "We have more important things to discuss! I'm dying of curiosity here."

Avery bit her lip. Okay. She was going to do this.

"I hope my story is worth all of this. But let's go."

Beth turned to Avery once they got into Beth's car. Avery didn't even wait for her to say anything.

"I slept with Taylor on Friday night."

Beth squealed.

"AHHHHHHHHH I KNEW IT!" Her face filled with glee, and

she clapped like a seal. "Wait, I need all the details. Where can we go?"

Avery thought for a minute. They couldn't go anywhere she might run into anyone she'd known forever, nor could they go anywhere she might run into Taylor or any of her friends. Hmm.

"Okay, this is a little random, but there's a champagne place about fifteen minutes away that I've been wanting to go to. And I don't think I know anyone who works there."

Beth started the car.

"Perfect, I love champagne. Just tell me how to get there. And don't say anything else until we're there, I need to concentrate on this story."

Twenty minutes later, they were seated in the corner of the restaurant's patio with a glass of champagne in front of each of them and a plate piled with thin, crisp, golden french fries in the middle of the table.

"To having that kind of smile on your face," Beth said, and raised her glass.

Avery laughed and raised hers, too.

"Now," Beth said after she took a sip. "Tell me everything."

So Avery told her. Not quite everything, but almost. She didn't tell her about the way Taylor's eyes had looked when she'd taken her clothes off, or how nervous and excited she'd been to undress Taylor, or about her anxieties about going down on Taylor. But she told her a lot.

And Beth's reactions could not have been more satisfying. Her eyes got big when Taylor said it was a flirting midterm. She gasped when Taylor said, *Now is when you kiss me*, and she let out a little squeal when they got back to Avery's apartment. By the time Avery finished, Beth had a huge smile on her face.

"Okay, I have many questions," she said, "but first, can we toast to this incredible first queer sex experience for you? It was incredible, wasn't it? No, I don't even have to ask that, I can see it in your face, let's toast." She held up her glass.

Avery giggled again.

"I'll toast to that."

Beth took a gulp of her drink and then grabbed a handful of fries.

"First question: Why are you here, with me, and not still in bed with her? I mean yes, the garden is very exciting in August, I wouldn't have wanted you to miss that zucchini, but I have a feeling Taylor offers a few more attractions."

Avery let herself think about that for a moment. Let herself imagine what it would have been like to spend all weekend in bed with Taylor. That sounded . . . heavenly.

She reached for some french fries to bring herself back to earth. She'd barely eaten any, she'd been so busy talking.

"I had work all day yesterday, and Taylor is . . . Taylor. She checked in with me yesterday morning, and we agreed that neither of us wanted a relationship. But we're still—"

Beth set her glass down.

"Wait. She brought this up already? Did you even have clothes on yet? Of course you agreed, she had the upper hand! I can't believe her. Just because she's more experienced doesn't mean she's allowed to be an asshole about it!"

Avery had the strange urge to give Beth a hug. The only person who had ever flown to her defense like that was Luke. It wasn't necessary, but still.

"No, seriously, it was okay. Truly. I know I'm not ready for another relationship yet. Even if I was, I don't think it should be with someone like Taylor." Beth was looking at her doubtfully, so she kept talking. "I swear, I'm not upset. I never expected Taylor to want any more than sex. And I don't want any more than that with her; anyone who gets serious about Taylor is asking to be crushed in the end. I'm glad we already talked about this so that things wouldn't be weird between us."

It must be so stressful to be in a relationship with Taylor. She knew Taylor too well at this point; she knew how it would go. The many women who'd had their hearts broken by Taylor could probably fill a convention hall; she didn't want to be part of that number.

Beth looked relieved and took another handful of french fries.

"Good, I take back my rage at her. I will no longer plot to destroy her. And I'm very pleased that she gave you some great orgasms." Beth raised her champagne glass to Avery again. "I know, I know, you didn't tell me the details, but I could tell by the way you talked about it and that smug smile on your face."

Avery felt the smug smile creep back and couldn't help but shrug.

"Well, I mean . . . all I can say is, to many more." She lifted her glass and touched it to Beth's.

"That's what I'm talking about," Beth said. She raised an eyebrow. "Okay, but that brings up another question. Are you going to do it again? With her, I mean. I know you don't want a relationship, but no one said you had to have a relationship to have good sex."

Avery made a face.

"In my experience, once you have a relationship, all you have is bad sex, which is yet another reason I'm in no hurry to get into another relationship."

Beth shook her head.

"Oh, honey. We need to talk about your relationships at some point, and yes, it's probably good for you to wait awhile. Also, you didn't answer the question."

Avery shook her head.

"No, it was pretty clear that she didn't think we should do it again, and I don't, either. It would make things too complicated, and I don't think I could really do a friends-with-benefits thing with her. But we're still doing the flirting lessons—I want to get better at this, and I definitely want to kiss more women." Avery couldn't believe she'd said that out loud, but Beth just lifted her second glass of champagne to her. "I hope she keeps introducing me to her cute friends so I get a chance to do it again with *someone*."

"Don't worry, I have no doubt about that," Beth said. "Who wouldn't want to have sex with you? You're hot, you're smart, you're fun, you're the whole package."

Avery held back her sigh. People always said this about her. Yet it was hard to believe them, since no one ever wanted to sleep with her.

Well. Taylor had.

Avery felt that smug smile spread across her face again.

"What are you smiling about *now*?" Beth asked.

Avery laughed, slightly embarrassed, but only slightly.

"Because I was going to roll my eyes at you and say, 'Then why does no one ever actually want to have sex with me in real life?' But then I remembered—"

"Someone did!" Beth finished for her. "And mark my words, that someone still does."

"Why do you think that?" Avery asked. Not rhetorically, she really wanted to know.

"Because of everything you told me," Beth said. "Yeah, she kind of blew you off, but she was also *into* it. Wasn't she?"

Avery didn't have to think about that. Even with her general insecurity about everything sex and relationship related, she knew the answer to that.

"Yeah," she said. "She was."

Beth nodded.

"Even if you two don't sleep together again, she still wants you."

Avery hoped Beth was right. Because she sure as hell still wanted Taylor. At least no matter what happened between them in the future, she'd know she'd already had her.

That would probably give her more confidence than any possible flirting lesson could.

ELEVEN

DESPITE THEIR GROWN-UP, MATURE CONVERSATION ON SAT-urday morning, Taylor was still irritated at herself for sleeping with Avery. She didn't want things to be weird between them, damn it. They'd actually become good friends over the course of the past month, and she didn't want to ruin that.

She should have thought of that before ending up in Avery's bed on Friday night. When was she going to fucking grow up and stop making bad decisions?

No, that was Erica's influence talking. Everything would be fine! She would keep things purely platonic on Tuesday night. No flirting, no glances at her cleavage, no accidentally touching her hair, or her shoulder, or her knee, or . . . none of that.

She decided they'd go to a queer social at a paint-your-own-pottery studio. Toddlers painted pottery; it was impossible to make it sexy. Simple, no stress, no innuendo, lots of other people, bright lights. They would go and each paint a mug or bowl or something. She would encourage Avery to chat with some cute women, and then congratulate her for a job well done on the way home. A nice way to ease back into teaching Avery how to flirt a few days after she'd flirted Taylor's fucking pants off. Literally.

Monday afternoon, when she was at the winery in the middle of four different things, Avery texted her.

AVERY

What should I wear tomorrow??

Right, she'd forgotten to do that. Okay, what was a good dress code and also a tiny clue? She hastily typed out a quick answer.

TAYLOR

something you can get dirty in

Oh no, she'd already violated her no-innuendo rule. Why was her brain like this? Was innuendo such a natural part of her conversation that she did it without even thinking? Probably. She meant she wanted Avery to wear something to *get* dirty in, not *be* dirty in; would Avery understand that distinction?

Okay, fine. She *did* want Avery to wear something she could be dirty in. Obviously, she wanted that.

But she didn't want Avery to think she wanted that. Because then Avery would think she wanted a repeat of Friday, and while she did very much want that, she also wanted no drama, and to stay friends with Avery and keep doing these surprisingly fun flirting lessons. She didn't think she would get all of that and get to sleep with Avery again, too.

AVERY

Lol ok

Okay. That response from Avery made her feel better.

TAYLOR

here!

She texted Avery, as usual, when she got to Avery's apartment on Tuesday night. When Avery got into the car, she just had to be casual, normal, not the way she'd been on Friday night.

The problem was, she couldn't remember what "normal" was like between her and Avery. She remembered what it was like at the beginning, with Avery nervous and stressed out and herself amused. And she remembered what it was like at trivia, with them easy and comfortable, and, okay, fine, lightly flirting with each other. But was their fun, flirty interaction at trivia what "normal" was between the two of them? Or had trivia been a precursor to the midterm that ended in sex? Very extended foreplay, if you will. She wasn't sure.

When did their relationship—their friendship—change from stilted and kind of awkward to relaxed and easy? Taylor couldn't remember. She wanted to go back to the relaxed and easy version of their friendship, but was that possible without the flirting and the potential sex? It must be. She had that type of friendship with other people, and she'd never had sex with them!

She had to be friendly to Avery, but not too friendly. How did she do that?

What the fuck was she doing? She was completely overthinking this, and she never did that. She was far more likely to severely underthink something. For example, Friday night when she'd had sex with Avery. Maybe if she'd thought a little more about that, she wouldn't be in this situation right now.

"Hey," Avery said as she got into the car. "Where to?"

"Hey," Taylor said. "Oh, we're going to—" Shit, that had been a close call. She'd been so frazzled she'd almost told Avery where they were going. "Ha, you thought you'd get me that time, didn't you?"

Avery grinned.

"I almost did. Nice save."

Taylor shook her head at herself as she started the car.

"Did I wear the right clothes for tonight?" Avery asked her. She didn't wait for an answer before she continued. "I've been trying to figure out where we could be going where I'd need to wear clothes I can get dirty in. First, I wondered if we were going to make wine somewhere, you know, do the foot-stomping thing, but it's not harvest yet. I always roll my eyes at that, but also it looks fun. I could have worn what I wear to garden, but all of my gardening clothes literally have dirt on them, so I had to find something else. Anyway, I thought maybe cooking classes? We'll see if I'm right."

Avery was talking a lot more and faster than normal. She must be nervous about tonight, too. That made Taylor feel better.

"You'll see," was all Taylor said. Avery pouted that very cute fat-bottom-lipped pout of hers.

"Fine," she said. "I've missed my chance to go upstairs to change, though, if I guessed wrong."

Taylor glanced over at Avery's outfit, but immediately she wished she hadn't. Avery was wearing a thin gray V-neck T-shirt and jeans, which could be unremarkable, except Avery's T-shirt was thin enough to be slightly see-through. When she was this close to Avery, and the sun shone down on her like this, Taylor could clearly tell that Avery was wearing a lacy black bra. Damn, that was so fucking sexy. What a fucking nightmare.

"You look fine," Taylor said, and turned her eyes back to the road. She couldn't look at Avery anymore.

But too late, she heard the harsh edge to her voice, one that she'd meant for herself, not for Avery. Avery must have heard it, too, because she didn't say anything else. That should have been a relief to Taylor, that her nervous chatter had subsided, but the silence between the two of them felt awkward. And now she felt bad for snapping at Avery. It wasn't Avery's fault that they'd had sex a few days before; Taylor was the one who'd had the stupid fucking idea to give her a flirting midterm. *You have to flirt with me*—what the fuck was the matter with her? Talk about playing with fire and getting burned.

She had to pull herself together. If she was going to keep doing these flirting lessons with Avery, like she'd promised, she had to put on her fucking big-girl panties and deal. She was very attracted to Avery, she knew that, she'd known that since the beginning; now it was far more out in the open. Oh well, they would deal with this like adults.

Why was this such a problem for her? She'd hung out with plenty of people she'd slept with in the past, and it hadn't been an issue like this.

Maybe because with Avery, unlike with all those other people, it didn't feel like they were done. Yes, she'd told Avery they shouldn't do it again, but she wanted to do it again. And again. That wasn't Avery's fault; it was hers.

She turned to glance at Avery again, who was staring straight ahead. She abruptly pulled over.

"Hey," she said when she stopped the car.

"Hey," Avery said. She hadn't seen that stiff, unsmiling look from Avery in a long time. She didn't like it.

"I'm sorry I was being weird," Taylor said. "I guess I'm feeling kind of awkward, and I wish I wasn't, and I snapped at you and I didn't mean to."

Avery's face relaxed.

"Okay. It's okay. Thanks for saying that. I'm feeling awkward, too. I just . . . I don't regret what happened—"

"Me, either," Taylor quickly replied.

"Good," Avery said. "I wasn't sure if . . . Anyway, I don't want it to mess up our friendship, because I've had a lot of fun with the flirting lessons, and I know I kind of pushed you into still doing them, so if you don't want to keep going, say the word. But I feel like—I don't know, maybe I'm wrong—we've become friends through this, and I don't want to lose that."

"You're not wrong," Taylor said. "We have. And me neither." She started the car again. "And no way we're stopping the flirting lessons. You're not going to get out of them that easily. I can't have your skills regress, not after all this work we've done."

Avery grinned at her.

"Okay, then. Let's do this. Whatever it is."

They drove on, in silence again, but this time the silence was more companionable. Relaxed, friendly, not tense and stressful. Taylor sighed an internal sigh of relief. She didn't know why it had been so important to her to make sure things weren't weird between her and Avery, and she wasn't going to try to figure it out now, but she was just glad they could go have a normal, ridiculous time painting pottery tonight.

She pulled into a parking place about a block away and turned to Avery.

"I have one more question," she said.

Avery's eyebrows went up.

"Go on."

Taylor bit her lip.

"Will you help me plan a baby shower?"

Avery burst out laughing.

"What? You're kidding, right? Did you lose a bet?"

Taylor could feel the wide grin spread across her face.

"Actually, yes. You see, I kind of had this bet with Erica that I could make it to Labor Day without having sex with anyone. If I won, she had to give me a spa day. And if she won, I had to plan her baby shower. And. Well."

Avery laughed louder.

"Oh my God. I was kidding, but you really did lose a bet. And of course I'll help."

That was a relief, what with Sloane ready to take over.

"Thank you. I know nothing about babies or baby showers; I'll need all the help you can give me. Especially since I have to cohost it with Sloane, who I'm sure already has all sorts of plans, and I . . . don't."

Avery grinned.

"Luckily, you came to the right place. A few decisions to make, off the top of my head: Do we want to paint onesies or bibs? A balloon arch or a flower arch? Should the games be tasting baby food, celebrity baby names, or guess the birth date? Should the favors be custom M&M's or custom matchboxes? Do we want—"

Taylor broke in.

"Balloon arch? Baby food tasting? Custom candy? What other horrors do you have in store for me? I was expecting to buy a cake and a few decorations and call it a day?"

Avery raised an eyebrow.

"Oh, Taylor. My friend. Thank goodness you have me."

AS THEY WALKED TO WHEREVER THEY WERE GOING, AVERY was still amused by the look on Taylor's face after she'd listed baby shower activities.

But also . . . Taylor had clearly told Erica that she'd lost the bet. Did that mean she'd told her she'd slept with Avery? Probably, right?

"I can't believe I managed to get myself in charge of a baby shower!" Taylor said as they walked down the street. "I guess I have to find a place to have it? Where do people have baby showers? I'm sure Sloane wants it at her house, but God no. I bet her house is, like, all off-white with lots of delicate crystal, and I would either destroy something or get hives as soon as I walked inside."

"Why don't you ask Margot if you could have it at the winery?" Avery asked. "She wants to start renting out the garden for events, doesn't she? This could be a good way to ease into having events there, and she'd probably be happy to start off with someone who knows the space and can let her know what works and what doesn't. And I doubt she would charge you much, if at all."

Taylor turned to look at her, shaking her head slowly.

"See, this is exactly why I needed you to help me. That's the perfect solution, and it would have taken me weeks to come up with it. I'll ask her at work tomorrow." She made a face. "I will not, however, tell her why I'm planning a baby shower, even though I know she'll ask."

Just then, Taylor stopped walking and opened a door with a flourish.

"Here we are!"

Avery stepped back and read the sign above the door.

"'Let's Paint!' We're painting pottery?" That didn't sound like a normal Taylor Cameron–style flirting lesson.

But Taylor nodded.

"Yep. There's a whole queer mixer tonight, so I signed us up. Wine and pottery and paint, what could go wrong?"

"Incredible." Avery looked at her outfit as she walked inside. "Aah, 'something you can get dirty in,' now I get it. But wouldn't *messy* be a better word than *dirty*?"

Taylor waved that aside.

"Close enough. I'm excited to see how colorful those jeans are by the end of the night."

As soon as they walked in, a very brightly dressed person greeted them.

"Hi! I'm Lupe! Did you two register for the event tonight, or are you dropping in?"

"We registered," Taylor said. "I'm Taylor Cameron."

"Hi, Taylor!" Lupe said. "So nice to meet you!" She turned to Avery expectantly, so Avery smiled at her, too.

"Hi, I'm Avery."

"Welcome, Taylor and Avery! We are so excited to have you here at Let's Paint! Have you been here before? No? Great, welcome in! I'll explain to you how it works! Head over to the wall and select the piece of pottery that you want to paint, and then you join your group at your table to paint! Someone will be walking around to help if you need it! At the end of the night, you leave it with us, we fire it, and in a few days, you can come back to pick up your beautiful new pottery! Any questions?"

Taylor looked slightly shell-shocked by how aggressively bubbly Lupe was, so Avery answered her.

"No questions for now. Thanks so much for the explanation, I appreciate it!"

She couldn't help herself with the exclamation points. They were catching.

Lupe beamed at her.

"You're very welcome! Time to pick your pottery!"

Avery nudged Taylor on their way over to the wall.

"You okay over there? I've never seen you so taken aback."

Taylor shook her head slowly.

"That was a lot more cheerfulness than I expected, that's all. I should have assumed from the exclamation point already embedded in the name of the place that this night would be full of people with that much enthusiasm, but wow, I still managed to underestimate it."

Avery patted her on the shoulder.

"Time for us to select our pottery, which you obviously wouldn't have known to do if she hadn't told you. Do you want a mug, a teapot, a cup and saucer, or—ooh, I need some new vases! I'm going to paint one of those."

Taylor picked a mug, like Avery knew that she would. Taylor didn't seem like a teapot or cup-and-saucer kind of person. She also didn't seem like a paint-your-own-pottery kind of person, which made Avery wonder what they were doing here. Did Taylor think *she* was a paint-your-own-pottery kind of person? She didn't think either one of them was that kind of person, for opposite reasons: Taylor was too cool, Avery was too bougie.

But this was the new Avery, remember? The new Avery flirted with people and made new friends and slept with women! She was going to paint her own pottery and like it!

Had Taylor thought of going to Let's Paint! tonight because she thought neither of them would be into it? Was she trying to create some distance between her and Avery?

Ugh, now she was being paranoid. Maybe Taylor thought it would be fun precisely because it wasn't the type of thing either of them would do on their own?

Yes, that was probably it.

"Put your name tag on." Avery nudged Taylor as they walked to the back of the room. There should be more name tag events in this world, it made everything easier.

"Right," Taylor said, and slapped her name tag on her chest.

When they joined the group at the big table in the back, Avery looked around for two seats together, but everyone was clustered down at one side of the table, and it would have looked weird and unfriendly for them to sit at the end. Plus, the whole point of this was to flirt, so they had to be in the middle of the action, right? She didn't need to sit next to Taylor.

Even though she wanted to.

She shook her head at herself and started to walk over to the other side of the table, when Taylor nudged her.

"Let's grab that corner," she said, and pointed to two unoccupied seats that someone had been standing in front of.

They slid into them, and Taylor raised her eyebrows at Avery in a way that Avery knew meant it was time for her to start flirting. Fine.

"Hi!" she said to the table at large. "I'm Avery, and this is my friend Taylor."

General hellos followed. The person next to Avery turned to her.

"Hi, I'm Cat, and my pronouns are she/they. What are you painting?"

Avery smiled at Cat. They had short, curly hair, with a handful of slightly faded pink streaks, and many piercings in their ears. Well, at least the ear closest to Avery.

"Hi, Cat, and I'm she/her. I'm painting a vase, but I'm not sure what I'm going to do with it yet. I guess it depends on where I want it; if I'm going to put it in my living room, I might want to paint it orange, or pink, or yellow . . . you know, something bright. But in my bedroom, I'd want it to be darker and moodier. What about you, have you done this before? What are you painting? Oh, a mug! What are you going to do to it?"

Avery was talking too much; she knew she was. Like in the car with Taylor. She had been nervous then, and she knew why, but she didn't know why she was nervous now. Earlier it had been because she was seeing Taylor for the first time since they'd slept together. But now, she had no idea; she'd stopped getting nervous about flirting lessons a while ago.

Right, that's why she was nervous. Because Taylor was right next to her. It had been one thing to flirt with Taylor watching before, but now it felt different.

She laughed at herself. It was just a weird fucking situation— she was sitting here, holding a piece of pottery, next to her friend whom she'd slept with a few days before, and said friend was there to help her try to get someone else into her bed? That was legitimately something she'd never come close to dealing with before.

At this point, she had the option to be stressed and feel weird about this, or just have fun with it. And she'd been stressed and felt weird for most of her life, so this time, she was just going to fucking have fun.

She'd just had sex with Taylor—*Taylor*—which gave her a huge ego boost, and her entire mission was to flirt with adorable Cat and paint pottery and drink some of this not-terrible white wine they'd just handed out? Excellent, she could do that. A month ago, she never would have even thought that. Maybe Cat wouldn't be interested, or wouldn't flirt back with her, or whatever—so what? She'd still had sex with Taylor a few days ago!

In the time she'd taken to have this slight mental breakdown and rebuild, Cat told her she hadn't decided what colors to paint the mug yet, but she knew she was going to make the inside a different color from the outside.

"I follow all of these pottery people online, and watching them throw things and paint is so soothing, and one of them always paints the inside of her mugs and bowls a contrasting color, and it looks so cool, so I thought I'd try that."

"What a great idea," Avery said. "Maybe pink, to go with your hair?"

Cat brushed back her hair and smiled shyly.

"Oh, thanks. I was actually kind of regretting these pink streaks; they seemed so bright, and I wasn't sure if they were really me, but I like that idea."

Avery tucked her own hair behind her ear.

"Well, I only just met you, so I can't tell you if they're 'you' or not, but I love the pink streaks."

Cat reached for the pot of pink paint.

"Thanks. It was a whole breakup-related hair thing, you know how it goes. I didn't want to cut it, like I did last time." She laughed and shook her head. "So, this time I got pink streaks, probably because I told my ex I was thinking about getting them and she told me she hated the color pink, and it was so infantilizing, so of course I got them to spite her. But then I regretted them. Classic story, I know."

"Sounds familiar," Avery said. "A while ago, I got some bookshelves, those white IKEA ones, and I wanted to paint them one color on the inside, in the back of the shelves, and then another color everywhere else. I'd seen the idea somewhere and I thought it would be cute. But my ex thought it was a stupid idea, that it would look bad and I'd be wasting my time. At the time, I said fine, never mind. But the week after I moved out, I painted those shelves."

"And," Cat asked, "how did they turn out?"

Avery sighed.

"I wish I could tell you that they turned out perfectly, but the first day I bought the wrong paint, which I realized when I—too late—googled 'how to paint IKEA shelves.' I had to go back and return that paint and buy a different kind. And then I taped the shelves wrong and had to retape after I'd already started painting. That was messy. But after a few other fits and starts—and many, many trips back and forth to the hardware store—I did it, and I actually love the way they look now. They were just what I pictured in my head."

Cat smiled at her.

"It sounds like they did turn out perfectly, then."

Avery stopped what she was doing and looked at Cat.

"You know what? You might be right about that."

Cat picked up a paintbrush.

"Amazing how it works out sometimes like that, isn't it? I'm sort of a recovering perfectionist, and I'm trying to get rid of those tendencies—at least for the things where it's okay to learn and play and mess up, you know what I mean? I can understand that you felt like it's not perfect because you had bumps in the road. But I'm trying to embrace that imperfection along the way is part of any good process."

Avery picked up her glass of wine—which already had paint on the outside of it—and held it up to Cat.

"That's probably the most profound statement ever uttered inside of Let's Paint! Cheers."

Cat blushed but reached for their own glass.

"Thanks, also cheers to my therapist, who I got that from. But hey, cheers to me for going to her."

Avery took another sip of her wine, and then looked down at her paintbrush.

"I also want to paint my apartment walls. I've been planning on it for a while. My landlord gave me permission and everything, but . . ."

"It seems like a big commitment?" Cat asked. "I get it."

As Avery and Cat sipped and painted and talked, Taylor chatted away with the woman next to her. Dark brown skin, short hair, bright red lipstick, very beautiful. Avery wondered—not for the first time—what Taylor's most recent ex looked like.

Not that it mattered. She was just curious.

Cat mixed a tiny bit of pink with some white paint, and then added one more drop of pink.

"Um," they said, staring down at the paint. "How long ago was your breakup?"

It was funny that Avery had to think about it now.

"In the spring, although it feels like it was a lifetime ago. I think I mentally disengaged with him long before I actually broke up with him, so it didn't take me that long to move past it, you know? Like, obviously things about it still affect me, but I feel like that's the case with every breakup. I'm so much happier without him that I've never questioned the breakup for a second. What about you?"

Cat sighed.

"Six weeks ago. I wish—" They broke off and then looked up at Avery.

"I probably shouldn't say this to someone I'm attracted to and am chatting with at a queer mixer and all, but I wish it had been easy for me like it's been for you."

Did she just say she was attracted to Avery? When she said "someone I'm attracted to," she meant Avery, didn't she? She must; she wasn't talking to anyone else right now.

Avery straightened herself up. Of course she was! People were attracted to her, even though it was hard for her to realize it. Taylor's friend Callie! Taylor's friend Liz! Taylor herself! And now Cat!

Cat, who was still talking about their breakup.

"The first few weeks I was . . . a mess, even though I knew it was the best decision for me. I'm doing a lot better now, which is why I'm here. I've been out a few times since the breakup—I mean, out on purpose, I work in wine, so sometimes work is going out, you know how it is."

Avery nodded.

"I'm an event planner, I definitely do."

Cat laughed.

"I bet you do. Anyway, I saw something about this on Instagram, and thought maybe painting pottery would be as soothing as watching people do it? At least, it seemed like a lower stress way to meet people. What about you, have you done this before?"

Avery shook her head.

"Nope, this was my friend Taylor's idea. I'm excited to see what her mug ends up looking like. So far, it doesn't seem like she's making much progress."

"I heard that," Taylor said. "And I am, too, making progress. I'm coming up with a plan. My new friend Blake over here is assisting me."

Avery leaned around Taylor to wave at Blake.

"Hi, Blake, I'm Avery, Taylor's friend. And this is my new friend Cat."

"Hi, Avery and Cat, nice to meet you," Blake said. "And yes, Taylor was about to do something very boring to her mug until I intervened."

"I'm trusting you, Blake," Taylor said. "Don't make me regret that."

Blake just laughed and gave Taylor a look that Avery one hundred percent recognized. It was a "damn, I'd love to see you naked" face. Avery mostly recognized it because she was sure she'd felt it on her own face many times while talking to Taylor, especially last Friday night.

"She's a ringer over here!" Taylor said, pointing at Blake. "An artist in our midst. Artists aren't allowed to come to things like this! It's like if Adele dropped in to a karaoke bar."

Blake dipped her paintbrush in the white paint, still laughing.

"As much as I enjoy being compared to Adele, Taylor is exaggerating. I'm not a potter, or even a painter—I'm a photographer. It's an art form, yes, but it's a lot different than this."

Taylor brushed that away.

"It's a type of art form, you just said it. You have an eye for these things, I very much do not. I'm grateful you're here; thanks for your help, I needed it."

Avery talked herself down from the flash of jealousy that she felt as Taylor flirted with Blake and Blake flirted back. *Avery* was the one who had wanted to keep the flirting lessons going after they'd slept together, remember? She knew what Taylor was like, and she'd told her—and Beth—that it would be fine. And it was, mostly. This was just weird for her.

On the bright side, this was the ideal flirting lesson, to be able to watch Taylor work her magic at close range. Maybe Taylor was doing this for her benefit!

Avery laughed at that patently ridiculous idea and joined the conversation again.

The four of them talked for the next hour as they painted. Avery's vase ended up being blue and white stripes with a blue interior. The stripes were slightly crooked, but Avery reminded herself that she was the only person who would notice. Taylor's mug was a sort of ombré reddish brown, which Blake assured them would be beautiful after it was fired.

When they finished placing their pieces on the shelf to be fired, Cat stopped her on the way back to the table.

"Do you want to get a drink sometime? Or coffee, or something?"

Avery wanted to turn to grin at Taylor in triumph. People asked Taylor out almost every time they went out; this time someone asked *her* out.

"Yeah, that would be great," she said instead. She tried to strike a balance in the tone of her voice between totally chill and incredibly enthusiastic but sounded robotic as a result. She smiled at Cat, hoping they hadn't noticed that. "Why don't I give you my number and we can figure out when and where?"

Cat pulled out their phone and typed in Avery's number, and then Avery felt a buzz in her pocket.

"There, I texted you, now you have mine, too," Cat said. "Um, well, see you soon, then."

"Looking forward to it."

She and Taylor fell into step on the way back to the car. Taylor turned to grin at her once they were a few doors away from Let's Paint!

"And you were skeptical of the pottery painting mixer."

"I was not!" Avery said. "I trusted you. I thought it wasn't very you, that's all."

Taylor's eyes were full of amusement.

"Mmm, likely story. Cat seemed pretty enamored of you."

Avery rolled her eyes at Taylor.

"I could say the same about you and Blake. Are you going to see her again? What's her story?"

Taylor shrugged.

"I don't know. She says she'll stop by Noble sometime to see me, so we'll see if that happens." She unlocked the car as they approached it and changed the subject. "I didn't know that you painted those bookshelves at your place."

"Oh yeah." Avery got into the car. "It started a whole decorating thing for me. I'd always wanted to have a nicer living space, one that felt cozy and also a little fancy, you know, but at first I couldn't afford anything—or at least, I thought I couldn't—and Derek was so boring and never wanted to do anything. I had followed all of these decorating people on Instagram for a while, and when I was still with him, it made me just feel sad and resentful. But when I moved out, I realized I could do something about it, so I did."

"But wait, you're telling me that all the furniture and decorations in your apartment are things you've gotten since the breakup? That was only a few months ago!"

"Yeah." It felt good that Taylor seemed so impressed. "I haunted garage sales and antique fairs and Facebook Marketplace for furniture and stuff, and I found a ton of good deals. I was slightly obsessed for a while there."

Taylor smiled at that.

"And your place is so cute now. At least, what I remember of it." She sent a sideways grin to Avery, who let herself grin back.

"Thank you, I appreciate that. I worked hard on it."

"Have you really been thinking about painting it?" Taylor asked.

"Yeah, my landlord said she doesn't care as long as I paint it white before I move out. She didn't paint before I moved in; I was kind of in a rush to move in, so I told her I'd do it, and managed to negotiate being able to paint any color. But I've been frozen on which color, so I haven't done anything. But lately . . ."

"You've been thinking what the hell?" Taylor asked.

Avery smiled and nodded.

"It's silly—no wait, I'm going to stop saying that, let me start again. There's this artist I follow on Instagram, and she always says, 'It's just paint.' And I realized that's true. It's just paint! It's not permanent. If I hate it, I can paint over it."

"So why haven't you done it yet?" Taylor asked.

Avery glared at her.

"I'm getting there, okay? I even bought a few testers of paint colors and some brushes to see what colors I like. I just haven't . . . quite put it on the walls yet."

Taylor let out a long, deep sigh.

"Do you need me to come over and stand there while you open those cans of paint and try them out on your walls? Say the word, and I'll do it."

Avery didn't hesitate.

"How about right now?"

Taylor's head turned with a jerk.

"Right now?"

"I'm all inspired after painting that pottery! But I know if I'm alone, I'll chicken out." Taylor didn't think she was trying something, did she? No, she'd made it clear nothing further would happen between them. Friends helped their friends paint, no big deal. "But if you can't tonight—"

Taylor laughed.

"No, you're right, you will chicken out if you're alone. Okay, let's do it. Can we pick up some takeout on the way, though? The wine was good at that thing, but the snacks were subpar."

"And there were hardly any of them! How about pizza?"

TWELVE

TAYLOR WOKE UP THE NEXT MORNING IN AVERY'S BED.

She was snug under Avery's linen sheets and fluffy comforter. A gentle breeze blew in from the open window. A soft, herbal scent was in the air. Avery's arm was draped over her hip, with Avery's hand resting at the top of her thigh. Taylor sighed softly and let her eyes flutter closed.

They snapped open again. She'd woken up in Avery's bed. Again. After sleeping with Avery. Again.

She hadn't meant to. They'd painted pottery, for the love of God! Nothing against pottery or painting it—she was sure there were plenty of sexy potters out there—but she had not expected anything remotely sexy or flirtatious to happen at Let's Paint! A store with a built-in exclamation point didn't seem like it would be a hotbed of sexual tension.

And yet she'd ended up in Avery's bed anyway.

Taylor had been so proud as she'd listened to Avery almost effortlessly chat up the pink-haired lovelorn Cat, who responded to it like she was a flower and Avery was the sun. Taylor hadn't been jealous as she'd listened to Avery's very Avery way of flirting. She was perfectly happy to sit next to Avery all night, to listen to their conversation so she could give Avery tips later, all the while remembering how Avery's skin felt, how pink her bottom lip got after Taylor kissed her, how hard her nipples were between Taylor's fingers, how soft and sweet and surprised her sighs and moans were. As she'd listened to Avery talk to Cat, she was impressed with how far Avery had come and, fine, a little smug that while Cat looked at Avery like she wanted to eat her up, Taylor already had.

But damn, had she felt triumphant when Avery left with *her*, and not Cat.

Avery sighed softly in her sleep. Taylor really had only meant to come back here last night to help Avery paint. Seriously. But then Avery had changed into a thin old tank top and shorts to paint—while making yet another joke about clothes to get dirty in—and she had looked so fucking hot in them. And after they'd painted the test patches in the bedroom, she'd cocked her head in the cutest way to look at the different shades of pale green, and Taylor hadn't been able to help herself. She'd kissed her. She had to.

If Avery had stopped her then, or said, *Are you sure?* or *I thought we decided* . . . maybe that would have been it.

But Avery had responded to her without hesitation. She'd kissed her back, this time with the knowledge and self-assurance of recognition, of familiarity. They'd moved quickly from kissing standing up with their clothes on, to kissing standing up with their clothes off, to kissing on the bed with their clothes off, to fucking for hours.

Now it was morning, and here she was curled up in Avery's

bed, where she'd never intended to be again. And she wanted to stay right where she was.

And you know what? Nothing was stopping her from doing exactly that.

She felt a stirring next to her, then Avery's hand moved from its perfect spot on her thigh and slid backward. Taylor put her hand on it to stop it from moving to Avery's side of the bed.

"Oh, you're awake," Avery said. "I was trying not to wake you up."

Taylor turned over to face her. This time, Avery hadn't done her middle-of-the-night washing of her face and moving their clothes into neat piles. She had taken out her contacts and put her hair up in a bun, but that had been after round one last night. Taylor liked her like this, a little squinty, with creases in her cheek from the pillow, not quite put together, but still Avery. But then, Taylor was discovering she liked Avery most ways.

"Good morning," Taylor said. She moved her hand up to rest on Avery's bare hip.

"Good morning," Avery said, a sleepy smile on her lips.

"We find ourselves here again," Taylor said.

"We do," Avery said. "I hope this doesn't mean you have to plan another baby shower."

Taylor laughed.

"No, thank goodness. Just the one."

Avery didn't make any move to get up, and neither did Taylor. They just lay there, looking at each other, Taylor's hand caressing Avery's skin.

"What are we going to do about this?" Avery finally asked.

"I have an idea," Taylor said, moving her hand up along Avery's torso. "What if we . . . kept doing this?"

"What?" Avery started to sit up, but Taylor pulled her back down.

"Hey, I'm comfortable here," Taylor said.

Avery laughed.

"So am I. Sorry, I was just surprised. That's not what I expected you to say. So . . . what, you're saying you want to be friends with benefits, or something? Because I—"

Taylor shook her head.

"I don't believe in friends with benefits. Either you like each other and you're fucking, which means you're dating, or you don't like each other and you're fucking, which means you're just fucking. If you try to pretend there's a middle ground, it all goes to shit. I'm saying I like you, and I want to keep hanging out with you, and I definitely want to keep fucking you." Her hand moved up to the side of Avery's soft, pillowy breast.

Avery stared at her for a second without saying anything.

"That's *really* not what I expected you to say. On Saturday morning, you said—"

"I say lots of things. Forget what I said on Saturday morning. I changed my mind."

Avery's eyes narrowed.

"Saturday was only four days ago. Are you sure about that?"

Taylor nodded.

"I'm sure."

And she was. Not that her reasons from Saturday weren't still valid, they were. But sometimes things defied reason. Plus, those had been the reasons *not* to sleep with Avery again. There were probably just as many reasons that she *should* sleep with Avery again, and continue to sleep with Avery.

For instance, she had a hell of a good time with Avery, in and out of bed; Avery always surprised her, usually in a good way; she always enjoyed Avery's company whether they were doing fun things (going to the bookstore, dancing) or boring things (loading boxes at the winery, trivia, fucking pottery painting); the sex was good and had the potential to be great; Avery made her laugh all the damn time, and vice versa; and she hadn't been this comfortable in someone else's bed in a very long time.

"Hmm," Avery said. "You sound so definite."

Taylor smiled as she looked at naked, tousled Avery, with that firm, daytime Avery sound in her voice. The contrast delighted her.

"I am," she said, moving her hand again. "But I'm just me. How do you feel? On Saturday, you said you weren't ready to date anyone, I don't want to push you. What do you want to do?"

Avery's eyes half closed, then opened.

"I was going to say we should stop the flirting lessons, because it was going to be too hard for me to keep hanging out with you once we'd done this again. But that was when I thought . . ."

Her voice trailed off.

"And now?" Taylor prompted her. She thought Avery wanted the same thing she did, especially since Avery was still naked in bed with her right now, but she couldn't be sure.

"I can't concentrate while you're doing that!" Avery said, looking down at Taylor's thumb, lazily moving back and forth across her nipple.

"Does that mean you want me to stop?" Taylor asked, looking at Avery's hard nipple, not stopping the motion of her thumb.

"No!" Avery said in such an irritated voice that Taylor leaned forward to kiss her. Avery wrapped her arm around Taylor's neck and kissed her back hard.

"Is that my answer, or do we need to talk about it some more?" Taylor asked.

Avery pulled back and looked at her for a minute without saying anything. Taylor waited for her answer.

"Mmm, yeah, we probably should talk about it some more," Avery finally said. She ran a hand up Taylor's inner thighs and pushed her gently over so she was on her back. "I think we have a lot to talk about, don't you?"

Taylor looked up at Avery, whose lips hovered over hers, and whose hand rested in between Taylor's thighs.

"Like what?" Taylor asked her.

"Well, dating sounds great, because I like you, too, and I certainly want to keep fucking you," Avery said. God, why was it so hot to hear Avery talking even a little dirty?

"Excellent," Taylor said. "Why does it seem like you're about to say 'but'?"

"But," Avery said, and Taylor groaned. Only partly because Avery's fingers were gently caressing her. "I'll be sad to give up our flirting lessons."

Avery's fingers were still softly moving up and down. Too softly. Oh my God, the bitch was teasing her.

Okay, that was fair. She probably deserved it.

Taylor grinned at her.

"Oh, we don't have to give those up. And now you can practice on me all you want."

Avery nodded.

"You bring up a great point. I have a suggestion. Maybe part of that 'practice,' as you call it, can also be sex lessons."

"Sex lessons?" Taylor started to sit up, and this time Avery pushed her back down.

"Yes, sex lessons." Avery slid one finger inside of her, and Taylor opened her legs wider. "You see, as I said last time, I don't really know what I'm doing here—"

"You seem to have a pretty good handle on it," Taylor said.

Avery smiled at her.

"I appreciate that, but you know me, I always strive to do better," she said. "Plus, I have a lot to learn about what you like."

Taylor settled back and enjoyed the feeling of Avery's fingers inside of her, sliding slowly up and down, circling, dipping in and out.

"Hmm, well, something that you may or may not know about me is that I love morning sex," Taylor said.

Avery moved her other hand up Taylor's torso.

"See? I didn't know that. What do you like so much about it?"

Taylor's eyes closed for a second as Avery's thumb brushed across her nipple.

"Mmm, just about everything. It feels sort of illicit, like we're supposed to be doing something else, but instead we're in bed together, and it's only ever because we want to be. It always feels either lazy and comfortable, like we have all the time in the world, like right now, or it's rushed and urgent, because we both have to get somewhere but we desperately need to fuck first, and that's hot as hell. Either way, I'm having a great time."

She watched Avery as she talked. Avery was so focused on her, so intent on feeling her way around Taylor's body, and Taylor fucking loved it. Her eyes were closed, but Taylor could tell she was listening to her. She couldn't remember the last time someone had really paid attention to her the way Avery did. It felt good. All of this felt good. Taylor was suddenly very pleased with her snap decision to keep this up with Avery.

"Well," Avery said as she moved down Taylor's body. "My goal is definitely for you to have a great time."

She pushed the covers back, and Taylor opened her legs all the way so that Avery could settle in between them. She leaned back on Avery's big pillows and looked down at Avery. She loved this view. She was glad the pillows were so fluffy so she could watch her.

Avery started off slowly, just by dropping small kisses on the insides of her thighs, and then a few eager licks along Taylor's lips. But soon, her tongue danced in quick circles around Taylor's clit, and those very talented fingers of hers moved in and out, at first slowly, but then faster. She pinched Taylor's nipple softly; when Taylor gasped at the sensation, she could feel Avery smile. Then she moved to really concentrate on Taylor's clit, and Taylor slid her fingers into Avery's hair. Taylor moved against her as she licked and sucked, and then they moved together, faster and faster as the pressure built inside her, until Avery sucked just a little harder, and the whole world exploded around her. Taylor arched her back and held on to Avery, who kept licking and sucking her as the waves of pleasure shook her body, until finally they both collapsed against the bed.

Avery crawled up next to her, and Taylor pulled her into her arms.

"That was worth another baby shower," Taylor said. "At least."

Avery laughed and stretched out next to Taylor.

"Let's wait until after you've done one baby shower to say things like that, but I very much appreciate the sentiment."

AVERY RESTED HER HEAD NEXT TO TAYLOR'S. SHE FELT TRIUM-phant, sexy, on top of the world.

Taylor grinned at her.

"I'll update you after I do the one."

God, that grin just did things to her. Now she didn't have to hide that Taylor's grin did things to her, or that she looked forward to seeing her every Tuesday, or how much she had wanted to have sex with her again after Friday night. She'd pretended—to Beth, sure, but also to herself—that she didn't care, that one night was fine, that she didn't really want or need to do it again. None of that had been true.

She kissed Taylor softly, and then sat up.

"I have a meeting soon, unfortunately. I'm going to make coffee, you want some?"

Taylor opened her mouth, then stopped herself. Avery laughed.

"Oh, that's right, I forgot, you're a coffee snob, aren't you? Fine, you can come into the kitchen with me and look at my coffee-making apparatus and see if it's good enough for you."

Taylor sat up and crossed her arms over her chest.

"I wasn't going to say anything! I was just going to say, 'Yes, I'd love some coffee, thank you!'" She swung her legs off the bed. "But since you offered . . ."

Avery laughed out loud as she pulled a robe on. She took another one out of her closet and tossed it to Taylor.

"Here. It gets chilly in my kitchen in the mornings."

Taylor shrugged the robe on and followed her into the kitchen.

"What else do you have today other than that meeting?"

"A bunch of calls all day, and I'm having dinner with Luke." Where she would probably tell Luke about whatever this was going on between her and Taylor. Would Taylor have a problem with that?

Taylor didn't react. Instead, she examined Avery's coffee maker, and then sniffed her bag of ground coffee. Maybe she hadn't heard her.

"Not terrible, but can I—"

Avery took a step back.

"Yes, you make the coffee."

Taylor opened a drawer and pulled out a measuring spoon.

"Dinner with Luke, huh?" So she had heard. "What does he know about all of this?"

Avery took the oat milk out of the fridge.

"Nothing yet. I mean, I told him about the flirting lessons, but not . . . about Friday night. I haven't seen him since then, and this felt like an in-person conversation."

Taylor laughed as she measured far more coffee than Avery would have into the filter.

"I wish I could be a fly on the wall when you tell him. He's going to flip out."

Oh good, Taylor wasn't going to be weird about her telling Luke. Not that she thought Taylor would be, but you never knew.

"He sure is," Avery said. "Don't worry, I'll tell you what he says."

"YOU'RE DOING WHAT WITH TAYLOR?" LUKE HALF SHRIEKED. Avery was glad she'd decided to have this part of the conversation in the car.

"I mean, do you want me to go into detail, or . . . ?"

Luke shook his head vehemently.

"No, that's not what I meant, you know what I meant!"

Avery giggled. She couldn't help it.

"Yes, I know what you meant, but I'm pretty sure you know what the word *dating* means."

Luke glared at her.

"That's not how you said it. You made this dramatic pause before you said *dating*, like there was another word you were thinking about putting in there and didn't."

Avery giggled again. It was way more fun to tell Luke about this than she'd thought it would be.

"Well, yes, we did . . . another word before we decided we would start dating, but you get weird when I tell you about doing that word, so I didn't mention it."

"*I* get weird? You get weird, too! Remember when I—" Luke shook his head again. "You're trying to get me sidetracked. Back to the point. You and Taylor? I thought she was just teaching you how to flirt? I thought you knew you didn't want to have anything with her because you knew she was kind of a heartbreaker? What happened to all of that?"

Right, this was why she'd been worried about telling Luke.

"I guess her flirting lessons worked too well." Avery shrugged. Luke looked at her. She should have known she couldn't get away with that with him.

"Okay fine. Nothing happened to all of that, it's still true. But really, this is just a casual thing. She doesn't do serious, I know this, she knows I know this, but that's okay, I don't want a serious relationship right now anyway. We have a lot of fun together, and when we did you-know-what, that was a lot of fun, too, so we decided to keep doing both things. Actually . . ." She let out a sigh. "After we did you-know-what the first time, we both said we shouldn't do it again, and we would go back to the flirting lessons, but that didn't last very long, so we decided to go with it. Don't freak out about this. I'm a big girl, you know."

"I'm not freaking out," Luke said. "Taylor's great, I like her a lot, you know I do. I just don't want you—"

"To get hurt, I know," she said. "But Taylor's the first person in a long time who I've dated that I've had actual fun with. I don't expect this relationship to lead anywhere, it's not like you and Margot; I know what Taylor's like. I'm not going to be one of those people who thinks I can change Taylor, I swear. But it's been a hard few years; I want to keep having fun."

The worried look faded—a little—from Luke's face.

"I'm glad you're having fun," he said. "I want you to keep having fun, too." He opened the car door. "Come on, let's go get something to eat, I'm starving."

Avery got out and fell in step with Luke as they walked toward the restaurant.

"Not coincidentally," she said, "she's the first person in a long time I've dated who you like."

Luke grinned at her.

"That hadn't escaped my attention, either." He threw his arm around her and pulled her in for a hug. "I'm really happy for you," he said. "I should have started with that. I haven't seen you this relaxed and happy in a long time. You used to laugh like that all the time, and it's only now, seeing you do it again, that I realized you'd stopped. I'm glad that laugh of yours is back. I'm glad you're with someone who makes you laugh like that."

Avery stopped walking and hugged him back.

"Yeah," she said. "Me, too." She took a step away from him. "Now can you stop it with all this mushy stuff and buy me some tacos?"

Luke opened the door of the restaurant with a flourish.

"Absolutely."

TAYLOR WALKED INTO THE KITCHEN AT NOBLE FAMILY VINE-yards on Thursday morning and found Elliot at the coffee maker. She breathed a sigh of relief.

"Oh great, you made the coffee."

Elliot pulled out a mug and poured her a cup.

"Finished brewing a few minutes ago; I was late today."

Taylor picked up the mug and breathed in that wonderful, strong dark coffee smell.

"I'm glad you got here before Margot, anyway."

"He did *not* get here before Margot," Margot said, walking in with a thermos in her hand. "Margot has simply ceded the control of the coffee maker to the two of you and brings her own from home. Did you think I didn't know you both rush to make coffee before me so you could make it to your weird specifications? I know you weigh out the coffee by the gram, I refuse. I've seen the looks you share when I put milk and sugar in my coffee. I know when I'm outnumbered."

Taylor and Elliot looked at each other, and then all three of them burst out laughing.

"Sorry, sis," Elliot said. "We didn't want to hurt your feelings, we just both like each other's coffee better than . . ."

"Better than mine, I know, I know. Anyway, good morning to both of you. Busy day all around today." She turned to Taylor. "Speaking of, we have a few VIPs dropping in later. Definitely not the day for it, of course, but what can you do?"

Taylor followed Margot back to her office, her coffee mug in hand.

"They always pick the worst possible days to drop in, but at least it isn't Saturday."

Margot held up her hand.

"Bite your tongue, I'm sure some will come on Saturday, too."

Taylor made a face. Margot was right. It was August and high tourist season, and every day was booked solid at the winery. Which was great for the health of the business but made it a very busy time for all of them. And probably a bad time to ask Margot about the shower. Unfortunately, she had to do it.

"Oh, um, there was something I wanted to ask you about," she said.

Margot looked at her warily.

"Go for it."

Hmm, she'd possibly picked the wrong morning to make fun of her boss's coffee. Doing it right before asking her if she could host a baby shower at the winery perhaps wasn't the best idea. Why did she always have to be a smartass at exactly the wrong time? Classic Taylor.

"So, I'm hosting my best friend's baby shower—yes, I see your face, it's true—and I was wondering if I could do it here at the winery? Outside in the garden, if you think that would work? I understand if we're too busy, or you think we're not ready for events, though."

"Oh." Margot's brow cleared. "I thought from that look on your face that you needed time off this weekend or something. Yeah, sure, of course. That's perfect, actually; I've been wanting to have more events here, and that'll be a good test run to do something smaller than the anniversary party. And with you in charge, I won't be stressed about it."

That had been exactly what Avery had said Margot would say. Not that it took mind reading to know that; if she'd been thinking straight, she would have thought of this herself.

"Fantastic, thank you," she said to Margot. "That'll make this whole thing much easier."

Margot went over to her big wall calendar.

"When and what time?"

Taylor pulled out her phone.

"Great question. Let me ask Erica. I'm guessing sometime in September?"

TAYLOR

> margot said yes to having the shower at noble, what did you say were the best dates for you again?

She might as well slip some other news in, too.

TAYLOR

> fyi, avery's going to help me with the shower, she's great at this stuff. she'll make sure i won't just set a case of wine down with a congrats sign and call it a day. by the way, we're dating now

Maybe she was being petty to ignore what Erica had said about Sloane helping out, but whatever.

Erica's first text came in right after Taylor pressed send on her second.

ERICA

> Yay! Tell Margot I said thank you! I was targeting the last weekend of September! Late afternoon? I know Sloane was excited to host it at her house, so if it doesn't work to do it at the winery, then we could still do it that weekend at Sloane's . . .

Over her dead body.

"Does the last weekend of September work?" she asked Margot. "Sometime in the afternoon? It'll be hot then, but there's shade over in that garden area."

And then the second text arrived.

ERICA

Excuse me what??? When did this happen? What happened to she'll fall for me too hard and I'm not ready for anything and neither is she and on and on?

Taylor slid her phone back into her pocket.

Margot picked up a pencil as Taylor's pocket buzzed. She ignored it.

"Works for me. Let's say Sunday afternoon? Obviously, no charge for you; you're doing me a favor. This will be a good dry run for events here."

Taylor saluted Margot.

"I'll make sure all goes well, boss, don't worry." She picked up her coffee mug. "See you later, you know where to find me."

Margot sat down at her desk.

"Holler if you need me."

By the time she'd gotten into the tasting room, her pocket had buzzed two more times.

ERICA

Helloooooo

Omg you cannot drop something
like that and leave me hanging
like this I am going to murder
you

Taylor Elizabeth Cameron!

When Erica started using her full name, she was approximately twelve seconds from calling her.

TAYLOR

i was checking with margot about the
date! she says the last sunday of
september works

and yeah i remember what i said, i
changed my mind

i like her, what can i say?

She knew that would disarm Erica. But it also had the advantage of being true.

ERICA

I can't believe you didn't tell me about
this immediately

Awww ok

> But wow I should have bet you that if you actually started dating Avery, you'd have to be godmother. Lost opportunity on my part

Taylor laughed out loud at that.

TAYLOR

> you did yourself a favor there. imagine me as your child's godmother. you can't, can you?

> also you need to tell me who i should invite to the shower and all of that

Erica took the Avery thing better than she'd expected. These texts hadn't had the judgmental tone she'd had sometimes lately. A lot of times lately.

ERICA

> Maybe you and I and Sloane and Avery can all get together to plan the shower!

That was honestly the last thing she wanted to do.

TAYLOR

> sounds good. ok winery is opening in fifteen minutes, talk later

ERICA

Ok! And I'll send you an email with an invite list spreadsheet and my registry links later today!

An invite list spreadsheet. Oof. Thank God she had Avery to help with this, otherwise she would be very bitter about losing this bet.

A few hours and many winery guests later, she heard the chime of the tasting room door and looked up, her customer service smile on. And then she relaxed.

"Did you hear that it was busy today and decide to come by to help out?" she asked.

Luke grinned back at her.

"No such luck, I'm here to pick up Margot. Her car's in the shop so she's borrowing mine."

Taylor waved him toward the employees-only door.

"You know your way around; head on back to her office. Good to see you."

Luke took a step in that direction, but stopped and came back over to her at the bar. The grin on his face faded into a tentative smile. Ah. Right.

"She told you," Taylor said.

Luke nodded.

"She did. I think it's great. She seems really happy."

Taylor raised an eyebrow at him.

"But?" She liked Luke a lot, and she knew the feeling was mutual, but she could tell he had something else to say.

He shook his head.

"But nothing. Avery seems happy, and that's the most important thing. The only important thing, really." He paused for a second. "I really care about her, you know."

"I know," she said. "It's nice."

Luke smiled faintly, but went on. "Avery has been there for me . . . anytime I needed her, and a few times when I thought I didn't need her but was wrong. She doesn't ask for help much, but when she does, I'd do anything to help her. She's a great person. A special person."

This conversation should feel strange, but somehow it didn't.

"I know she is," she said.

Luke looked at her hard.

"I really hope you do," he said. "She's gotten pretty hurt in the past. I don't want her to get hurt again."

Why did he assume that she would hurt Avery? What had she done to deserve that?

Plenty of things, actually. Fine, Luke, that was fair.

It was very sweet that Luke cared this much about Avery to corner her for a little talk. If Luke were a different kind of guy, she'd call this a warning. But then, if Luke were that kind of guy, Avery wouldn't be his best friend.

"I know you don't," she said. "I don't want her to get hurt, either."

Luke nodded once. Twice.

"Okay." He took a step back. "I should go get Margot. I just . . . I just wanted to say that."

Taylor grinned at him.

"Okay," she said, slightly mimicking his tone of voice. She hoped it would make him smile, and it did. "Good talk."

Luke nodded again.

"Good talk."

He disappeared through the employees-only door, and Taylor smiled to herself. That had been very sweet. She couldn't wait to tell Avery about it.

Though Avery would probably think Luke was being overprotective, when he was just being a good friend. On second thought, that conversation could stay between her and Luke.

THIRTEEN

FRIDAY NIGHT, AVERY HAD PLANS WITH TAYLOR. A DATE WITH
Taylor? Yes. Right? What should they do? Where should they go?
Taylor had planned all their flirting lessons; it was her turn to plan
something, now that they were officially . . . whatever they were.
She wanted to surprise her, do something Taylor wouldn't expect.
But what? She racked her brain for the answer.

When it finally came to her, late on Thursday, she laughed out
loud. Then she texted Taylor.

AVERY

We still on for tomorrow? What time?

Taylor texted back right away.

TAYLOR

yes. 6:30 or 7?

AVERY

> Great. What's your address? I'll pick you up at 7. Wear something that makes you feel powerful.

She pressed send before she could chicken out.

Almost immediately, the three little dots popped up to show her Taylor was typing a response.

TAYLOR

> turning the tables on me, i like it

> and that's a challenge if I've ever heard one. i guess we'll see if I'm up to it

Avery could see the amused, slightly wry look on Taylor's face as she typed that. She grinned at her phone. She was pretty sure Taylor was up to the challenge.

ON THE WAY TO TAYLOR'S PLACE, AVERY SECOND-GUESSED herself. Would Taylor find this idea as fun as she did? What if she thought it was stupid? She wouldn't say it, but Avery would know. Shit, she should have done something easy like a sports game or something.

Did Taylor even like sports? Not that she knew of, but still.

Well, it was too late now.

Her phone buzzed as she pulled up in front of Taylor's building.

TAYLOR

i'm sure you're going to get here early. i'll be outside in five minutes, which is ten minutes early for me, and ten minutes late for you

Avery looked at the clock: 6:55 p.m.

AVERY

Just got here. No rush!

Taylor walked outside seven minutes later. She had on jeans, a studded belt, combat boots, and a white sleeveless shirt. She saw Avery, smiled wide, and walked over to the car.

"Hi," she said as she got into the car. She leaned over and kissed Avery on the lips, and Avery kissed her back. They were definitely *something* now, if Taylor greeted her with a kiss on the lips like it was an everyday kind of thing.

"So, I didn't say 'dress like the hottest thing in Napa Valley,' but I'm going to thank you for doing that nonetheless," Avery said.

Taylor smirked at her.

"Where do you think I get my power?"

Avery glanced down, and Taylor laughed.

"No, not from my boobs! Okay, not *only* from my boobs."

Avery could feel herself blushing.

"That's not what I was looking at! I was looking at your whole outfit—not just your boobs! Just to see what you meant."

Taylor's boobs did look great, though. But then, they always did.

Taylor just laughed and put a hand on Avery's thigh.

"I can't wait to find out where we're going."

Avery started the car, even though the pressure of Taylor's hand on her thigh distracted her so much she forgot where they were going for a second.

"Don't you have any guesses?"

She could feel Taylor smile at her, even as she looked straight ahead.

"What do I get if I figure it out?"

Avery pretended to think about that.

"Hmmm. I think it's only fair that if you figure it out, I'll go home with you tonight."

Taylor's smile got bigger.

"Okay, then, what happens if I don't figure it out?"

Avery put her hand on top of Taylor's.

"Well, that would be very sad for you. I guess, as a consolation, I'll go home with you tonight."

Taylor let out a deep sigh.

"Oh wow, so the stakes are high, then. Let's see . . . powerful . . . maybe it's a rock climbing gym? But you don't seem like a 'rock climbing gym date' kind of person. Do you think *I'm* a rock climbing gym kind of person?" Taylor paused and looked at her. "No, impossible that you'd think that. Okay, not rock climbing."

Avery smiled but said nothing.

"You're not going to tell me? Okay, that's fair. But I've convinced myself that it's not rock climbing. Maybe a butchering class? I have always wanted to learn how to do that, so good for you if it is."

Avery tucked butchering class away in her mind for the future.

"Hmmm," Taylor went on. "Butchering class is a promising idea, but I don't know if they even have them this late in the day. I feel like butchers have to get up early, like bakers and farmers, though I have no idea if that's true. But if I'm right about that, it's not a butchering class. Maybe, like, woodworking? You need to be powerful to do that . . . though I feel like you would have given me a different prompt if it was woodworking."

Avery raised an eyebrow.

"Like what?"

Taylor shook her head.

"I didn't think you'd say something phallic, please, you would never. Maybe something about almond or olive or walnut or something to make me think you were talking about food."

Avery thought about that for a second, then nodded.

"That could be the kind of thing that I would do."

Taylor smiled.

"So, no woodworking, then. I didn't really think it was that, but it's good to check something off a list." She held up a finger. "Ooh, powerful: superheroes are powerful. Is it the new superhero movie? You know I love those things. And it has Anna Gardiner in it, and you know how I feel about her."

Avery did know. She'd thought of that and then rejected it for being too obvious. Plus, you didn't really get to talk during a movie, and one thing she liked about going out with Taylor was getting to talk to her all night. But now she regretted her decision; Taylor sounded so excited by the idea of going to see that movie. Maybe she should have gone for the obvious choice.

"Or . . ." By the time Avery had parked her car, Taylor had come up with three other options, none of which was right. She looked around when Avery turned off the car, and Avery touched her hand.

"The bad news is that you didn't guess it. But the good news is that means I'm coming home with you tonight."

Taylor leaned over and kissed her softly on the lips.

"You are an excellent consolation prize." And then she kissed her again. And again.

"Don't you want to know where we're going?" Avery asked in her ear.

Taylor brushed her thumb against Avery's lip.

"Right now? Not particularly."

After not long enough, Avery made herself pull away.

"Come on," she said to Taylor. "We don't want to be late."

Taylor tucked Avery's hair back behind her ear and opened her door.

"Fine, but only because you just told me that you're coming home with me later."

Avery laughed as she got out of the car.

"I was always coming home with you later."

Taylor reached for her hand.

"I didn't want to take that for granted."

That look on Taylor's face, that frank, honest tone in her voice, made Avery believe, maybe for the first time, that she and Taylor were really doing this. She'd been a lot more anxious about tonight than she'd recognized: anxious to plan a good night for Taylor, anxious to show that she was good enough and cute enough and cool enough to actually date Taylor and not just be her pathetic bisexual buddy who didn't know how to flirt with women, anxious that Taylor would realize that she was boring Avery Jensen and wonder what she'd ever seen in her.

But in all of that anxiety, she'd forgotten who Taylor was. Taylor liked her, just for her. Taylor didn't care if she was cool or not, because Taylor herself was too cool to worry about what other people thought. And Taylor wouldn't care what she'd planned, she'd have fun no matter what they did.

Avery squeezed Taylor's hand.

"It's this way," she said. "Let's go."

They were at the end of the block before Taylor saw the sign. She burst out laughing.

"You didn't," Taylor said.

Avery grinned at her. That had been the exact reaction she'd been hoping for.

"I sure did," she said. She opened the door of Axes R Us, and ushered Taylor inside.

Avery felt very smug as the guy at the front desk checked them in, led them to their lane, and gave them the whole safety rundown.

Finally, he left them alone in their lane with the huge target at one end and two big axes at the other. Taylor looked at her with such warmth in her eyes that Avery felt a fluttering in her chest. Ah, that's why they called it butterflies.

"I'm going to be laughing about this forever, you know that, right?" Taylor said.

Avery took a step back and picked up an ax.

"I certainly hope so."

Taylor picked up her own ax and weighed it in her hands.

"This thing is somehow both heavier and bigger than I expected. I don't know why, I guess anyone would expect an ax to be big and heavy, but the whole 'throwing' aspect made me think it wouldn't be that bad. I guess I'm not a very good lesbian if I didn't already know that."

Avery put her ax down and swung her arm around to loosen it up. She had a feeling Taylor would be good at this; she didn't want to embarrass herself.

"Okay," she said. "Let's do this."

Taylor held up a hand.

"Wait. We need some stakes. What does the winner get?"

Avery had an idea about that. But before she could say anything, Taylor laughed.

"Not that, you dirty girl. I saw that look on your face. *That's* a given."

Avery blushed, then she thought for a second.

"I know. Loser has to get up tomorrow and go get the winner the breakfast of her choice."

Taylor held out a hand.

"Done. Perfect. You're very good at this."

Avery tried not to show how flattered she was by that, and then realized how silly it was that her first instinct was to not let Taylor know she was pleased by a compliment. Right, she was doing that thing again, where she hid her feelings. Maybe she could try to practice being more open about them with Taylor, since everything with Taylor was just practice anyway. It was practice dating, not serious dating. Could she practice this, too?

She smiled at Taylor after probably too long a pause.

"Thank you. I like it when you tell me I'm good at things." Wow, that sounded awkward. She'd ignore that for now. "No more delay tactics. Let's do this."

As it turned out, they were both terrible at throwing axes. Avery's first throw made it only halfway to the target, which made Taylor laugh out loud—something that would have infuriated her from Derek, but with Taylor, she just laughed, too. Taylor's first throw was better, but it still came nowhere near hitting anything.

Avery picked up the ax for the second time.

"I think I need to do more of a windup." She swung the ax around a few times, but right when she was about to release it, she was startled by a grunt from the lane next to theirs.

"What—" She looked over and saw two very burly men in that lane. Taylor turned to her, eyes full of laughter.

"I think we've got some actual wannabe lumberjacks over there."

"UUUUUUHHHHHH." One of them released his ax, and it flew across the room straight into the target. Avery pressed her lips together so she wouldn't burst out laughing as she watched him walk to the target and pull out his ax.

"You're staring," Taylor said. "Stop looking at them."

Avery turned back to Taylor, who was giggling so hard Avery thought she was about to fall over.

"I was trying to learn some techniques," Avery said. "They can hit the target, at least."

Taylor walked over to Avery and put her mouth close to her ear.

"Learn all the techniques you want, just save the noises for later."

The low, throaty sound of her voice was so fucking sexy that Avery wanted to throw the stupid ax down immediately and drag Taylor back home.

She put her hand on Taylor's waist and smiled at her.

"I look forward to that, and to learning other kinds of techniques."

Taylor looked at her with such heat in her eyes that if she said the word, Avery actually *would* drop her ax and drag her home immediately.

"I'm counting on it," Taylor said. "Now." She gestured at the ax in Avery's hand. "Show me what you've got."

She took a step back, and Avery went through her ridiculous windup routine again. But since she'd seen the grunter do it, she felt more justified. When she released her ax this time, it flew toward the target.

"Ah!" she yelled as her ax hit the very edge of the target.

"UUUUGGGGGGGGH," the second burly man grunted as he threw his ax.

That time, Avery and Taylor both dissolved into uproarious, almost silent, laughter.

The four of them—Avery, Taylor, and their two grunting buddies—kept throwing axes for about an hour. Surprising herself, and, she was pretty sure, Taylor, Avery handily won their bet, though Taylor did at least hit the target twice.

"Was it as good as you wanted it to be?" Avery asked as they walked to the car.

Taylor grinned at her and put her arm around Avery's waist.

"Better. The grunting really took it over the top. Now I understand why people like it. It's weirdly fun to throw axes around. I don't need to do it again—my ego isn't up to that—but I get it." She looked sideways at Avery. "We *are* getting something to eat now, right? After all that exercise, I'm starving."

Avery shook her head slowly and took a step back.

"I'm honestly insulted that you thought you had to even ask that question."

Taylor laughed and put her arm around her again, and Avery grinned. It was so refreshing to be with someone with whom she could joke around like this. She was now realizing that she'd dated far too many people who she'd never truly relaxed with enough for that. Either for her to make fun of them, or for them to make fun of her.

"You're so right, I'm sorry, that's on me," Taylor said. "The question I should have asked was whether you had any plans for where we're getting food, or if that was a game-time decision."

Avery unlocked the car doors and they both got in.

"Well, I didn't want to be dictatorial on the matter, but I was thinking burgers?"

Taylor let out a deep sigh.

"Thank God. Please take me to the burgers immediately."

AFTER BURGERS AND FRIES AND MILKSHAKES, THEY DROVE back to Taylor's place. Taylor was a little uncertain about what hyper-organized Avery would say about her apartment.

"I've never seen your place before," Avery said. "Are you hiding something in there?"

Taylor nodded as she unlocked the door.

"So many things, you have no idea. Mostly that I'm a total slob, don't tell anyone." She pushed open the door. As Avery looked around, Taylor winced as she saw her place through Avery's eyes. She'd cleaned up—some—but her place was still pretty messy. Like, that pile of shoes in a jumble by the door—Avery would have had them neatly lined up or even on little shelves. She definitely would have organized those stacks of books, and would never have half-opened mail strewn around. And she absolutely would have remembered to water her plants in the past week.

"I wouldn't call you a slob," Avery said. "It's not that bad. It's not even bad at all, it's nice. And I love all of your plants."

Taylor laughed as she pulled off her boots.

"I love my plants, too, though I'm a terrible plant owner, I always forget to water them. But I haven't killed one yet, so I keep buying more. Callie always gives me a discount, I can't help it." She took her wallet out of her pocket and tossed it on the mail-covered table. "Want something to drink?" She didn't wait for an answer and walked back to the kitchen. Avery took off her sandals and followed her.

"Let's see, I have wine, obviously, rosé and white; beer, which I've never seen you drink, but you could surprise me; sparkling water in lime, watermelon, and no flavor; ginger beer; and then I have stuff to make, like, a gin and tonic or vodka tonic or whatever, if you want that; or just ice water. Or . . ." She trailed off as she looked at Avery. She was staring hard at a spot on the floor, with an odd expression on her face. She clearly hadn't paid any attention to what Taylor had been saying.

"Hey," Taylor said.

Avery looked up. "Oh. Um, I'll have sparkling water. Lime, please."

Taylor took a can out of the fridge and handed it to her.

"Everything okay?"

Avery nodded, then shrugged. "Yeah, of course."

Taylor's face must have shown that she didn't believe that.

"Okay, everything's *mostly* okay," Avery said. "But, um. I'm just feeling a little anxious about tonight. This is all so new. For me, I mean. So, I guess I'm kind of jittery. It's no big deal."

Taylor took her hand, led her to the couch, and pulled Avery down next to her.

"I'm glad you told me, instead of being anxious and pretending everything was fine," Taylor said. She couldn't even count the number of times someone she'd been dating had done that, and every time she *knew* there was something wrong. But it wasn't just other people; she'd done that, too, when she knew saying what she really felt would hurt someone's feelings, or start a fight, when all she wanted was to have sex and go to sleep. She was glad that, at least so far, she and Avery weren't doing that with each other.

"I, um, I'm trying to be better about stuff like that," Avery said. "With you, I mean, but also in general. I have a habit of blowing off my own emotions, and that's not good for me. I know this is . . . we're just casual, it's not like I think . . . but I want to practice saying how I feel. But it's, um, hard to change bad habits."

Taylor put her arm around Avery.

"Tell me about it," she said. "My bad habits are probably far worse than yours, and yes, it's been very hard to change them."

Avery turned to face her.

"You have bad habits?"

Taylor laughed at the shocked tone of her voice.

"You're kidding me, right? You can even ask that question, while you sit here in my messy apartment? I have a million bad habits. I'm disorganized, I'm bad with money, I'm terrible at commitment, I haven't had a relationship longer than a few months in years, I'm barely a functioning adult. Meanwhile, look at you, queen of the spreadsheets, in an apartment you only moved into a few months ago that looks like it should be in a magazine, an upstanding member of society and everything. It's kind of ridiculous that you're spending so much time with someone like me, honestly." Wow, she hadn't quite meant to say all of that.

Avery rolled her eyes.

"Now it's my turn to say, 'You're kidding me, right?' Other than spreadsheets, which is not a thing that really matters, tell me one thing that I can do better than you."

Taylor dropped her arm and turned to face her.

"I can list so many things, but how about we start with this one: You have your own business! And you're not even thirty! Years younger than me! Only a few, but still. Then there's me over here, who has had a dream of starting a business for years, but that's all it is, a dream."

Avery widened her eyes.

"You've had a dream of starting a business for years? Doing what?"

Damn. She *really* hadn't meant to say all of that. She'd just been blabbering away in an attempt to soothe Avery's anxiety, and she'd accidentally confessed this big secret.

She must have shown that in her face, because Avery quickly held up a hand.

"If you don't want to talk about this with me, I get it. That's okay, my feelings won't be hurt."

"No, it's not that." Taylor sighed. "It's not that I don't want to talk about it with you. I just haven't really talked to anyone other than Erica about this, and I'm kind of tender about it, I guess." It felt scary to talk about this, though she didn't want to say that to Avery. "My sort of grand, someday ambition is to open a little wine bar up here. One that focuses on local wines, obviously, where people can taste a few side by side without having to drive around to different wineries or buy a huge meal, a place people can drop in and have a glass or two and eat some snacks. I feel like the valley needs a place like that, something unpretentious, all about wine, but not in a snooty way, approachable for both locals and tourists."

She could feel herself getting more excited as she talked about it and had to bring herself back to earth. She knew that practical, organized Avery would if she didn't. Avery would probably point out all the problems with her plan, and how Taylor didn't have the experience or expertise for this, and how much it would all cost, and how impossible it was. She knew that already; she didn't need Avery to tell her.

"But don't worry, I know that that's something that goes right into the 'dreams that won't come true' category," she said. Hopefully that would be enough to forestall Avery from what Taylor knew she was going to say.

"But why?" Avery asked. "I love this idea! You'd be so great at that!"

Taylor turned to look at Avery. Her eyes were wide and excited.

"Just listening to you talk about it makes me want to go to your wine bar right away," Avery said. "You're so great at the customer service stuff, and you're right, we do need a place like that. I can't wait for this to happen."

She hadn't expected her to say that. She hadn't expected Avery to be supportive of this idea that she'd had for a long time but thought of as impractical, unrealistic. She hadn't expected Avery to believe in her this much.

"You're not just saying that?" she asked.

Avery shook her head. She wasn't smiling anymore; her expression was completely serious.

"Of course not. I wouldn't do that to you. I think it's a great idea, and I think you can do it. It'll be a lot of hard work, and it'll probably be really scary, and you'll have to learn a lot of new things, but you're not afraid of hard work. You can do all of that."

Avery was right about how hard it would be. Was she right that Taylor could do it?

"Back to the thing about bad habits, I've been trying to get better at money stuff, to understand it a little more, so I'm not just nodding and smiling along when people talk about taxes and stocks like they're speaking Latin. But wow, is it hard for me." She didn't look at Avery when she said that; she didn't want to see the pity on her face.

"You know, there are good classes you can take," Avery said. "About that kind of stuff, but also other things about how to run a business. That's what I did."

Taylor sat up straight and looked at her.

"You did?"

Avery nodded.

"Yeah, I had no idea how to do any of this stuff, either. Sure, I have an orderly brain, but it's not like my parents knew any of that, neither of them owned a business. I still feel like I barely know what I'm doing."

Incredible that someone like Avery could think that.

"I've thought about taking classes, just about how to run a business, or a bar," Taylor said. "So many bars and restaurants close within the first year, it's such a risky thing to try to do; I would want to know what I was getting myself into. But I don't even know where to start."

"But you have lots of friends in that business who you could ask, don't you?" Avery asked.

That had occurred to her, of course it had. But . . .

"But if you asked them, you'd have to tell them that you're thinking about doing this," Avery said.

Avery knew her better than she thought. Taylor nodded.

"I get that," Avery said. "I'd worry about that, too. Well, I can share the research that I did, this was a few years ago, but it should still help. Oh!" She put her hand on Taylor's. "You know who the perfect person to talk to about this is? Margot! She'll know exactly what you should do, she knows everybody. And she'll totally be in your corner."

Margot. Of course. Why hadn't she thought of that?

"She's the perfect person, you're right," she said. "If I work up the nerve, she's definitely the first person I'll talk to."

Avery slid her fingers through Taylor's and squeezed tight.

"You should," she said. "And thank you for telling me about this. I'm glad you felt like you could talk to me about something so important to you." She smiled at Taylor. "See, there's both of us working on our bad habits."

Taylor kissed her on the cheek.

"I'm proud of us," she said.

"Me, too," Avery said.

Taylor cupped Avery's cheek, and then kissed her lips.

"Do you know what it's time for?" She let her hand move slowly down Avery's body. Avery's eyes fluttered shut.

"What?" she asked.

"It's time for me to take these clothes off you."

Taylor started slowly, leisurely. The other times they'd had sex, she'd felt almost frantic about it, like she'd better do it fast before one of them came to their senses. But tonight, she knew this wasn't their last time, so it felt like she could take a deep breath and enjoy all of this. After Avery had planned a hilarious night of ax throwing, the least she could do was to make sure she had a fantastic time here, too.

She reached for Avery's delightfully apropos plaid shirt, and slid first one button undone, then another. She was surprised that Avery even had a plaid shirt, but maybe she kept it around when she had to play dress-up, just like Taylor had a ladylike cardigan somewhere in her dresser. Avery had tucked the front of her shirt into her jeans, because of course she had. Taylor grinned as she unbuttoned Avery's shirt to reveal a hot pink bra.

"God, I love how you always have the best surprise for me under there," Taylor said as she traced the lace of the bra with her fingertip.

Avery watched the movement of her finger with a smile on her face.

"I wasn't sure if you cared about lingerie. It's good to know that you do."

Taylor sat back so she could savor Avery in that bra.

"Why, because mine is always so boring? I don't care about it on myself, but I love it on you."

She moved her fingers up and over and all around Avery's

breasts in that bra, tracing the lace and making circles around her nipples until Avery shivered.

"Oh, do you want me to take this off of you?" she asked innocently.

Avery glared at her.

"You said you were going to take it off of me five minutes ago!"

Taylor reached around her to unhook it.

"Mmm, does that mean you didn't enjoy the last five minutes?"

Avery reached out and pinched her nipple softly, and Taylor felt a jolt of pleasure.

"What do you think?"

Taylor's eyebrows went up.

"I think you liked that a lot. Let's see what else you like." She took both of Avery's nipples between her fingers as Avery watched her. Avery's eyes were wide, her lips were pink, her mouth was slightly open. Taylor pinched them, one after the other, like Avery had done to her . . . well, maybe just a little harder, but not *too* hard. Avery gasped, then giggled, then closed her eyes in pleasure.

"Mmm, you like that, too, don't you? I thought that you would. I like it, too. It's fun to pinch, just a little, to bite, just a bit." She demonstrated as she talked. "What do you think?"

Avery's cheeks were pink, and she didn't quite make eye contact with Taylor.

"I, um, think—"

Taylor stopped. Waited. She didn't want to rush Avery, either way.

Finally, she looked at Taylor.

"I, um, I do like it."

Oh. Avery wasn't scared to tell her she didn't like it. She was embarrassed to tell her that she did.

Taylor moved her hand to Avery's cheek.

"If you don't want to talk about this—to talk like this—we don't have to. You don't have to like it, just because I do."

Avery kept her eyes on Taylor's.

"I do, too. I'm just . . . nervous about it. That I'll sound stupid, or something. But I don't want to not do it because of that."

Taylor felt a wave of affection for her. For how scared and confident and shy and sweet and assertive she was. She kissed Avery softly on the lips.

"My God, you're so sexy. I can't get over it."

Avery kissed her back.

"You told me that at our first flirting lesson. And I didn't believe you then, I thought you were just saying it, trying to raise my confidence a little."

"And now?" Taylor asked, reaching for Avery's huge, silly, fantastic belt buckle.

"And now I believe you mean it," Avery said. "I feel so sexy when I'm with you. I've never felt like this with anyone before. I've felt pretty or whatever, but not sexy." She reached for Taylor's belt, too. "It feels amazing."

Taylor loved not only that she'd done that for Avery, but also that Avery had told her about it. It felt like such a gift, for Avery to share that with her. She wanted to say that to Avery, but she didn't know how. Instead, she unbuttoned Avery's jeans.

"That's always the goal. For you—for both of us—to have fun." Taylor grabbed Avery's hand and pulled her up from the couch and toward the bedroom. Avery kicked her jeans off on the way there and giggled. When they got into the bedroom, Taylor pulled open the bottom drawer of her nightstand.

"I was wondering—no pressure—if you thought playing around with one of these might be fun?" Taylor asked her.

Avery looked at the assortment of toys in the drawer. Taylor was prepared for any reaction: shock, embarrassment, refusal, tentative agreement. But Avery surprised her yet again. She stared down at the toys for a while, and then looked at Taylor with dancing eyes.

"Only one way to find out," she said. She reached in and grabbed one. "How about this one?"

The sight of Avery, clad only in a pair of hot pink bikini underwear, fondling a very large vibrator was one of the hottest things Taylor had ever seen. She took her own pants off immediately.

"Um, yes, that one is great," she said. She pushed Avery down onto the bed, and Avery fell backward, still with that laughter in her eyes. Taylor pulled off her shirt and grabbed the vibrator from her, right before she knelt on the bed next to Avery.

"Hey, no fair, I wanted to play with that," Avery said.

Taylor hooked her fingers around the waistband of Avery's underwear and pulled them off.

"Don't worry, you'll get to play with this, all right," she said. She turned it on, first to low power, then stronger, and Avery giggled.

"I've only ever heard that noise when I've been alone in my bedroom," she said.

Taylor pushed at her knees, and Avery opened her legs wide.

"How do you like hearing it when you're here in my bedroom?" Taylor asked. She slid the toy slowly in and out of Avery. She could see Avery's face so well from this vantage point.

"I like hearing it," Avery said. "But I like feeling it even better. And I *really* like watching you do that."

Taylor smiled as she moved the toy faster, harder.

"That's good," she said. "Because I *really* like watching you do this."

Avery opened her legs wider, and Taylor came in closer. She

kept it up with the toy as she bent down to suck on Avery's nipples, first one, then the other. Avery let out a soft moan.

"You . . . have to promise me something," Avery said.

"What?" Taylor asked.

"That I'll get to do this to you next."

Taylor grinned as she pinched one of Avery's nipples.

"I promise."

FOURTEEN

TWO WEEKS LATER, TAYLOR GROANED AS SHE TURNED OVER in Avery's bed.

"Do we really have to do this today?"

Avery laughed as Taylor nuzzled into her.

"You're the one who lost the bet, you got us into this mess."

Taylor threw a leg over Avery's hip.

"First of all, it was your fault I lost that bet. Luring me into bed with your come-hither eyes, you should be ashamed of yourself. Secondly, I didn't realize that losing the bet meant not only that I'd have to plan a baby shower but that I'd have to plan it with *Sloane* and especially that I'd have to go to a Saturday-morning brunch at nine with Sloane and Erica to discuss said baby shower. Every word of that sentence is antithetical to my very being! A meal at nine a.m. isn't even brunch! That's just breakfast! I don't care if it's on a Saturday."

Avery opened her mouth, and Taylor put her fingertip on her lips.

"And don't say, like I know you're about to, that it's so early because I have to be at work at ten thirty, I know this, it will not make me feel better. Thank God you're coming with me, is all I can say."

Avery moved her hand down the side of Taylor's body. Taylor closed her eyes and let herself enjoy the feeling of Avery's skin against hers, Avery's arms around her, Avery's hand caressing her. She'd said all of that in a half-joking tone, but she wasn't joking at all about that last part.

"I mean that, you know," she said. "I'm really glad you're coming with me today."

"I know you are," Avery said. "Me and my baby shower–related spreadsheets are going to make you look good."

That's not what Taylor had meant, but she let it go.

"That, and your sparkling personality, and your ability to elbow me if I start to say something deeply rude to Sloane."

Avery raised her eyebrows.

"Only if you start to say something *deeply* rude?"

Taylor sighed.

"Okay, fine, anything rude at all. You're not going to let me have any fun today, are you?" She kissed Avery once, and then again, longer this time. "How much time do we have?" she said in Avery's ear.

Avery looked at her watch and kissed her hard.

"Enough. Barely. I know how long you take in the shower."

"Hey! I can hurry up in the shower if I have to. I can't believe you're going to use my good hygiene habits against me."

Avery giggled as Taylor rolled over on top of her.

Afterward, she kissed Taylor's neck.

"We need to get up. I want to look nice today. I'm meeting your best friend for the first time, and I don't want her to think that I just rolled out of bed and to this brunch like I don't care."

Taylor kissed her shoulder.

"It's breakfast. And you always look good." Wait. Taylor turned so she could see Avery's face. "Are you nervous about meeting Erica?"

Avery didn't meet her eyes, in that way that she did when she was stressed.

"Um, sort of. Yeah, I mean . . ." She sighed and finally looked at Taylor. "Yes, of course I am. I've met your other friends, and they were all nice to me, including after they knew we were together, so I assume she will be, too. But she's your best friend, and that's different. Plus, I didn't know I was meeting your other friends in advance that first time. I didn't have time to get nervous."

They'd gone back to trivia this past Tuesday night, and the crew there swarmed them like they were the paparazzi and Taylor and Avery were a celebrity couple. She'd stuck to Avery's side most of the night, not because she was worried that one of her friends would hit on Avery again—she knew they wouldn't—but because she'd worried that one of her friends would quiz Avery about their relationship. They had that habit.

She hadn't needed to worry, though—the night had turned into an impromptu birthday party for her, which surprised her a little and touched her a lot. She hadn't made a big deal about her birthday to Avery, because she didn't want to stress her out about it, but she'd underestimated Avery, who had managed to sneak a cake for her into the bar. It had been a really fun night.

Erica hadn't been there, though. Which, there was no reason Erica should have been there, it's not like she regularly went to trivia anymore, especially now that she was pregnant and going to bed even earlier than she used to, and it hadn't been a planned birthday party for her or anything. Still, it was weird that she was only now meeting Avery for the first time. Taylor had barely heard from her in the past few weeks, other than her happy birthday text. She hadn't even really asked about how things were going with Avery. And things were going great, actually. They saw each other multiple times a week, and it felt good, not suffocating; they had a blast together; and the sex got better every time. But Erica wouldn't know any of that. The most they'd communicated was to plan this stupid brunch. Breakfast!

"Don't stress about meeting Erica. She can be kind of judgy about people I date, but I've told her only good things about you, not that there's anything else to tell. But she's pretty wrapped up in baby stuff right now, so I'm sure it'll be fine. If Sloane wasn't going to be there, she might grill you a little if I go to the bathroom or something, but I'm sure she'll be focused on all the shower stuff today. I wouldn't worry about it."

She could tell from Avery's face that she was even more worried. Great, she'd handled that all wrong. Time to deflect.

"Go get in the shower so we won't be late."

Avery looked at her watch and fled to the bathroom.

Even though they were early—well, her version of early—Erica and Sloane were there before them, already at a booth. And, even more irritatingly, they were sitting across from each other, which meant that Taylor didn't get to sit next to Avery.

Not that she was one of those people who insisted on sitting next to the person she was dating. She'd always made fun of those people when she saw them at restaurants, two people at a table sitting next to instead of across from each other. Did they have to be within touching distance at all times, even for an hour-long meal? Did they really need to snuggle in public that badly? But today was different. She needed to sit next to Avery so she could kick her under the table when Sloane annoyed her, or so Avery could grab her arm to stop her from a smartass comment. Oh well, they'd sit across from each other; they could exchange glances and Avery could kick her under the table if all else failed.

"I hope you already ordered coffee," Taylor said when she got to the table. She slid in next to Erica, leaving Avery to sit next to Sloane. She almost felt bad about that, but then, Avery would be better at chatting with Sloane than she would be anyway. "Erica, Sloane, this is Avery. Avery, this is Erica, and that's Sloane."

Avery smiled at both of them.

"It's so nice to finally meet both of you, I've heard so much about you. Thanks for letting me crash your shower-planning brunch, I can't wait to help out."

This is why she needed Avery around. She was so diplomatic.

Taylor was usually good at this stuff, too, but for some reason, Sloane got under her skin.

"It's nice to finally meet you, too, Avery," Erica said. "And we did indeed order coffee already, because I know you too well not to." Taylor rolled her eyes at Erica's dramatic sigh but gave her a sideways hug. Erica hugged her back and turned to Avery. "I didn't know how you took your coffee, so I didn't know what to ask for. Are you a purist like Taylor?"

Now it was Taylor's turn to sigh dramatically. Avery laughed and shook her head.

"Nope, I take milk in it. Oat milk." She grinned at Erica. "As I'm sure you can imagine, I've heard a lot on this matter."

"Oh, I don't have to imagine, I've heard it all myself." Erica and Avery both laughed, and Taylor glared at them.

"Weaklings and traitors, both of you," she said under her breath. That just made them laugh harder. Good, honestly. She wanted them to bond a little, and what helped two people bond better than making fun of the person they had in common?

The server came over, and they all ordered more quickly than she'd expected. She'd been certain Sloane would ask a long series of questions about how local the eggs were and if the kale was hand massaged or whatever, but she ordered her chia pudding without any delay. Thank goodness, Taylor was already starving, and even though the coffee at this place wasn't her favorite, the food was great.

"Okay!" Sloane said brightly as soon as the server walked away. "Time to plan for the shower! To start us off, I checked the list of RSVPs before coming here, and so far, we have twenty-one people coming, with ten maybes, and nineteen who haven't responded."

"Some of those nineteen are definitely coming," Taylor said. "They'll RSVP eventually."

"I see." Sloane pressed her lips together, like the concept of not RSVPing immediately was foreign to her. "Next: What does the space look like? I've never been to Noble. I thought I'd take over decorations if that's okay with everyone?"

There was nothing Taylor wanted to do less than deal with baby shower decorations, but she cringed to think about what Sloane's idea of decorations would be. But before she could object, Avery jumped in.

"Great idea!" Avery flipped open her notebook. "I took the liberty of making a few lists for us, I hope that's okay?" She looked from Erica to Sloane, and when they both nodded and smiled at her, she went on. "So, we have decorations, food, games, photos, presents, and cleanup. Why don't we discuss each one a little bit and see who will be in charge of each? But please, let me know if there's something I forgot to add to the list."

This must be what Avery was like at work. Clear, organized, and a total boss.

"I'll take care of food," Taylor said quickly, before Sloane could take that, too. "And I have a friend who is a photographer, I could see if she's free to take the photos? She's great."

They got through most of Avery's list even before their food came. Taylor attempted to stay engaged in the conversation about balloons and flowers and decorating onesies. She'd said if she'd lost the bet, she was going to organize this baby shower, and she was going to organize it, damn it.

"As for games," Avery said, "I think we should discuss those without the guest of honor around, don't you?" She turned from Taylor to Sloane with a sly smile on her face. "I feel like there should be *some* surprises for her."

Erica pouted.

"Hasn't Taylor told you that I hate surprises?"

Taylor elbowed her.

"I told her, but sorry, you can't be in control of everything. We'll discuss the games over text, right, Sloane?"

Sloane smiled and nodded, before she turned to Erica.

"But don't worry, we won't make you do anything humiliating."

"Oh yes, I forgot to say that," Avery said. "Absolutely no sniffing a poopy diaper or measuring your belly or anything like that. I promise."

"Sniffing a poopy diaper? Measuring her belly? Excuse me? What the fuck usually happens at baby showers?" The other three just laughed at Taylor's outrage.

"See, this is why I knew I could trust you to do my shower, despite everything," Erica said. "Those are some very popular baby shower games."

"The diaper has a chocolate bar in it, it's not really poop, but it's still gross," Avery said. "And the belly measuring is so people can bet on how big her belly is."

"Well, we are definitely not doing anything like that, don't worry," she said to Erica. "Look, I may not be a baby shower expert, but this I can tell you—there will be no references to poop, and there will be no body-shaming for anything I'm involved with planning."

Erica threw an arm around Taylor and laid her head on her shoulder.

"I promise, I definitely knew that last thing, and I never thought the first thing would ever occur to you."

Avery got up, a wide smile still on her face.

"I'm going to run to the bathroom."

Sloane slid out of her seat.

"I'll take this opportunity to go, too."

As soon as they were safely out of earshot, Taylor turned to Erica.

"So?"

She might as well get Erica's opinion on Avery right away.

"I like her," Erica said. "I didn't really expect to. I figured she'd be mooning after you like everyone else."

"Everyone else doesn't 'moon' after me," Taylor said.

"But she has her shit together, and she's also nice, and funny," Erica said, ignoring Taylor's interjection. "And she's clearly into you without worshipping you—which isn't good for you—and she's got a good head on her shoulders. She's almost too together for you, honestly. Don't get bored with her and break her heart before my shower, that would mess everything up."

Taylor sat back.

"What? Do you think I'll break up with her because she's too grown-up for me?"

Erica's expression softened.

"No, of course not, I was just joking. How are things going with her, anyway?"

Taylor couldn't help the smile that came over her face.

"I mean, you saw, she's great. Maybe it's because we hung out so much this summer before anything happened between us, so we really got to know each other, maybe it's because we got used to being so honest with each other, but it's just really easy and good. It's definitely more than I can say for my last relationship."

Erica laughed.

"Definitely more than anyone could say about your last fifteen or so relationships, you mean." Wow, low fucking blow. But before Taylor could react, Erica changed the subject. "Okay, about the food, I was thinking that since the shower is in the late afternoon . . ."

"That the food would be afternoon tea kind of food, with little sandwiches and scones? I know. Come on, I haven't known you this long not to know that. I already called Callie and asked her if she'd come out of her catering retirement just for you, since I know she does that stuff well, and she said yes. But fifteen, that's not—"

Erica's face lit up.

"Callie said yes, really? Oh my God, do you remember those scones she made after that one breakup? They were incredible."

Erica was not going to distract her by talking about those scones, even though yes, Taylor did remember them, and yes, they were amazing.

"She already agreed to make mini versions of them. But—"

"What are you two so excited about?" Sloane slid back into the booth, and Avery followed her.

"The food for the shower. Callie is going to make it all, a whole afternoon tea situation, and we've both had her scones before, they're amazing."

Fine, she'd let it go for the moment. Erica always had something to say about people Taylor was dating, and she usually laughed it off. She should laugh this off, too. She *would* just laugh this off, too.

But it wasn't just that Erica had brought up her past relationships in that snarky way. Or that what she said about Taylor had felt pointed this time. It was also that Erica had barely asked her anything about her and Avery, and then had changed the subject right back to the shower. Like, okay, yes, she was bad at relationships, everyone knew that, it's not like she thought this thing with Avery would last, but still, she'd been looking forward to talking to Erica about Avery! About how when she thought about her, she had that fluttery, warm feeling in her chest; about when she was on her way to see her, she couldn't stop smiling; about when she woke up next to her, she didn't want to leave. About whenever she spent time with her, she discovered something new that she liked about her, whether it was the way she'd carefully picked the enormous spider up out of her sink with the edge of a magazine and deposited it outside, or the way she'd cackled when Taylor had told her the story of the one time she'd tried to ride a motorcycle, or the sharp tone in her voice on the phone when a vendor had tried to overcharge one of her clients.

Taylor grinned when she thought of the satisfied look on Avery's face when she'd gotten off that phone call. Erica nudged her.

"What are you smiling about?" Erica asked as Avery and Sloane chatted with their server as they paid the check.

"Oh, I was just thinking about the other day. Avery was—"

Erica smiled wider and shook her head.

"Taylor. Keep it PG, my child is listening."

Seriously?

"It's not that kind of a story. I wouldn't even start to tell that kind of a story with her right across the table from me, come on."

Was this how Erica was going to be forever now? Sure, she'd

been kidding, but was she going to cut Taylor off every time she thought something might be about sex because her child was listening? Her child was still months from being born!

Taylor glanced at her phone and stood up.

"As much as I would love to stay longer, duty calls. I have to be at work in twenty minutes." She nodded at Sloane, and then made herself smile. "We'll text about details, okay? And let me know if you want to come by the winery so you can see the lay of the land." She kissed Erica on the top of her head. "See you soon."

Erica smiled up at her.

"See you soon. Love you." She turned to Avery, who'd also stood up, and was talking to Sloane. "So nice to finally meet you. See you soon, I hope."

Avery smiled at her, a very sweet, slightly shy smile.

"I hope so, too. Excited for the shower."

Taylor slid her hand into Avery's as soon as they walked out of the restaurant. Taylor liked her job, a lot, but she wished that instead of going to work, she was heading back home with Avery.

"I think she was happy with all those plans—your plans, obviously," she said to Avery as they walked down the street to their cars. "Thanks for making those lists and stuff. She liked you, FYI. I know that was going to be your next question."

Avery laughed.

"God, am I that transparent? How embarrassing."

Taylor shook her head.

"No. I just know you, that's all."

Avery squeezed her hand.

"To be fair, I wasn't going to ask if she liked me, though of course, that's what I wanted to know. I *was* going to ask what you two were talking about when Sloane and I went to the bathroom, and then I was going to say, 'Was it about me?' but I think I just got my answer."

"You did, and really, yes, she liked you, a lot. Honestly, I think she's wondering what a together, accomplished smoke show like you is doing with someone like me."

Avery stopped at her car and pulled Taylor to a stop along with her.

"You can't be serious. I'm with you because you're kind, straightforward, smart, funny, and very, very hot."

Avery didn't usually say things like that. She wasn't a person who gave compliments easily or often, so from her, those felt huge. Taylor raised a hand to Avery's cheek.

"Um, wow, thank you." She leaned forward and dropped a kiss on Avery's lips. "I wish I didn't have to go to work right now."

Avery smiled and kissed her back.

"Me, too. You coming over tonight?"

Taylor nodded.

"Just text me when you're done with work, okay?" She let go of Avery and took a step back. "See you soon."

Her walk to the car with Avery was so nice that it almost made her forget what Erica had said. Almost.

AVERY HAD A VERY LAZY SUNDAY MORNING WITH TAYLOR. They woke up and had sex, and then drank coffee and ate some of the leftover baked goods that Taylor had brought back from work the day before, then watched half of a movie, took a nap, and then had sex again. It was easy and relaxing and comfortable. Too comfortable. Avery had to remind herself not to get used to this. That Taylor only did casual, short-term relationships, so this thing between them was a ticking clock, no matter how good it felt.

Taylor leaned over and kissed her upper arm. She had a way of doing that, of kissing Avery on the part of her body closest to her, and Avery liked it so much. It made her feel like Taylor valued every part of her, that every part of her mattered.

"What are your plans for the rest of the day?" Taylor asked. "You don't have to work?"

Avery shook her head.

"Wild, isn't it? I had an event every day this week. It's nice to get an actual weekend day off, for once. I'm meeting Beth at the garden this afternoon, but that's all." She was looking forward to going to the garden today, even though she didn't want to leave this haze of soft pillows and warm cookies and Taylor's soft, warm body.

"Can I come along?" Taylor asked. "To see your garden, I mean? I won't stay—I just got a text from my old boss begging me to fill in tonight, and since you're busy, I'll do it, but I'd love to come by and see this bed that you keep talking about."

Avery giggled at the way Taylor said "bed," but also to cover her surprise. She didn't realize Taylor would be that interested in her garden. It made sense, she'd talked about it a lot this summer, but she'd always assumed she'd bored Taylor when she did so.

"Sure, of course," she said. "I'd love to show it to you. And for you to meet Beth."

Avery had to warn Beth so she didn't lose her shit. When Taylor was in the shower, Avery texted Beth.

AVERY

> Taylor might come by to see the
> garden today, be cool

Beth responded with just a series of exclamation points. Oh no. But it felt good to walk into the garden with Taylor. To see her marvel that she'd driven by there a million times and had never known that garden was there, to point out the people Avery had told her about for the past couple months, to show her their very own garden bed with the plants in it that they'd raised from tiny little seeds.

And it felt good to introduce her to Beth. Beth was already there when they arrived—Avery was sure she'd rushed to the garden as soon as she'd gotten the text, just so there was no possibility she'd miss her chance to meet Taylor, but she just smiled and looked up from the cherry tomato plant when they got over to the bed.

"And this is Beth," Avery said. "Beth, this is Taylor."

Beth came around the garden bed, pulled off her gloves, and shook hands with Taylor.

"Nice to finally meet you," Beth said. "What do you think of our garden bed?"

Taylor's eyes danced when Beth said that, and they all laughed. But as Avery looked at their garden bed, she wished she'd known in advance that Taylor would come to see it. She could only see the problems with it: the blighted tomato plant, that one squash that wouldn't thrive no matter what they did, the lettuces that had bolted, the wilted flowers that they hadn't deadheaded yet, the herbs they'd planted too close together. Taylor would wonder why she'd wasted all this time.

Taylor walked around the bed, and Avery and Beth walked with her. "I had no idea it was this impressive," she said. "When Avery said 'garden bed,' I pictured something the size of, like, one of those half wine barrels. Not all of this. It's huge. And you guys have so much in here."

Avery and Beth beamed at each other. It was true, they did have so much in there.

"We have a lot to do today," Avery said. "So much harvesting, and, Beth, I hate to say it, but I think we might need to just concede defeat on that tomato and pull it."

Beth nodded.

"I know, I was thinking the same thing, but I didn't want to say it."

Taylor smiled at them and put her hand on Avery's back.

"I'll leave you to it, then." She leaned up and kissed Avery softly on the lips, then took a step back. "Talk to you later?"

Avery nodded.

"Yeah. Thanks for coming by. I'm glad you got to see it."

Taylor grinned at her.

"Me, too."

When Taylor walked away, Avery turned back to the garden bed, but she could feel Beth's eyes locked on her.

"Later," she said.

"Oh, that's for sure," Beth said.

Avery put her gloves on and went to work. This time of year, there was so much to do. Weeding, hand-pollinating, harvesting, cleaning up leaves with fungus or black spot, clipping off branches that looked like they were about to break and take the rest of a plant with them. Soon, they had basketfuls of cherry tomatoes, zucchini, cucumbers, jalapeños, and radishes, and there were a bunch more ripening on the vines.

"What are you going to do with all of this?" Beth asked her as they divided up their fruits and vegetables. "I still can't believe that we managed to grow so much."

Avery pushed back her hat and looked around at the garden, at their little plot, at the other plots, and all the activity going on. It seemed like everyone in the community garden was here. All day people had been walking by and greeting them, complimenting their successes, and commiserating with their failures. Lots of people had shared their fruits and vegetables with them, so they had even more varieties of tomatoes, and so many zucchini that Avery didn't know what she was going to do with them all. People really liked to give away their zucchini, she'd discovered, and she felt like she couldn't say no to any of it. But even that felt good. She was so happy and proud of herself that she was a part of this.

"I know, me, too," she said. "Even with the stuff we tried that didn't work, we got so much, it's amazing. As for what I'm going to make, I guess some sort of zucchini bread with all this zucchini that we somehow have—maybe I'll figure out how to do that later?" She bit her lip and then smiled at Beth. "I'm trying to teach myself how to become better at baking, and I feel like zucchini bread is a good thing to practice on, right? Since we have so much, I feel like if my first attempt is a failure, I can just try again?"

Beth clapped her hands and stood up.

"Zucchini bread is the perfect thing to make when you have a ton of zucchini and you want to learn how to bake. Plus, I have a great recipe. Come over to my place and we can snack and bake and debrief, which you know I've been dying to do for the past two hours." She stopped and looked at Avery. "That is, unless you have plans with your hottie, in which case I excuse you."

Avery laughed.

"She's working tonight, so I'm in."

Thirty minutes later, Avery pulled up in front of a cute little corner house on a side street, and Beth threw open the door.

"Come in, come in." Beth ushered her into the house.

There was a big tomato, cucumber, and herb salad on the kitchen table that Beth had made from their garden bounty, and Avery contributed some cheese and prosciutto and bread she'd picked up on the way.

"Okay," Beth said after she'd sliced up the baguette and deposited it on the cutting board next to the cheese. "*What* is going on with you and that impossibly hot woman? I thought you were just sleeping together, but that goodbye kiss was more than sleeping together." She spread a bunch of cheese on a piece of bread and looked at Avery expectantly.

Avery blushed and laughed.

"We're mostly just sleeping together. I mean, I guess it's sort of more than that, but not really—Taylor doesn't do serious relationships, I've known that forever, so I guess it's just casually dating. Which is fine, I didn't want anything serious either, especially since—"

Beth brushed that off.

"Yes, yes, now that we're done with all the disclaimers, tell me the good stuff."

Avery laughed. And then she let herself smile.

"I don't even know what to say—things are just so easy with her. That's probably because it's not serious, so I'm not spending time worrying about the future or stressed about everything. Though, I mean, I am kind of stressed about how long this can last, partly because it feels too good to be true, but mostly because it's Taylor, so I know it can't last very long. But other than that, it's great. We spend a ton of time together—we take turns now surprising each other for dates, which is fun, but sometimes she'll just come over after work, or I'll bring takeout to her place or whatever, and we'll just hang out, and it's just so . . ." She couldn't think of the right word to describe it. "It's . . . I don't know, I haven't had a relationship like it. Like, I'm excited whenever I see her, and I have a great time with her, but also being around her doesn't stress me out? I'm weirdly proud of myself; part of the point of the flirting lessons in the first place was to learn how to do casual, no-stress relationships, and I did it, and it feels great." She made a face. "Sorry, that was probably too much information about my relationship baggage, but I'm so used to being quietly tense around the person I'm dating that it feels amazing to me that I don't feel that way, like, at all."

Beth spooned some salad onto her plate.

"First, we've been bonded by soil, okay? There is no such thing as too much information. Second, I am so glad you're finally dating someone who you can relax and be yourself around, that's huge. But third . . ." She waggled her eyebrows at Avery. "Now that we've established that there's no such thing as too much information . . ."

Avery laughed at the look on Beth's face. Then she gave in. She'd been dying to talk to someone about this.

"Beth. The sex is so good. Just . . . *so* good. I didn't know sex could be this good! I mean, I guess I knew that it could be for some people—I read romance novels and everything—but I thought some of it was hyperbole, you know? But it's that good with Taylor. I know you know this, but God, having sex with a woman is fucking incredible. Have women who have sex with women been walking around in the world on this cloud of incredible sex forever and I just didn't know? It's like there was another world that I didn't even know existed!"

Beth started laughing midway through Avery's speech and didn't stop.

"Absolutely yes, there has been another world going on of women walking around being totally satisfied by their sex lives. You just confirmed something to me that I've always suspected about straight people: this is why they're so uptight—the sex is so bad!"

Avery couldn't stop giggling.

"I don't think all straight people have bad sex—maybe it was just me?"

Beth shook her head.

"It absolutely was not just you. I promise. But I also promise that not all women are as good as your hottie Taylor apparently is."

Good Lord, she was giggling far too much lately, but she couldn't stop herself.

"She is *really* hot, isn't she?" Avery thought about Taylor this morning, that look in her eyes as she'd turned toward Avery in bed. "Do I think it's so good because the sex I've had before was so mediocre that anything seems good to me?" And then she shook her head. "No, this is Taylor we're talking about. I guess this is the advantage of having my first real sexual experience with a woman be with someone who has a lot of experience. But . . ." She bit her lip. "I hope it's as good for her as it is for me. It probably isn't, right? See, this is the *problem* with your first real sex with a woman being with one who has a whole lot of experience." She shook her head. "Sorry, sorry, you wanted the fun stuff, not my insecurities, you don't need to answer that." She stood up. "Are we ready to make zucchini bread?"

Beth stood up, too.

"Sure, but you're not getting away with that. Have you talked to her about this?" Beth handed her the basket of vegetables. "Wash and dry the zucchini while you answer that question."

Avery stared down at the sink. Why had she even brought this up?

"We did, a little bit, at the beginning. I mean, the first time." It felt scary to be this vulnerable with someone else, but she'd already started. "I told her I was nervous, and she was really great about it. And since then, she's said some complimentary things about, um, how much she's enjoying herself, so it's not that she makes me feel bad, to be clear! I always feel good when I'm with her. It's when I'm not with her that I wonder what she's doing with me." She picked up a kitchen towel and carefully dried the zucchini. "Oh God, I was going to stop, and I just kept talking, what is wrong with me?"

Beth took the zucchini from her.

"You're having normal human emotions, that's what's not wrong with you." Beth sent two zucchini through the food processor, and they came out in a perfectly grated pile.

"I guess, but this isn't even a real relationship. I like her, I *really* like having sex with her, I'm having a great time, but it's all very relaxed. I think that's why I'm not stressed around her, because I know it can't go anywhere, so I'm not constantly worrying about what's going to happen or if I'm being a good enough girlfriend or whatever."

Beth dumped the shredded zucchini in a colander, then handed two loaf pans to Avery.

"Grease these. Okay, so . . . easier said than done, I know, but maybe you could talk to her about it? Do you think she'll tell you the truth?"

"Yes," Avery said immediately. She scooped up some butter and started on the first loaf pan. "She's always honest with me." She finished greasing one pan and started on the other. "Maybe that's the problem, that I know she'll be honest with me, so I don't want to bring it up because I'm afraid of what she's going to say?"

Beth measured out flour and salt and baking powder and didn't say anything.

"Fine!" Avery said. "I know what you're thinking, I'll talk to her! Are you happy?"

"Very," Beth said.

Avery set the loaf pans down. She was ready to change the subject.

"What are you and Greta going to wear for your wedding, do you two know yet?"

Beth handed her a carton of eggs.

"Crack four of these into this bowl. Greta and I just call it 'the party,' so we won't slip and call it a wedding around someone else. But yeah, we know what we're wearing." She smiled down at the bowl of flour. "We went shopping together, actually. I know that's not how you're 'supposed' to do it, but we've done a lot of things you're not 'supposed' to do, and it's worked out great for us, so what's one more thing? It was a really special day for both of us, I'm so glad we did it that way."

Avery was so happy for Beth. And she was suddenly sad that she wasn't invited to Beth's wedding. Ugh, why did she feel like that? She and Beth had been friends for only a couple months, it was a small wedding, and she'd never even met Greta. Why *should* she be invited?

"That's so great," she said. "I'm glad that planning for the . . . party has been a happy time for both of you. Especially since so often I see people having the opposite experience."

That look on Beth's face when she thought of Greta, and their wedding, that look of total happiness and peace and love and security . . . she wanted that. Not now, not yet. But someday.

Beth took the bowl of eggs from her and measured sugar into it.

"Now for my favorite part, beating sugar into these eggs. And thank you, again, for suggesting the surprise wedding. I don't think either of us would have had the idea on our own, and if we'd had either a big regular wedding or a quick courthouse one, we both would have been so unhappy—one of us because it wasn't what we wanted and we'd hate every minute of it, and the other because our partner would clearly be so miserable. So, truly, thank you so much for talking to me about all of that when you'd literally just met me, and thank you for coming up with the ideal solution for both of us."

Avery felt the ridiculous urge to cry. Maybe because she was so happy for Beth, maybe because she wished she could see the surprise wedding herself, maybe because that kind of happiness felt so far away for her.

"Well, you're welcome. I'm glad I could help."

Beth smiled at her.

"Now, let's get this zucchini bread into the oven and sample some of the fruits of our labor, no pun intended."

Avery groaned, and Beth cackled.

FIFTEEN

AVERY SIGHED AS SHE LOOKED THROUGH HER CLOSET AND tried to figure out what to wear to go out with Taylor. *Something that makes you feel flirty*—not helpful, Taylor! What could she mean by that?

Wait. She knew Taylor well enough to guess what she meant by that. She meant something that Avery felt great in, that she felt like herself in, but maybe a tiny bit more risqué than she'd wear in her daily life. Something that when she wore it, she looked in the mirror and felt both nervous and excited.

With that in her mind, she flipped through her closet again and stopped at a dress she'd bought a few years ago but had yet to wear. It had a deeper V-neck than she usually wore, and a skirt that moved beautifully when she walked in it, and she remembered that when she'd initially gotten the package and tried it on at home, she'd walked around in it for a while, delighted by the way it felt on her and how she felt in it.

But somehow, she'd never worn it out of the house. It wouldn't be right for a work event, and she hadn't been to any social events in the last few years where it made sense to wear it. But every time she did a closet purge, she always kept that dress, because she loved it so much.

She had no idea if it would be appropriate for whatever she and Taylor were doing tonight, but to hell with appropriate. She was going to wear this dress that she liked because yes, she absolutely felt flirty in it.

As soon as she opened her front door to Taylor, she knew she'd made the right choice. Avery could feel the heat from Taylor's eyes as they swept up and down her body.

"Where the fuck did you get that dress, and can all of your clothes come from there for the rest of your life?" Taylor finally asked her.

Avery laughed and beckoned her inside.

"I can't believe this, but you're ready and I'm not. Let me just finish my hair." Taylor looked pretty great herself, in black tuxedo pants, silver oxfords, and a silky black sleeveless top. Avery wanted to reach out and stroke her, even more than she did usually.

"I hope I interpreted the brief correctly?" she said as she combed product through her hair with her fingers so her curls wouldn't get too frizzy in the early September heat.

Taylor smiled at her from outside the bathroom doorway.

"If you feel flirty in it, then you interpreted it correctly," she said, a cryptic smile on her face.

Avery glared at her, and Taylor just laughed.

"You know what I mean!" Avery said. She started to walk out of the bathroom, but Taylor didn't step out of her way. She just stood there with that knowing smile. Avery had no choice but to kiss her. Kissing Taylor felt like a treat every time she did it; she couldn't believe that she could pull Taylor close and kiss her, anytime she wanted to. She remembered that first time, how much she'd wanted it, how nervous she'd been, how much of a daze Taylor's touch and smell and lips and taste had put her in. She still put Avery in that daze, every single time.

"Mmm, I see that this dress definitely makes you feel flirty." Taylor's hand went to her waist. "It makes me feel flirty, too. Did you know that would happen?"

Avery slid her hand up underneath Taylor's shirt and moved her fingers over her soft, smooth skin, before she gently brushed her thumb over Taylor's nipples.

"I didn't know that," she said, "but I really hoped it would happen. And I don't know if you gave yourself the same assignment that you gave me, but that outfit of yours definitely makes me feel flirty, too."

Taylor's eyes smiled into hers. If there was a way to bottle the feeling that Taylor Cameron gave a person, she'd make a million dollars on just one sale.

"Good," Taylor said. "I hoped it would. But as much as I would like us to keep going with this flirting practice right here, we have to go. I don't want to be late."

Avery kissed her one last time, and then picked up her bag and slid her feet into her sandals.

"This had better be worth me missing out on some very important flirting practice," she said. Taylor laughed that low, throaty laugh that made Avery want to drag her into the bedroom immediately. Instead, she grabbed her hand on the way out the door.

When she got into the car, she remembered her promise to Beth, and sighed to herself. She'd meant to bring this up the last time she'd seen Taylor, but she'd been stressed about work, and she hadn't wanted to have a difficult conversation when she was in that kind of a mood, so they'd just eaten takeout and watched *Drag*

Race. Which meant she had to do it now. She would feel like she'd broken a promise to Beth if she didn't.

And to herself, for that matter.

"Can I ask you a question?" she asked. She was asking a question by asking that, wasn't she?

Taylor shot her an amused glance.

"You know you can. What's up?"

How should she phrase this? She wished she'd thought this out earlier.

"Do you like having sex with me?" Shit, that wasn't the right way. "I mean, don't answer that, let me rephrase that. That first time, I said I didn't really know what I was doing, and then another time you said I'd gotten pretty good at things, but I just want to know . . . because to me, the sex is really, really good, great even, but I don't know, I mean, I'm not sure if you feel that way, too, and if not, I want to know what I should do, or—" Oof. This sentence had gone on long enough. "I meant to say all of that much better."

Taylor turned and glanced at her, a stricken expression on her face, and then pulled over and stopped in what Avery wasn't sure was a parking spot.

"Have you been unsure of this the whole time?" she asked as soon as the car was in park. Then she held up a hand. "Wait, let me answer you first. Yes, yes, I absolutely like having sex with you. I like it a lot. A lot, a lot." She put her hand on Avery's. "A thing that you might not know about me, probably because you're not like this, is that I don't stay in situations for very long where I'm not enjoying the hell out of myself. Many people see this as a character flaw, and I don't necessarily disagree with them, but that's how I am. And that means that I enjoy the hell out of myself all the time when I'm with you, and that absolutely includes when we're having sex. Yes, sure, you're not that experienced, but experience isn't everything. You pay attention, and you listen to me, and you remember what I like, you tell me what you like, and you're up to try new things. And most of all, you make it clear that you're enjoying yourself—which I know isn't easy for you—and that makes me enjoy myself. And that makes having sex with you both exciting and a lot of fun. And my God, Avery, I'm so sorry if I've said or done anything to make you feel like I didn't feel that way, please tell me what I did, and I'll never do that again."

Well, damn, now Avery was on the point of tears. No one had ever said anything so kind and blunt and wonderful to her.

"No, no." She shook her head. "You didn't, I promise. And I never feel like that when I'm with you. But sometimes I get . . . anxious that I'm not measuring up, and I didn't want to say anything because it felt stupid to say something, so it just became a thing I would worry about and then forget about, and the cycle would repeat. I only brought it up today because I said something about it to Beth, and she made me promise to talk to you about it."

Taylor intertwined her fingers with Avery's.

"Remind me to thank Beth for that." She kissed Avery. A long, slow, shimmery kiss. When she pulled away, she traced the outline of Avery's lips with her fingertip. "I really want to keep doing this, right here, but I'm excited about our plans tonight. Remember where we were later, okay?"

Avery smiled at her.

"I will."

TAYLOR PUT HER SEAT BELT BACK ON AND DROVE OFF, HER hand still tightly clasped with Avery's. Had Avery believed her?

She hoped so. Everything she'd said was true, and she and Avery were always honest with each other. But she knew Avery had some trust issues, and it made sense that she was insecure about sex. Taylor should have been better about going out of her way to praise her, but would that have felt condescending? She hoped things were good now.

When they pulled into the community center parking lot, Avery laughed as she looked around.

"Another event here? This is the same place we did the dance class, isn't it? That was really fun."

Taylor tried not to smile too hard.

"I thought so, too."

When they got out of the car, Taylor could tell Avery was looking around at everyone else in the parking lot, trying to figure out who they were and where they all could be going.

"I can't tell if I'm overdressed or underdressed," Avery said to her as they walked toward the auditorium.

"You are dressed just right," Taylor said to her. "I thought I made that pretty clear back at your place?"

Avery's lips crinkled up in that way they did when she was trying not to smile and failing.

"That's not what I mean! You aren't the only judge of how appropriate my outfit is, you know that!"

Taylor grinned as she looked Avery up and down again.

"No, *you* are the only judge of your outfit, I'm just the happy appreciator of it, that's all."

Avery smiled for real this time. Then she looked around, and her eyes widened. Taylor followed her gaze and saw that she was looking at the sign outside the auditorium. She turned to Taylor, a slightly confused look on her face.

"Dance class again? I'm not complaining, I loved it the first time, but . . ."

"But why are we doing another salsa class when we've done it already?" Taylor finished that question for her, and Avery nodded. "Because I thought it would be even more fun if we got to dance with each other this time."

She didn't say what she felt, didn't quite have words for that, but when she'd seen the email about this class, she'd remembered how she'd felt at the last class, watching Avery dance with all those people who weren't her, and how, in retrospect, she realized how much she'd wanted to dance with Avery that night. Now she could, and she didn't want to pass up that opportunity.

Avery turned to her with a soft, sweet smile on her face.

"You're absolutely correct," she said. "That will be even more fun."

Avery opened the door and waved her inside with a bow.

They went into the auditorium, and everything was the same as their first class—the sign-in was the same, the teachers were the same, their funny patter at the beginning of class was almost the same. But everything between her and Avery felt totally different. Instead of walking around the class, chatting with people she knew, encouraging Avery to chat and flirt and smile with her dance partners, and trying to ignore how much she wanted to dance with her, to hold her in her arms, touch her, she had Avery to herself. She didn't usually feel that way about people she was dating. She liked to be around them, sure, but she also liked to socialize with a crowd, to mingle and flirt and chat with whoever else was around. But tonight, she was happy to stay right by Avery's side, with one hand in hers and one arm around her as they danced together.

At first, they stumbled, made the wrong moves, laughed at themselves, and then tried again. As the night went on, they learned each other's movements, Taylor stood up straighter, Avery relaxed her hips, and their feet moved in unison, Avery moving back as she moved forward, and vice versa.

She put her hands on Avery's hips when a new song started.

"Okay, now it's time to shimmy. I know you have it in you, I want to see it."

If she'd said that to Avery two months ago, Avery would have looked terrified and stricken, but tonight she just laughed.

"I'm glad *you* know I have it in me, because I'm not sure *I* know that."

Taylor leaned forward until her lips were against Avery's ear.

"You know you have it in you, too. I've seen the way your hips move when my mouth is in between them."

Avery let out a tiny gasp and pulled back with a scandalized look on her face, but the laughter in her eyes belied the frown on her lips.

"Taylor! You are a very naughty girl."

Taylor pulled her close.

"I know you're not just now figuring that out."

A giggle escaped Avery, and they grinned at each other.

"NOW!" Elena boomed out.

Avery's hips shimmied and sashayed as her feet moved in time with Taylor's, their eyes locked, their hips moving in sync as they danced. It felt like they were moving as one body, they were so in tune with each other. Taylor felt like she could keep doing this forever. When the music stopped, she didn't want to stop dancing.

"How was that?" Avery asked, a shy smile on her face.

Taylor honestly had no idea how to answer that.

"That was so good that I can't fucking wait to get you home tonight," she said. That was true, but there was more to it.

Avery dropped a quick kiss on her lips.

"Me, too," she said.

Avery wasn't a PDA person—a peck on the lips in public from her was like actual groping from someone else. Taylor could feel the ridiculous way she was smiling at Avery. Of course they were going to have sex that night when they went home; that was basically a given at this point. And yet, she was as full of anticipation as a kid on Christmas Eve.

They laced their fingers together as they walked to the car after class.

"I'm glad we did that," Avery said. "It was a lot of fun."

Taylor smiled at her.

"I thought so, too."

Avery turned to her on the way back to her place.

"I was wondering . . . We haven't talked about this in a while, but have you talked to Margot? About your business idea, I mean."

Taylor shook herself back to earth.

"Oh. Right. Um, no, not yet. It's so busy at the winery right now, when I'm around Margot, it's because we're both working hard, and when she's there and not in the tasting room, she's usually on the phone or in meetings. But I'm going to do it, really."

Avery put a hand on her knee.

"I know you are. I'm not, like, nagging you to do it, or anything. I was just wondering. I know it's important to you."

Taylor put her hand on top of Avery's.

"No, I know you weren't. And thanks. I appreciate that."

She parked right in front of Avery's building, and as soon as she turned off the car, she pulled her into a kiss. A long, sweet kiss that got a lot more than sweet by the time they both came up for air.

"Let's go inside now," she said in Avery's ear. "Because I've been dying to see those hips of yours move again for me, but up close this time."

Avery flung open her car door and jumped out. Taylor laughed all the way up the stairs.

SIXTEEN

AVERY WOKE UP THE MORNING OF THE BABY SHOWER TO TAYlor nuzzling into her neck.

"That tickles," she said, trying not to giggle.

"Mmm, good to know," Taylor said. She kissed the nape of Avery's neck, and then ran a hand down her body. "Does that mean you want me to stop?"

Avery kept her eyes closed and smiled to herself. She loved waking up in bed with Taylor.

"I didn't say *that*," she said.

"Well." Taylor dropped a kiss on her upper back. "Sometimes people don't like being tickled, so I wanted to make sure you weren't one of those people." Taylor kissed her all along her spine, gentle little kisses that made Avery's whole body tingle.

"I don't like being tickled by most people," Avery said, which was true. Most people didn't know how to stop, but Taylor did. "But I like everything you do to me." That was also true, but it was something she probably wouldn't have said if she'd been fully awake. She didn't want Taylor to think she was falling too hard.

She didn't want to fall too hard. She wasn't, actually, falling hard at all. It was just that she was having great sex on a regular basis, so of course she wanted to be around Taylor all the time. But that didn't mean anything. This thing was going to end, at some point, she didn't know when, but probably soon, and she knew that. She wasn't one of those people who were going to get their heart broken by Taylor.

"What a coincidence," Taylor said as she kissed the small of her back. "Because I like everything you do to me, too." Taylor dropped a kiss right in the center of first one ass cheek, and then the other, making Avery giggle again. She turned onto her back to find Taylor grinning at her.

"What can I say, I love your ass," she said. "It's so soft and round, and it fits into my hands so well."

Avery couldn't help but smile as she looked at Taylor. Taylor made her feel so good about her body. So good *in* her body. Part of it was absolutely that Taylor clearly liked her body so much and had since the very beginning. She'd given Avery compliments that were so casual and matter-of-fact that after a while, Avery couldn't help but believe her. But a big part of it was also that *she* found Taylor so attractive that it helped her realize how Taylor—and other people—could be attracted to *her*. She loved the dimples in Taylor's thighs; the curve of her belly; her strong, solid arms; and her round, substantial ass. She discovered something new about Taylor's body almost every day.

"You know," she said, "there are other parts of my body that are soft and round and fit into your hands well."

Taylor's mouth dropped open in mock surprise.

"Are there now?" She moved her hands back up and cupped Avery's breasts. "Mmm, were you talking about these?"

Avery closed her eyes as Taylor's fingers moved around the

outsides of her breasts, and then slowly inward, until they circled her nipples.

"I was," she said. "My God, I love it when you do that." She sighed as one of Taylor's hands drifted down to move between her legs. "And I *really* love it when you do that. How did I get so lucky?"

Taylor chuckled as her mouth followed her fingers.

"We make our own luck, you know." Taylor pushed Avery's legs open, and Avery propped herself up on her elbows. As much as she loved it when Taylor went down on her, she loved watching her do it almost as much. The way her hands lingered on her inner thighs; the way she smiled with anticipation every time, like she couldn't wait to do it; the way she manipulated Avery's body like she was playing an instrument; that sly little grin on her face when she slid first one finger inside, then a second; how serious she looked when she really got into it, like it was the most important thing in the world.

And then Avery's vision blurred; she couldn't hold herself up anymore. She had to give herself over to how her body felt, like nothing could ever feel better than what Taylor was doing right now, but then Taylor went faster, and then faster, and Avery could barely breathe, her whole body tensed up, and then she gasped and dug her fingers into Taylor's shoulder and arched her back as the waves of pleasure hit her, so good it was almost painful, so good she had no idea what noises she was making and didn't care, she just wanted to prolong this as much as she could. And then with one final gasp, she collapsed, still holding on to Taylor.

When she could talk again, she turned to Taylor and smiled.

"And that was before you knew anything about the surprise I have for you today," she said.

Taylor's eyes opened wide.

"A surprise? That sounds exciting. Is it that I don't have to go to the shower after all? Is it that there's going to be one of those dunk contests and I'm going to get to dunk Sloane? Ooh, ooh, or is one of the games going to be a pie-in-the-face game, and I'm going to get to—"

Avery put a finger on Taylor's lips, but she couldn't help but laugh.

"Stop it. Sloane isn't that bad. And you have to go to the shower, you're hosting it, you lost the bet, remember?"

Taylor sighed, then grinned that devilish grin of hers.

"Oh, trust me, I remember. Fine, what's my surprise?"

Avery laughed as she flipped over on top of Taylor.

"You don't know the meaning of the word *surprise*, do you? You'll see, after the shower."

Taylor let out a loud groan.

"*After* the shower? But what if I can't wait that long?"

Avery didn't answer that, she was too busy with Taylor's breasts. She sucked one nipple into her mouth and heard a gratifying moan from Taylor.

"Are you saying you want me to stop this?" she asked, after she released Taylor's nipple. She rubbed it back and forth between her fingertips, and watched Taylor watch her fingers. "Because I don't want to stop, but I will if you want me to."

She started to move her hand away. Taylor grabbed it and put it back.

"You have an evil streak, has anyone ever told you that? It's one of the things I've liked about you from the beginning. And no, fuck you, don't stop a single thing you're doing."

Taylor pushed her head back down, and Avery laughed.

Later, she lay in bed with her coffee and watched Taylor get dressed.

"I'll be at the winery by eleven," she said. "I think Sloane is planning to get there at the same time."

Taylor took a gulp of her coffee. She'd begrudgingly admitted that Avery made decent coffee, an enormous compliment coming from her.

"I'm going to be very glad when this is over, you know that, right?"

Avery laughed out loud.

"All of Napa Valley knows that. Probably most of Sonoma, too."

Taylor walked over to the bed and kissed her hard.

"Okay, see you soon." She walked to Avery's bedroom door and stopped. "And if I haven't said it enough, thank you for everything that you're doing for this shower. This would be a nightmare without you."

Avery knew Taylor was grateful for her help, but it still felt very good to hear that.

"You're very welcome. See you later."

Taylor opened her eyes wide.

"Don't you think it would be just as much of a surprise if you told me about it now?"

Avery burst out laughing.

"It absolutely would not be, but nice try."

Sloane was already at the winery when Avery got there, even though Avery was right on time. Taylor was going to have to get over this thing about Sloane at some point. She was pretty sure Taylor resented how close Sloane was with Erica, but right now, Taylor and Sloane were companionably setting up the decorations in the garden, so Avery just joined in to help Taylor put up the umbrellas to shade the food tables, and all three of them set up the balloon backdrop. (They'd decided on balloons, since flowers would wilt in the late September heat.)

Then Callie arrived with the food, with Erica and Sam right behind her. Avery had been curious to meet Sam, whom Taylor seemed to like just fine but never really mentioned. Avery understood why when she met her; Sam was very nice but quiet. Erica was definitely the extrovert in that pair. Sam smiled at Avery without being effusive but seemed very appreciative of all their hard work.

Avery had been nervous to be at Erica's shower, where she felt like she didn't really belong. It would be one thing if she were actually the event planner, but she was there as Taylor's sort-of girlfriend, and everyone else already knew one another except for her. Would they all give her a look like they were wondering who she was and what she was doing there?

But no one did that. There were people she knew—Taylor's friend Callie, of course, and Liz and Dani and Nadia, whom she'd met at trivia, and they all gave her hugs and said how happy they were to see her. And everything at the shower went according to plan. They made flower crowns, and all wore them—even Taylor. They played the games that Taylor and Avery and Sloane had come up with, and when people laughed until they cried at the answers to the "invent a new baby food flavor" game, they exchanged pleased glances.

"Time for the toasts," Avery whispered to Taylor. Taylor nodded and caught Sloane's eye, and they both went over to Erica and Sam. Sloane tapped her wineglass in an attempt to get everyone's attention, but that accomplished nothing. Then Taylor whistled, and the crowd quieted down immediately.

"Does everyone have a glass of something?" Taylor asked. She didn't wait for an answer. "Good. Thank you all so much for coming. As many of you know, baby showers are not, shall we say, my usual milieu—" Everyone laughed, including Erica. "But Erica and Sam and their upcoming baby mean so much to me that I would do anything for them, and that includes throwing a baby shower."

There was more laughter, and Taylor grinned at the crowd. She looked right at Avery, and her grin got bigger. Avery couldn't help but laugh again; Taylor might not be big on baby showers, but she was great at talking to crowds, that was for sure.

"And I'm serious about that," Taylor continued. "Erica and I have been friends for what feels like forever—she's been there for me in just about every way imaginable, and I am so very happy for her and Sam and am thrilled to help them welcome their new addition to the world. Cheers to all three of them." Everyone lifted their glasses as Taylor turned to Erica. Her smile and eyes both softened. "Auntie Taylor can't wait to meet you."

By the end of Taylor's short speech, her eyes were, if not full of tears, at least slightly damp, and Erica was openly weeping. She stood up and pulled Taylor into a hug. Taylor patted Erica's stomach and said something to it that made Erica burst into a fresh set of tears and pull her into another hug.

Once Erica had stopped crying, Sloane cleared her throat.

"I also wanted to say a little something. Most of you don't know me that well—Erica and I are relatively new friends, we only met earlier this year after Erica and Sam moved in next door to me. Even though I'd been in the neighborhood for over a year, I felt like I didn't really know anyone yet. I can be kind of shy, and I work from home, and my daughter is still pretty little, so I wasn't going out and meeting a lot of people. And then Erica and Sam moved in, and it felt like my whole life changed. I was . . . in a very lonely place then, with a stressful job and a baby, and Erica's friendship has meant so much to me." She stopped, swallowed, and went on. "Erica, I am so grateful for your friendship, and I'm honored that I was able to help you and Sam out in any small way with this shower. To all of you friends and family of Erica and Sam, but especially Taylor, thank you so much for welcoming me, but I would have expected nothing less from any friend of Erica. Erica, thank you for everything, and I know I speak for all of us when I say that I can't wait to meet that baby of yours!"

They all toasted again, and Erica sobbed even more. Erica hugged Sloane, while Taylor smiled at the two of them. She caught Avery's eye and shrugged. Taylor walked across the party to her side.

"Okay, fine," Taylor said in her ear. "You were right about Sloane. She's not that bad. I may have been wrong there."

Avery smiled and put her hand on Taylor's back. When was the last time someone she was dating had admitted to being wrong? She didn't think it had ever happened.

"That was a very sweet speech she gave, it's true. But yours was better."

Taylor looked half-pleased, half-embarrassed.

"I don't know if that's true, but thanks. It was . . . I mean, Erica's friendship means a lot to me. I feel kind of like a jerk now after being so bitchy about Sloane. Maybe I'll tell Erica that. Not now, she has to open her presents. Plus, that would probably make her cry, and I feel like she's going to be dehydrated if she cries any more; but later."

Avery rubbed the small of Taylor's back, and Taylor put her arm around Avery's waist.

"Good idea," Avery said. "And thank you for the reminder." She raised her voice. "It's time for presents!"

***

TAYLOR FELT SO MUCH WARMTH AND LOVE FOR ERICA AS SHE watched her open her presents. In the end, she was glad that she'd thrown her this shower, and that she'd been able to be a big part of this important day for Erica. She was even glad she'd thrown the shower with Sloane. And miraculously, it had gone well.

The miracle workers, of course, were Avery and Sloane. Either Avery or Sloane could have thrown a shower all by themselves and done an incredible job, but Taylor certainly couldn't have. Could they have thrown this particular shower, which had been a great meld of Erica and Sam, without her? No, but she didn't fool herself that they would have managed just fine on their own. But she was glad that she'd been a part of this, for Erica's sake, and her own. And most importantly, Erica seemed to be having a great time.

Taylor saw Erica's mom pat her on the shoulder, before walking over to Taylor.

"Unfortunately, we have to leave now, but the shower was lovely," she said to Taylor.

"Oh, thank you so much, I appreciate that, and I'm so glad you enjoyed it," Taylor said. "Anything for Erica."

Erica's mom nodded and gave her a firm handshake before she left. Erica looked up and watched them leave and then winked at Taylor. Now Erica could truly relax. She had a pile of gifts next to her, which Sloane—because she was Sloane—was neatly stacking into a set of fancy reusable bags that she'd conjured out of nowhere. Honestly, thank God for Sloane.

Taylor saw Erica pick up the enormous package wrapped in plain brown paper and watched her open the card. She mentally read it along with Erica.

"Don't ask me to change any of these. Love you, Taylor."

Erica grinned at her, and Taylor grinned back.

"I have a feeling I know what these are," Erica said, and tore open the package. Every possible variety of diaper came tumbling out.

"A year's supply," Taylor said to her. "Just tell me which one your favorite is, and I'll start sending them your way."

Erica held out her arms to Taylor, with more tears streaming down her face, and Taylor shook her head.

"No time for tears, we can hug later! Keep opening!"

Erica laughed, wiped her face, and reached for another present.

A few minutes later, Sam whispered something to Erica and stood up. Erica frowned at her and started to whisper something back, then sighed and put a smile on her face. Taylor recognized that face. That was the "Erica is pissed but trying not to show it" face. What was going on?

Sam walked over to Taylor.

"I have a work call that I can't miss, so I'm heading home, but thanks so much for everything you've done for this shower. I know Erica is thrilled. You or Sloane can give Erica a ride home, right?"

Ah, that's why Erica was pissed. Taylor had a feeling that this work call—if not exactly fabricated—could have happened at a different time. Sam had even less of a tolerance for things like baby showers than Taylor did.

"Yeah, I'm sure one of us can get Erica home," Taylor said. "And as for the shower, I'm happy Erica is having a good time; I was glad to do it." Sam met her eyes, and they both laughed. "Okay, I was glad to do it in the *end*. Why don't Avery and I help you get some of these presents in your car, so that Erica doesn't have to worry about that later?"

Taylor, Avery, and Sam each grabbed two of the bags full of presents.

"I don't know what most of this stuff even is," Sam said on the way to the parking lot. "Guess I have a few months to figure all this out."

"Seven weeks!" Avery said. "That is, unless Erica is late."

Was that a flash of panic that she saw in Sam's eyes?

"Seven weeks," she said. "Right. I should know that."

When they got to the car, Avery nudged Taylor.

"Do you want to head back and grab the rest, while we load everything into the trunk?"

"Good idea."

Taylor could hear the chatter from the party as she walked back from the parking lot, and she smiled when she heard Erica's high, infectious laugh. Even if she'd been upset about Sam leaving, she was okay.

"Okay, quick," Liz said. "Before they come back, what do we all think of Taylor and Avery?"

Taylor stopped abruptly. She was torn between walking around the corner right then so they would all know she'd heard or waiting to see what they said. As she hesitated, the decision was made for her.

"I like Avery!" from Sloane. "She's great!" from Callie. "A little uptight, but not bad" from Nadia. "Avery's awesome, but Taylor usually has pretty good taste." That one was from Erica. Taylor wasn't sure if she'd added that last part because more than one of Taylor's exes was at the shower, but she was grateful that Erica had stuck up for both her and Avery, and that the general response to Avery had been good. She was also grateful that Avery hadn't heard all of this. It must have been hard for Avery to come to this shower, filled with people who all knew Taylor well, as her new girlfriend. She'd probably assumed that people would be gossiping about her, but it was one thing to assume that and another to hear it.

"Exactly," Liz said. "Taylor does have pretty good taste, and Avery is great, but Taylor also never stays with anyone for very long. So how long do we give *this* relationship?"

Wow, thanks for that, Liz. As Taylor heard the laughter that followed Liz's question, she got more and more irritated, especially since she could identify most of those laughs. There was Liz's laugh, Kelsey's laugh, and—what the fuck?—Erica's laugh. Erica? Seriously? Why was she laughing at that?

"I say only a few more weeks, if that," Liz said. "She's a little too innocent for Taylor, I think. Taylor will get sick of that soon."

Despite her annoyance, Taylor laughed to herself at the thought of what Avery would say if she heard Liz call her innocent.

"I was going to say she seemed too well-adjusted for Taylor," Kelsey said. "Not enough drama. I bet this will be over by the end of the month."

What the hell, Kelsey? Now you couldn't have torn Taylor away from her eavesdropping spot.

"Kelsey has a point," Erica said. "And so does Liz. She's not Taylor's usual type; she might get bored with Avery."

There she was with the fucking getting-bored thing again. Why would anyone think Avery was boring? Taylor had never once been bored in her presence!

"I don't know, Taylor seems to really like Avery," Sloane said.

Sloane was standing up for her? That was unexpected. Now Taylor felt even more guilty for being a bitch about her.

"You know Taylor, she's no good at relationships," Erica said. "I bet this pregnancy will last longer than their relationship." She paused for a second. "Actually, really: Would anyone bet that their relationship will outlast this pregnancy? If so, raise your hands."

What the fuck, Erica?

There was lots of laughter, and then silence, presumably while people were raising their hands. God, Taylor wished she could see through these damn bushes. After a few moments, Erica laughed. "Okay, if their relationship outlasts this pregnancy, each one of us will buy the two of you dinner. If it doesn't, you two have to buy the rest of us dinner. Nothing too fancy, no French Laundry here, we don't want to bankrupt you two!"

Everyone laughed in agreement, while Taylor just stood there, stunned. Not only had Erica suggested this bet, but she was on the side betting against Taylor. It was one thing when she and Taylor bet about Taylor's love life, but this was different.

She couldn't believe that, of everyone there, the one person who she knew was on her side was Sloane.

"Okay, we have a few more presents!" Speaking of Sloane, she was apparently eager to turn the conversation back to the actual point of the shower. Taylor turned and walked back toward the parking lot, but Avery was already coming toward her.

"Sam had to go," Avery said. "What took so long?"

Taylor opened her mouth to tell Avery everything she'd just overheard, when a few guests walked out of the party toward the parking lot. Shit, she couldn't do this here, now.

"Oh. Um, I had to run inside to go to the bathroom, sorry." She grabbed Avery's hand and walked back into the garden and forced a grin onto her face.

"What did we miss?" she asked. She was pleased to see that Erica didn't meet her eyes, but that didn't really make her feel better.

Taylor got through the rest of the shower by mostly keeping herself busy cleaning up and helping Sloane with the presents, but every time she looked at Erica, she got angrier and more hurt. No, betrayed. Erica should be on her side. *She* was always on Erica's side. And she'd thought Erica had always been on hers—had she been lying to herself about this over the years?

It hurt that Erica thought of Taylor's dating life as fodder for gossip, as something to bet about with other people, to laugh about with other people. It hurt that Erica thought of Taylor and her life as so juvenile that she would make fun of her and her relationship like that. It hurt that Erica had so little respect for her.

She didn't say anything to anyone about the conversation she'd overheard; this was Erica's fucking baby shower after all. She didn't want to make a scene in the middle of it. But once the guests left and it was just her, Sloane, Avery, and Erica, she felt like she was going to snap.

"Sloane, why don't you take Erica home," Avery said. "Taylor and I can handle the rest of the cleanup. The guest of honor should probably get some rest."

Bless Avery. If Taylor had said that herself, she absolutely would not have been able to keep an edge out of her voice.

"Yeah, we can take it from here," Taylor said, and was relieved that her voice sounded normal. "It's hot out here, get yourself back inside in some air-conditioning and unpack all of your presents."

Sloane looked uncertain.

"You're right, I should get her home, but I don't want to leave you two to do all the cleanup! I can come back after I've dropped her off."

Taylor draped an arm around Sloane.

"Sloane, you've already done so much for this shower. Go home and relax, really. Thank you so much for everything." She pulled Sloane into a side hug. She meant that far more than Sloane would ever know.

Sloane looked down at her, a hesitant smile on her face.

"It's been great doing this with you, Taylor. And you, too, Avery. Thanks for being so welcoming." Oh great, now Taylor felt guilty for how not at all welcoming she'd been to Sloane.

"It's been great, Sloane," Avery said. "I've had so much fun, and everything went so well." Taylor took a step back so Avery and Sloane could hug. It would have been natural for her to turn to

Erica at this point to give her a hug, but she just couldn't do it. Instead, she grabbed a box from underneath one of the food tables and started stacking dirty dishes in it.

"And don't worry about the cleanup, Sloane," Taylor said. "Callie had a hookup with a rental agency for these dishes, so we only have to pack them all up as is and drop them off. And the rest of this stuff, we can clean up easy."

Please, just let them leave. She wanted to be able to clean up and get out of here before she exploded.

"I'm going to run inside and get another box," she said. She waved in the general direction of Erica and Sloane. "Bye, guys! Great party, see you both soon!" And then she fled toward the winery building before she'd have to give Erica a hug.

By the time she got back to the garden, Erica and Sloane and all the presents were gone, and Avery was busy stacking chairs together.

"They got everything?" Taylor asked Avery as she filled up another box with dishes and wineglasses.

"I think so," Avery said, "though I'm sure we'll find something left behind; it happens at every party." Avery finished stacking chairs and came over to help her with the dishes. "I hope it's okay that I sent them home, but you looked like you'd had enough, and even though you seem to have softened toward Sloane, I thought it might be easier if we did this part ourselves."

Taylor smiled at Avery. She was deeply grateful for her in that moment, which made her rage at Erica even more acute.

"I can't even tell you how okay it is that you sent them home," she said. She dropped a quick kiss on her cheek. "Actually, yes, I can and I will, but that'll wait until after we've gotten out of here."

Avery grinned, with a little raise of her eyebrows. Oh, Avery thought she'd meant something sexual, when she was being completely literal. Did Avery think she only ever thought about sex? Wait. She forced herself to calm down. She was prone to innuendo like that; it wasn't Avery's fault for thinking that. And Avery had no idea what had just happened.

"Come on," she said. "Let's finish cleaning this up so we can get out of here."

Sloane had done a good job cleaning up the wrapping paper and ribbons and gift bags. For what felt like the thousandth time that day, Taylor mentally blessed Sloane and then laughed at herself. If someone had told her a week ago that she'd send countless blessings to Sloane on the day of the shower, she absolutely wouldn't have believed them.

"Oh!" Avery picked something up. "Here's an unopened card for Erica and Sam; it must have fallen behind the table without anyone seeing it."

"That's not like Sloane to have missed it," Taylor said. Avery made a face at her, and Taylor laughed. "No, I wasn't being sarcastic, I swear!"

Avery slipped the card in Taylor's back pocket.

"Well, you can give it to Erica the next time you see her."

Sooner than Taylor would have thought, they were done cleaning up and just needed to bring the folding chairs and tables back into the basement of the winery building. And who should come strolling outside at that moment but Luke.

"How'd the shower go? Need any help?"

"We definitely do," Taylor said. "Can you help us carry this stuff? Once we finish this, we're done."

Luke picked up a folding table in each arm, while Avery and Taylor each grabbed a stack of chairs.

"How is it that you always turn up here at the winery to help out right when we need you, even though you don't work here anymore?"

Luke grinned.

"Well, at first it was because I was in love with Margot, and now it's also because I'm in love with Margot." Taylor and Avery both laughed at him. "Other than that, though, I was out of town and just got back, so I swung by the winery to say hi, since I know she can't leave until late. But she's schmoozing with some VIPs, and I saw you two out here, and I thought I might as well make myself useful while I wait for her." He looked from Avery to Taylor as Taylor opened the door to the basement. "What more do you two have to do other than get the rest of the stuff out there back in here? Because if that's it, you guys take off, I'll take care of this."

"Luke, you don't have to do that—" Taylor started. But Avery talked over her.

"You're the best, thank you so much. And yeah, we've taken care of everything else, and there are some great leftovers up in the staff kitchen." She grabbed Taylor's hand. "Do you have everything?"

"Yeah, but he doesn't have to—"

Avery tugged her outside.

"Bye, Luke! Thanks again!" she called over her shoulder. She smiled at Taylor as she hurried her toward the parking lot. "Don't argue, just let him do it. Aren't you ready to get out of here? He needs something to keep himself busy until Margot is free. Win-win."

Avery had a point. Who was she to try to keep a man from doing her work, especially something she didn't particularly want to do?

Once they were both in Avery's car, Avery looked at her expectantly. It took her a few seconds to realize why, but she finally got it: Avery must know something was wrong. That's why she'd gotten rid of Sloane and Erica, and that's why she'd been so eager to let Luke take over. Thank goodness she could finally relax and not have to keep up the pretense that she wasn't angry and hurt.

"Well?" Avery said. "Aren't you going to ask?"

What was she talking about?

"Ask?"

"About your surprise?" Avery said.

Oh. She'd forgotten about the surprise. All she'd been able to think about for the past hour and a half had been Erica's bet against her.

"Right. My surprise."

She tried, and failed, to say it with some excitement in her voice. Fuck, now Avery looked hurt. Taylor was furious with herself. Avery was excited about this damn surprise, and Taylor probably would be, too, if she hadn't overheard her best friend shitting on their relationship an hour and a half ago.

"Sorry, I didn't mean to say it like that," she said. "Can we try that again? 'Oh right, my surprise!'" She winced. Great, now she just sounded sarcastic. "I'm sorry, I swear it's not you, I'm—"

"It's fine," Avery said, in a voice that made it clear that it was absolutely not fine. *Fuck, fuck, fuck.* She wasn't good at this shit. Maybe Erica was right about her and relationships.

No, fuck that.

"No, seriously, Avery, listen to me. I'm sorry that I'm being shitty about your surprise, it has nothing to do with you. I'm upset about something that happened at the shower; I was waiting until everything was over to talk to you about it, and I was so focused on getting out of there that I forgot all about the surprise, I'm really sorry."

Avery's shoulders relaxed, and her expression softened.

"Oh. Okay." She started the car. "What happened?"

Taylor took a deep breath. She hadn't actually planned to tell Avery about this. She didn't want to spoil the shower for Avery, who had worked so hard, and she didn't want Avery to feel insecure around her friends. But now she had to tell Avery what she'd overheard. She didn't tell her someone had called her uptight; Avery didn't need to know that. But she told her everything else that Erica had said, and everything else she'd overheard.

"Well," Avery said when Taylor finished her story. "I'm now invested in making sure Sloane wins this bet. We just have to stay together long enough to prove the haters wrong."

Taylor burst out laughing. Leave it to Avery to make an unexpected joke to cheer her up.

"I'm serious," Avery said. "No matter when we actually break up, I swear I won't tell a soul until . . . let's see, at least three days after Erica has that baby. Just text me as soon as Erica has the baby, three days later, we're over. We'll make sure that Sloane and whoever that second person on our side was will get their free dinners."

Taylor tried to smile. Maybe that would get rid of that heavy, tight feeling in her chest.

"By the way, I admit I was wrong about Sloane," she said. "I'm glad I already started to feel warmer toward her before I heard her come to my defense; if I hadn't, I may have fainted." She sighed. "But I can't believe Erica did that. Bet about me like that, with all those people. Like, yeah, most of them are my friends, but she's my best friend, you know? I was sure she'd stick up for me, defend me. And instead of doing that, or even just being quiet and changing the subject—which wouldn't have bugged me that much, it was her baby shower, after all—she went the opposite way and made fun of me, too."

Taylor had always assumed that her friends thought of her as an immature, unfocused commitment-phobe, but to hear it like that, to know it for sure, really hurt. Avery reached for her hand. Taylor was embarrassed by how good it felt to hold on.

"You know they're all jealous of you, right?" Avery asked. "Like, they're your friends, and I like them, and they clearly adore you, but they're jealous that you're so hot and charming and magnetic—don't make that face, you know it's true. They wish they were like you, someone who can just snap your fingers and date any woman you want, present company included."

Taylor rolled her eyes.

"Thank you, but—"

Avery shook her head.

"Oh, I wasn't paying you compliments, I was just stating facts. Of course they're all jealous of you, of course they gossip about you, but it's not malicious. I'm sure that doesn't make you feel any better, but it's obvious to me. And, like, I'm not a huge catch or anything—" Taylor started to interrupt her, but Avery talked over her. "I know what you're going to say, I just had to say that because what I'm about to say makes me feel arrogant. But that night we went to trivia, before anything happened between us, and they were all flirting with me, and I was flirting back, and you told them nothing was going on between us? And then the next time we went to trivia, you and I were together. Has that happened with you before?"

Taylor sighed. She didn't like thinking this way.

"I mean, I suppose so." Avery gave her a sideways look. "Fine, yes, there have been times that everyone was hitting on one person, and they came home with me, but—"

Avery nodded.

"Right, exactly. I'm not saying that means your friends should have said any of that stuff, that sucks that they did! Especially that Erica did! I'm just telling you why."

Taylor digested that. She understood, she supposed, why Avery was saying this. But—

"But these are my friends! Erica is my *best* friend. And she's happily married and about to have a baby! Are all of them so jealous of my, what, ability to get women to sleep with me that they regularly talk shit about me behind my back? That makes no sense! Especially since they're all far more accomplished and good at life than I am."

Avery squeezed her hand.

"No, they're not. But from what you told me, they weren't talking shit about you. I'm sure they talked some shit about me that you didn't tell me—thanks for that—but most of what they said sounded like good-natured teasing of a friend, stuff they'd all say to your face. Am I wrong about that?"

Taylor wanted to say yes, but she forced herself to stop and think about it.

"For most of them, that's probably true," she admitted. "Like, they wouldn't have bet on how long my relationship would last if I'd been there, but the rest of it, maybe. But Erica . . . no."

"That's the one you're really upset about," Avery said.

"I was expecting her to jump in to defend me," Taylor said. "Not . . . not put my love life up for a bet. And then bet *against* me."

Taylor let go of Avery's hand and turned to look out the window. She never cried, but she knew that if she kept talking about this, about how betrayed she felt by Erica, how much her words had hurt, she might break down. Sure, they hadn't talked as much recently, but she didn't think that much had changed between them. She couldn't handle seeing the kind, concerned look on Avery's face; she couldn't deal with her gentle touch right now. She would fall to pieces.

"I, um . . ." She cleared her throat. "Am I dressed appropriately for my surprise? You didn't give me a dress code." She tried to put enthusiasm in her voice. This time, it seemed to have worked. Or at least Avery went along with her tacit plea to change the subject.

"Oh, don't worry, I took care of that," she said. "I have clothes for both of us in the trunk."

Clothes for both of them? Hmm. Trying to figure this out was a good distraction. It was a hot late-September afternoon in Napa Valley. Avery's sundress would be perfectly appropriate for just about anything they could possibly do.

Or were they going somewhere they had to really dress up? If they were doing a fancy dinner somewhere, Avery would definitely want to wear something other than her sundress. Maybe that was it. But ugh, Taylor hoped not. After dealing with the stress of the shower, plus everything that was jumbling around in her head because of that stupid, mean bet, Taylor was prematurely exhausted by the thought of sitting through a stilted, three-hour white-tablecloth meal. Hell, the thought of sitting in a *chair* for that long was tiring. She wanted to sit on a couch, recline on a chaise, flop in a bathtub, curl up in a bed, lie on the floor—any of those options would be far better than sitting in a chair for a fancy meal.

She sighed internally. If this was a fancy dinner, she was going to be enthusiastic about it for Avery's sake. She wouldn't lie to her; she'd never lied to Avery, and she wasn't going to start now. But she also didn't want Avery to feel bad. She would find something nice to say about it. Multiple nice things, even.

But she'd thought Avery knew her so well, that they were so in sync. If Avery would plan a surprise like this for her, then how well did Avery know her? What could have even given Avery the idea that she wanted to do something like this? Did she know Taylor at all? Was Erica right that they'd be over soon? Why did the thought of that make Taylor so sad?

Did Erica know something that she didn't about how well Avery knew her? Had Taylor been on a sex high that had made her ignore red flags? Is that what happened when she didn't have sex for months, she would fall hard for the next person she had sex with no matter what?

Was Erica's bet like some self-fulfilling prophecy? Like, because she'd overheard it, it meant that it had to happen? Or maybe it was a curse. Wait, but that would mean that Erica had cursed her.

She was officially losing it.

She looked up with a jerk when the car stopped. She hadn't even noticed that they'd turned into a parking lot. She took a deep breath, ready to smile.

"We're here!" Avery said. "Time for a spa day—or, late afternoon, rather—at Calistoga's famous hot springs, and Calistoga's famous mud baths."

"Spa day," Taylor said slowly. "Mud baths."

Avery nodded.

"You told me that if you won the bet with Erica, she would have had to treat you to a spa day, and I didn't want you to lose out on that, so . . ."

Relief flooded through her body. It wasn't a fancy dinner. It wasn't somewhere she would have to sit in a chair! It wasn't somewhere she would have to dress up. It was somewhere she could decompress and relax and lounge. It was something only someone who knew her well and had listened to her would plan for her.

"Mud baths!" she said again. And then she laughed so hard tears came to her eyes.

"Um, Taylor?" Avery said. "Is . . . are you . . . I thought . . ."

Taylor put a hand on her cheek.

"You thought right. This is exactly what I needed." She flung open her car door. "What are we doing still sitting in the car? Let's do this."

Taylor jumped out of the car. As they walked toward the spa, she reached for Avery's hand.

"This is a perfect surprise," she said. "One question: When you said you packed clothes for both of us, what did you mean?"

Avery patted her tote bag.

"Swimsuits. Right in here."

Taylor laughed again. She slipped her arm around Avery's waist and pulled her in for a hug.

"Swimsuits. Of course."

They checked into the spa and changed into their swimsuits, and then went out to the hot tub before their treatments. It was toward the end of the day on a Sunday, so there were only a few people in the very large hot tub, leaving Avery and Taylor a big corner to themselves. Taylor leaned back against the jets and closed her eyes.

"Wow. This . . . *this* is perfect." She reached for Avery's hand under the water and squeezed it. Avery squeezed hers back.

Taylor let her eyes drift closed. See, this was exactly what she needed after that baby shower. She never would have thought of it for herself, but reclining in this hot tub, with the promise of whatever the mud bath would be and then a hot shower and a massage afterward, was even better than a chaise or a recliner or the floor, or any of the other things she'd thought of in the car on the way here. She shook her head and laughed at herself. How could she have even thought that Avery would want to take her to a fancy dinner after that shower?

Why would Erica bet against her staying in a relationship with someone who knew her this well, someone who cared for her like this? Betting against her didn't just mean she was sitting on the sidelines waiting to see what happened; it meant she was actively cheering for the end of Taylor's relationship with Avery so she could win her bet.

Taylor opened her eyes. Avery was next to her, relaxing against the jets, her straw hat on to protect her against the late-afternoon sun like the practical, organized, stylish person she was, and Taylor smiled. She was nowhere near getting sick of those qualities of Avery's.

Did Erica think Avery would get sick of her? Taylor was well aware of her own faults: she was bad with money; she was too impulsive (which sometimes was a good thing, but okay, fine, wasn't always); she was a little too convinced she was right all the time; other people called her fickle; and yes, she relied on her ability to charm people to get her what she wanted too frequently. Would Avery get sick of those things? Or was there something else that Avery hated about her that she didn't even know because Avery wasn't good at conflict?

Why the fuck was she spoiling this great time by being consumed with all this fucking insecurity?

Taylor forced herself to shake off her negative thoughts. Avery had planned this fun day for them; Taylor wasn't going to ruin it. She refused to let anything interfere with her first mud bath experience.

After a while in the hot tub, they went back to the dressing room and changed into their enormous spa robes. Taylor grinned at Avery when she tied hers.

"I'm impressed that they gave me one that's big enough to fit me; most of these 'one size fits all' robes at spas leave me half naked."

"That's awful," Avery said. "What do you do then?"

Taylor grinned at her again.

"Oh, they have bigger ones on the men's side; when I walk around half naked for a while, they usually find one for me."

Avery burst out laughing.

When it was time for the mud bath, a staff member led them out of the changing room and to the back of the spa.

"You *can* wear a swimsuit in the mud bath if you prefer, but I don't recommend it," she said to them. "I tried it out when I first started here, and I never got the mud out of that swimsuit."

Taylor smiled and glanced over at Avery. She was also smiling, but she looked a little nervous.

"I'm fine without one," Taylor said.

"Um, yeah, me, too," Avery said.

The staff member threw open a door. "It's through here."

Taylor wanted to giggle when she walked into the room. The rest of the spa was all white linen, flowers, soft music, cucumber slices; this room was industrial, utilitarian, gray concrete. It made her feel like this was the old-school version of the spa, and she was into it. Whatever happened in this room, this was the real deal.

The floor was covered in black rubber mats, with buckets everywhere, and there were four huge, deep tubs, full of thick black mud. When she'd imagined what a mud bath would be like, she somehow hadn't thought it would be this intense. Now she was even more excited.

"Taylor?" one of the women standing by a tub said, and Taylor stepped forward. "I'm Gloria. I'll take your robe. Sit here right on the edge, and then turn around and lower yourself into the bath."

Taylor lowered herself, very awkwardly, into the tub full of steaming hot, very heavy mud, as Avery did the same in the tub next to hers. Finally, she was all the way in or, rather, on the mud, at which point Gloria picked up a bucket and scooped more mud over Taylor's whole body until she was covered from her neck to her toes. She turned to look at Avery, who was also now packed tightly into her mud bath. As soon as their eyes met, Taylor burst out laughing, and Avery followed suit.

"This is the most amazing thing I've ever done in my entire life," Taylor said. She lifted her hand out of the mud and squeezed a handful of it. "This is like . . . when I was a kid, I used to love going to the beach and playing in the sand, especially when it was a little wet, and this is like the grown-up, much more expensive, and also much dirtier version of that." She laughed at the look on Avery's face. "Nonsexually dirty, to be clear."

Avery giggled.

"I was about to say. This is so deeply gross and fantastic at the same time." She lowered her voice. "Though, speaking of sex, I feel like I'm going to have mud in every single crevice of my body after this."

"Oh, without a doubt," Taylor said. She leaned her head back against the pillow at the edge of the tub and let herself relax into the sensation. At first, this had felt like a gimmick, but after a few moments of feeling the warm, heavy weight of the mud surrounding her body, in this cozy tub, with Avery right next to her, peace overtook her. She wasn't thinking about the shower, about the bet, about what Erica said; all she was thinking about was how happy she was to be here, right at this moment.

She could have stayed in the mud bath for hours, but eventually, they had to get out, take very thorough showers, and move on to their massages. They were some of the last to leave the spa that evening, and then they drove straight back to Avery's apartment and collapsed on the couch.

"So," Avery asked after they'd ordered takeout. "Good spa day? How did you feel about your first mud bath?"

"I'm not sure if anything in my life has ever felt that good that didn't involve sex," Taylor said, which made Avery burst out laughing.

Taylor smiled at her.

"But seriously, thank you. For thinking of it, for arranging it for today, when you knew I'd need it, for everything you did for the shower—it was all perfect."

Avery curled into Taylor's side, and Taylor wrapped her arms around her.

"You're welcome," Avery said, and kissed her on the cheek.

Taylor could still feel the knot in her stomach from what happened at the party, and part of her wanted to call Erica now, ask her why she would do something like that, why she would root against Taylor's happiness, why she thought so little of her. But she made herself push that aside. She had Avery's silky-smooth body tucked against hers, and she was still slightly dazed from the mud bath and massage; she was too happy and peaceful to think about Erica and her bet right now. Plus, she had better things to do.

She put her hand on Avery's thigh.

"You know," she said, "even though that massage didn't involve sex, that doesn't mean everything today has to be like that."

Avery nuzzled her neck.

"Mmm, I like the way you think."

Taylor slowly pulled Avery's dress up above her knees. Avery put her hand over Taylor's and slid it up her thigh to her ass. Her bare ass.

Taylor's dramatic gasp wasn't even pretense.

"Avery Jensen! *You* aren't wearing underwear?"

Avery kissed her neck and giggled.

"I forgot to bring an extra pair with me, and after my massage I didn't want to put the pair I'd been wearing all day back on, so . . ."

"You naughty girl," Taylor said, with a gentle smack of Avery's ass that just made her giggle more. "And here I was, about to tell you how hot I found it for us to be naked and getting massages at the same time, and how I was thinking about you glossy with that massage oil, and the whole time you were walking around naked under that dress. Does this mean that on our drive back here I could have done this in the car?" She slipped a finger inside of her. Avery shifted to give Taylor more access, and Taylor took full advantage of that.

"You definitely could have, yes, if you'd wanted us to get into an accident and possibly arrested," Avery said.

Taylor smiled and looked at Avery. Her eyes were closed, and a smile was on her face.

"Do you know what I thought about at the spa?" Avery asked her.

"No, but I have a feeling that I really want to know." Taylor moved her fingers a little faster inside of Avery.

"I thought about how much I wanted to do this to you when we were in the hot tub," she said. "I wanted to pull those little shorts of yours down and push your legs open, and watch you right there, with my fingers inside of you, and see your face as you arched your back in that way that you do, and hear those little soft sounds you make when you're getting close. And then, right when you were almost there, I would make you sit on the edge of the hot tub, and I would put my face in between your legs and my mouth on your pussy and see how long I could make you come for."

"Holy fucking shit, Avery!" Taylor was scandalized, and very, very turned on. Avery had so far been tentative with dirty talk, but she had apparently lost those inhibitions.

Avery looked both smug and extremely proud of herself, as she should. She pulled herself up so she was kneeling over Taylor, pulled her pants off, and pushed her legs open. And then she gave Taylor three orgasms in quick succession.

Taylor was still gasping for breath when Avery's phone rang.

"I think that's our food." Avery jumped up. "I'll run down to get it."

Taylor sat on the couch, half naked and fully satisfied, as she waited for Avery. Usually, she was the initiator in their relationship when it came to sex; she'd always assumed that was partly because she was more experienced and confident, but also because that's how their personalities shook out. Avery was the quieter, shyer, more conservative one; Taylor was the loud, outgoing risk-taker. But tonight, for whatever reason, Avery was driving around without underwear and taking the lead in sex, and Taylor fucking loved it. Maybe it was because Avery thought Taylor needed a treat after that shower, maybe it was because Avery finally believed Taylor when she had said she enjoyed the hell out of their sex life, but whatever it was, Taylor was very fucking grateful for it.

"What's gotten into you?" she said, when Avery strolled back into the apartment, a big bag of food in her hand. "*Not* that I'm complaining, I'm doing the opposite of complaining, I'm just wondering if there's something I did so I can do it again."

Avery flashed her a grin.

"It was probably the mud bath," she said, and took the food into the kitchen. Taylor followed her.

"If it was the mud bath, I want us to go at least once a week," Taylor said.

Avery laughed again.

"Or maybe it's just that now I know that we have a hard stop in seven weeks, I want to enjoy this for as long as I have left," she said.

A hard stop in seven weeks? Taylor paused halfway through putting rice on her plate and looked at Avery.

"Huh?" At some point today, she'd lost her ability to be articulate.

"You know, because of the bet?" Avery looked at her, and then her smile faded. "Sorry, I can tell that you don't want to talk about the Erica thing more tonight. Forget I said anything."

Taylor shook her head slowly.

Avery had been serious when she'd said they should break up after Erica had the baby. Taylor had thought she was joking. And she was lighthearted about it, like it didn't bother her at all.

"What if I don't want to break up in seven weeks?" Taylor asked her.

"Oh, I thought about that," Avery said. "Don't worry, if we break up before that, I won't tell anyone. Well, I'd probably tell Luke, but I'd swear him to secrecy. I'm invested in Sloane winning this bet now."

Whether Taylor wanted to break up wasn't the issue—*Avery* definitely wanted to break up in seven weeks or less. Assumed they would break up in seven weeks or less. Had already thought about what they'd do about this stupid bet if they broke up before the seven weeks and three days were up. And she told Taylor about it in that casual, no-big-deal way, like it didn't matter to her, wouldn't matter to her.

"Oh," Taylor said.

SEVENTEEN

WHEN AVERY WOKE UP THE NEXT MORNING, TAYLOR WAS GET-
ting dressed. That was rare; Taylor almost never woke up before her.

"Where are you going?" Avery asked. She hoped it was to go
pick up pastries. Taylor had done that before, though she usually
waited until after they both woke up (and had sex) to do so.

"I'm taking off," Taylor said as she pulled her shirt on. "I have
to get to the winery to pick up my car, and then I have some stuff
to do today before work."

Avery sat up.

"I'll drive you there."

"Don't worry about it," Taylor said. "You had a busy day yesterday. Go back to sleep, I'll see you later." She flashed a smile at
Avery and walked out of the bedroom. That was also unlike Taylor. She was probably still upset about the whole Erica thing and
needed to be alone, so Avery just let her go.

Taylor had been really hurt by that bet, which kind of surprised Avery. She would have expected Taylor to shrug it off and

not worry about what other people said about her. Taylor's reaction to the bet made Avery realize she'd been wrong about her vision of Taylor: she did have insecurities like everyone else. She'd told Avery that, more than once; Avery supposed she hadn't really believed her. Should she have insisted on driving her this morning, just to see if she was okay? She hated that Taylor was hurting. She would text her later to check in.

But also . . . she was weirdly glad that she knew the expiration date for their relationship. Maybe it was because she liked structure, clarity, deadlines; she knew Taylor never stayed with anyone for very long, but no one had really told her how long "not very long" was. Everything had been going so well for the two of them, and they'd been having so much fun; she knew that if things kept going like this for much longer, she ran the risk of getting crushed when Taylor decided she was bored with her and it was time to move on. And she didn't want that.

Now that they had an end date, she felt more secure. No surprises, no chances of getting hurt or too attached. At the most, seven more weeks of fun times and great sex, then Taylor could go off and date the next person who raised an eyebrow at her when she poured wine, and Avery would use her newfound flirting skills to attempt to date someone else.

Avery looked at the clock and snuggled back down into her bed. She had at least an hour before she had to get up. And even though the day before had been fun, it had been long and exhausting, so she was grateful for the break she'd given herself in her schedule. Unfortunately, now that she was awake, she was *awake*. After ten minutes of trying to go back to sleep, she got up and made coffee, and got back in bed to spend the next hour peacefully scrolling through nonsense on her phone, which she didn't often have the leisure to do on a Monday morning. Her phone was still on do not disturb, and she didn't let herself check her email yet—she wanted a few more moments of relaxation—but she did click over to check her texts, and found one from Luke from a few moments earlier.

LUKE

> How'd the surprise go? What's your week look like? Dinner tomorrow night maybe?

Luke had known about her surprise for Taylor, which was why he'd jumped in to take over the cleanup after the shower. She owed him one.

AVERY

> Surprise was great, thanks for the assist. And yeah we haven't hung out in too long, let me check my calendar

She couldn't do Tuesday night, though. Tuesday night had been her night with Taylor ever since they'd started the flirting lessons, and they'd kept it like that after they'd started dating. Even though they usually saw each other on the weekends and at least one other night a week, they always got together on Tuesdays.

AVERY

> What about lunch tomorrow? I have a busy morning but a window between 1 and 3 if that works for you

She couldn't wait to tell him about the bet that Taylor had

overheard. If she was being honest with herself, when Taylor told her about the bet, she'd gotten a flash of pride. She'd tried to push that away in the moment, since Taylor was clearly upset about it and needed to vent. But *she* was never the person other people gossiped about. She was Goody Two-shoes Avery Jensen, always responsible, always dating the nice, boring guy, always doing what was expected of her, always the person who said "yes, please" and "no, thank you." She never dated the person whom everyone gossiped about, the person people said, *What do you think about those two?* about, the person people placed bets on. And now she was, and it felt great.

Was it kind of weird and intrusive that people were that interested in her relationship with Taylor that they were placing bets about it? Sure. It was still exciting. Not that she'd tell Taylor that; Avery didn't want her to think she was making light of something that bothered her so much. But she couldn't wait to tell Luke about this.

LUKE

Done. Let me know where and I'll be there

The next day, Luke texted her after he got to their favorite sandwich shop.

LUKE

I'm in line—Italian sub or fried chicken sandwich? Or one of each and we share?

She texted him back once she'd parked.

> One of each and we share, and chips too. Just parked, I'll grab a table out back

Luke grinned at her when he came outside.

"Hey!" He put their food down and gave her a hug. "I feel like it's been forever. You're so busy now with *Taylor*." He said her name like he used to say the names of people she'd had crushes on in high school. She, in turn, reverted to elementary school and stuck her tongue out at him. They both burst out laughing.

"Oh, I'm the busy one?" She couldn't help but tease him. "You spend every spare second with Margot, and you begrudge me time with Taylor?"

He smiled that besotted smile that always came over his face when Margot came up, and shook his head.

"You know I don't begrudge you time with Taylor. You seem so happy with her."

Avery laughed again.

"How do you know? You've barely seen us together."

He shook his head again.

"I can tell. You're so comfortable with her, so relaxed, so . . . you. But that's not all—you just seem happier in general ever since you started dating her. You laugh a lot more. You have more fun. Your voice even sounds different. It's really nice."

She hadn't expected this from Luke. She wasn't sure what to make of it. She supposed she did feel different now and had all summer. Was that because of Taylor? Partly, probably. Some of it was because of doing the flirting lessons with Taylor; they'd given her more confidence in herself, they'd made her feel less stressed about every interaction, they'd made her feel more . . . herself. Which wasn't what she'd expected from them. But yeah, some of it was definitely from dating Taylor.

"Speaking of Taylor, I have to tell you what happened at the shower. Wait, give me half of a sandwich."

He handed her half of the chicken sandwich and opened the top of the sparkling water he'd gotten her.

"I have no idea what could be so exciting that happened at a baby shower, but I'm all ears. Did everyone find out the baby isn't the father's? Oh wait, it was a two-mom shower, that wouldn't work. Did someone cheat at one of the games and then someone else found out about it and there was a whole brawl? Granted, I saw no evidence of a brawl when I got there, but that doesn't mean anything; you and Taylor are both pretty efficient at cleaning up. Did someone spike the punch? But why would they have to, the shower was at a winery. Okay, I give up."

Avery took a bite of her sandwich and chewed it slowly before she looked up at Luke.

"Are you done? Do I get to tell my story now?"

Luke thought for a second.

"Yep, done. Please go ahead." He unwrapped the other sandwich and gestured for her to talk. She rolled her eyes and tried to hide her smile.

"Okay, so Taylor and I left for a few minutes toward the end to help Sam load up the car, but Taylor came back before I did. *Well,* she overheard the rest of the people there gossiping about the two of us—what they thought of our relationship, what they thought of me, stuff like that."

"What do they think of you?" Luke asked.

Avery shook her head.

"Taylor only told me good things, though I'm sure she was holding something back. But then, Erica—the guest of honor, pregnant lady, Taylor's best friend of many years—proposed a bet on how long our relationship would last. Mine and Taylor's! And then they all bet on if we would last longer than her pregnancy!" Luke didn't look as amused by this as she'd assumed he would be. "It's okay, you don't have to be mad about this on my behalf, I'm not upset about it. Taylor is, though. She's upset that her friends were gossiping about her—which I get—and she's pretty hurt that Erica proposed the bet in the first place. I understand all of that, but I also think it's kind of funny. When Taylor told me about it, I had to be nice and understanding and come up with a solution for her, but I think it's wild that people are betting about my relationship, you know?"

Luke tore open a bag of potato chips.

"I guess I can see that, but I'm more in Taylor's camp here. These were her friends, right? Wouldn't it feel weird to you and make you feel bad if your friends were all betting against you? Or if your friends thought your relationship was something to place bets on and laugh about?"

Avery reached for a chip.

"I get that, but this is Taylor we're talking about here. She's always hopping from relationship to relationship—I'm sure her friends have met so many of her girlfriends of the month, you know? Hell, half of them have *been* her girlfriends of the month! I knew that going in. Everyone and their mother flirts with her—sometimes literally! She knows that about herself, though I guess it bothers her that other people like talking about it."

Luke looked at her with some concern in his eyes.

"Does that mean that this relationship isn't serious? Because I hoped . . ."

Avery laughed.

"Taylor doesn't do serious, come on, I know this. You know this, too! As a matter of fact, we decided that because of the bet, we're going to stay together until three days after Erica has the baby, and then break up. And Erica isn't due for seven weeks, which honestly is far longer than I thought we'd stay together."

Luke crumpled up his sandwich wrapper.

"Oh. Huh, okay. You already have a breakup plan. Was this Taylor's idea?"

Avery shook her head.

"No, mine. She was upset about the bet, and mad that most of her friends bet that we wouldn't last until Erica had the baby, so I said we should make sure the people who bet on us would win. Hilariously, the only person we know who was on our side was Erica's friend Sloane, who Taylor spent all summer despising."

Luke nodded slowly.

"Right, but why does this mean you have to break up? I know that you say Taylor doesn't do serious, but . . . you seem to really like her, and she seems to be really into you, and there are lots of people who 'don't do serious' until they do, you know? Like, is this what you want? A casual relationship that you already have an end date for? Because it doesn't seem like that's what you want."

"There's nothing wrong with wanting that," Avery said.

"But is that what *you* want?" Luke asked. "I don't know, after seeing you with Taylor . . . Are you sure you don't have real feelings for her?"

Avery started to deny it, to say of course she didn't, of course she wanted something casual. The look on Luke's face stopped her. He looked so supportive, so concerned for her, that she couldn't do it. She was trying to be more honest about her feelings, wasn't she? She knew she could trust Luke.

"Okay. To you, and to you *only*, I'll admit that if I let myself, I could have some real feelings for Taylor. And yes, there have been a few times when I wished that she did serious relationships. But she doesn't. And I *haven't* let those feelings get big, I *am* okay with this relationship staying casual. I don't want to be one of the many people who has had their heart broken by Taylor Cameron. You don't have to worry about me, Luke, I promise."

If she let herself hope, even a little bit, she could easily convince herself that there was something real between her and Taylor, that she really cared, that their relationship could last. But if she did that, when the end came . . . it would be awful. That breakup would be far worse than the breakup with Derek. By the end, she was so unhappy with him that her heart had been just fine when they broke up. But if she let herself think that she and Taylor . . . No, she didn't even want to think about it. It was much more civilized to have a nice, agreed-upon date for when they'd break up. No drama, no tears, no heartbreak.

"Okay," Luke said. "But have you and Taylor talked about this? Not the bet or the breakup plan or whatever, but that neither of you thinks this relationship is serious or has the potential to be?"

Luke was going to keep pushing on this, wasn't he?

"We don't have to talk about it. We've talked about a ton of relationship stuff for months now, long before we were even dating. She and Erica had a bet before we started dating that Taylor couldn't make it all summer without sleeping with someone, because that's the kind of person she is. I knew that's what I was getting into. I need to sow my wild oats for a while, not jump back into a serious relationship. And she's the first woman I've dated, after all. I want to do more of that."

Luke nodded again. Avery was starting to hate that nod.

"What?" she said. "Just say it, since I know you're going to anyway."

He offered her the open bag of potato chips, and she took a handful.

"I just don't want you to give up on a relationship that could be something more because you're scared of getting your heart broken." She started to say something, to tell him that wasn't it, but he went on. "With Derek, you realized afterward that you were much happier without him in your life than you were with him in your life, right? Well, with Taylor, you're happier with her in your life than you were without her, aren't you? I guess . . . Look, I don't want to be that guy who is all coupled up now and so is trying to preach about love and relationships and act like I know better than you, because I've never known better than you about anything, and I'm not going to start now. But I don't want you to ignore your own feelings and try to take the easier way out when you actually want something else."

Avery shook her head.

"Luke, I know you care about me, and I appreciate it, but I'm having a great time with Taylor, and that's all. I wanted to have fun in this last year of my twenties, and that's what I'm doing, I'm having a blast. I know you're happy now, but I am, too. I'm happy just the way things are, I don't need to change things to be happy, okay? Now, tell me about your trip. How's the new job?"

Luke gave her a long look. And then, like she'd known he would, he let her change the subject.

"The job is good so far," he said. "I keep expecting something bad to happen, my shoulders tense up every time I check my email, but everything has been far better than I expected. As for the trip . . ."

Avery sighed with relief as she listened to Luke's story. It had been a mistake to open up to Luke about her very occasional thoughts of what could be between her and Taylor. Casual, fun, great sex, seven weeks to go. Just what she wanted.

———

TAYLOR WAS COLDLY FURIOUS AT BOTH ERICA AND AVERY. SHE spent Sunday and Monday replaying what they'd each said, to remind herself why she was angry and why they deserved it. Every so often, hurt began to seep through the anger, both hurt and sadness, but when that happened, she replayed a particularly enraging part of one of the conversations in her head, and that reignited her anger.

Usually, when she was this angry with someone, she would bring it up immediately so they could hash it out. Often when she got this angry at someone she was dating, she would just break up with them, because what was the point in staying in a relationship if it was going to be difficult? But this all felt different. She was angry at Erica, yes, but she was also too hurt to even talk about it yet. She had to sit with this before she did something wildly embarrassing like burst into tears when she saw Erica.

As for Avery, the whole point was that Taylor *didn't* want to break up with her. That's what hurt so much—and made her so angry: Avery had decided that they would break up and when, without even talking to Taylor about it or asking her how she felt.

Was this a taste of her own medicine? Probably.

On Monday, Avery sent her a few texts, all of which Taylor either ignored or responded to briefly. Her texts were light and cheerful, which only enraged Taylor more. But then on Tuesday afternoon, she pulled out her phone to see a text that made her want to throw her phone across the room.

AVERY

What time tonight?

Right. It was Tuesday, the night they always hung out. And because Avery thought everything was totally fine between them, she assumed they had plans. But Taylor couldn't see Avery tonight, she had to calm herself down first, or deal with Erica first, or something. Whatever it was, she hadn't done it yet.

TAYLOR

can't tonight

She should probably say more to Avery. If she were mature and grown-up and all of those things, she would, but she felt neither mature nor grown-up right now.

AVERY

Oh, ok

Then the three little dots popped up next to Avery's name to show that she was typing, and stayed there for a long time before her next text came.

AVERY

See you later this week then

Now Taylor felt guilty for blowing off Avery, and then furious for feeling guilty. Why should she feel bad about that? Avery seemed perfectly happy to have their relationship end seven Tuesdays from now! Why would Avery even care that she was blowing her off? Avery didn't care about her at all!

She stayed at the winery late that day, doing only sort of necessary cleanup and organization, and got bad takeout on the way home.

Late the next afternoon, Erica texted her. Not to the group chat they had with Liz and Callie and that whole crew—Erica had texted that chat for days with photos from the shower and how much she loved them all and then pictures of the nursery set up with presents and blah blah. Everyone else had hearted and awwwed and yayed about that stuff, but Taylor had ignored it all. She wondered what they were saying about her in the group chat she was sure they had without her in it. But no, Erica's text today was just to her.

ERICA

> Hey! Did you or Avery happen to see an extra envelope around when you guys were cleaning up after the shower? I only ask because my aunt apparently gave me a big gift card, and my mom will lose it if I don't send a thank you note, but I can't find it anywhere.

Shit. That envelope. Where the fuck was it? Taylor looked in her bag, but it wasn't there, and then checked her pockets and pulled out a frayed—but still intact—envelope from her back pocket. Right, Avery had stuck it in her back pocket when they'd left the winery that day. It was a miracle that it hadn't fallen out when she'd washed them. Good thing she was wearing those same pants today.

TAYLOR

yeah i've got it.

Normally, she would apologize for forgetting something like this and not texting Erica right away, but she wasn't fucking sorry. Hadn't she thrown Erica that fucking shower only to have her curse her relationship? Erica was the one who should be sorry.

ERICA

Awesome! Want to drop it by on the way home from work? Sam isn't home, I could order dinner? I haven't gotten to see just you in a while.

Oh, she wanted to see *just* Taylor?

TAYLOR

Taylor had a pit in her stomach when she left the winery that afternoon. She didn't know what she was going to do when she got to Erica's, if she was going to chicken out and just drop off the card and go, or stay and talk about everything, or something in between. She hadn't said she was going to stay for dinner tonight; she could make an excuse and say she had to meet Avery or something. But if she said that, would Erica smirk and then Taylor would know what she was smirking about and then let it all out? Had Erica smirked every time she'd brought up Avery for the past few weeks or months? She couldn't remember.

Plus, Erica had been distant for months. Taylor had blamed

either Sloane or Erica's pregnancy for all of that, for the disappearing acts and the ignored texts and the condescending tone from Erica about lots of things, including Taylor's failed celibacy bet. But had Erica decided that since she was a grown-up married woman who owned a house and had a baby on the way, she was too mature for her mess of a friend who lived in an apartment and had a mediocre credit score and jumped in and out of people's beds at the drop of a hat? Maybe. Maybe Erica didn't want to be her friend anymore.

Taylor felt a tear threaten to spill out of her eye. Goddamn it.

Erica had been there for her when she'd lost two jobs in a row and hadn't been sure how she was going to pay her rent that month. Erica was the only person other than Avery she'd told about her secret dream to own a wine bar, and Erica had cheered her on. Erica had laughed and cried and mourned and celebrated every big moment with her for years. Erica, *her* Erica, wouldn't smirk when she brought up her girlfriend—if she had, Taylor would have noticed, would have said, *What the fuck?*

Granted, she wouldn't think that Erica, *her* Erica, would have made that bet in the first place, but unfortunately, she'd heard it herself. She had to ask Erica what the fuck was going on.

She pulled up in front of Erica's cute little house, right next door to Sloane's much bigger one, and squared her shoulders as she walked up to the front door. Erica opened it almost as soon as Taylor rang the bell.

"Hey! I wasn't sure if the doorbell was you or our pizza, and honestly, I was more excited for it to be our pizza, no offense, I'm starving. I got two of them, since I feel like I could eat an entire pizza myself—even though I have awful heartburn now, sorry, you'll have to excuse the TMI, but then, I feel like there isn't really TMI between the two of us, anyway? Sorry that I'm talking nonstop,

I haven't left the house all day, and with Sam gone, I haven't talked to anyone in person today and I feel like it's all just exploding to get out. Do you want Diet Coke? It's in the fridge, I put some in there for you."

Taylor didn't even try to get a word in edgewise as they walked into the kitchen. She could tell the chatter was because Erica was nervous; they hadn't been friends for over ten years for nothing.

When Erica finally stopped talking, Taylor pulled the card out of her bag and handed it to Erica.

"Here's your aunt's card," she said. "I overheard that bet you made that my relationship with Avery wouldn't last longer than your pregnancy. Avery decided that we should make sure we dated until a few days after you gave birth, just so you would lose the bet, and I suppose that would be nice revenge and all, but I don't really want revenge, I really just want to know what the fuck, Erica? Why did you do that?"

As soon as Taylor said she overheard the bet, Erica dropped into a seat at the kitchen table and put her head in her hands. She didn't look up until Taylor finished talking.

"Shit." She bit her lip. "I'm so sorry. I'm sorry you overheard that. It was—"

In her whole previous speech, Taylor had been calm and measured and to the point like she'd wanted to be, but as soon as Erica said she was sorry, Taylor snapped.

"I don't fucking care about your apology," she said. "I don't want you to apologize to me, I don't care how sorry you are. What I care about is that you're my best friend, and you think it's funny to bet with other people about me like that? You sit there at your fucking baby shower all happy and on top of the world because you have everything you've ever wanted, and you mock me and what I have and what I want? While I'm carrying your fucking baby presents to the car you are actively rooting against my relation-ship? And you won, congratulations, because when I told Avery about your bet, I found out that she doesn't really care when we break up, and it feels like you cursed me and I don't understand any of this."

She couldn't help the tears from falling, which made her an-grier. She compensated for them by raising her voice. It made her feel like shit to yell at a pregnant lady and make her cry, but hey, at least she wasn't the only one crying.

"I didn't mean to . . . I'm so sor—" Erica stopped herself and took a shaky breath between her tears. "I'm not going to apologize again, but can I explain?"

Taylor felt wildly guilty when Erica took that shaky breath. But wait a fucking second. What the hell did *she* have to feel guilty for? Erica was crying for good reason, because she'd done something fucked up and Taylor had found out about it.

"Explain what? Why you told a big group of our friends—and some people who barely know me—that I'm such a joke of a person that it's fun to bet about my life? And that my love life exists purely to entertain you and give you something to laugh about? Is that what you're going to explain, or is there more to it?"

Erica looked so hurt, which both gave Taylor a jolt of satisfac-tion and made her feel like an enormous asshole all at once.

"I don't blame you for being mad," Erica said. "But please, can we talk about this? Will you sit down and listen?"

That was what she'd come here for, after all. Not the yelling, which she hadn't meant to do. Taylor brushed the back of her hand against her face and sat down at the kitchen table across from Erica.

"I know the bet was shitty," Erica said. "I mean, I didn't realize you'd care this much, you didn't tell me you cared about Avery this much, but—"

"You never asked!" Taylor shook her head. "No, I said I'd let you talk, keep going."

Erica nodded.

"I'm not going to make excuses. But I guess I was just . . . resentful. You've been spending so much time with Avery lately, and I've hardly seen you. I've been miserable all summer—all year, actually, but especially this summer—and you didn't seem to care."

"I didn't know!" Taylor couldn't help herself from interrupting. "Yeah, I know you had a hard time earlier this year, with the miscarriage, but it seemed like you were feeling better, and you got pregnant again! I didn't know you were miserable."

"You didn't ask!" Erica said. "Okay, you did ask at the beginning, but then everything seemed to go back to normal for you, when it felt like nothing would ever be normal again for me. You were all normal happy Taylor, dating people and breaking up with them and bemoaning how many people there were in this world who wanted to date you, and it was so hard for me to listen to that. I desperately wanted to have a baby, you knew that, and then I got pregnant and had a miscarriage, which almost broke me. And you were great when I had the miscarriage, you were, but then I got pregnant again, and I've been terrified for every second of this pregnancy that something else would go wrong, and you didn't seem to care that much."

Taylor hadn't known any of this.

"I cared. Of course I cared. But I didn't realize you felt like this."

Erica sighed.

"I know. It felt irrational, so I didn't talk about it. I tried to keep my mind off it, but how do you keep your mind off something when your whole body is changing exactly because of that something? The only thing I could try to do was to make plans for the baby, but you absolutely did not care about my plans for the baby; you have no interest in babies. Which is fine, I don't expect everyone in the world to have an interest in babies, but it was all I could think about. But, like, your punishment for losing our bet was that you had to throw me a baby shower, since the idea of doing that was so repulsive to you; imagine how that made me feel."

"The baby shower was your idea!" Taylor said. Shit, she was yelling again. She took a deep breath. "I didn't know it bothered you," she said. "We always make bets like that. Are you telling me you've been mad at me about this all summer? Is that why you made that bet?"

"No!" Erica was crying again. Or still. "That's not what I'm saying! I wasn't mad at you, just kind of hurt, but I brushed it off, because you're right, we always make bets like this, and plus, I know you, and I know you didn't mean anything bad by it. I'm not trying to excuse myself here, I'm just telling you how I felt. You wanted me to be the exact same Erica I've always been, but I'm not that person anymore. I talked about baby stuff with Sloane because she was the only person I *could* talk about baby stuff with, and you were so snotty and resentful about Sloane and how I was going to turn into a suburban mom just like her, and wasn't her life depressing, and on and on."

Well. Erica had a point there.

"Okay, yes, I was a bitch about Sloane, I admit it. But that was . . ." Fuck, she had stupid tears in her eyes again. "That was because I thought you were replacing me with Sloane. You moved into your cute little house, and you had your perfect relationship with your wife, and you had a baby on the way, and here I am, your fuckup friend over here who still isn't really sure what she's going to be when she grows up and doesn't know how to have an actual relationship. I thought you were . . . done with me. Or, maybe keeping me around as an example of who you used to be but didn't want to be anymore. Someone to tell all your rich friends stories about: 'Let me tell you what my wild friend Taylor did this time, she's always hilarious!'"

Erica got up, grabbed a box of tissues and put it in the middle of the table, then sat back down.

"Tay. I would never." She shook her head. "My relationship with Sam isn't perfect. Not even close. That's another reason this year has been so hard for me."

Taylor looked up at her.

"What? You guys are having trouble? I didn't . . . I had no idea."

"I just held it in," Erica said. "It's been so scary. We both dealt with the miscarriage really differently—I fell apart, and she was stoic through it all. And she's also been totally stoic and . . . unfeeling through this whole pregnancy. She's been out of town a ton for work, and generally just working a lot. I know she has a tough job, and I know she works really hard. But she's missed a bunch of doctor's appointments—you saw how she even left the shower early. And we keep fighting about all of that. We finally had a blow-out fight after the shower; she said it's because she's so worried about the baby and about how childbirth will be for me that she's trying not to think about it. We're going to get back into couples therapy, we honestly never should have stopped, but it was one more thing, you know?"

Taylor nodded. That's why she'd quit going to therapy a few years ago herself. One more thing to schedule and remember to do and pay for and stress about.

"I wish you'd told me about all this." She shook her head. "No, I wish I had been a better friend to you; I'm sorry you didn't feel like you could tell me all this."

Erica wiped her eyes.

"It wasn't that, I was just in the middle of it and so I felt like I had to hold it all in, because if I let it out to someone, it would be real, you know? Anyway, I said that thing about the bet after Sam left the shower early—which she hadn't told me she was going to do—and I was mad and resentful, and I took it out on you and I know you don't want me to say this but I'm so, so sorry. But also . . . you were spending so much time with Avery this summer, and I felt like you were replacing me with her, and then you guys were dating, and you seemed so happy. And I guess I was kind of jealous of you. That your life seemed so fun and easy and carefree, the way my life used to be. And I know, I know it's not actually like that, I tried to remind myself of the ways it wasn't like that, which I guess meant I kept acting shitty to you without meaning to. I really am sorry I did that."

Taylor didn't mind Erica's apology that time. She reached for a tissue and handed it to Erica, then grabbed another one for herself.

"Thanks for saying all of that," she said. "And thank you for the apology."

Erica wiped her eyes and squeezed Taylor's hand.

"Okay, what were you talking about earlier about how I cursed you or whatever? What's going on with you and Avery? I know I'm into tarot, but I can't actually curse anyone, you know that, right?"

Taylor laughed at that so hard that tears rolled down her cheeks. Probably not only from the laughter.

"I was just being histrionic." She stopped and wiped her eyes. "But look, I feel like you're selling yourself short; I think you could do it if you really put your mind to it."

"Thanks, but that didn't answer the 'what's going on with you and Avery' part of that question, you know."

Yeah, she knew.

"Avery made it pretty clear that she doesn't want to be in a relationship with me, not a real one. Sure, she's had a lot of fun with me, but that's all she wanted; some fun and flirting lessons and some experience with women and a little—probably a big—ego boost."

Erica folded her hands together and sat back.

"What do you mean she 'made it pretty clear'? What did she say that makes you think that's how she feels about you?"

Taylor shrugged.

"After we left the winery, I told her about what I overheard, and how you bet against us and how Sloane was the only person who was on our side—also, yes, I was a bitch about Sloane, I completely acknowledge that, I'd already told Avery that she was right about Sloane even before I overheard that."

Erica smiled.

"Yeah, she seems like one of those people who would have a house in all white and beige and never let their children get dirty and who would be super uptight, I know. And she is a little uptight, but she's not those other things, and she's been a really great friend to me. I'm glad you realized that she's actually pretty cool."

Taylor nodded.

"Yeah. Me, too. But anyway, when I told Avery about the bet and what everyone said about us—well, me, mostly—she just laughed and said, 'Oh well, let's make sure the people who bet on us win, and the other people lose, so we'll break up a few days after Erica has her baby!' And I laughed, because I thought she was joking, but then she said it again a few hours later, and I realized she was serious. She also doesn't believe in us, like everyone else at that party."

Erica was silent for a minute.

"Then I guess the question that I have for you is, how do you feel about Avery? Because her reaction is bothering you a lot more than I would have guessed that it would. Do you want more with her? Do you think your relationship could be serious?"

Erica said all of that in the same tone of voice people use when they're trying not to frighten baby animals. Taylor couldn't even be offended.

"Um." She took a deep breath. "The thought of not being with Avery . . . it really hurt. Things have been so good with her. She just . . . she likes me, she accepts me for who I am, who I am right now, you know? Like, we're so honest with each other, we're so comfortable with each other, I can talk to her about things that I don't talk to most people about. Some of the stuff that I don't like about myself or find frustrating about myself are things that she likes about me, which I still can't believe. I want to spend as much time with her as possible, which isn't the way I've felt about most people I've dated. You know that. You know I like my space when I'm dating someone. But with Avery, it feels like I can have space while I'm around her. That I can bring her along to hang out with my friends and I still get to relax and have fun, that I can just sit on the couch and do nothing at her place with her sitting on the other corner of the couch working or watching TV or whatever, that it's fun to even do things like go to the stupid grocery store with her. I thought I had to have everything all figured out about my life, before I tried to build any sort of life with someone else, but now . . ." Taylor pushed her fingers through her hair. "I guess that should all be in the past tense, though. Because now that I think I want this thing between us to be big, serious, something that could go the distance, it's only because I found out she wasn't thinking that way at all."

Erica shook her head.

"Okay, wait, are you determining this just because Avery made a joke about how you guys should break up so I would lose the bet? Did you talk to her about this?"

"Yes! I told you! She brought it up again, and that's when I realized she wasn't joking, except for how she thinks everything about our relationship is a joke! She thought the whole bet thing was funny—she tried to be nice about it because I was clearly so upset, but I could tell—and she even had an idea for what to do if we wanted to break up before you have the baby! We just wouldn't tell anyone so we could make sure the people who bet on us win the bet. Isn't that great? This relationship feels different to me; I don't want to give up on it, but it's just a big joke to her. Whenever we break up, it doesn't matter to her at all."

"But it matters to you?" Erica asked. "When you break up, or if you break up at all?"

"YES!" Taylor couldn't help but yell. "What have I just been saying to you?"

Erica nodded.

"Mm-hmm, and why does it matter to you?"

Taylor glared at her.

"Erica, is this some sort of bullshit Socratic method thing that you learned from your lawyer wife or your couples therapist or your tarot books or something?"

Erica just smiled at her.

"Answer the damn question, Taylor. Why does it matter to you?"

"Because I think I'm falling in love with her, that's why! Is that what you wanted to hear? Fine, I said it, are you fucking happy now?" Taylor stood up; she didn't know why. To leave, to go hide in shame, because it was easier to yell when she was standing up, maybe all of the above.

Erica's smile got wider.

"Then why the fuck don't you tell her that?"

"Because that sounds fucking scary!" Taylor fell back down into her chair. "And once I say how I feel and she says she doesn't feel the same way, it'll be out there, and I'll know it and she'll know it, and we won't be able to go along as we have been, so we'll have to break up, and I'll be miserable, and fuck, this is bullshit, why does anyone do this?"

She and Erica both burst out laughing. Taylor let the tears she'd been holding back stream down her face, and Erica handed her tissues as they both laughed and cried.

"Maybe you should try telling her?" Erica said, in the don't-scare-the-baby-animal voice.

Taylor shook her head.

"I fucking knew you were going to say that." She crumpled up her tissues and dropped them onto the table. And then she stood up.

"Fine. I will." She turned and walked out of the kitchen. Then she turned around, went to Erica, and pulled her into a very tight hug. "I love you so much, you know that, right?"

Erica kissed her cheek.

"Yeah, I do. I love you so much, too. And, Taylor, I'm so sorry. For the bet, and for being such a resentful little shit, and for not talking to you about what was going on with me, and for so many other things."

"I'm so sorry for being a bitch," Taylor said. "And for not listening to you, and not being the best possible friend I could be to you, and so many other things."

Taylor took a step back, and then leaned forward and bent down to Erica's belly.

"Sorry for yelling at your mom and for using all that bad language, I promise not to do it again." She thought for a minute.

"Well, the yelling, I definitely won't do that again. The bad language, I can't make any promises."

Erica gave Taylor a hard hug, and then pushed her toward the door.

"Go, before you lose your nerve."

Taylor glared at her.

"Okay, I'm going!" She turned to leave and then turned back around. "Wait, I have one more question. Who was the other person who bet on me and Avery?"

Erica laughed.

"Callie. Now I'll owe her dinner, too. And, as we both know, she'll make me pay."

They grinned at each other, and then Erica took Taylor by the hand and pulled her to the front door.

"Now. Go."

EIGHTEEN

AVERY FELT AT LOOSE ENDS ON WEDNESDAY AFTERNOON. SHE
hadn't seen Taylor the night before, the first Tuesday since the
winery party that she hadn't, and the first Wednesday since
the pottery class that she hadn't woken up with her. She hadn't
even heard from Taylor since that terse text the day before saying
she couldn't go out that night. Taylor always texted like that,
though. Avery shouldn't make a big deal about this. She wasn't
going to make a big deal about this.

It was Luke's fault that she felt so lost and ill at ease just because she hadn't seen Taylor since Monday morning. He'd brought
up all that stuff about whether Avery had feelings for Taylor and
wanted a real relationship with her, and it had made her think
about what could be, and it had made her needy. She spent a lot of
time alone, she had no problem with being alone, she was fine!
She'd see Taylor whenever; it was no big deal. They were no big
deal, wasn't that the whole point?

But she still felt off. She didn't have any meetings or calls for
the rest of the day, she had everything squared away for her events

for the weekend, and she didn't have any plans tonight or tomorrow night. So she did the only thing she could think to do. She went to the garden.

There were a lot of people there, which was nice. She had people to smile at as she walked by, people to wave at across the way, so she wasn't alone anymore, but she didn't have to talk to anyone. She wasn't really in the mood to talk. Instead, she got to work. She weeded, pulled off mottled leaves, harvested ripe tomatoes and discarded the fallen ones, plucked zucchini out of their hiding places, snipped herbs, pulled up a few radishes, and planted more radish seeds and cilantro seeds, hoping they'd sprout and grow for the next few months. Finally, she picked some flowers to bring back home to be a bright spot in her newly painted living room. They—she and Taylor—had decided on a soft pink and had painted it themselves. It made her happy every time she walked inside of it.

"Hey!" Beth said. Avery jumped, jolted from her thoughts about that night she and Taylor had started to paint, and what happened later. "I didn't expect to see you here until later."

"Oh," Avery said. "I had some downtime, and it was such a nice day, so I thought I'd come by early to . . . putter around a bit."

Beth dropped her garden basket at the edge of their plot and surveyed the work Avery had done.

"It looks great, doesn't it?" she said. "Who would have ever thought we could do this? Not me. And yeah, it's a gorgeous day, that's why I came over here early, too. Greta and I just finished doing some tastings for our New Year's Eve party, and I was going to go home and get some more work done before coming here, but it was too nice outside to waste the afternoon."

Avery looked back down at the tomato plant as soon as Beth brought up their wedding. God, she was being so stupid about this.

Why were her feelings so hurt that she wasn't invited? She and Beth had known each other for only a few months, anyway. The same amount of time she'd known Taylor, practically. That wasn't enough time to expect anyone to have strong enough feelings of friendship for someone to invite them to their wedding. Or strong enough feelings of . . . other things for someone to want a real relationship. She had to pretend that she wasn't upset, that everything was fine, that she was just happy for Beth. She knew how to do that; she was an expert at pretending that everything was fine.

"Oh, that's great," she said. But it didn't come out right, not how it was supposed to, not how it used to. Maybe now that she'd been actively working on not pretending about her feelings this summer, on being more honest, with Taylor, with herself, she didn't know how to pretend anymore.

Beth looked at her. And then she smiled tentatively.

"Um, speaking of the New Year's Eve party," she said. "We aren't sending out formal invitations, because, well, we don't want people to think something's up. But you know you're obviously invited. Right?"

Avery's head shot up. She didn't even attempt to stop herself from smiling.

"Oh. No, um . . . I wasn't sure. I thought since we didn't really know each other that well . . . and you didn't mention it, so . . ."

Beth shook her head.

"Didn't I say we were bonded by soil? You'll be there, right?"

Avery grinned back at her.

"Wouldn't miss it."

"Good. Maybe you can bring that hottie of yours."

"Oh." Avery said. "We won't still be together by New Year's Eve, but thank you." She tried to make light of it, even though she wasn't feeling light about it. "Your party will be a perfect place for me to practice flirting. Just make sure to invite some good options for me, okay?"

"Why are you so sure you two won't still be together by then? You seem to really like her, and from what you say about how she is toward you, she seems to really like you, too."

Avery tried to ignore the tears that came to her eyes when Beth said that, pretend them away, crush her feelings down into a little ball.

But she was tired of doing that. She didn't want to do it anymore.

The problem was, now that she'd opened the door to thinking about her feelings for Taylor, the answers were all too clear in her mind.

"I do really like her," she said to Beth. "But from the beginning, we said this would be a casual thing. I'm realizing I might want more than that. I guess I'm kind of sad about that today."

"What if she wants more than that, too?" Beth asked. "Have you even asked her?"

Avery sat down on the edge of their garden bed.

"Why did you have to ask me that?"

Beth laughed and sat down next to her.

"I guess that's a no. What are you waiting for?"

Avery bit her lip. She was waiting for the same reason she'd waited so long to break up with Derek, for the same reason that she'd been so well-behaved throughout her teens and twenties, for the same reason she hadn't asked Beth if she was invited to the wedding. She was waiting because it was less scary to wait than to take action.

"I'm waiting so I can become someone who can have strong feelings and be vulnerable and bold, but also never gets her feelings hurt." She was waiting to become a different person. "How do you become like that?"

Beth put her hand on Avery's shoulder.

"I hate to break it to you, friend, but you can't."

Avery dropped her head in her hands.

"I was afraid you were going to say that."

"You have to talk to her, you know," Beth said.

Avery didn't look up.

"I don't know that. Okay, fine, I do know that, but can I live in ignorance about that for at least one more day? I mean, two days, twelve days, thirty-five days, any of that would be better than one day, but give me one day? Can't I just immerse myself in the garden or in baking more zucchini bread or learning how to make jam with these peaches that James dropped off for us or something, anything other than thinking about this?"

Beth stood up.

"Yeah. Come on."

Avery looked up at her, relief washing over her.

"Really?"

Beth nodded.

"Yep. Promise me you'll remember tomorrow, and deal with it tomorrow, but for now, turn off your phone so you won't check it forty thousand times tonight, and let's get out of here."

Avery stood up immediately.

"Oh, thank God."

———

TAYLOR DIDN'T KNOW WHAT TO DO. SHE LEFT ERICA'S HOUSE and went straight to Avery's apartment, but she didn't answer her door or her text, and her car wasn't there. She must be out somewhere, but Taylor had no idea where. Probably if she'd responded to any of Avery's texts that week in something more than monosyllables, she might know where the fuck Avery was, but that was one more mistake she'd made; there was nothing she could do about it now. She was probably at some work event, or maybe at her garden, or out with Luke, or something, but Taylor couldn't call Luke to see if he knew where Avery was, because he would think something was wrong, and shouldn't she know that herself? She *did* drive by the community garden to see if Avery's car was there, but no luck. Eventually, she just went home and texted Avery again.

TAYLOR

hey! let me know if you want to go out
later or want me to come over

She started to reread her text, to see if she should change the wording or delete that exclamation point or whatever, but even thinking about that made her roll her eyes at herself, so she just pressed send.

And then she waited. And waited. And waited. She had obviously been cursed by someone, that was the only explanation for this. It could have been anyone, honestly. Anyone she'd dated and broken up with could have cursed her, or maybe they all had. Because now when she was all hyped up to confess to the person she was falling in love with that she was falling in love with her, she couldn't fucking get in touch with her? That was definitely cosmic payback in some way or another.

And now she had all this time to just . . . sit here and think about this. Think about how Avery had been so nonchalant about the whole idea of them breaking up, about how she had no idea what Avery's feelings for her were, about how this whole thing with Avery had started with her giving Avery flirting lessons so she could learn how to be more comfortable asking women out and dating them, and that maybe Avery viewed this relationship as the first of many relationships with women, and her actual feelings weren't really engaged in this thing with Taylor at all. About how she was about to tell Avery how she felt, and she had no fucking idea if Avery felt the same way or how it would go.

And now there was no fucking way to know except to sit here and wait for Avery to text her back.

Finally, her phone buzzed, and she grabbed for it.

AVERY

Sorry, I was at the garden, and then I had dinner with Beth. I have to get up early tomorrow, but can we do tomorrow night?

Tomorrow night? She had to sit with this until tomorrow fucking night? Good God, this was a nightmare.

She wanted to text Avery back that no, she needed to talk to her right away, she didn't care if she was tired and had to get up early in the morning. Why did it even matter if she had to get up early in the morning anyway? Taylor had slept over at her place lots of times when Avery had an early morning meeting; they dealt with that just fine!

But she knew that number one, that was probably not the way to handle this situation, and number two, Avery turned her phone on do not disturb as soon as she even thought about getting ready for bed, so it wouldn't do her any good anyway. She picked up the phone.

"She had dinner with her *garden* friend tonight and is going to bed early, what am I going to doooo?" she whined as soon as Erica answered.

"Oh, honey," Erica said. "I'm so sorry. Do you want to come back over here and eat some of the food I ordered for us and watch a very stupid movie and tell me all about it?"

"God yes."

She stayed at Erica's for four hours; they put a series of stupid movies on in the background, ate a lot, and talked and cried a lot more.

When Taylor left, very full of pizza and Diet Coke, Erica gave her another hug.

"It's going to be okay, I promise," she said.

Taylor shook her head.

"You can't know that."

Erica nodded.

"I can, because I know you, and I know us. I can't promise that everything with Avery will turn out all right, or even that everything with Sam will turn out all right, but I can still promise it's going to be okay."

Taylor tried to hold on to that throughout her sleepless night.

The next day, she had no idea what the fuck to do. This wasn't the normal "when should I text her?" game she always refused to play—she didn't want to be pushy or make Avery think something was wrong, but she did, very urgently, want to see her and talk to her that night.

Finally, at three in the afternoon, right before Taylor was about to cave, Avery texted.

AVERY

Were you still interested in getting together tonight?

Did that seem weirdly stilted? She thought it seemed weirdly stilted. Maybe Avery knew what she was going to say and wanted to get it over with because she would then have to tell Taylor that she didn't feel the same way. She knew Avery didn't like confrontation. Wait, was that why she hadn't been around the night before and why she "had to get up early" and therefore couldn't see Taylor? Because she didn't like confrontation and so she'd been trying to avoid Taylor, and then finally she was like, *Fine, I'll get it over with*?

Oh God, she was doing that stupid overevaluating text messages thing, she never did that, she didn't like being that person! Plus, why would Avery know why Taylor wanted to see her? She'd been the one who had assumed they were hanging out on Tuesday night, and Taylor had blown her off that night. Unless she'd wiretapped Erica's house—which not even this unhinged mood would let Taylor pretend to believe—Avery would have no idea what Taylor planned to say to her when she saw her.

Okay, but once she'd even thought the word *wiretap*, she was officially unhinged. Time to stop thinking. Thinking was overrated anyway.

TAYLOR

> pick you up at 7? wear your favorite outfit

Shit, shit, she'd said that with no plan. What the fuck was wrong with her, *"thinking was overrated"*? She at least needed to have some type of a plan for tonight. If she was going to tell Avery she was falling in love with her, didn't she need to be sweeping and romantic or something? Shit, did she even know how to be sweeping and romantic?

AVERY

No fair, isn't it my turn?

Okay *that* was a normal text message from Avery. Taylor felt a little bit of her tension slide away.

TAYLOR

nope, mine. but here: you can give me my dress code, and we can split the night

Avery's response came quickly.

AVERY

Perfect. Wear *my* favorite outfit.

Did she mean Taylor should wear the outfit of hers that Avery liked the best, or did she mean that Taylor should, like, dress up like Avery and wear Avery's favorite outfit? Unfortunately, according to the rules that Taylor had tacitly established months ago, no clarifying questions were allowed, so she just had to figure it out.

TAYLOR

done. see you at 7

Taylor pulled up in front of Avery's apartment at seven on the dot, wearing her favorite pair of jeans, the ripped ones that were a little snug in the ass, and a black T-shirt with the sleeves cut off. She wondered what Avery would wear, what her favorite outfit was, but the problem was that Avery had so many clothes that it was hard to figure out what her favorite outfit would be.

Taylor turned her car off and took a deep breath. She had a plan now, and she thought it was a good one, but it didn't matter how good or romantic or sweeping or whatever her plan was if Avery didn't feel the same way. She tried to act calm, she tried to be calm, but her heart was beating so fast it was like she was midway through running a marathon.

Well, she assumed it was like that; she knew nothing about actually running a marathon and wanted to keep it that way, but still.

"Hey!" she said in too high a voice when Avery opened her front door. And then she took a look at her. Her whole body relaxed, and her smile got wide. "You look incredible."

Avery was wearing that snug black sundress with the spaghetti straps that she'd worn a few times that summer, most notably on the night they'd first kissed. It wasn't like Taylor to remember something like that, but one thing that was burned in her memory from that night was sitting at the bar with Avery, staring at those tiny little straps, and wanting so badly to slide her fingers underneath them.

Did Avery remember she'd worn that dress that night? She hoped so. Avery was the type to remember things like that. But maybe she was only wearing it because it was her favorite dress.

Taylor leaned forward and kissed her. It felt so good to kiss her. Their bodies fit together so well. They hadn't kissed for days, not since Sunday night. They hadn't seen each other since then, which was probably the longest they'd gone since they'd started dating. She thought about that first kiss, how Avery had been hesitant to kiss her, to touch her, and then as soon as their lips had touched, she'd relaxed, grown more sure of herself. She'd been like that with everything, from dancing to painting to sex: anxious at first, needing a bit of encouragement, a little push to get started, and then as soon as she did, her confidence grew. She experimented, learned more, asked questions, messed up a few times, laughed, and then tried again and got better and better and more self-assured with each try.

That was one of the things she loved about Avery: Yeah, she was scared to take risks, to try new things, to push herself, but once she'd committed to doing it, she was all in. She didn't pretend she had all the answers, she let herself stumble, and then she would get back up and try again without being ashamed of herself for trying, and she would get better at it. That was something that Taylor could learn from Avery, actually. She tended to be too cocky, too convinced that she knew all the answers, when half the time she was crossing her fingers and hoping she was right.

She made herself pull back from the kiss. She couldn't get distracted tonight. At least, not right now.

"God, you look amazing," she said.

Avery smiled at her. "You already said that." She lifted her thumb and brushed it over Taylor's lips. "Rookie move—I already put lipstick on before you got here."

Taylor shook her head.

"Rookie move, indeed. Are you ready?"

Avery nodded.

"Let me just put my shoes on."

She slid her feet into flat sandals and grabbed her purse from the hook by the door.

"Where are we off to?" Avery asked as they walked toward the car.

Taylor threw what she hoped was an amused smile in Avery's direction, but her heart was beating wildly again.

"You think it's going to be that easy?" she asked.

Avery laughed, but it was her nervous laugh, the same one she'd used when they were at trivia that night around her friends, before she'd gotten more comfortable with them. Taylor wondered why.

"It's never that easy, but I keep trying," she said.

They were both quiet once they got into the car. Taylor thought of asking how she was doing, how dinner with Beth was, how work had been that week, but she was so full of what she needed to say to Avery, what she wanted to say to Avery, that she couldn't make small talk. Yes, she cared about how Avery's work was going, and yes, she cared about her garden and her gardening friend, but she couldn't ask her any of that, she couldn't talk about any of that, until she told Avery how she felt. When the big talk was all that consumed her mind, when the need to do the big talk was overwhelming her, small talk seemed ridiculous, unnatural. She had to get the big talk over with first.

Later—if things went well—she would tell Avery that maybe she had a point about small talk.

She pulled into a parking spot—not the exact space she'd wanted, but one a few spots down from it, and turned off the car.

"Okay, we're here," she said.

Avery got out of the car and looked up and down the street. They were back in downtown Napa.

"Oh, are we going back there?" she asked, pointing to the place they'd gone to the night of the flirting midterm.

Taylor shook her head.

"Nope, but good guess." Avery glared at her, but a tiny smile danced around the corners of her eyes. "After this long, you still think I'm going to tell you any more than that until we get there?"

Avery shrugged, but now the smile touched her lips.

"Hope springs eternal."

Taylor reached for Avery's hand, and they walked together down the street. They didn't talk as they walked, but this time the silence between them didn't feel heavy, loaded, the way the silence in the car had. Now they were just comfortable, walking down the street hand in hand the same way they'd done dozens of times over the past few months. The same way they'd done ever since that night, when they'd walked together toward the Barrel, the same walk they were taking right now.

The same, but different. Now it was two months later, it was darker, cooler, at least at night. Before, that other time, they hadn't even kissed yet. Before, they were just friends. Before, Taylor hadn't fallen for Avery. Now, everything was different.

When they got to the same block as the Barrel but were still a few feet from it, Avery stopped and let go of Taylor's hand.

"I'm sorry, I'm sorry, I know you have something planned, but I can't take it anymore. I have to say this, I have to get this over with, in case we . . . in case it changes things. I've been holding it in, but I have to get it out now or else I might never do it."

Taylor's heart dropped. Avery was going to break up with her, wasn't she? This was it. She was going to do it now, before Taylor could even say her piece. She wanted to fight, to say no, to say she had to plead her case first, but wow, how humiliating, to plead with someone to love her back. All she could do was look at Avery, her skin glowing in the streetlights, the warm breeze blowing her hair off her shoulder, and nod.

Avery took a long, shaky breath.

"I know that neither of us planned for this, between us, I mean.

And that we both tried to avoid it, push it away when it happened the first time, for all sorts of good reasons. And we both ignored all those good reasons, and decided to jump into something, because we couldn't help ourselves, because we were having so much fun and we wanted to keep having so much fun, but we both knew that was all it was going to be—fun, right?"

She looked hard at Taylor when she said that, and paused, like she was looking for a response from Taylor, so Taylor said what it seemed like she was looking for.

"Right."

Avery nodded.

"Right."

Were those tears in Avery's eyes? She couldn't quite tell in this light. She hoped that Avery at least felt bad about breaking up with her.

"The thing is—oh God, I don't want to say this, I hate everything about this, but I've already started, so I guess I have to finish, and this is growth, I guess, confrontation and doing something hard that I don't want to do, being vulnerable and all those terrible things." She let out a breath. "Sorry, sorry. The thing is, that conversation we had the other day, about that bet, Erica's bet, and how I said we should break up after Erica had the baby to ensure that Sloane won—"

"Yeah, I know which bet you're talking about," Taylor said. She was trying to let Avery say her piece, but she had to fucking get this over with.

"Of course you do. The thing is, that conversation brought up a few things for me, and I guess—I mean I know—over the past week I've realized that I don't want to break up."

Taylor's head shot up.

"What? What did you say?"

Had she heard her right? Maybe she'd heard only what she wanted to hear? Maybe it was those other people walking down the street saying something that she'd heard instead of what Avery had actually said? Or maybe Avery didn't mean what Taylor wanted her to mean?

"I don't want to break up. I understand if you do, I get it. I know that all you wanted out of this relationship was some fun, and we've had that, and I know what you're going to say to this, but I had to tell you . . . my feelings for you are more than just fun. I mean, that wasn't a good way of putting it, let me try again, I want—"

"I think I'm falling in love with you," Taylor said.

"What? What did you say?" Avery asked.

Now Taylor knew she had tears in her eyes.

"I'm falling in love with you. I realized it at the shower. No, I realized it a few days later, but at the shower, when I overheard that bet, I realized I hated the thought of breaking up with you. I hated the thought of breaking up with you in seven weeks, six months, whatever. I love having you in my life, I love talking to you and waking up with you and kissing you and laughing with you and coming up with surprises for you and being surprised by you, and I don't want to stop."

"Are you . . . Really? You're serious?"

Taylor couldn't help but laugh at the stunned look on Avery's face. Though, wow, she hoped, she really, really fucking hoped, that it was a stunned and happy look.

"Does this sound like a thing I would joke about?" she asked. "I avoided you all week—I even bailed on our Tuesday night—because I was so hurt that you would just casually refer to our breakup, like it was no big deal to you, like it didn't matter, like our relationship didn't matter to you. But then I realized that maybe I hadn't actually told you how much our relationship matters to me, since

I hadn't actually realized it for myself, and that I should probably tell you that before I determined that you didn't care about me the same way I care about you. And most of all, I realized that I cared about you—cared about us—too much to just give up on us. That I wanted, needed, to fight for us. So, I brought you here—" She gestured in the direction of the Barrel. "Or at least intended to bring you here tonight, to the place we first kissed, because I was trying to be romantic, even though that's not really my strength, so I could tell you that—"

Avery backed her up against the wall.

"Taylor?" she said. "Now is when you kiss me."

EPILOGUE

"REMEMBER TO ACT SURPRISED," AVERY SAID. "WE'RE THE only ones—other than the brides and the officiant—who know that it's a wedding."

Avery looked up in the mirror as she put her earrings on and saw Taylor behind her. She looked hot in that black velvet jumpsuit. Avery had convinced her to order it a few weeks ago—*Just humor me. I promise that if you hate it, I'll return it for you*—and as she'd suspected, it looked incredible on Taylor.

"We look good together," Taylor said as she looked at their reflections in the mirror. Avery was in a simple, sleek black dress. She hadn't intended for them to match, but it didn't really count as matching if they were both just in black, did it? "And I know it's a surprise, you've told me that at least three times today alone, I'm not going to forget!" She wrapped her arms around Avery and kissed the side of her neck. "But I do love being in the know."

Avery turned around in Taylor's arms and kissed her on the lips.

"I'm sorry I keep bringing it up. It's just that the surprise was my idea, and I'm thrilled it's lasted this long, so I'm paranoid that one of us will blow it before the actual wedding happens." She turned back around and picked up a lipstick from the dresser and put it in her gold clutch. "Let me just put my shoes on, and I'm ready." She slid into the strappy gold sandals that she'd worn to countless weddings and events and pulled her faux fur coat out of the closet. "Are you sure this coat isn't over the top?" she asked Taylor.

Taylor smiled her most lecherous smile.

"Mmm, all I can see when I look at that coat is that time I came over and you greeted me at the door in it and nothing else, so I'm going to say no, absolutely not. But maybe next time we should try that with that coat and those shoes, just to see if I change my mind."

Avery blushed. She still couldn't believe she'd actually done that.

"I hadn't seen you for almost a week! I was getting feral." She saw a thoughtful look come over Taylor's face and shook her head. "No, don't go getting any ideas—you don't need to disappear for that long again."

Taylor chuckled as they walked out of their hotel room.

"I didn't disappear, I was taking that intensive business class Margot made me take, excuse me, *encouraged* me to take, you know that. Plus, I believe I made you appreciate that move so much that you'll definitely want to surprise me that way again for no reason at all."

Avery thought back to that night and let her smile get very wide.

"That you did," she said.

They walked down to the elevator and pressed the button for the top floor. The party was on the roof deck and started at eight p.m., so they'd gotten a room for the night at the hotel.

"I'm so glad it didn't rain tonight," Taylor said.

Avery slid her arm around Taylor's waist as they got in the elevator.

"Me, too. Obviously, there were many contingency plans for if it did, but I'm glad we—they—didn't have to worry about that."

Taylor grinned at her.

"You know, it's just us in the elevator. You don't have to pretend like you haven't been planning this . . . party."

Avery touched Taylor's bottom lip with her fingertip.

"Hmmm, I thought you were going elsewhere when you said that it was just us on this elevator."

Taylor's eyes widened.

"Avery Jensen! I'm shocked!"

Avery smirked.

"What can I say, you created a monster."

The elevator dinged, and two other couples got on, so for the rest of the ride, they chastely held hands and traded very unchaste text messages.

Beth and Greta were there when they got out of the elevator, in their New Year's Eve best. The four of them exchanged excited looks and quick hugs, and then the two secret brides hugged everyone else and directed them toward the champagne. After they took glasses of champagne and a plateful of snacks, Taylor pulled Avery over to the side of the room.

"Now I'm paranoid that I'm going to spill something," Taylor said, "and I don't mean the champagne. So, we're going to stand over here and sip our champagne and eat some cheese and crackers and be antisocial so that I don't spoil the you-know-what."

Avery laughed and lifted her champagne glass to Taylor.

"Standing in the corner and being antisocial is my favorite way to go to a party; I'm so glad I've finally lured you over to my side."

Taylor clinked her glass with Avery's.

"When I have the hottest woman in the room by my side, what else do I need? Honestly, it's a little cruel of me to stand here like this with you, since I know everyone in the room is going to look at me and be jealous, but I'll do anything for you."

Avery turned to her with a smile.

"And here I was thinking how everyone here will be jealous of me tonight since I'm here with you. I can't even imagine how many people are going to slide their hotel room keys in that back pocket of yours. I'm going to count them at the end of the night."

Taylor took Avery's hand and tucked it into her pocket.

"Just keep your hand right here all night, then no one will get the chance."

Avery laughed and kissed her softly on the lips.

"You know how much I love you, right?" she asked Taylor.

Taylor leaned forward and kissed her.

"I sure do."

At nine thirty, Beth came over to Avery.

"Hey, Avery, there's more champagne downstairs, can you help me get it?"

Avery grinned at her. That was the signal.

"Will do."

Avery went to the elevator with Beth. Once they got off on Beth's floor, they giggled like teenagers.

"Taylor knows what she's supposed to do?" Beth asked.

Avery nodded.

"Don't worry, she's got this."

Twenty minutes later, after getting the couple into their bridal finery and escorting them to the service elevator, Avery got back to the roof and found Taylor. She was in the middle of the party, but Avery saw the way Taylor's eyes lit up as soon as she saw her.

She immediately said something to the person she was talking to and made her way through the crowd to Avery.

"Everything's set up here," she said to Avery. She took the microphone out of her pocket and handed it to Avery. "The music will stop at ten oh one on the dot; all they have to do is flip this switch."

Avery slid back behind the bar and handed the mic to Beth, and returned to Taylor's side.

"Oh, how were Erica and Sam and the baby?" Taylor had spent the day with them before coming to meet Avery.

Taylor grinned.

"That baby is so fucking cute I can't even get over it. Erica and Sam are still exhausted, but other than that, they're doing great. Things are really good between them. I'm so glad."

Avery put her arm around Taylor.

"Me, too."

"Though," Taylor said. "I'm starting to regret that whole 'year's supply of diapers' thing. Do you know how expensive diapers are?"

Avery giggled at the outrage in her voice.

Four minutes later, the music cut, and Beth's voice boomed out from the speakers.

"Happy New Year, family and friends! Thank you all so much for coming to our New Year's Eve party to celebrate Greta's birthday! We're so grateful that you're all here, for more than one reason. Because this is more than a party." Beth and Greta walked out from behind the bar, Beth in a flowy off-white gown, and Greta in a perfectly cut tuxedo. "It's a wedding. And we're so thrilled that you're all here to celebrate with us."

There was a huge gasp from the crowd. Avery held back a giggle at Taylor's very dramatic inhale.

Beth handed the microphone to their officiant, her minister

godmother, who was already at the front of the room, and they said their vows to many rounds of cheers. As soon as they kissed for the first time as a married couple, their officiant turned around and picked up two champagne glasses, and then handed them to the brides.

"A toast, to Beth and Greta!" she said. "A happy marriage to them!"

The whole crowd raised their glasses.

Three minutes later, Beth and Greta were on the dance floor. Taylor pulled Avery out there to join them.

A few minutes before midnight, Avery stood with Taylor at the railing as they overlooked the party on one side and the view of Napa Valley under the clear, starry sky on the other.

"You know," Taylor said. "This is maybe my favorite wedding I've ever been to. Simple, low-key, a ton of fun. I'm into it. Weddings aren't so bad if they can be like this."

Avery grinned at her.

"You see how much I'm broadening your world? First baby showers, then weddings, I can't wait to see what the next thing is that I'm going to change your mind about."

Taylor took a sip of champagne.

"Would you maybe want to do this sometime? Like, I don't know . . . with me?"

Avery carefully set her glass down on the railing.

"Taylor Cameron, are you proposing to me?"

Taylor shook her head.

"No, absolutely not. I'm not a Neanderthal, I wouldn't propose at someone else's wedding; even I know not to do that. When I do it, it's going to be a surprise."

"Did you say . . . when?" Avery asked.

Taylor smiled at her.

"You answer my question first."

"Yes," Avery said, without hesitating. "Now you answer mine."

Taylor set her glass down next to Avery's and leaned close to her, so close their lips were almost touching.

"Yes."

ACKNOWLEDGMENTS

I am enormously grateful to everyone in my life who has supported this book and all my books, and I'm so glad there's a place for me to thank you all. I am so very fortunate to have you all in my life.

Holly Root, thank you, as always, for your guidance, experience, intelligence, thoughtfulness, and humanity. You always support me in the best possible way, and I can't tell you what it means to me. Alyssa Maltese, thank you for your attention to detail in the face of my chaos, and for all your hard work; you're a gem! And thank you to everyone at Root Literary for all that you do for me and for so many authors.

Cindy Hwang, what a joy it is to have an editor like you. Thank you so much for caring about me as a person, as well as me as a writer, for wanting me to be able to write the best book I possibly can, and especially for giving me the time and space and support to write this book. Huge thanks to everyone at Berkley and Penguin Random House: Elizabeth Vinson, Erin Galloway, Kristin Cipolla, Craig Burke, Jin Yu, Anika Bates, Rita Frangie, Monika

Roe, Angela Kim, Megha Jain, Angelina Krahn, and LeeAnn Pemberton. You are the best publishing team any writer could ask for, and I'm so grateful for your creativity and advocacy on behalf of me and my books. And many thanks to Jessica Brock and Fareeda Bullert, I miss you both and I'm always grateful for everything you've done for me.

Thanks to Alice Lawson and everyone at Gersh for all the work that you do for my books. And thank you so much to everyone at Reese's Book Club for championing not just one book, but my career; I appreciate all of you so much!

To the many writers who have supported me, given me advice and pep talks, vented with me, gossiped with me, cheered for me, and been there for me, I am grateful for you all every single day. Thank you Jami Attenberg, Melissa Baumgart, Robin Benway, Akilah Brown, Nicole Chung, Alexis Coe, Heather Cox, Roxane Gay, Emily Henry, Mira Jacob, Leah Johnson, Ruby Lang, Danny Lavery, Tembi Locke, Jessica Morgan, Samin Nosrat, Taylor Jenkins Reid, Helen Rosner, Emma Straub, Julia Whelan, Tia Williams, and Sara Zarr. And a special, extra thank-you to Kayla Cagan and Amy Spalding for our retreats, our full moon moments, and that snippet of your conversation that gave me the first glimmer of this book.

I've been blessed with some of the best, smartest, and most supportive friends in the world. Julian Davis Mortenson, I never would have finished this book if it wasn't for our virtual writing dates, may they continue forever. Margaret H. Willison and Christina Tucker, thanks for cheering for me to write this book from the moment I first mentioned it, and for the many fit checks and ego boosts; a special thanks to Margaret for the astrology assist. Sara Simon, I don't know what I'd do without you. Thank you to Joy Alferness and the entire Alferness family, Kimberly Chin, Nicole Clouse, Nanita Cranford, Rachel Fershleiser, Alyssa Furukawa,

Janet Goode, Alicia Harris, Jina Kim, Kate Leos, Lisa McIntire, Maret Orliss, Simi Patnaik, Jessica Simmons, Melissa Sladden, Jill Vizas, and Kyle Wong. I love you all so much.

I'm so fortunate to have such a supportive family. Thank you to my parents, grandparents, sister, and aunts and uncles, and especially to my many cousins, whom I love so very much. You've all been the best cheerleaders a writer could ever have, thank you for everything.

I owe my career to librarians and booksellers. You have championed me and my books since day one, and I genuinely can't thank you enough. Here are just a handful of the extraordinary booksellers and bookstores that have done so much for me and my books: Cathy Berner from Blue Willow Bookshop, Katherine Morgan from Grand Gesture Books, Hannah Oliver Depp and Christine Bollow from Loyalty Books, and everyone at Bookmarks in North Carolina and Books are Magic in Brooklyn. But most of all, thank you, thank you to Brad Johnson and everyone at East Bay Booksellers in Oakland for everything you've done for me and for the literary community in Oakland and the whole Bay Area.

And thank you, thank you, thank you to all of my readers! Thank you for buying my books, for checking them out of the library, for telling your friends about them, for coming to my events, and for being so wonderful. You inspire me and uplift me, and you make all the hard parts of writing a book worth it. Thank you so much.

Finally, thank you to Rosie, the best dog in the entire world, who kept me company as I wrote this book, made me go for walks, and made me laugh every single day. Thank you for coming into my life just when I needed you.

FLIRTING LESSONS

JASMINE GUILLORY

READERS GUIDE

DISCUSSION QUESTIONS

1. What is your go-to move when flirting with someone you like? Do you consider yourself a big flirt?

2. Both Taylor and Avery feel stuck in their lives in different ways. Taylor feels like her friends are moving on to the next stage of their lives without her, and Avery feels like she hasn't done the normal things for people her age. Have you ever felt stuck in your life? How did you overcome it?

3. One of the first ways Avery starts to get out of her shell is by trying new things and going to new places, like joining a gardening club. What is a hobby you have always wanted to try?

4. Taylor has a lot of friends, including several that she once dated. Have you stayed friends with an ex before, or do you think that once you break up, you should stop talking for good?

5. What are your feelings about blurring the line between friendship and dating?

6. A big part of Taylor and Avery's relationship is planning dates for each other. What is your ideal date, and what date would you plan for someone you're dating?

7. Avery started her own event-planning business, and Taylor dreams of opening a local wine bar. Have you ever dreamed of starting a business? What would it be?

8. As much as this book is about romance, it's also about friendship. Both Avery and Taylor grow in and out of friendships. How have your closest friendships developed over time? Have you ever grown apart from someone who used to be a best friend?

9. Taylor's bet with Erica leads to an unintentional expiration date to Taylor and Avery's relationship. Have you ever been in a similar situation with your partner or a friend where they said one thing and you interpreted it to mean something very different? How did you resolve it?

10. Avery and Taylor have complementary personalities and skills. Do you think the idea of "opposites attract" is important in relationships? How do Taylor and Avery complement each other in their relationship?

Andrea Scher

JASMINE GUILLORY is a *New York Times* bestselling author. Her novels include *The Wedding Date*, *The Proposal* (a Reese's Book Club pick), and *By the Book*. Her work has appeared in *The Wall Street Journal*, *Cosmopolitan*, *Bon Appétit*, and *Time*. Jasmine is a frequent book contributor on the *Today* show. She lives in Oakland, California.

VISIT JASMINE GUILLORY ONLINE

JasmineGuillory.com

X TheBestJasmine

JasminePics

JasmineGuilloryWriter

Learn more about this book
and other titles from
New York Times bestselling author

JASMINE
GUILLORY

SCAN ME

**or visit
prh.com/jasmineguillory**